WHEN AN

Angel Falls

Vernon A. Nairn

LifeRich
PUBLISHING®

LifeRich Publishing is a registered trademark of
The Reader's Digest Association, Inc.

LifeRich Publishing books may be ordered through booksellers or by contacting:

LifeRich Publishing
1663 Liberty Drive
Bloomington, IN 47403
www.liferichpublishing.com
1 (888) 238-8637

ISBN: 978-1-4897-2613-1 (sc)
ISBN: 978-1-4897-2614-8 (e)

Print information available on the last page.

LifeRich Publishing rev. date: 11/15/2019

Contents

My thoughts, my words
With no deceit,
By way of studying human behavior
This is my belief!

The world has spiraled so deeply in its inequity, for in the face of stupidity, they deny moral values, reek with self-centered laws and the great book amendments with misinterpretations, wrapped in their personal greed. Selective first and second class citizens of all nations, on or with manipulations, by using the cover of limited capitalism to bring upon economical slavery; which seeks to replace salvation.

Dear Readers,

Although there might be striking similarities between major social media companies, figures, characters, names, places, and world events, I wish to remind you that, this is a work of fiction grounded in the author's instinctive beliefs that offer no preconceived predictions concerning the events that will unfold in it.

Prologue

Don't be fooled by the soft fairy tale beginning of this work, *When an Angel Falls*, as it offers you another theory on how we all came into existence. Because of the current calamitous state of the world that suffers from an obvious racial divide and a drastic decline in moral fortitude, there is a clear distinction between good and evil. From the Kremlin in Russia that undermined the democracy of the Western world, to the ISIS demonic plague that is wreaking havoc in Levant in the Middle East as well as in selective countries around the world, Satan and his demons appear to be tapping into a series of triangulations, using the social network, spearfishing tactics, and dog whistling conversion methods. This triangulation starts at the point of 2 billion social media followers, followed by a seven-step breakdown to the mark of the beast. This would be explained in detail in the story should you choose to read it.

The end of the world's cycle is fast approaching. This has prompted God to send his three "Top" angels, Gabriel, Raphael, and Michael, the Archangel, who is leading the team, to earth. They are on an assignment for Him! They would literally and physically destroy and rip apart anything that tries to derail their mission to right the wrong on the earth.

Stephan Smith, a morally, insightful man of faith, was touched by the angel Gabriel, and he, along with journalist Christopher Rogers, and detective Danny Stone, forms a team in California to shut down a series of wrongdoing perpetrated by white supremacists in an effort to disrupt Satan's major diabolical plot.

Thousands of miles away in London, England, Carla Wallace, a lawyer, who is accompanied by her cousin, Sandra Wright, who has the same moral strength and faith, was touched by the angel Raphael, and they, along with Brent Russell, an MI-5 agent, team up to stop a series of events designed to change the world as we know it.

Dunstan Archer, who worked as an elderly caretaker in Cleburne County, Alabama, was incarnated as Andrealphus, one of Lucifer's fallen angels. After Lucifer and his selective angels took up residence on the earth, Andrealphus soon realized that he was caught up in the politics and evil conspiracies of the day. Once he realized that he made a mistake, he decided to flee with hopes of getting back into God's good graces. He and both of his friends, Dr. Angela Romano and Julian Bates, took an adventurous trip to the Great Angel Falls of South America, Venezuela in order to assist Sam Watson his mentor, who was incarnated by Gabriel. Every effort had to be made to defuse the dark angel's plot. Filled with riveting, heart-stopping twists and turns, this tale is an eye-opener and a page-turner!

Freedom

How do we define freedom? Some say its independence or it is the power or right to act, speak or think in the way that we choose! Yes, we do have some freedom of choice. But unfortunately, in this materialistic world, we often live up to other people's expectations, which can impede our freedom.

It is my belief
Based on moral integrity, we are free to act on our gut instinct.
But to disconnect our moral fortitude from our basic instincts is fruitless. Those with the power, that is, who intentionally misinterpret the constitution for their own selfish and personal gain, are clearly in the category of those who are vehemently heartless. This is wrong! Now it is time to "Right the Wrong."

Chapter 1

The fast rolling speed of a luscious orange stopped lightly at Gabriel's feet. It had been over-thrown by Matthew who had been engrossed in child's play. Matthew, one of the many groups of children that flocked into the garden of heaven, appeared between eight to ten years old. He was a very inquisitive young boy with blonde hair, brown eyes, and a light-brown complexion. He often played with Maxine, a little girl who was about the same age. She had dark brown eyes, caramel colored-skin, and black hair that looked like sheep's wool. She played the role of a follower whenever they were together.

Both of them were now sitting at the feet of Gabriel, who sat on a very large rock alongside a running stream. Holding the orange in his hand, he began to explain the cycle of infinity to them:

> "Life in heaven and on the earth, and throughout the universe, is not a straight line that goes off into the distance—its beginning point never to be seen again. It is like this orange, which is round as a sphere—you know, just as round as a ball. Yet, there is a beginning and there is an end! Would you be able to find the beginning point if it were just a plain smooth ball? No, right?" he answered himself while confirming this with both of them.

"You would only know the beginning when you see the end, and that is subject to repeat itself. There cannot be a beginning without an end or an end without a beginning! This is evident to the world, and the universe. Don't you see that the stars are round? They revolved around one another. This is also true about our gifted behaviors. You are to do unto others as you would have them do unto you (a reciprocated act). If you do wrong then wrong will come to you; if you do right, well, I am sure you understand where I'm going with this. Do you remember that human beings once thought that the world was flat?" he asked.

Suddenly, a seemingly dark, ominous cloud blocked the rays of heavenly light in the turquoise blue sky, but it was only for a brief moment for then there was light again. It was the wingspan of Michael, the Archangel, who appeared over-head, drifting slowly through the air as if he were a large condor bird.

Staring up at him, Matthew asked, "Does he ever come down from the hills or the mountain tops and mix with you, Raphael, and the other angels?"

Gabriel slowly lowered his trumpet, which he so often used to blow light, melodious tunes to entertain the children in the garden, and responded, "Michael is a true, loyal warrior who feels that it is his duty to constantly protect us even though we are in heaven under the forever, watchful eyes of the Almighty God."

Maxine quickly chimed in, "But why? Aren't we are in heaven protected by the Almighty God?"

Gabriel then said, "I will say this and only say this once—you need not concern yourselves with this at such a young age. Archangel Michael has unfinished business to attend to in the universe."

At that very moment, the shadow of an image fell over Gabriel and his listeners. Looking up, they saw a very tall, slender and muscular-built angel with long golden locks. It was Raphael, an angel who often mixed and mingled with the mature dwellers of heaven. Then he spoke, "Gabriel, we have to talk!"

Gabriel slowly rose to excuse himself as he looked down and nodded at Matthew and Maxine. Then he walked away as he wrapped an arm around Raphael's shoulders. Gabriel's structure was an average one when compared to the other angels, but he was also very muscular. His hair, which was long, black and curly had a gold leaflet bandana around it. Angels were as tall as Goliath while most humans and the dwellers of heaven were David's height. They also had a mystical glow about them.

Gabriel's and Raphael's path took them up a steep slope, and there, on the first landing, Michael, the Archangel, descended before them. Physically, Michael was massive. He looked as if he had been carefully sculptured for he had a muscular build of great proportions; his skin was the color of bronze, and his hair fell below his shoulders in long, black, matted locks. He had a brutally handsome face that appeared to take on the hues or colors of all races. The ages of the mature or older dwellers of heaven seemed fleeting, while the ages of the younger ones seemed to be frozen in their mid-twenties. But Michael's age appeared to be different for at times he seemed frozen in his mid-thirties, and again in his mid-sixties, almost as if he took on the stresses of earth just as most humans do.

Raphael had summoned Gabriel to the meeting on Michael's request. Michael often communicated through telepathy, and when he spoke it was often very short. He spoke, "*It is time.*" This world's cycle was coming to an end. Hell had no fury like that of Michael's who was about to surgically rain down his wrath upon the earth. The onslaught would soon begin.

℮℘

Steven Smith flopped down on a park's bench. He was mentally exhausted, grief-stricken and filled with despair. He slowly rested down a bag of groceries that he had purchased from a corner store where he often shopped. It was not too far from the park and was a block away from his apartment. It's Saturday, November 5th, 2016 at 8:00pm in Orange County, California, three days away from the presidential election of the United States. From his vantage point, he stared blankly at the basketball court where he had often played one on one games with guys of the neighborhood.

Steve was born in the Bahamas, which is a small country comprising a chain of islands east of Florida, USA. He, aged 53, was of a dark brown complexion, 5'10" tall, with a powerful build that always seemed to be pushing the limits of his athleticism. In grade school, he was known as 'Rocket' because he ran so fast. But he never gained this recognition until his mid-teens when he trained himself to become a runner and a unique creative dancer. He was born in poverty but was able to lift himself out of it through his paid performances. His mind wondered as he mulled over every situation that had put him in his current dilemma—he was working between jobs as a skilled construction worker. His wife, Crystal, who recently had a stroke, was hospitalized and bed-ridden. To add insult to injury, their insurance was on the brink of dropping them just as the fine print said, which they had overlooked. Then he looked up into the sky trying to pick out the little and the bigger dippers, that is, the formations made by the stars that could be seen on a clear night. Then he spoke aloud, "Lord, please show me the way." As a young man, and during his first marriage, Steve had studied theology but had strayed away from its truths after his divorce.

The park seemed to be strangely quiet. The bench on which he sat was very close to a side street. He occasionally heard a car pulled up to the stop sign and then turn up the main street.

e/o

Pete and Billy were arguing with each other about which turn to make in their dark blue paneled van as they drove down a brightly lit street in Orange County. With a quick right tug of the steering wheel, Pete turned onto a side street.

"Whoa!" a loud voice yelled out from the back of the van. It was followed by a thud on the left side panel of the industrial van. It was Joe's 300 pound big belly, tattooed up to his bald head. A white guy, he was sitting on the floor of the van. "Chill out you guys! Are you trying to kill me back here?" Joe asked.

"We could only hope!" Pete said as he drove slowly, gazing left to right. He was also a Caucasian, a well-built, six feet tall man with a bald head.

Again, Joe sounded out from the back of the van, "Let's open the bottle!"

"We're not trying to get a DUI right about now!" Billy fired back, a 5' 8" Caucasian who was a military marine.

They were a part of a violent group of white supremacists—a mixed group of skinheads who were cooking up a sinister plot. Although this group, unlike other mainstream groups, is known to have a warped sense of reality, these guys were planning to take things a little bit too far.

As the van took another right turn, its head lamps' high beams shone brightly across the park's basketball court, and then on the bench.

"There, there, right there!" Billy shouted. They were searching for a black male.

Steve was sitting on the bench. Pete shut off the head lamps as he pulled to the side of the road. Then there were the faint sounds of the rollers, slowly rolling out of the van's side door that could barely be heard. Collecting his thoughts, Steve pulled himself together when he realized that he had had perishable items in his grocery bag. Slowly, he began to pick up the bag as he stood up and stretched an arm. Suddenly, he glanced to his left and through the corner of his eyes he saw Pete approaching with an unlit cigarette dangling from his lips. Steve was an on and off smoker, so immediately he began to look for a match or a lighter on himself to assist him for being a gentleman was second nature to him.

Without warning, a sound filled the air, WHAM!! Steve was sucker punched from the right. A deafening quietness engulfed him as white flashes of fire-flies blurred his vision. His knees, then his right cheek hit the pavement. Without warning, Joe sneaked up behind Steve and floored him with one blow. Proud of himself, he pumped his fist into the air, jubilantly celebrating as if he had just scored a shot on the basketball court. Within seconds, Steve caught himself, got to his knees, and taking a track starting running position, he took off, tackling the first human object that stood before him. Billy was swept off his feet and was taken at least eight yards back before both he and Steve hit the ground with Steve on top flailing blows. Instantly, he felt an electric shock, and his body stiffened, jolted a few times, and then he flopped down too weak to resist. Pete stepped back, holding a Taser, and calling for Billy to apply the chloroform.

Two hours later, Steve woke up to a nasty smell. It was the foul scent of the black hood that covered his head.

"Wakie, wakie, sleepy head," Pete said softly as he removed the hood from Steve's head. "I guess you have a lot of questions," Pete mumbled. Steve slowly gazed at him, his vision blurred as he looked left to right trying to make out his surroundings. He figured out that he was being held in an industrial storage warehouse. Yes, he wanted to ask a lot of questions but a cloth was tied across his mouth preventing him from doing so. A few minutes later, Pete gave him a shot that put him out again.

He woke up eight hours later to a lot of movement and commotion in the warehouse. It was 6:00 am, and a part from Pete, Billy and Joe, there were four other guys fitting the same description of his abductors. They were all focused on their mission. Three of them positioned 55 gallon drums on a crate, using a dolly, while the other one used a folk lift to lift the crate onto the back of the box truck.

To Steve's left, about 15 feet away, there was an office that had a clear glass window. Inside stood Rod, his head nodding as he talked on a cell phone. He was a six feet tall, slender built man in a beige suit. Rod was what some people called, 'a go to man' with nefarious ways who worked for an important high-ranking government official. He hung up his phone and placed it in his top inner coat pocket. Then he looked down at John who was sitting behind a desk and who had also hung up from a call on a land line. John, a Caucasian in his sixties, was a blonde, heavy set, chain smoker. He was also the boss of all the guys in the warehouse, including Pete and his crew.

"We have to move fast because we are running short on time!" Rod said.

At that moment the big doors rattled as they began to open so that a squealing tires, speeding white van could enter; it came to a quick stop. Its doors immediately opened with one quick jolt and a group of six skinheads exited it—four of them physically handled and threw two African Americans to the ground. With an astonished and puzzled look on his face, Steve stared at them.

The door of the office slammed shut as Rod and John walked out to them. "Is this it?" Rod asked.

"Yep, you wanted three! We got three," Pete said.

Rod snapped, "Let's do it then!"

"Okay guys, we got to move because the rally's in two hours, and we got a long drive ahead of us. Clean up your personal mess! Remember, you can't leave any fingerprints! But I need those niggers' fingers on everything, the doors, the lift, the dolly, the office phones and the explosives. Remember, this is supposed to look like they set this up! Come on, set it up

Pete looked down at Steve and said, "You are wondering what is happening right now, right? You have a lot of questions I would imagine. Well, I think I can fill you in with some answers on some of those questions. You guys think you can come into this country and take over. Don't you know that the White race is supreme? You think you can taint our color and make it impure, and we would allow this to go unchecked? In short, you are going down on a lie!

7

Now, isn't that something? What we are setting up here will spark a race war—a racial divide will be created beyond your imagination."

"Isn't that ironic?" Steve said softly.

"What do you mean?" Pete fired back.

Then Steve replied, "Well, you are talking about the colors being tinted and tainted, when in your view, if you mix a drop of black paint in a pail of white paint, it is no longer white even though the naked eye cannot see it. Don't you see the irony? You are painting yourself into a corner. The outcome of all of this was set in motion long before we existed, and perhaps, it will continue long after we both leave this planet! It's inevitable!"

Wap! Pete punches Steve in the face, "Smart mouth! We'll see!" Pete mumbled.

"Hey hey, no exterior bruises!" Rod shouted out, and then added, "Okay guys, we are running out of time. Get to work!"

Four of the thugs paired off and picked up the two abductees they had brought in. Apparently, they had abducted them while they were jogging because they were in warm up suits. Pete carefully placed a duffle bag on the floor, while the other guys started to remove firearms from the bag, 9mms, AK 47s and a pistol grip shotgun. They then removed clips and live rounds of ammunition from the weapons so that they could forcefully place the abductees' prints on the firearms without being shot themselves.

The plan was to make sure that the three African Americans, whom they had kidnapped, would be implicated in a sinister plot to drive a van full of explosives onto the grounds of a campaign rally attended by thousands of Whites who were supporting the underdog, the elected candidate for President of the United States of America, Ronald Thick. They were to drive the van to a predetermined side street near the campaign rally's site. Then they were going to make it look as if they had unraveled their plot at the very last moment by driving up on them and engaging in a gun fight, which was set up for them to ultimately win. They believed that this would create extreme tension across the board among tens of millions of white and black supporters—it would create such a racial divide that they hoped would spark a race war.

Suddenly, Pete shouted out, "Bring that AK here!" He held out his hand as he looked down at Steve and said, "You people like guns don't you? Yeah, you're an AK 47 man!"

Steve then looked up out of the corner of his eyes and retorted, "And you, you are a disgrace to the rest of your race!" Then he raised his head and looked Pete dead in his eyes and spat out in a cold calculated voice, "IGNORANCE IS BLISS!"

Pete quickly pulled out his personal 9mm, and pulled the slider, but right then, Rod stepped up from behind and held his hand. He spun him around and said, "Are you out of your fu----- mind? This guy is getting into your head! Learn to focus."

Meanwhile in heaven, Michael, Gabriel and Raphael held hands and formed a tight circle as white clouds swirled around them in the skies. An unusual high velocity wind picked up, and then there was a loud thunder clap as a black hole appeared. Then God shouted out, "GO!" It shook the very foundation of the earth.

Meanwhile, miles away in Riverside, California, at 6:30 am, four-year old Tommy interrupted his mother during her morning routine that occurred before she got dressed for work. With a cigarette and a cup of coffee, she would sit out on her patio watching re-runs of the news that had aired on TV the night before. With a tug on her bathrobe, little Tommy caught her attention, "Mommy, Mommy, look, a falling star!"

She looked up and whispered, "Make a wish! Make a wish," she repeated. At that very moment, the star split into three, one looked as if it was on a course, coming directly towards them, while the other two went off into the distance. A ripple of light flashed but there

9

was no thunder. Tommy's mother looked down at him and asked, "What did you wish for?"

Tommy looked up with his cute little rosy face and said softly, "I wish that all the bad people would go away!"

She picked him up and hugged him tightly.

Chapter 2

The soft crackling of dry leaves, and the crunching of small pebble stones sounded under the slow rolling tires of Christopher Rogers' Acura as it pulled up and stopped on a hilltop side street. This gave him an advantage as he had a clear view of the industrial warehouse. Christopher Rogers, a Caucasian, who had short reddish hair, some would call it a carrot top, was just a little on the heavy side. Considered to be very enthusiastic, he was an inspiring journalist and reporter, and a favorite among his colleagues.

It's Sunday, November 6th, 6:20am. Thirty minutes ago, Chris barely glimpsed the third abduction as he drove to his favorite park for his usual workout. He kept his distance as he followed the white van to the location of the warehouse. Chris' enthusiasm had often led him to cover great stories in the past, and now, he was probably in a very unique position to cover the greatest one ever.

The warehouse was strategically selected because the area surrounding it was quiet and barren. Chris slowly placed his left foot outside his vehicle, and then pulled himself upright to a standing position. He had leaned back into the car to retrieve his equipment bag from the back seat for in his line of work, you never leave home without it. After locking his door, he created a path down a slope through some bushes—it was a direct path to the warehouse. The warehouse was located in a two-corner entrenchment, and the slope ran eight feet lower than its rooftop. He closed in carefully as he stepped over and held onto low hanging tree branches, occasionally slipping on loose gravel. When he got to the edge of the slope, it was then that he realized he had another clear vantage point—it was a high window with a view that looked directly down on the operation that was taking place on the inside. He quickly gripped a tree, and looking down on the thirty foot sharp drop below, he sat down, positioning his feet with his right leg stretched out, and locking his knee on the exposed tree's root. He then proceeded to open his bag for his camera, selected video and then began to record. His face took on a look of astonishment as he zoomed in closer.

With a hard thrust, Pete kicked over the chair Steve was sitting in. Still in restraints, Steve rolled over onto his left shoulder to break the fall. The others were forcefully shoving and pushing the other two abductees toward the back of the 16ft. box truck, which was filled with the explosives for the rally. As they placed them into the truck, Pete quickly untied Steve from the chair, and with his hands still tied, he walked him over to the back of the box truck, and then shoved him into the back with the others. A strong smell of ammonia nitrate filled the air of the truck. Chuckling maliciously, he sarcastically whispered to all three, "I wouldn't sneeze if I were you!"

Chris quickly rested his camera down, and then took out his cellphone to dial 911. After giving the dispatcher the address, he immediately went back to recording the scene. At that very moment, there was a sudden loud bang as if fifty concussion grenades had been simultaneously set off, and then there was a white flash. It was such a scary moment that most of the guys, including Rod, wet themselves. Then silence filled the room as the lights flickered. Slowly, the image of Gabriel appeared. He stood firm and tall with a light glow about his body, almost as if he were a gigantic fluorescent stick. With a look of disgust, his eyes wandered about the place, and even though his feminine features made him look very handsome, he looked ferocious and tremendously strong. Then he looked down at John, who was lying at his feet. He apparently had met his demise from a heart attack on hearing the initial bang. Rod was aimlessly crawling on the floor; he appeared to be disorientated. Finally, he seemed to collect himself, and as he shakily rose to his feet, Gabriel reached out his hand to help him, and suddenly, without warning, threw him across the room. Gabriel then picked up a pull and lift strap that was lying on the tail end of the forklift. It was Pete who fired the first shot from his pistol grip shotgun, but it was to no avail, for as though on cue, Gabriel began whipping that awful crew with the strap! Their cries and echoing screams of centuries of old demons, as well as the sounds of that lion's tamer whip, reverberated throughout the room.

Flashbacks of the evil engulfing the world throughout the ages sent Gabriel into a fit of rage that had been harnessed and held back throughout time. He had never been able to release it as the wishes of the Almighty God had restrained him. Gabriel was wailing relentlessly as the strap tore deeply into the flesh of the sinister crew. The blood splattered past images of the demonic faces of Hitler, grand wizards, and other demonic leaders, and then as it drained down the walls, the images slowly disappeared, leaving pools of blood splatter everywhere.

The lights had suddenly stopped flickering, and then they dimmed, creating a ghostlike setting. Gabriel looked through the open tailgate door of the box truck at the three African American abductees who were cowering behind the drums that were filled with high explosives. He then lowered his hands, and dropped the strap as his rage subsided and a look of calm appeared on his angelic face. Softly, he said, "God said, 'Vengeance is mine! I will repay....'" He slowly reached out his hand towards Steve, and then said, "Come with me."

Steve carefully and reluctantly rose to his feet, and reached out and held Gabriel's hand. Then, as quickly as Gabriel had appeared, they both disappeared, leaving the other two, who were now safe, but bewildered and frozen in fear over their ordeal, and Steve's and Gabriel's disappearance.

Chris quickly shuffled to his feet, and with the sounds of the distant sirens approaching, he made his way back up the path he had created earlier, got into his car and sped off so that he could blend in with the first responders. It only took a few minutes for the officers, who had arrived in their marked cars, to assess the carnage inside. They quickly yellow-taped the area. It almost seemed as if they had arrived in the blink of an eye, as Chris looked around and noticed all the news station vans that had gathered at the scene. He then thought to himself, they must have heard the word 'massacre' in the news dispatch that had obviously been leaked by a radio dispatcher; it had spread like wildfire. Shortly afterwards, two homicide detectives' unmarked cars pulled up. Chris immediately locked onto whom he believed to be the lead investigator, based on his demeanor, for he appeared to have taken charge of the investigation. Forty-five year old Detective Danny Stone was 6'3" tall, handsome and slender. He had jet black hair and blue-gray eyes. 15 years in homicide, he was a no-nonsense detective whose track record as a homicide investigator spoke for itself. He lifted the tape, and entered the warehouse to examine the scene.

ℯ໑

Meanwhile......

It was a beautiful view from the peak of Mount Whitney, in California, but it was cold as hell! Gabriel turned to Steve and said, "Sit!"

Steve rubbed his arms due to the cold, and quietly asked himself, "Where am I?" He then locked his eyes onto a large rock, headed towards it, and sat down.

"You have no idea what is going on right now, do you?"

"No!" Steve exclaimed as he uttered beneath his breath, "Jesus, it's cold!"

Gabriel quickly responded, "Gabriel, Gabriel is my name, although it was nice of you to mention Jesus. He is fine, but this world and its deviants are not! Although it is common and even acceptable at times to make mistakes, you, Steve, and many like you have been chosen because of your moral fortitude. The world is increasingly filling up with people who have agnostic beliefs, even though Lucifer is to blame for this, given his determination to derail God's plan. Yes, God has given you free will, but there is no man that walks the face of this earth, who can truly and honestly say that he does not know the difference between good and evil. He or she chooses to turn a blind eye to that which is good and right because it is easier to do so! But make no mistake about it—that is a big mistake in our eyes."

Steve then looked up at Gabriel and said, "I always told myself that I had to keep the faith, but now that I've seen and heard you, I believe." Tears began rolling down his cheeks as he continued, "I am truly blessed, so I thank you and the Lord above for allowing me to have this privilege of a lifetime to experience this first hand. Steve went silent as he crossed his arms to cover his shoulders from the bitter cold. Then he said, "I guess you are my God-sent Angel! Are you?"

"You can say that," Gabriel replied.

Trembling from the cold, Steve rejoined, "Well, are you going to let me freeze up here?"

Gabriel looked down at him, smiled and said, "Come, let us walk in faith." He reached out his hand to assist Steve, who slowly stood up. That mere touch engulfed the surrounding air with warmth!

Grateful for it, Steve breathed softly, "Thank you."

As they walked across Mount Whitney's rough terrain, Gabriel declared, "There are three of us here on the earth, Michael, Raphael and myself, and we have been given specific tasks to perform here. You, my friend will assist me with our message. It is all about the numbers—two billion to be exact. When we leave here, you will understand, and get the answers to those questions that boggles the human mind. For example, your life, or the world, or this universe, is a *bent curve* whose beginning and end are tied together. It's a simple circle that continuously loops around and around. In your case, when you find the beginning, you will also find the end. Everything in this world is based on reciprocation—you do wrong, wrong will come to you; you do right the same applies." Then he paused to let that sink in.

He nodded his head as he continued speaking, "Just think about it, your basic movement requires a back and forward motion; you turn or move like a pendulum, so too does reciprocation. Don't you see? Infinity in your mind appears to be a straight line that goes off into the distance, never to return, but that is not so. It does return!

Steve, now smiling, said, "I have to think about that! Right now, I'm not getting it!"

Gabriel's eyes widened as he looked at Steve, amazed at how he had responded. Then he said, "Be that as it may, you need not become bogged down with such thoughts right now. To be honest with you, it's simpler than you think! At this point, all you need to do is simply accept it as true, and, later, everything will slowly manifest itself. Now go, and don't worry for I will accompany you from time to time."

Steve looked at Gabriel with a concerned look on his face and asked, "Do you want me to walk from here?"

Gabriel smiled and answered, "Yes, walk in faith!" Immediately afterwards, Gabriel vanished into thin air.

Not at all surprised at Gabriel's disappearance, Steve turned, and began reluctantly walking down the side of the mountain. He felt a little more optimistic about his life based on all that he had seen and heard. Then his thoughts shifted—he needed to get to the hospital to see how his wife was doing. As he picked up the pace, suddenly, and without warning, he slowly vanished into thin air.

It took most of the morning before detectives, forensic, and EMS personnel got an unbelievable understanding of what had taken place at the warehouse. Although Chris had extensive video coverage when he replayed the video footage, there was a hazy glare over Gabriel, who had orchestrated the horrific scene. There were no survivors other than the two African Americans. The scene graphically displayed the carnage—the torn flesh of the dead, and the severed body parts. The cause of death was obvious—the crew had bled out. The strap had apparently cut through their main arteries, evidenced by the massive amounts of blood at the scene. It took hours for the homicide detectives to walk through, collect evidence, and complete their assessment.

A few hours earlier, Detective Danny Stone had had a soft interview with the two African Americans. Then he had to release them to the care of the medical team for further examination, in the event that they were not physically or mentally fit to be transported to his precinct for in depth interviews.

Detective Stone was very zealous. As he walked toward his car, he indicated to the chief coroner that he was cleared to bag the body parts. Then in his peripheral vision, he noticed that Christopher Rogers, who had revealed himself from the thick of news reporters and journalists surveying the scene, was waiting patiently to speak with him. Chris began walking towards him in his effort to intercept him before he left. He wanted to privately tell him about his footage. He quickly converged on Detective Stone, and quietly said, "I have video footage of the slaughter that took place inside that warehouse!"

Detective Stone stopped in his tracks, and looked directly at Christopher and asked, "What is your angle?"

"I have no angle! It's just that this is a unique and very unusual crime, if a crime was committed here!"

"What exactly are you trying to tell me?" Detective Stone asked.

"Look, you need to see the video for all of this is new to me. I am having trouble trying to understand it myself," Chris exclaimed.

"Okay, meet me at the station at 575 Anton Blvd," Detective Stone said, handing him a card.

Christopher interjected, "There was a third African American in that warehouse! I know you'll want to speak with him. But I need you to keep this private as I did not mention this to my colleagues."

"Okay, I'll see you in one hour! You got the address?" Detective Stone asked as he jumped into his car and closed the door.

Christopher nodded and then turned to look at the onlookers and reporters, who were watching as EMS personnel bagged the bodies and placed them in waiting emergency vehicles. He slowly walked back to his car.

Just as Chris was about to turn off the final surface street to hit the ramp for the highway, he exclaimed, "Oh shit!" fumbling blindly in the back seat for his jacket. He had just realized that he was not wearing it! That was the jacket he wore with his favorite hooded workout suit. It had been a gift from his girlfriend, which he was still fond of even though they had just broken up. He banked an illegal U turn on the traffic light change, and sped back to the warehouse.

It was 10:30am. Steve was spinning around in circles on the road, trying to figure out where he was as he had suddenly appeared there. He didn't recognize the warehouse at first from the outside, and then slowly he realized that he was where it had all happened several hours ago. Two TV station news reporters, who were standing next to their vans, were still out there reporting the breaking news. No one had noticed Steve's magical appearance. Confused, and not having the mental capacity to explain how he'd gotten there or what he had experienced in the past 14 hours, he decided to leave the scene. Just as he was approaching a T-junction, a gray Acura made a turn at such a high rate of speed that it damn near ran him over. After stepping back out onto the side of the road, he turned and threw both of his hands into the air, with a "What the hell........" gesture. To his surprise, brake lights, and then reverse lights lit up. "Now what?" he thought. Since he was not a contentious person, he was prepared to forgive and forget the driver who almost hit him. The car pulled up alongside him.

A voice sounded out, "It's you! I saw everything and videotaped it all! We have to talk! Get in, and I will take you wherever you need to go."

Steve paused for a brief moment, stared at him, not really trusting him at first, and then he thought of Gabriel, and realized that he would be protected no matter what. As he got into the car, he wondered what was going to happen next!

Chapter 3

Steve opened the door, and got in. As Christopher pulled off, he introduced himself, blurting out in one breath, "My name is Christopher Rogers, a journalist and a reporter. I have a video! I saw it all! Where did you go?"

Steve stared at Christopher for a few seconds, and then said, "I'm Steve! I'm so bewildered right now, that I don't know where to begin!"

"Take your time," Chris said, as he pulled alongside a news station van, and parked. As he got out of his car he whispered, "Stay in the car! I'll be right back!" He turned away and walked over to a low wall on which he had sat earlier, waiting for the opportunity to introduce himself to Detective Danny Stone. It was where he had taken his jacket off because of the hot sun, and had laid it across the wall, inadvertently forgetting it.

Christopher returned with his jacket. As he drove off, he began talking about the video footage, where he was when he took it, and the talk he had had with Detective Danny Stone. Then he explained why it was important that they both see him right away. "My video footage is just that as the audio was limited—it only recorded a loud bang, and then one gunshot! But you can fill me in on the conversation that was going on in there!

With a stern look on his face, Steve began to speak, "Christopher...."

"My friends call me Chris!

"Okay Chris, I have to make a stop first! Steve mumbled softly.

"No problem, where?"

"155 South Main Street," "the hospital," Chris shot back. "My wife is there! I have to see her! It won't take long!"

"No problem! May I ask what is wrong? Why is she there?"

Steve looked down at the floor board of the car, and said softly, "She had a stroke."

Chris shot a quick look at Steve, "I'm truly sorry to hear that!" He quickly attempted to change the mood by adding, "I see you are a fruit lover! You can go ahead and peel that orange, if you like! Here, use this," giving him an empty Starbucks bag that was in the car from the previous day.

Looking very surprised, Steve stared down at his right hand, unaware that he had been carrying it the entire time. "Where on earth did I get this?" he thought to himself. Then he smiled, deep in thought. "Gabriel," he whispered softly to himself. He turned to Chris, "Yes, apples, bananas, and oranges, I love them all!" He took the bag, placed the orange in it and said, "Thank you, I will eat it later." Then he quietly turned to look out of his side window. He stared blankly outside of it as the old Christian song, '*He's got the whole world in his hands*' rang out in his head.

Meanwhile.....

Some 8 hours ahead, (GMT), at 1:55pm, about 5,318 miles away in London, England, the echoing sound of a car door closing, followed by the beeping sound of a car alarm filled the air. On the third floor of Heathrow Airport's parking garage, Carla Wallace hurried towards the elevators. She was hoping to find a parking spot on the ground level, that would parallel with Terminal 3, the arrival section, but unfortunately, she didn't find a spot until she got to the third level. A sigh of relief came over her face as she pulled into an empty spot. When the elevator opened, she stepped into it, and immediately after pushing the button, she mumbled, "In a perfect world, her cousin, Sandra, would be walking out as she walked in."

A criminal defense attorney, Carla Wallace was born on October 26 1979, in Sussex England. Of a soft caramel complexion, with brown eyes and black hair, she was 5'9" tall, and athletically built. Although considered very young, given the many cases she had won, which was mainly through her zealously determined approach, she struggled to maintain her moral compass as a lawyer who defended known criminals.

Soon after the elevator doors closed, a voice said softly, "Fear not, for I come in peace."

"Jesus!" Carla blurted out as she jumped and turned around in fright. "Where did you come from?" she asked.

Raphael smiled and said quietly, "No, it's not Jesus. I am Angel Raphael."

Carla stood there frozen for a few seconds, observing the phenomenon that stood before her. As she did so, she kept repeating to herself, "Oh, my God! Oh, my God!"

Raphael smiled again and said, "Wrong again! But tell me, how many times did Jesus return to the earth?"

"What?" Carla asked with a puzzled look on her face.

Smiling, Raphael replied with an all so gentle voice, "Concern yourself not."

Right then the elevator jolted to a stop between the first and second floors. The lights dimmed for a moment, and then, all of a sudden, the elevator lit up with a very bright light. Raphael began to speak, "In this world, there are many terror attacks! Another one is about to take place if we don't foil it! Come, I am you, and you are me!"

Unexpectedly, Carla found herself standing outside of Terminal 3. A strange, warm and powerful feeling engulfed her as her eyes took in the sights around her. Then they locked onto a Range Rover that had pulled up to a screeching halt. Simultaneously three doors opened, and three men in trench coats quickly exited the vehicle. Terrorists no longer used the cover of darkness for stealth approaches. Now, all they need are a few seconds, and a heavily crowded area to do their damage.

Carla immediately found herself standing before the leader of the trio. Her body language could stop the world. Angel Raphael was inside Carla's body! With a strange look on their faces, the men froze for they realized that there was something other than normal about her as she stood before them. Suddenly the winds picked up! The high winds revealed the assault rifles that they had strapped beneath their coats.

Then an incarnated Carla said, "Do you truly believe that killing innocent people, who don't share your beliefs, will open the door to heaven, that is, your twisted idea of heaven? Do you?" Carla declared, "Well, allow me to open that door for you, just you," as she placed her hands on the leader's head. Immediately he froze as if he were a deer caught in a vehicle's headlights. The other two also had that stunned look on their faces as they watched helplessly while the skin on his face began to blister with air pockets. The water bubbles surfaced on his skin as the internal boiling temperature increased. Small pockets of flames burst through his clothing, which quickly burned away, along with his flesh.

By then, onlookers were noticing the commotion as the airport police approached, drawing their weapons. One of the officers shouted at Carla, "Raise your hands above your head, and step back!" Right then and there, they quickly trained their weapons on the remaining two because they began to draw their assault rifles. Since time was not on their side, they were quickly gunned down.

Carla slipped back into the crowd, and became herself again for Raphael had disappeared just as quickly as he had appeared in the elevator. She was completely dazed because she could not tell anyone what had happened or why she was at the airport. However, her memory slowly came back to her as she started to walk quickly through the frightened and puzzled crowd. A few minutes later, feeling dismally depressed, she slowed down.

Then a voice shouted out, "Carla, Carla!" It was her cousin, Sandra. As she approached, she asked, "What the hell is going on? I heard gun shots!"

Carla replied, "I'm not sure, but we need to get out of here!" Grabbing one of her bags, she took the lead, making a beeline towards the parking lot elevators.

High above, on the open rooftop's parking level, there was a guy videoing what had just happened. He was a part of the *Fringe* group, and was supposed to video the assault and intended massacre that had been foiled. With a frustrated look on his face, he quickly flicked a lit cigarette to the ground, bagged his camera and jumped into a black Ford transit 100 T280 industrial van and sped off. As he was turning off the down ramp of level 3, he spotted Carla and Sandra rushing across the parking lot with their bags in tow towards Carla's car. He pulled to the side to observe them.

As Carla and Sandra pulled out of the airport's parking lot, he proceeded to follow them, keeping his distance. A solid three minutes passed without anyone saying a word. Then Sandra spoke, "Is this a bad time? Aren't you happy to see me?"

"Oh, Sandra, I'm so sorry! Of course, I am!" she paused for a moment and then said, "Sandra, honey, something just happened! I'm struggling with it! I'm trying to make sense of it all! Give me a moment! I would probably have a better understanding of it by the time we get to the condo."

Sandra reached over and tapped Carla lightly on her arm, "Girl, you missed your turn!"

"Damn!" Carla exclaimed, frowning as though in deep thought.

Sandra Wright, a thirty-six year old British born mulatto, was a junior high school teacher. She had dark brown hair and brown eyes. She was pretty, yet a little on the heavy side. She lived in Atlanta, Georgia, where she had spent the last five years.

"Carla, where are your towels? There is none in the linen closet!" Sandra shouted out from the bathroom.

"Sorry, they are in the dryer! Hang on!" After she had given Sandra a set of towels, she poured herself a glass of wine. Still in a daze, she walked out onto the balcony. She lived in a two bedroom, two bath, second floor condo, in a pristine gated community complex. As she looked off into the distance, she thought about what had happened to her earlier that day. As she pondered over the strange events, her thoughts were heavily focused on Raphael, whom she assumed was her guardian angel.

It was really quiet for the only sound she heard was the faint sound of the shower running. Suddenly, it was interrupted by a soft voice, speaking over her left shoulder, "Were you truly happy winning those cases for known criminals?" Raphael asked quietly.

"Oh, my God, you're back!" Carla cried out, spinning around to look at him.

"There you go again, using the wrong name! Didn't I tell you that my name is Raphael?"

Carla immediately followed up with questions of her own, "What did we do? What happened to me?"

Raphael rested his right hand lightly on her right shoulder, "We saved at least one hundred lives today, and you, my dear, are the heroine of today's top story. They might not know it now, but later they will find out! Yes, you are my *rising star!*"

Carla stared at him in disbelief, realizing right then and there that her life had changed forever. She knew too that after the authorities viewed the surveillance footage, they would be looking for her.

"So I ask again, were you truly happy?"

"What?" she asked with a puzzled look on her face. Then she remembered, "Oh right! You mean am I happy in my profession, right? I chose to follow in my dad's footsteps, thinking we were that much alike! But I guess we're not that much alike! It doesn't bother him but it does bother me! No, I can't say that I am ecstatic about my life right now. But now that you are here, I see that that is about to change. I always did confess that I have some moral fortitude."

"Carla, my presence alone should tell you that it won't take much for me to convince you that that is true especially when you see what I have to show you, and tell you." He reached out for her hands, "Give me your hands." As she placed her hands in his, he told her, "You will feel a sensation which will be followed by an affirmation of the truth. The puzzling questions that you have will slowly untangle themselves for you will get the answers you seek. Carla, it's all about the numbers! God has sent three of us, Michael, Gabriel and myself, down to triangulate our subjects. We don't have much time! You have to find them before they find you!"

"Who is them?" Carla asked.

"A lot of eyes were on you at the airport!"

"Yeah right! MI-5 agents are probably all over this by now," she mumbled under her breath.

"Now you have to go! You will find them quicker than they can find you! Now go!" he ordered.

"Go where?" she asked.

"Follow your instincts! It's important that you go through the motions! Don't worry, I will be with you."

Before Carla could respond to him, he was gone! Then she saw Sandra, who was standing to her left. "You heard that? You saw him?"

"Yes, I did! Pinch me because I must be dreaming!"

"Come, we have to go!" Carla said as she scrambled for her bag.

Meanwhile……

Back in California, Gabriel was very busy. He walked in onto a pornographic movie set with an incarnated elderly man, named Sam.

The director looked at him in disdain and asked, "Who are you? What are you doing here?"

"Who am I?" Gabriel intoned, staring sternly at him. <"I am Gabriel, the Messenger!"

"Okay then give it, give it to me! What do you have for me? Director Jones snarled.

Gabriel cried, "You reveal naked bodies for sex and cheap thrills; you create and blanket man's weaknesses in your dark world of..."

At that very moment a porn star, a young girl, walked out onto the set and began to disrobe. As her robe fell to the floor, so did her flesh, revealing muscles and bones. Gasps sounded throughout the room, as Gabriel turned towards the director and said, "Message sent!"

He walked over to the girl and picked up the robe as she, now on her knees, began crying and screaming as she looked at herself in a mirror that was directly in front of her. Sam, incarnate, knelt beside her, picked up the robe, and draped it over her. Then he said, "Stop it! Stop crying! Calm down!" He held her by her chin and said, "Look at me, and stop crying! You are okay, see..." He turned her head towards the mirror and added, "Fear not my child, for now you see how truly naked you can be."

Then he stood up, looked towards the director and said, "Message received." He looked back down at the girl and said, "Let's see where you go from here!" As Sam walked away, the optical illusion that the director and the young girl had witnessed frightened them but it also gave them pause to look deeply within themselves to see just how morally bankrupt they had become.

✑

Meanwhile......

At the hospital, Steve looked down on Crystal, his wife, who was asleep in her private room. He held and squeezed her hand as she slowly opened her eyes. "Hi, Sweet cakes," he crooned, smiling at her. When are you coming home?"

"Soon, soon, I hope, very soon, she breathed softly as she looked up at him and smiled.

"Oh, I have something for you!" Steve said as he took the orange out the bag, showing it to her.

Crystal smiling from ear to ear, exclaimed, "How sweet of you? But I never knew Starbucks sold fruits!"

"This is a special fruit from another world," Steve laughingly said. "Wait a minute, I have to wash and peel it for you," as he excused himself and headed to the bathroom.

Crystal was a forty-six year old assistant manager of an apartment complex in Orange County, California. Initially, her employment's insurance kicked in and was going well, but after reading the fine print, they both realized that she would have to give up the luxury of her private room that had been her home away from home for two weeks and three days.

When Steve returned, he sat down in the chair next to the bedside table. He slid the trash can between his feet after peeling the orange, and then stood over her to hand-feed her each plug, piece by piece. He wanted to be very careful as he did not want to alarm her given her delicate condition. He chose not to bring up his recent episode because, deep within the recesses of his brain, he had made himself believe that he was acting a scene in a play. So he quietly said, "We have been sent an angel, you know!"

She smiled again and with a strange, but very strong response, replied, "That's nice, but no, I didn't know that."

Steve smiled at her innocent, but seemingly sarcastic response, and said, "You seem to be getting better already!"

Right then the nurse walked and said, "I am sorry we have to cut this visit short. The doctor is on his way to run some tests."

Steve looked down at Crystal, held her hand tightly for a brief moment and said, "I will be back real soon."

She nodded at him as he left the room.

❦

Chapter 4

C hristopher had fallen asleep while watching TV in the waiting room. Then he awoke to find Steve staring down at him. "What? You think I got a burning bed," Chris grumbled, looking up at Steve as he jumped up and stretched!

"If I was thinking about it, it may have been my first thought," Steve said with a smile. "Okay, let's go see this detective," Steve said as he held on to Chris' shoulders, directing him towards the elevator.

As the elevator door opened at the ground level, Chris turned to Steve, "So tell me how is she?"

"As well as she could be at this stage in her recovery," Steve replied, a worried look appearing on his face.

As they walked quickly across the parking lot, Steve began thinking out loud, "Gabriel, Gabriel, where art thou?"

"What are you grumbling about?" Chris asked, staring at Steve with a puzzled look.

Steve smiled, thinking to himself how funny he must have sounded as he spoke in biblical terms. As they walked alongside the car, Steve turned to Chris, "Didn't you tell me you have video footage, but poor audio of that horrific scene?"

"Yes!"

"So you must have seen that big guy with the fluorescent glow! Right?"

"Yes and no! I forgot to mention that my video was great with the exception of this white glow! But with my naked eyes, I saw that out-of-space looking.....not sure what it was, or who it was!"

"That's Gabriel, the Messenger Angel!"

"You're kidding me, right?" Chris looked up with a surprised look on his face.

"Why are you looking so surprised? You saw him with your own two eyes! He took me away with him you know! I spent at least 40 minutes with him. This is deep! Are you a believer?" Steve asked.

"What?" Chris exclaimed. "God, the Bible, heaven—you know, all that good stuff we were taught as we were growing up! Well, I hope you had the same upbringing. Oh yes, I am a straight up believer," Chris said.

"Good," Steve responded. "Because what I am about to tell you will seem unbelievable!" Then he looked Chris directly in his eyes and asked, "Can you explain what you saw and videoed?

"I can!" a voice sounded out from behind them both.

As they turned in the direction of the sound, Steve said, "Who are you?"

The voice answered the question with questions of his own, "Who am I? How is your wife?"

Steve, still puzzled, wondered who he was talking to. "Oh, by the way, did you eat that orange?"

"Gabriel, is that you?" as he wondered about the man standing before them.

The man smiled and continued with his purposeful dialogue, "It was and still is my intention to set things in motion. She will be fine for now, but we have to undo what has been set in motion. This presents a much larger picture for us!"

Yes, it was Gabriel, incarnated as Sam, the elderly man. Angels tend to seek out and host good hearted people, who have fallen on hard times or suffered hardships through very little fault of their own. Sam Watson, 70 years old, was 5'10" tall. He had long, black, uncombed hair, and green eyes. He was a street pan handler, who had fought in the Vietnam War, but through the system, he was dealt a bad deal and had fallen on hard times.

"Thank God, you are here," Steve sighed in relief.

"I do like the way you and the others thank God a lot, though much of it is just paid lip service. You have no idea what He has done to keep your moral compass holders from drifting into the abyss," said Gabriel.

"Well, I truly thank you and God," Steve said, his voice filled with compassion. "Gabriel, meet Christopher."

"Christopher, the carrier of Christ, it's my pleasure to meet you! Well, that is what the Greek say! Do you truly carry Christ within your heart?" Gabriel asked as he reached out for both of their hands. Then he said, "Envision this…." A warm flow of energy passed through their fingertips, and then throughout their bodies. All three stood there as if they were in a moment of prayer, and then came the images of heaven, world battles, and wars that occurred throughout man's existence, thousands of years came through in flashes—significant highlights of great sins of the world, past and present, appeared and disappeared; there was a clear distinction between good and evil.

Releasing their hands, Gabriel said, "This is not what God intended from the onset. If you notice there are two types of people in this world, those with empathy and those with apathy. You both, along with many others, fall into the category of empathy. Those who are apathetic couldn't care less about their fellow brothers and sisters. Even though they appear to be academically inclined given that they have the ability to study and think, they are still ignorant for they do not understand or seem to realize that good basic human behavior is rewarded in this life and in the afterlife."

Gabriel paused for a moment, and then declared, "I am a Messenger! My time with you is limited! I have to go where I am called! In this world there are ongoing calamities, but with the exception of Michael, we, as angels, can and do alter them for true believers. However, you, as human beings, together with those who are morally empathetic, can prevent them, or minimize their impact! In fact, we can eliminate them. Remember, it's all about the numbers! You will find the answers too many of your questions about the many ongoing plots around you. You have to look to the basic tool, the internet that is used to attract attention worldwide. Look for strange behavior after each unfortunate aftermath, and then follow that lead. Now go! Your basic instincts will guide you!"

"Wait up!" Steve exclaimed, "You said with the exception of Michael…"

"Yes, with the exception of Michael," Gabriel replied, looking up at the skies. "His only restriction is our Father. No barrier on earth can stop him! He is focused on one thing, and that is to take the head off the one who is responsible for this mess! You have no idea how long he has waited for this moment! Hell has no fury in comparison to MICHAEL'S WRATH! Yes, he is here, high above us and he is unleashing that wrath." Gabriel then turned and started to walk away.

"Where are you going?" Steve asked.

Without turning, Gabriel said, "I am a Messenger; I have to get my messages out there!" His image became a shadow, and then he faded away.

Chris was standing motionless as if in a daze!

"Come, snap out of it! Let's go see this Stone guy!" Steve said, tapping the roof of the car.

As they drove off, Steve mumbled to himself, "This is going to be hard to explain!" Then he thought, affirmation, yes, he was afforded affirmation's wide scope and he had the knowledge to explain what had just happened.

჻

Meanwhile…

Back in London, England, Raphael reappeared in the back seat of Carla's car.

"Holy shit," Carla shouted as the car ran slightly off the road when she saw Raphael in her rearview mirror. "You are going to defeat your purpose if you keep reappearing that way! Or, is it your purpose to give me a heart attack?"

Sandra, who was seated in the front passenger seat next to Carla, was so shocked that she couldn't say a word!

"Calm down! I am sorry! I guess I would need a host, preferably, a loner, someone who would appreciate positive changes in his or her life," Raphael declared.

Both Carla and Sandra looked back and nodded in agreement. Instinctively, Carla made a right turn that went down a hill that had a left curve leading to an embankment.

As they came to a T-junction, Raphael quietly said, "Stop!"

Both girls turned their heads to the left and immediately knew why. Sitting on a bench and looking down at a grassy slope near a running stream, was a young man in his late teens or early twenties, or so he appeared to be from that distance. In a blink of an eye, Raphael was suddenly there sitting with him.

"There he goes again!" Carla said aloud, her voice filled with sarcasm. "That is one Angel who sure loves to startle people! That boy damn near fell off the bench!"

Looking up and down at the boy, Raphael whispered, "I am so sorry if I frightened you. I really have to, how would you say it? Brush up on my approach!" Then he immediately held his hand out and said, "Hi, my name is Raphael. I come in peace, and you?" Raphael asked.

"Paul," the young man said as he shook Raphael's hand.

"You know, in the twists and turns of your great book, they first called you Saul, which was your Hebrew name. But then after the resurrection, you were converted to Christianity. Paul, you are not small in size but I can see you are a humble man.

A Roman family name, Paulus or Paul, which means small or humble, Paul was looking at Raphael with a strange expression on his face.

Raphael said with a smile, "Paul, I can see you don't know much about the Bible or ancient history for that matter. As you can see, I am not your average man." Right then a glowing light engulfed him as he continued to speak. "I see you are sitting here and you are in despair, wondering where to go, and what to do. I say to you, worry no more, the world as you know it is fast approaching a major change! Here and now, from this day forward, nothing will be a wonder to you. Come, come with me! I am now you, and you are me!"

The girls were so taken by the scenic view around them that they didn't notice someone had gotten in the car until a voice from the back seat said, "Drive!" Both Carla and Sandra turned to look at the back seat to see a handsome young man sitting there.

"Hi, I'm Paul!"

"Hello, I'm Sandra and this is Carla my cousin!" Sandra reached out for his hands as she stared at him with flirting eyes.

Paul raised his hands to signal her to stop speaking, and quickly said, "I am also Raphael! Now we need to go!"

"Where to sir?" Carla asked sarcastically.

"Instinct, Carla instinct! You will know when you get there."

As mentioned earlier, the horrific events taking place in the world have to do with an intricate set of numbers, that is, they follow a number sequence. All three of the Angels' messages were similar— the world's catastrophe's focal point is based on numbers, 2 billion to be exact, which will eventually cap off and start growing at its peak. In the beginning it will be used to misdirect voters for political gains, and then will grow to set off a chain of merciless events, all by simply using the most used social media network. Even though the numbers surpass the starting point of 2 billion, the meltdown process has already begun.

In this case, one third of the 2 billion represents one third of the angels who followed Lucifer in his bid to take over the Kingdom of heaven. Michael, the Archangel, took his stand with his band, and ran them out of heaven. Self-exalted, they purposely chose the dark side and became demons, there was a few that joined their leader who had manage to surface from the black hole, called hell, to live on planet earth. One third of 2 billion gives you a rounded off figure of 666,000,000. The .7 at the end of the correct calculation gives you the steps. Drop seven sets of 10% that represent the seven deadly sins, (cardinal sins), which will bring you to 66.6. This figure represents the 66 operatives on each of the six populated continents, with the exception of Antarctica, not having and ongoing population. Multiply the last 6 by 66, which will give you 396, that is the number of dark fallen Angels including Lucifer, that had manage to break from the black hole that they were cast down into, which is commonly known as hell. They have set off, over a period of time, massive destruction and mass killings mainly with explosives and other lethal means to establish a deep fear within the world's population, all in an effort to gain control so that they could set up a new world order.

Today's media and social network circus make it so easy for criminal minds to tap into the lives of the weak-minded. In this case, it will be done through spearfishing tactics, dog whistling and hypnotism. They will set up 6 continents, with 66 triangulated points on each country, with their states, cities, province and boroughs; their targets are the churches that sustain true believers. They want to destroy their faith and moral fortitude. But I say to those within this Category, "Do not fear for even though this will be the biggest challenge you will ever face, you will be victorious!"

Chris took a quick glance down at the card Detective Stone gave him to check the address. "This is it!" he said, pulling into the main entrance of the police station. "We are here to see Detective Danny Stone," Chris said to the station's clerk as he slipped the card back into his wallet.

The officer got up, pushing the door open to the detective's office floor, and shouted, "Stone! Has anyone seen Stone?"

"Right here," Stone replied, walking from the restroom area.

"Two guys are out here to see you."

"Great, send them back here," Stone said, pulling two chairs to his desk.

As Chris and Steve approached the desk, Detective Stone reached out his hand and said, "Christopher, I'm glad you can make it, and who may this be?"

"The third guy, Detective. Meet Stephan Smith," Chris said, pulling up a chair to sit down.

"Steve, can I call you Steve?" Detective Stone asked.

"Yes, everybody else does," Steve replied.

"Okay Steve, so tell me what went down out there?"

"I guess it was around 8:00pm as I had just finished shopping for a few grocery items from the corner store. I headed to the park and sat down on a bench because I wanted to reflect a little on my personal dilemma. Suddenly a guy approached me. At first, I thought he was looking to light a cigarette, but the next thing I knew I was floored by a sucker punch. After seeing stars, I was able to regain my footing and drilled the first person I saw in front of me to the ground. The fight went on for a few seconds, and I guess I was shocked with a stun gun, and then held down and a rag, which I guess was soaked with chloroform, was used to cover my nose and mouth. I awoke I think a few hours later but wasn't able to see my watch because my hands were tied behind my back. Then I found myself looking into the face of this weird and cold looking White guy who taunted me with racial epithets. There were a few other White guys, who appeared just as cold and calculating, walking about. They seemed to be members of a White Supremacy group."

Then Detective Stone jumped in, "I just completed interviews with the other two victims in this case, and they seem to be in the dark about what was really behind all of this. They both said they were jogging and then abducted, thrown into a van and taken to a warehouse. Soon after that they were piled into the back of a box truck, and then there was a calm that seemed like a blessing in disguise. It was followed by a glowing God who looked like a man. Oh, by the way, Chris, you did bring the video clip right?"

Chris responded, "Yes, I have it right here."

Then Detective Stone looked back at Steve and said, "Okay, where were we? Right, the glowing God who looked like a man."

"I'm going to get to that," Steve said. "Taking a needle to my arm, they drugged me again. It was 6:00am when I woke up. I knew this because I saw the clock on the wall through the office glass window. There stood before me was the same guy who had drugged me; he taunted me again using the same types of epithets he'd used before. Detective Stone, this is where it gets complicated. What I'm about to tell you, you will find hard to believe! Yes, it was a God-like man or should I say it was a God-sent man who saved us! He was no ordinary man! He was an Angel, Gabriel, the Messenger to be exact!"

"You are kidding me, right?" Detective Stone asked with a smile. "A man walks into a warehouse, and with a nylon rope strap he made a whipping and thrashing motion as he tore off the flesh of a group of guys, walks out and leaves them all to bleed out and die? You are telling me he is an Angel?"

"A no nonsense Angel!" a voice said that could be heard from across the room. There stood Gabriel/Sam looking at a large noticeboard filled with the photos of wanted criminals. He appeared out of nowhere because the entire room had dropped what they were doing, a look of sheer surprise on their faces as they stared at him.

Gabriel walked towards Detective Stone's desk, and as he got closer, he said, "They are not your average people, those supremacists! To think that they could change would be naïve on your part. They are deviant demons whose sole purpose is to demoralize mankind and condemn them, that is, all those who do not share their beliefs or are a part of their group, to second and third class citizens all around the world. They believe and say that they are the superior race, and where ignorance is bliss, they claim that they are here to fight for the human race. In short, this group triples the extremism of the others who are like them."

"And who are you?" Detective Stone asked.

Steve jumped in saying, "That's him, Gabriel."

"Is he the shining, glowing Angel you spoke of? He looks like an old bum!" Detective Stone said softly.

"Be careful what you say if you want his blessings. He's incarnated," Steve replied softly.

Danny Stone stood up to greet him as Gabriel reached out his hand to shake his. He held it for a moment, and then said, "Daniel Adamo Stone, a junior but not quite. You are the son of Daniel Abele Stone, whose father, before migrating here, changed his surname from Ascanio to Stone, which is an Anglo Saxon's name. He wanted to fit in. You are following in your father's footsteps, who, unfortunately, met his demise in an early career shoot out. My condolences!"

Detective Stone was mesmerized as Gabriel the messenger incarnated Sam stood before his very eyes. He stood silent for a moment, trying to make sense of what he had just heard and witnessed. Whatever doubts he may have had in his mind, they completely vanished after that simple, but short conversation. Then he said softly as he scanned the room, "Gentlemen, we need to continue this in a more private setting. I have to do some work on this case, and do a bit of research. I will call you to tell you when and where we will meet again."

Passing his card and the video clip to him, Chris said, "You won't be able to without this number."

Detective Stone's eyes widened as he reached for the video clip and the card. "Jesus, in taking all of this in that you guys put before me, I had totally forgotten about the video clip. I am going to keep this under wraps! You two and your new found friend here, "Sam' you can call me Sam, Sam said, Okay Sam, please we cannot let anybody know you had anything to do with this and we can't let this leak out to the press particularly with this divine intervention in the mix. I have a brother-in-law in the FBI and I will personally sit with him on this." They then shook hands and parted ways.

Chapter 5

It is 11:00am in Los Angeles, California, and Robert Forbes, Director of the world's giant social media, WorldNet, walked into the boardroom where five board members sat waiting for him. Robert, a forty-five year old, 5'10," Caucasian with sandy blonde hair, looked as if he lived in the gym. "Gentlemen," he said, as he dropped the month to month report on the boardroom's table. "Congratulations! After being stagnant for the past two months, we are finally closing in on that 2 billion worldwide social network of media users. We would have been in Cuba in a big way by now had those bigots in the Senate and Congress given the President a path to do his job. But I truly feel that God, in short order, will fix their business for them. But back to the good news, we are now at 1,999,500,000 and quickly climbing."

The room barely echoed the sounds of the few who applauded. "Malaysia," Robert shouted out as his eyes wandered across each board member's face, "Where are we?"

Meanwhile......

In London, at the MI-5 main office, Director, Frank Buckley stepped onto the floor amidst ringing phones and computer screens of satellite images. Looking around, he said, "Ladies and gentlemen, at 2:00pm today, at Heathrow's Terminal 3, a young lady literally smoked out a terrorist cell. By all accounts, according to eyewitnesses, cc footage, and the swift action of airport police officers, it was effectively done. Evidence suggests that she also burnt one of the subjects with something, but she did it without using an accelerant."

Right then the major floor screen started running the cc footage as he continued, "We need to know who she is, and where she is right now."

It took about two minutes before an agent stood up from behind a computer screen; she had a print out with the description that she had ran through facial recognition. She gave it to Sheila Hall, head of the MI-5 field agents. Sheila Hall, aged fifty-six, was 5' 10" tall. A diligent worker, who ate and slept her work, she had brunette shoulder length hair and brown eyes that conveyed an authoritative confidence. She read aloud, "Carla Wallace, thirty-seven years old, born October 26th, 1979, is a legal criminal attorney. She's a lucky girl for according to the date, she just recently made partner last month on her birthday at Depuch & Depuch Law Firm. I don't see any weapons or field training on her sheet."

"Well, how was she able to seek out a terrorist cell when she's just a lawyer?" Frank asked.

"Maybe it was by accident, but it was pure luck for us," Sheila responded.

"Well, find her!" he said as he turned to open the door to leave the room.

Meanwhile.....

Somewhere on the streets of London, Brent Russell, an MI-5 field tactical agent, cried out, "Aaah shit," because he had carelessly reached for his ringing phone, and spilled a cup of Starbucks coffee on his pants while making a wide turn in his car. He stopped on the curb, and reached into his glove box, frantically looking for napkins to clean up the mess he had made. "Hello, hello," he said, answering the phone. Immediately he froze in his multitasking when he recognized the voice on the other end.

"Mr. Russell, this is Sheila Hall. We have a situation. I am sending you information, with a photo of the subject, right now to your phone. It will explain in detail our situation. This will be your priority. I am switching you out with another agent to work your present assignment. I have chosen you for a reason, and I need not explain! Agent Russell, do what you do best! Work it!"

Brent Russell, who was thirty-eight years old, was 5' 11" tall. A black man of mixed African descent, he was born in Edinburgh, a city just outside of London. He was the product of a mixed race single mother who raised him. His mother was English and his father was African. His father was a hit and run, one night stand young man, who had just finished college. He had flown back to Africa the following morning, promising his mother that he would return, but he never did. She had long lost contact with him, and he had never made any attempt to contact them. This prompted Brent to take his mother's maiden name, Russell. His aptitude and field tactical skills tested off the charts. I guess you can say that these results were all the reasons Sheila needed to give him this particular assignment.

Brent started the downloading process on his phone, and then he looked down at the mess he had created. He stared around aimlessly until his eyes locked onto a diner across the street. He drove back onto the road, and made a U turn to enter the parking lot of the restaurant. As he entered the diner, his main purpose was to use the restroom to get cleaned up and then leave. Several minutes later, he changed his mind about leaving, and decided to sit down in a booth near the door, so that he could study his new assignment. He was so engrossed in his reading that he was startled when the waitress stood over him to take his order. He said, "Coffee, just coffee, please."

ల∕ల

Meanwhile.....

Back in the outskirts of London, Carla, who was driving for

a little over 15 minutes, felt as though they were going around in circles.

Suddenly, Sandra moaned, "God, I'm so hungry!" It was almost as if God had heard her for immediately she spotted a diner on the right side of the road.

"Good timing girl, I'm feeling a bit famished myself," Carla said, as she swung to her left to enter the parking area.

As the three of them walked up to the diner, Raphael/Paul mumbled, "Don't be surprised at what you are about to encounter inside there!"

"What are you talking about?" Carla asked, as she pushed open the door of the restaurant.

Raphael/Paul didn't answer.

As they walked in, a voice was heard from the booth near the door, "Wow! Wow! Is this amazing or what?"

With confused faces, Carla and Sandra looked down on a handsome black male, while Paul wandered away and sat at the counter. Brent Russell was looking up at Carla and then back at his phone comparing Carla's photo with the person he was looking at. Then he said, "Carla Wallace," as he showed his identification, "have a seat please!" He looked up at Sandra as she hesitated. She was uncertain as to whether or not she should do as he'd asked.

"You too," Carla immediately started to say as they both sat down.

"So you think me and that video footage you have on your phone are freaking amazing, huh? Hah, hah!" she smiled mischievously.

"Wait until you hear about, and see the bigger picture!" Right then all three of them looked up in surprise to find Paul staring down at them.

"Who is he?" Brent asked.

"Him? Oooh, he's a big ball of fun all rolled into one!" Carla said jokingly.

"You think this is funny especially when you consider the

situation you're in right now?" Brent sneered with an angry look on his face.

"No! But when you hear his story, you will understand why I am a bit at ease," Carla replied softly.

Sandra then stood up and said, "Carla, you got that right! I'm starving. I'm going over there to order something to eat."

Paul then sat in Sandra's chair, and reached out his right hand to shake Brent's. "Hi, I'm Paul and you are, Agent Russell of MI-5, who is about to haul the lot of you off to headquarters right now, if you all don't start making sense."

Brent stared at him as he continued speaking, "I speak affirmatively and with authority from a divine perspective—2 billion…." as they both released their handshake. Paul declared, "You are a smart guy, that is the reason your boss briefed you on the phone about that situation, without having to see you in person. What you saw on that cc footage is miniscule compared to what I am about to tell you!"

Then Paul repeated, "2 billion is just the tipping point!" He started to explain but was interrupted by Agent Russell's phone that started ringing.

c/☺

Meanwhile…..

Back in California, and sitting on a prestigious seat in the Senate, John White, who was an activist and advocate on gun rights, had pushed heavily against the ban on assault weapons for the NRA. John was on a family outing at the mall with his wife, Barbara, and their three kids, ages 8, 11 and 13. They were walking out of the mall when Barbara turned and said, "I'm going to take the kids back to Haagen-Dazs to get them ice cream." He grinned when he heard the cheers of 'yeaaah' from the kids in the background. She added, "You can bring the car around to the front entrance!"

"Okay," John replied as he watched them head back into the mall's main entrance.

The walk was about 4 minutes; all in all, it took about six minutes for John to drive up to the front entrance door. As he waited, he occupied his time by playing with the stereo set. Suddenly, sounds of gunshots rang out, and then a wave of people exited the mall like stampeding cattle. He opened his door to exit his vehicle when he heard the sounds of screams, and the shouting of names, that were coming from the dense crowd. John ran through the crowd that was pushing him back and forth, and left to right. He forced his way into the mall, screaming his wife's name as the gunshots suddenly stopped. As he ran and got closer to the ice cream parlor, he suddenly froze in his tracks when he saw the carnage before him. There were cries and screams coming from the wounded—regular shoppers who were crawling aimlessly about the floor—as first responders ran to their aid. Then he saw security officers, and two plainclothes police officers, with weapons drawn; they were holding their badges high as they stood over the shooter's body. An AR-15 automatic rifle was lying a few feet from the slain shooter.

John was spinning around looking frantically for his wife and kids. Then he heard shouts and cries from three of his kids, who were fast approaching him. "Daddy, Daddy, Mommy is hurt," they shouted as they ran towards him. John turned to follow their lead as they quickly ran to his wife's motionless body lying in a small pool of blood. He dropped to his knees and cried out, "Barbara, Barbara wake up!" But it was to no avail. It was soon clear to him that she had expired. Seconds later, a man knelt beside John as he, in a daze, whispered, "Why me? Why me?"

The man gently put his hands on John's shoulders. John turned to him; it was Gabriel/Sam. "Why me you ask? Would you much rather it be somebody else, while your life goes on unchecked?"

With tears in his eyes, John asked, "Why are you telling me this right now?"

Sam replied, "Don't you see?"

John looked at the man and asked, "Do I know you?"

"No, but I know you," Sam replied. "Now, you get to see firsthand the carnage that automatic weapons can cause in the wrong hands, and yet with a stroke of a pen, you could have prevented this one! You are going to get a pass on this one, not because I see your grief, but because, right now, you will truly see and understand the grief of others." As Sam looked John dead in his eyes, he simultaneously placed his hands on Barbara's forehead and said, "You are going to do the right thing from this day going forward."

Immediately Barbara started to choke and cough as she gasped for air. John's elated attention to his wife distracted him so much that he didn't hear Sam's last words as he walked off. They were "message sent, message received". Seconds later, John was gently pushed aside, as one of the EMS team said softly, "I am truly sorry Sir; we will take it from here."

John's attention was then drawn to Sam as he walked off into the distance. His silent thoughts drowned out the screams and chaos that surrounded him. Then a feeling of humility engulfed him. He knew right then and there the changes that had to be made.

Christopher jumped a little, when he felt the vibration of his phone, which was followed by a ring. "Hello!" he said, answering the phone.

"Christopher, Detective Stone here. Let's meet tomorrow, 8:00am at Starbucks on von Karman Avenue near Karman Plaza. We just got a call about a mall shooting! There might be a connection or this might be another terrorist attack!"

"Okay," Chris replied as he repeated the address. Chris turned to Steve for they had been driving somewhat aimlessly, and told him what Detective Stone had said, and then he added, "I guess you would have to get home to clean up because you truly had a long run of it!"

"You are right about that," Steve said as he riddled off his address. Chris took a series of turns and headed in the opposite direction. "By the way, what are your thoughts on this election?"

Steve paused, lowered his head and said, "You know, everything that we are going through right now is hinged on this election."

"Why would you say that?"

"Well, my most recent experience is all based on race, and the many racial wars we've been seeing over the past few months. Think about it, on its face we see a racial divide throughout this nation. Neighbors that you thought had your best interest at heart, are now revealing their true colors, simply by choosing to follow someone that has been proven, time after time, to have racial hang ups. It's a far cry throughout the world! There is a clear distinction between the differing opinions people hold about this election, and these individuals include those who have, and those who do not have a moral compass.

"Chris, at eight o'clock tonight, 24 hours would have passed since the beginning of this eventful day. I can truly say that I have seen the light!

Then, deep in thought, they both stared away from each other.

∞

Meanwhile....

It was 3:10pm, London's time, as Brent got up from the diner's table, aimlessly wiping his pants with the napkins he had taken off the table. He realized that this was the main reason he had stopped at the diner to begin with.

"You guys are coming with me, right? You have to explain the rest of this in detail down at headquarters, I am too much in a daze in following you on this right now

I cannot be a lone ranger in this! I have to defer to you."

Brent's phone began to ring, again "Hello!"

"What is your assessment?" Sheila immediately asked on the other end.

"I have done better—I got her, and I'm bringing her in now."

"That is amazing! How were you able to find her so fast?"

"You wouldn't believe me if I told you!"

❧

The security services, commonly known as MI-5 (Military Intelligence, section 5) is the United Kingdom's domestic counter-intelligence and security agency. It is a part of its intelligence machinery along with the secret intelligence service (SIS), MI-6, the government's communication headquarters (GCHQ) and the defense intelligence (DI). MI-5 is directed by the joint intelligence committee (JIC), and the service is bound by the Security Act, 1989. The service is mandated to protect Britain's parliamentary democracy and economic interests from terrorism and espionage within the UK.

❧

Meanwhile….

It is night, 3 hours and 30 minutes ahead of London's time, as Michael, the Archangel, stood tall on the 18,406 feet mountain peak of Mount Damavand in Iran. With an alert look on his face, arms opened wide, and muscles swelling, he gave a gigantic clap that sent a series of thunders and lightning flashes that spanned the Middle East. But there was not even a cloud in the skies of Afghanistan, Syria, Pakistan, or even as far north as Russia. It was a message to all ISIS leaders, and cruel dictators, because frightening images of Michael appeared under the lightning glow in the corners of their bedrooms or sleeping quarters. It was evident that demons were seeded deep within those who clearly walked with apathy throughout the world, whether they were dictators, law makers, politicians, hedge funders or murderers, of both genders, and of every race, creed and color. Their eyes, filled with a grayish yellow tint, quickly opened as Michael's face flashed within their presence. From that point on, an eerie feeling came upon them all for they knew, deep down inside, that their days were numbered.

In the city of Mosul, Iraq, a radical Sunni Islamist group, known to be responsible for beheadings, was huddled in their makeshift quarters. Three radical Sunnis stood over an Iraqi Christian informant, preparing to execute/behead him. They planned to capture it on live video at the crack of dawn. This was one of the methods they commonly used to strike fear in non-believers.

Not far away in another corner of the same room, a frightened Iraqi informant, who was held in restraints, was curled up in a fetal position as radicals mercilessly taunted him. Suddenly, a strong wind blew the front door open, even though, strangely enough, it wasn't a windy night. One of the radical Sunni soldiers went to close and latch the door when he was suddenly 'sucked out' by some strange unknown force. Puzzled and confused, the remaining soldiers watched as the half-opened, creaking door slowly opened wider. Astonished, they all jumped back in fright when they saw who stood before them in the doorway—a massively built person stood there with a light glow around him. It was Michael, the Archangel, standing there with an angry look on his face. He was holding in his left hand the head of the Sunni soldier. Michael then tossed the head at their feet and said, "Pick it up!"

They stood there frightened and motionless. Michael then stepped into the quarters, and pointing his glistening sword at them, he repeated himself, "Pick it up!" Michael then turned as if to walk away, but with lightning speed, he swung the sword back and forth. Their bodies fell and their heads rolled. Michael then stood upright, calmly looking down at their lifeless and headless bodies. Then he slowly knelt down, reaching out his hands to the frightened informant. He gently brushed away the restraints from his hands as though they were crisply burnt tree vines. As the informant struggled to stand, Michael helped him up, and embraced him. Then they both vanished.

ॐ

Chapter 6

A daisy tune sounded off on Steve's cell phone alarm. He rolled over in his bed to shut it off. "Seven o' clock," he said aloud, "time to get up." Soon after, his phone's ringtone rang out, "Hello," he answered with a mumble.

"Rise and shine," Chris chimed out on the other end.

"I need a half an hour," Steve said.

"That's all you got! It's going to take 20 to 25 minutes to get to that address."

It's Monday, November 7th, the eve of Election Day, 7:55 am. Both Steve's and Chris' eyes scanned for a parking spot as they drifted through the parking lot of Starbucks. "Right there," Steve said. Chris quickly pulled in, and to their surprise, there was Detective Stone sitting in his car next to them. He was smiling at them.

They locked their cars, entered Starbucks, placed and received their orders, and then took their seats. Detective Stone asked, "Turner Diaries?" as he added sugar to his coffee. He looked up when he didn't get an immediate response. "Turner Diaries are you familiar with the Diaries' plot?" he asked, looking directly at Steve.

"If my memory serves me right, it has something to do with race......race wars, right?"

"Is that a question?" Detective Stone inquired, looking at Steve.

"Yeah, race wars, that is it," Steve added.

"It's a little more to it than that! The National Alliance leader,

William L. Pierce, under the pseudonym, Andrew McDonald, wrote about it. The Turner Diaries tells the story of a White supremacist guerilla army, an organization that sought to overthrow the American government, leading social institutions, including the media, Hollywood's Anti-Defamation League (ADL) and Jewish nongovernmental organizations such as the International Fellowship of Christians and Jews. I was up most of the night reading up on this. Steve, the group you and the other two encountered is a section of this guerilla army. They were in the process of revamping their unit. I did a further analysis of the crime scene, and examined the phone records, and I must say, at the very least, they are disturbing. This goes deep!"

"How deep?" Chris asked.

"Slow down," Detective Stone replied, looking at Chris as he realized that his question was coming from the natural instinct of a journalistic mind. "I'm stepping out of the bounds of protocol discussing this with you. I have started an immediate investigation on this, even as we speak! Okay, let's put this Turner thing aside for now, and take a look at this divine intervention that seems to trump all that I have mentioned here."

"I wouldn't say that," Steve said quickly.

Detective Stone turned and looked directly at Steve. He had 'a why look' on his face.

Steve exclaimed, "This is all tied together! Look, our God sent Angel Gabriel whose parting words to both Chris and I were, 'We, as Angels, can alter a destructive course for true believers, but as human beings you have the ability to collectively choose what it is you want to do so that you can prevent it!' And listen, this is the part I like, Angels and human souls together can erase it from the very heart of a calamitous creation."

"So where is our Angel anyway?" Detective Stone asked as he tore at the Danish he had ordered with his coffee.

"Somehow, I believe that he is in me in more ways than one!" Steve replied. "Hey Chris, you know I had failed to mention to you where I had been for those 40 minutes after that explosion! Well, I guess that I was so freaked out and dazed that I went blank during that time. In fact, I didn't think about it! But he took me to the peak of Mount Whitney, which was as cold as hell! By the way, that's a figure of speech! I'm sure you know what I mean! Then he, in his glowing, angelic form, touched me, and told me that I now have all of the basic knowledge I need to understand why we are where we are today! I have it! I have the moral fortitude to fight whatever comes my way! We have it! Don't you see that this is the reason all three of us are sitting here today?" Steve voice softened as he said, "Believe it!"

Eventually, his eyes wandered to the news that was being broadcast on the TV's screen. Then he added, "Oh, I almost forgot, earlier on he also mentioned to us that he, as a Messenger, must travel to take God's message around the world. I took that to mean that we should not expect him to be with us all of the time."

"Oh, my God," Chris exclaimed as he gestured with his head towards the entrance door as a beautiful girl, dressed in a sexy outfit, walked in.

"Ho, ho, ho, hold back on your testosterone kid," Steve breathed, holding down on Chris's shoulder. "In light of what we are going through right now, you still letting that kind of stuff blind you?"

"I am not blind about this! I can see clearly now!" Chris responded.

"Cut it out Chris, and get serious now," Steve said jokingly, shoving him. "Check this out," Steve quipped as he gestured for their attention. "Look, please don't get me wrong about this because I am not going to profess to be a saint about it! There have been lots of times in my life that I have taken a second look at a female's physique. There is nothing wrong with wearing tight clothing! When people work out that is what they wear, right? Yeah, it's cool to show off how much in shape you are, and yes, she's sexy and beautiful, but I think her outfit is too revealing! Actually, she's making a sexual statement, all brawn, and no brain, (that is, of course, if she is not an undercover police officer). She's big bucks, fast car type of girl that is as close to selling sex as she can get! Now if she is all that I have mentioned, then to me she is shallow; she has no substance, and to hook up with her would result in a short lived future!"

"Damn Steve, that's cold," Chris said, shaking his head. "But it's true, because if you go up to her, and try to exchange pleasantries, she will blow you off. On the other hand, a woman who is also beautiful, but conservatively dressed, will welcome your compliment, smile and say, 'thank you'."

Detective Stone sat there smiling at both of them as they conversed, and then suddenly his attention was drawn to the flat screen TV that was replaying the news of the shooting at the mall. He snapped his fingers. "Guys focus, check this out!" he said, pointing at the screen. "The count is now thirteen dead. Where was your Angel?"

"Weren't you listening? It doesn't work that way," Steve said, partly focusing his attention on Detective Stone, and partly on one of the reporters on the screen who did not seem to fit in. Then he said, "Hey look, do you see something strange about that reporter, the second to the last one on the far right? He is not trying to question the Chief of Police, like the others. It seems as if he is more focused on talking to the other reporter as he just handed him a card."

"I know that guy," Detective Stone said.

"What guy?" Steve asked, turning to look at him.

"The one who just received the card. He's James, the reporter. He's always the first to rush up on me at crime scenes, asking for certain information, knowing quite well that I'm not going to give it to him."

Steve suddenly went quiet, and then whispered to himself, "This is interesting! Gabriel did say that we should watch out for strange behavior after each unfortunate aftermath."

"What are you talking about?" Danny asked, staring at Steve with a puzzled look.

Then Chris chimed in, "Yeah, that's right! He also said we should follow its lead."

Looking at Detective Stone, Steve asked, "Do you have James' contact?"

"I.....don't know! He must have given me a million cards, but I just discarded them. He was a bit annoying, but I may....have one. Let's see!" Danny began digging through his wallet. "Oh yes, here we go! This is it, James Carey."

They all went quiet as simultaneously, they began thinking about what to do next. Then Steve broke the silence, "I think we may have been given the reins to start the process of healing this world. Call him," Steve said. "This can be the beginning of something really significant! Call him, and let's set up a meeting."

Detective Stone sat quietly, pausing for a moment as he looked hesitantly at the card.

Noticing his seeming unwillingness to call James, Chris spoke up, "I understand your reluctance because we as reporters can be a bit annoying. But you have to understand that that goes with the territory. It's a hustle! Who knows? He might turn out to be someone you like, like me. Ha! Ha! Ha!"

They all chuckled. Detective Stone stared at the ceiling, tilted his head, and said, "O.....kay, here goes nothing," as he dialed James' number. "Hello James, Danny Stone here. Okay James, let's not get excited! I don't have anything for you concerning our last meeting, but I do need to talk to you. Where can we meet?" He started shuffling through the pocket of his coat that was lying across an empty chair, for a pen and a pad. Logan Park, 1009 North Custer Street, got it!" He hung up the phone, and then looked at the two humble gentlemen sitting before him. "Who is getting the check?" he asked.

Steve turned his head and looked at Detective Stone from the corner of his eyes and said, "Not my broke ass."

It was 10:05am when Detective Stone turned into Logan Park's parking lot, followed by Steve and Chris. While they stood alongside their vehicles looking around aimlessly for James, they talked about how beautiful the day was.

"There he is," Danny said as he started to walk towards a young man sitting on one of the park's benches.

The young man leapt to his feet when his eyes caught Detective Stone's. He extended his hand to grasp Detective Stone's hand, giving him a vibrant handshake. James was very enthusiastic about meeting the detective. "To what do I owe this pleasure?" James asked, smiling at Detective Stone.

"We will see if there is any pleasure in this," Detective Stone replied as he turned to introduce Steve and Chris.

"I know you! You are a reporter too," James said as he held out his hand to shake their hands. "Yes, Christopher Rogers, Anaheim News," Chris said.

After they had exchanged pleasantries, Detective Stone began the dialogue on the subject of the ongoing plots. You were covering the mall shooting yesterday, weren't you?"

James shot a quick glance at him with a how did you know look, and then quickly answered, "I was all over that! It appears that somebody was all over you too," James then paused, looking at Detective Stone, trying to determine where he was going with this.

"Look, we may need your help on something we are working on. Just a short while ago we were watching a replay of the shooting at the mall, and saw you in the clip. There was a reporter that stood out from the rest. We noticed that he was trying to talk to you about something, and then he gave you a card. Can you tell us what that was all about?"

James, who wore black-framed glasses, was a skinny, blonde twenty-nine year old devoted journalist and reporter. He stood there staring briefly at all three of them, and then he said, "He asked me if I was in the game."

"What game?" I asked, and then he gestured toward my friendship bracelet. It appeared as though its design and colors were symbolically significant to him. I just sort of played along with him then I said, "Games, I love games!"

Then he gave me his card and an invite to a meeting the group had scheduled for tonight. But I was not going! I was just playing along based on the invite.

"Here is the card! I haven't even looked at it."

Detective Stone took the card and read, "Focal group, section 1/6, Peter Davis, and there's a telephone contact—bla, bla bla! That's it! James, listen, we are working on something that may or may not be tied to the warehouse killings and that botched White supremacist plot. You must have heard about it! Do you want in? Now, wait before you answer that because I have a question, and you must be truthful when you answer it. Are you a racist?"

James stepped back as if taken aback, and then he looked at all three of them standing there, and said, "Hell no! Listen, I'm young and adventurous, and if it's for the greater good, I'm in."

Detective Stone gave James a fist bump and replied, "That's great! Now I need you to go to that meeting tonight, in light of tomorrow's elections. I think I speak for us all," as he looked down at the card again, "when I say that this Peter Davis may be a part of this extremist White supremacist group who are involved in ongoing plots to spark several race wars. He may have been trying to recruit you, but their main method of recruitment is via social media—Face book, Twitter, Snap chat, and all the others that fall into this category, not to mention people in journalism and reporters like you, who are willing to bend the truth. There may be risk involved with this infiltration, so are you still up to it?"

"Look, listen, lately I have been noticing a lot of tension in some regarding this type of talk in neighborhood bars, and I believe a definite racial divide has been stoked. If it's for the good of this nation, and other nations that share the same concern, I am in," James rejoined.

"Okay, it's 9:22am, and I have to earn my pay! Got to go," Detective Stone said as they all started to walk back to their cars.

"James, here is my card. Call that Peter guy, and tell him you are interested. Go with the flow, and give me a call the minute you get an address and a time. Steve, and Chris, I will call either one of you, when James gets back to me." As he turned to open his car door, he added, "We will catch up later!"

As Steve and Chris drove off, Steve said, "Chris, I know you have to get back to work, so just drop me off at the hospital. I will make my way from there."

"No problem," Chris responded. Right then Steve's phone started ringing; it was accompanied by a low battery flashing light. "Hello," Steve said, almost dropping the phone in his haste to answer it.

"Mr. Smith, this is Nurse Green. We need you at the hospital urgently!"

"Oh damn, I'm on my way! Oh boy, oh boy, this doesn't sound too good! Pick up the pace please Chris!"

"You got it," Chris responded.

◌◌

As Steve entered his wife's room, there was an eerie feeling, along with the silence, that was interrupted by the beeping sound of the ventilator that was monitoring Crystal's vital signs. Then sounding very compassionate, Dr. Greenslade whispered to Steve. "Mr. Smith, I am so sorry! Your wife went into a coma 35 minutes ago. We are monitoring her vitals but to be quite honest it doesn't look good. After reading our Glasgow coma scale, which is a standardized tool that aids us in assessing comatose patients through an evaluation of the gag and corneal reflexes, her brainstem reflexes have stopped working, and a test was given to stimulate her breathing. Mr. Smith, your wife cannot breathe without the ventilator. I'm going to step out now and give you two a few minutes alone."

Shortly after the doctor left, I heard the nurse outside the door saying, "Excuse me sir, you cannot go in there right now!"

"Why not?" the voice said, pushing the door open.

Steve turned to see Sam walking through the door with the nurse following close behind him.

"Sam, I 'm so glad you came!"

Looking from behind Sam's back, the nurse asked, "Do you know this gentleman?"

"Yes, trust me, lady, he's okay!"

The nurse then turned to leave, and Steve grabbed Sam and hugged him as if he were a long lost father. Then he stepped back as tears filled his eyes, "Sam, they are saying Crystal, my wife, is brain dead. What can you do?"

Slowly, Sam walked over to Crystal's side, paused for a while, and then put his hand on her forehead. His eyes wandered about the room, and then he turned to Steve and said, "You have to let her go!"

"But why?" Steve cried out, becoming distraught.

"Her physical condition is irreversible. Steve, let her go! Look, I can bring her back, but she would not be the same; she would be in constant pain, and I would be going against my Father's will for her as the process is already set in motion."

Before Steve's battery went totally flat, he managed to call her sister, Anne, who did not live not very far away, and who had Crystal's son, Joey, moved in with her from out of state during his mother's ordeal.

When Anne arrived, she rushed in and immediately rushed over to Crystal's side. As tears flooded her eyes, she cried, "Don't leave me, Sis! Don't leave me Sis!"

Steve walked over to console her, and softly explained to her what the doctor had said. Anne Peterson, a nurse, was a 42 year old blonde who had unique blue eyes. She worked at another hospital in Riverside, and was Crystal's youngest sister and only sibling. Both parents had passed away, separately, a few years back. They had an aging aunt who was only able to visit twice since the ordeal, due to her physical complications and the fact that she lived out of state. Anne understood exactly what Steve was relaying to her because of her background in medicine. She walked to the door and then opened it and beckoned to Joey to come in. Joey, aged 17, had curly black hair and brown eyes. He was a 6'2" tall mulatto who was in shape physically—he looked like a strong, healthy basketball player. Joey was always reluctant to see his Mom in that state, but with some coaxing, he finally walked in. Through all of this somehow, Sam had walked out unnoticed.

Shortly afterwards, there was a soft knock at the door, and then it was pushed slowly open. Dr. Greenslade stuck his head in, and said, "May I?"

Steve gestured with a nod, and he entered with the nurse following behind him. She was holding a clipboard that had a form attached to it. The doctor took the clipboard from the nurse. "Mr. Smith, there is no rush, but whenever you decide to do so, we will need you to sign this form."

Steve immediately took the clipboard, glossing over the material, knowing full well what had been asked of him. He looked over at Anne, who was holding Joey in her arms. She nodded as he beckoned for a pen. After he had signed, the doctor walked over to the ventilator, pointing out the on and off switch. Then he quietly left the room. Joey started to cry, so Anne quietly walked him out.

In the meantime, Sam had quietly snucked back into the room; he turned, locked the door, and then looked at Steve and said, "Steve, give me your hand. You will be completely convinced about your decision when you see this transition."

As Steve held Sam's hand, the room's setting changed—it was similar to the projection of an advection and convection that split in two like a layer of fog. They appeared to be suspended in outer space in the lower section of the room, and in the upper area of it, they seemed to be looking up at the blue skies. Crystal sat up, and then stood up in the midst of the dark outer space area. Smiling, she was looking directly up at the blue skies, where a gathering of celestial angels were reaching out their arms to receive her. Crystal was 47, but her image appeared as if she was 27. Suddenly, Sam let go of Steve's hand, and the room returned to normal. Steve walked slowly over to Crystal's bedside, bent over and kissed her on her forehead, and then he reached over to flip the switch. The flat line's beeping sound was his confirmation as he said to himself, "She is truly happy now."

Chapter 7

Meanwhile back in London at Thames House, the MI5 headquarters was buzzing with activity. A full minute of silence filled the interrogation room as Sheila Hall stared directly into Carla Wallace's eyes from across the table. Then she spoke, "So you want to explain how you, a lawyer, were able to seek out and put down a terrorist cell?"

Carla looked down at the table, and then up at Sheila. "Not me, it was divine intervention, and if I may add, beyond your imagination! That's of course, if you believe!"

"Believe!" Sheila shot back with a puzzled look.

"Yes, believe in God."

Brent, who was standing alongside Sheila, bent lower towards her and said softly, "The kid outside seems to have a broader insight on whatever you want to call this." He was referring to Raphael/Paul.

"Well, why isn't he in here?" Sheila asked as she turned to look at him.

Brent immediately turned, opened the door and beckoned the agent outside to bring him in.

Sheila was rapidly tapping her fingers in a piano playing motion, when Paul walked in at 3:55 p.m. Sheila said, "Have a seat, Mr. ...."

"Cornell, Paul Cornell," Paul said, as he pulled a chair and sat down. "Good afternoon, Sheila."

"Mrs. Hall to you," Sheila said in disdain, as she slid her chair back to stand.

Paul's eyes followed her as she walked around the interrogation table. Paul responded, "You have 326 districts, 36 metropolitan boroughs and very little time, because within those 36 boroughs, there is a terrorist cell of six. They were split into two groups as a part of a contingency plan. They brew separate terrorist acts, unlike that terrorist group at that little airport incident, who appeared to be a fringe terrorist group, and whose act was as miniscule as a teardrop. It pales in comparison to any act perpetrated by the operative cell of six."

"You seem to be a well-versed, young man," Sheila said as she walked behind Carla, resting her hands on her shoulders. Then she lowered her head to whisper in her ear, "am I too believe..."

Suddenly, Paul jumped in and said, "Sheila..."

Brent immediately bent over Paul, gripped his shoulders and said, "You better be careful dude!"

Paul ignored him, gripping Carla's hand as he stood with the four of them. It was a complete body connection. Then he said, "Your name Sheila means *heavenly blind, vision this.*" As he spoke, the room became filled with virtual images, and because he held Carla's hand, strengthening that physical connection, she was the only one at first who could see the images or vision.

Then all four of them saw a vision of two separate operations that appeared in the interrogation room. It looked as if they had had hidden cameras in the terrorists' rooms, which allowed them to watch them in real time. In the two separate operations, there were six individuals, males and females, in two separate groups of threes. They were predominantly of Middle Eastern descent. Some were looking at maps, while others were wiring up explosive devices. Both Sheila and Brent, because of their training, focused on their surroundings, that is, they examined the rooms where the operations were taking place, looking through the windows inside out, in order to pinpoint their exact location.

The vision in the interrogation room disappeared as Paul released his grip on Carla. Sheila and Brent turned to each other with a look of amazement on their faces. Sheila immediately sat down alongside Paul, and turning her chair to face him, said, "You are going to help us with this, aren't you?"

Paul looked directly at her and said, "I'm helping now, or should I say Raphael is helping you for you have to understand I am the Angel Raphael incarnate. He speaks through me. Without him I am just Paul Cornell, a lost twenty year old trying to find my place and meaning in this world." Then a dominant voice sounded out from Paul, "We, as Angels, have limitations on what we can do! We can alter a destructive course, but to change an event, we have to work with those of you who are moralistically inclined."

Sheila then stood up, and running her hands through her hair, asked, "Agent Russell, what did you see in that vision?"

Brent responded, "From my in-depth study of the scenes, I saw that one of the rooms had the look of a common one bedroom flat and the other one seemed to be very exquisite room in London. I also saw a cathedral that I made out to be St Paul's Cathedral through that window."

"Great observation," Sheila exclaimed, and then said, "I saw the same things but through one of my windows, I saw London's South Bank University. Brent, go get the address of that neighboring rental complex next to those sites that have direct window views." Then she looked at Paul and said, "I need you to get me back into that vision to have another look."

Paul looked at Sheila strangely, not saying a word.

Sheila said, "Please?"

"I can't! He's not here! I don't feel him!"

"Oh, my God," Sheila said, holding her head, "Can we get him back?"

"I don't know! Listen, while he was a part of me, he did give me a complete understanding of his other related duties on earth, and one of them has to do with healing. Maybe he went out there to heal the sicknesses of true believers, who knows? But there is a memory that I have retained from that vision."

"What is it?" Sheila asked with a hopeful look on her face.

Paul responded, "On one of the maps, St Paul's Cathedral was circled. I think the message Angel Raphael is sending us is if we follow his guidelines, we can figure it out. In short, he has given us a window, but we will have to open the door."

Sheila went silent to ponder her dilemma. Five minutes later, Brent burst back into the room, "I got a list—close to London's South Banks University are the South Banks Converse Apartments with a window view on 7th Union Street, London, SE 2 1SZ, UK, and close to St Paul's Cathedral is the Kings Courtyard, which is a modern apartment in the hotel location on London's EC5V 4AF."

"That's the exquisite one," Sheila said. "That's good! We also have a target. Paul saw a map in the vision with a circle around the St Paul's location. Sheila suddenly stopped talking, experiencing an epiphany. Then she said, "Oh, my God, I see where this is going. There is a 6:00pm mass, and a graduation at the university around the same time. We have to move fast! Agent Russell, get a team together for briefing!"

"You got it," Brent said as he turned to head out the door.

"Agent Russell," Paul shouted out, stopping Brent in his tracks.

Paul approached him and said, "We have to talk more about that number sequence as there is a possible link there!"

Sheila then looked at Brent with a puzzled expression on her face as if she were asking, "What number sequence?"

Walking towards the door, Brent breathed, "I will explain later!"

Paul sat back down as Sheila looked down on both he and Carla as they sat there. "Listen, I apologize for my harshness, but you have to understand that we can't take situations like this lightly. Carla, you and your girlfriend can go!"

Carla jumped up, saying, "She is my cousin!"

"Okay, you and your cousin can go, but Paul I need you here in case our God sends His angel again! Carla, I will have an agent take both of you back to your car. Oh, I will need your number!" Carla shuffled through her bag, pulled out a card and handed it to Sheila, and then she suggested, "Oh, by the way, Mrs. Hall, I would much rather your driver drop me at my firm because I need to pick up a case file. You see, I took a week off because my cousin was visiting me. There is an up and coming trial that I need to do a bit of homework on. It is also a lot closer than the diner. I can get a colleague to take me to my car afterwards."

"That's fine with me," Sheila said as Carla stood looking down at Paul.

"Oh, here's a card for you too! I also need your number, Paul," Carla said.

Paul gave it to her as she keyed it into her phone.

"Keep in touch," Carla said as she turned to walk with Sheila to the door.

Sheila suddenly stopped and turned to Carla, "Oh, should our angel show up, this is my card; it has a direct line on it. Call me anytime."

℘

For Your Consideration

Remember, there are 66 world terrorists or operatives in each of the 6 populated continents. Multiply this by 6 and it gives you 396. There are 396 incarnated fallen Angels throughout the world.

"If this is so, how can there be a God?" many would ask.

The king of evil has a way of recruiting followers. He uses cruel methods, and one effective way that is known throughout the world, is the sicknesses that prey on children, who are cancer patients, and/or who are starving as a result of famine which is caused by imperialism and environmental degradation.

It is my belief that shortly after the creation of mankind, Satan was cast into a black hole known as hell. From there he managed to escape with hundreds of fallen Angels who live on this earth. Then he immediately stepped in to physically convert and mutate a few to convince the many by designing, building and creating exploitation and strife, which would clearly show his superiority. It is an attempt to convince, and rid the world of the souls that remain on the earth. Thank God for the many who have stood, or are still standing firm because they have realized that *all that glitters is not gold.*

⟨⟩

Samantha Bates struggled to adjust her hospital bed with the wired remote control so that she could reach her TV remote that had slipped between the bed and its frame. Eight years of age, she was a cancer patient at the Elvina London Children's Hospital. Samantha was suffering from leukemia; she had been undergoing chemotherapy for a month, and was wearing a knitted cap because of her extensive hair loss. Suddenly, the room's lighting dipped and dimmed, and the TV mysteriously turned off. Then a voice was heard from the darkest corner of the room.

"What is your aspiration in life?"

In shock, yet feeling a sense of comfort and safety, Samantha peered into the darkened corner and saw Raphael in his glowing, angelic form. Her radiant smile matched his glow. Then she said, "I do not understand the question."

"Okay, what would you like to be when you grow up?"

Samantha struggled to sit up so that she could get a closer look at the comforting image that sat before her in the corner of the room. "I always wanted to be an airline pilot, like my Uncle Bob," she replied. Then she lay back in her bed twiddling with her fingers, "Well, that's not going to happen because I'm sick you know. I have leukemia."

Sadly, Samantha had acute myeloid leukemia, (AML), and

based on the doctor's diagnosis, and conjecture, she had about eight months to live.

"Oh, that's not good," Raphael said as he stood with his arms outstretched. The room then became bright as daylight, and the multi-colored furnished room became a glowing white as Raphael approached her bedside. Samantha looked up at him and reciprocated his smile. Raphael placed his hand on her head and said, "My, what beautiful hair you have!"

Samantha, shot a quick look at him as if to say, "What planet are you from?" Then she smiled and said as she pulled her cap off her head,

"I am bald! See!"

At that very moment Samantha sprang up in shock when her hair fell, draping over her shoulders. Raphael reached out his hand to hold hers and then said,

"You are going to be that airline pilot."

Right then the sound of a light knock, and then the clicking of the door knob sounded. With a warm smile on his face, Raphael looked down on Samantha and said, "I have to go!" Then he vanished.

On his rounds, the doctor walked in and stopped dead in his tracks when he saw Samantha's flowing hair. He reached down for her chart, and thinking out loud, said, "Am I missing something here?"

Poetic justice

Satan has put many unwarranted diseases on suffering adults and innocent children to cast doubt about the existence of God. However, through the mysterious, phenomenal healing of innocent children and adults throughout London, which was Raphael's doing, those same sicknesses would be cast onto evildoers who truly deserve them. Although many true believers, who became very sick, have passed and, of course, a few more will pass away, they have hope because Jesus Christ has prepared a place for them, a place where their names are etched in gold. For every child or adult that Raphael heals, six evil dwellers of this earth, who are from all walks of life, will be inflicted with the same diseases. To try to convince someone otherwise is not an option for this is war!

Yes, Raphael is the Angel that heals!

Raphael's campaign of healing had spread a repeated glow throughout the city. He left a wake of unexplained phenomena throughout many of the children's hospitals and private homes in London. They were a spin off from Samantha's visit. This process has spread, and will continue to spread, throughout the world. Those who do not believe or who walk in apathy will die like wilted flowers.

Sandra stopped dead in her tracks when she looked through the glass door and saw that it was night. "Damn Carla, it's only 4:25pm and it's dark outside! I forgot about the early nightfall!"

Carla turned to her and said, "Welcome to London, England. Because of the extreme time conditions here, the few friends that I have, that is, the ones who have kids, find it difficult to allow their kids to walk home from the school's bus stop because of this early nightfall. And in the summer it doesn't get dark until 9pm, which encourages later bed times. Sandra, how quickly you forget! Your head clock is going to get twisted while you are here," Carla said with a smile.

It was an hour later when Carla's friend and colleague dropped them off at the diner. As they turned to watch the taillights disappear, Sandra said, "Carla, give me a minute, I have to use the restroom." She turned away, walking quickly towards the diner.

Unbeknown to them however, there was a car parked across the street with one occupant in it who was observing them. Jeff Stuart, aged 48, was a slender built man with brown eyes and short black hair. He was a native sleeper, that is, he was born in the UK but had moved away only to be co-opted and used by the

Russians because of his ideology, and profession as an IT specialist in data communications. In fact, he was the overseer and recruiter of the airport's radical fringe terrorist group who had attempted the massacre that went awry. Their undercover operations was based in the UK. One of his duties was to stand back and watch possible enemy targets. Should anything go wrong, he would give a report to their main base that is somewhere in England.

While Carla waited, she decided to dig for Sheila's card so that she could enter her number on speed dial in her phone. She rested her bag on the hood of her car to shuffle through it, and soon pulled out the card. Suddenly, the same black van that had followed them earlier pulled up and came to a screeching stop. Two occupants exited it from the side door and grabbed her from behind. She started to kick and scream but to no avail because they out-muscled her and muffled her voice. Then they quickly threw her into the back of the van, and placed a hood over her head. It was quick, but poorly executed, because their orders were to abduct the two of them, not just one of them, and also it was a one way in, and one way out parking area, so they had to turn the van around.

By that time Sandra was on her way outside. She immediately summed up what had just happened because she did not see Carla where she had left her. Noticing a tussle from the rear window of the van, she immediately read the license plate, memorizing the number. Then she ran towards Carla's car, simultaneously digging in her bag for a pen to write down the number. She threw her bag onto Carla's car hood, and pulled out a piece of paper and began to write. After securing the license plate number, she took her phone from her bag, but then realized roaming was not set up on it. Slapping her head in frustration over her dilemma, she gazed down and noticed a business card lying on the ground. Picking it up, she immediately read Sheila Hall's contact information. "Thank God," she whispered to herself. She immediately ran back into the diner screaming for a phone.

Back in the speeding van, Stanley conveniently did not make physical contact with Carla because of what he had witnessed earlier on at the airport, and he never even mentioned it to the two who had physically abducted her. They had tied her mouth, hands and feet and placed a hood over her head. Stanley made rapid right and left turns in order to get onto the M25 in order to head southeast to Surrey.

℘

It was 4:50pm. Brent Russell took the lead in the briefing room after they had located the apartments where the terrorists had set up their operations. He drew on the chalkboard the tactical strategic moves on the hot spots of the apartments, which they had seen in the vision.

Sheila stood up and walked over to the chalkboard to assist him. "We need two separate teams of twelve on each location, six to breach and secure the crisis site, and the other six to serve as backup," she advised. Then she turned to Brent and said, "Contact MPS so that they can set up roadblocks in and out of both locations."

"You got it," Agent Russell said as he turned to another field agent and said, "Derrick, you head up the team on 7th Union Street." Suddenly, he clapped his hands and said," Okay gentlemen, tick tock, we're running out of time. Let's do this."

Brent and his team gained access to the adjoining room of the terrorists at King's Court. Using sign language, they communicated silently with one another as one of the agents went outside the room and secretly knelt down at their door and snaked a mini video cam under the door to study the occupants' position and activities.

This terror group seemed to be so fixated on blowing up things because the room looked as if they had just accidently triggered one of their bombs in it. Pizza boxes and fast food rappers were scattered all over the floor. The agent adjusted the cam's neck to focus on the occupants, while the other five watched the video feed on the monitor in the adjoining room. One of the three terrorists was sitting on the couch watching the news and eating a banana; a banana clip machine gun was leaning against the corner of the couch. Another was putting explosives into one of the three luggage bags that was sitting on the dining room table, and the third was a female, who was standing and staring out the window; she had an automatic pistol shoved down the back of her skirt.

Brent called Derrick, who was leading the 7th Union Street operations, which was coded Operation Yellow Tail, to find out if they were in position, and they were. It was important that they breached the same time in case the sting operation went badly—they did not want the terrorists to send out an alert signal. Brent laid his hand on the shoulders of one of the top sharpshooters they called, Hawk, and said, "It's now or never!" That was the cue, so they all took their assigned positions as the lead shooter walked to the door, checking his weapon. Then he opened the door slowly, signaling to the other agents to follow him. They were all simultaneously sound-checking their two-way ear communication devices as they quietly walked in a single file to exit the room.

One agent stayed behind to watch the monitor for any dramatic changes that may occur in the room. The breaching teams stood quietly outside the terrorists' door, having already numbered the occupants 1, 2, and 3, for each assigned shooter. Brent then signaled the agent with the battering ram and the other with the concussion grenades to breach. "Bam!" It was the sound of the door crashing in. It was followed by a "boom" from the concussion grenade. Then a "tap, tap, tap" could be heard—that sound came from Brent's and the other two sharpshooter's automatic hand laser guided weapons.

Precision work—that was all it took to put down all three of the occupants. After the surprise attack, the room looked as if it had undergone a small laser show as the red laser beams from their automatic weapons shone through the dissipating smoke. Then all three of the shooters shouted out, "Clear."

Immediately Brent ordered the team to collect evidence. While Brent was pulling his phone out to call Derrick, he reached out for

Hawk, held his right arm and said, "I need you to collect all of the cell phones and get them down to the lab immediately. Go!" After speed dialing Derrick, Brent held the phone to his ear and said, "Derrick, give me some good news!"

On the other end of the line, Derrick replied, "Operation Yellow Tail, down and out!"

Chapter 8

As Agent Russell walked down the steps of the King's Court, ripping the Velcro-grip bulletproof vest off, Sheila approached him with a congratulatory handshake, "Well done, Agent Russell! But we have another problem! I got a call from Sandra! Carla has been abducted!"

"When did this happen?" Brent asked, looking shocked.

"During the operation, I got the call twenty minutes ago. I have already sent an agent to the diner to pick Sandra up. They should be back at headquarters by the time we get there."

"Let's go!" Brent said, walking quickly to his car.

"I will see you back there! We only have a short time before the trail goes cold," Sheila added. "I told Sandra not to call her; she's a sharp girl for she got the plate number also, and I already have an agent trying to track Carla's phone as we speak. I'm hoping she was able to hide it!"

"Great!" Brent said, "I'll see you there."

Carla sat quietly on the floor of the back of the van as the driver drove cautiously; making rapid turns through the streets of London. The two abductors in the back were sorting through her bag's contents that were scattered on the van's floor. They were mainly looking for her phone or any other electronic device that could be tracked. Somehow however, they had overlooked her phone when they had patted her down because she had quickly and secretly slipped her compact phone in her bra between her breasts, when they first jumped her. It was also a good thing that she had just left her office where everybody knew she would be off for the week. She prayed that nobody called her before someone realized that she was missing and track her phone. Suddenly, the van turned onto the M25 motorway ramp, and picking up tremendous speed, it headed southeast towards Surrey.

℮∕℗

When both Sheila and Brent walked through the door of the Operation's floor of the headquarters, Sandra immediately ran to Brent, embracing him and crying, "Brent, they took her! What are we going to do?"

"I am so sorry, but calm down, we will find her," Brent promised.

Agent Valdez, who was assigned to track Carla's cell phone, called Sheila and Brent over to his station and told them he had picked up a track, and according to the cell towers, the van was heading southeast on the M25 motorway.

Then Agent Ailes walked up to them with a printout that had the information he had obtained from the license plate. He started to read from the sheet: "Stanley Wilson is the owner of the black van.

It's not even reported stolen—I have checked, but we have his home address. Stanley Wilson, a British born native, aged 42, is 5'9" tall. He has black graying hair that he keeps in a ponytail; he's single and has no children. An IT specialist, he specializes in computer data processing. He's also heavily influenced by Russian ideology. Even though he is a sloppy dresser, and careless at times in his work, he is dedicated to his duties as a member of the *sinister* group."

Suddenly, Brent snapped his fingers and pointed at the agent and said, "You got his cell number, right?"

"Yes," the agent responded.

"Track it," Brent said with a snap of his fingers.

"Why can't we call her?" Sandra asked.

Brent turned to her and said, "Because they will take her phone and destroy it. We are hoping she was able to hide it, and it looks as if she has, and, in that way, we will be able to track her." Brent then turned to one of the agents on the floor and said, "Bring Mr. Cornell in here!"

The agent responded, "Who?"

"Paul Cornell, the kid, bring him in here," Brent ordered. Then he turned to Sheila and said, "We need the chopper!"

Sheila replied, "You got it," as she quickly keyed in a number into her phone.

Brent added, "Sandra, you have to stay here. Boss, I also need Paul to come with me, just in case our Angel decides to make his presence felt."

Then, all of a sudden, Agent Valdez shouted out, "Got a hit and a track on the phone!"

"Where?" Brent asked, as he spun around to approach the agent's station.

Valdez then turned to Brent and said, "The phone is in that van, Stanley Wilson is our abductor."

A minute later, Agent Ailes walked in with Paul.

Brent turned to Ailes and thanked him. Then he turned to Paul and said, "Paul, let's go! Hope you're not afraid of heights."

"Where are we going?" Paul asked.

"You get to play an MI5 agent. Come on, man up!" Brent said.

As they ran across the helicopter pad towards the helicopter, they could smell the kerosene burning from the jet screaming engine. Valdez and Ailes, who had the tracking devices, accompanied Brent and Paul. Night had fallen, but they would not have a problem because the aircraft has infrared equipment. It was Paul's first flight in a helicopter, so he was looking around excitingly as if he were a child on a carnival ride. They took flight at 6:15pm. But the abduction had taken place an hour ago—that was how much farther ahead they were, yet the chopper could cover that distance in 15 minutes.

Jeff, the guy who had been sitting in the car across the street, had been observing both Carla and Sandra when Carla was abducted. He had been frantically trying to call Stanley on his cell phone but to no avail. He had somehow lost him in traffic a while back. The phone had accidently fell out of Stanley's pocket and onto the floor board between the two front seats of the van. Stanley wasn't able to hear it because it was set on vibrate. Jeff's urgency mounted as he had seen Sandra watching the van as it drove off, and she might have possibly seen and memorized the plate number. The problem was there was a clear connection between the van and that phone. Jeff seemed to know the van's destination as he was already in hot pursuit on the M25 motorway, trying to get a visual on it.

A few miles from his destination, Stanley decided to call ahead. After digging and looking around for his phone, he suddenly glimpsed it lying on the floor. It was flashing a ring signal. When he finally picked up the phone, Jeff started screaming at him on the other end, "Get rid of your phone!"

Stanley responded, "Why?"

"You left the other girl back there, which you shouldn't have done! She saw you pulled off! Two words, license plate—duh ass....... Just get rid of it!"

"Okay, Okay, I'm pulling over right now at a self-guided tour park."

Right then, Jeff got a visual on the van. Stanley had pulled the van into the self-guided tour park's parking lot. He quickly got out, stuck the phone under the front tire, got back in, and drove over it. Seconds after that, Jeff pulled up, got out of his vehicle and walked directly to the van. When he slid open the side door, the sound of a phone's dying battery sounded off. All four of them looked at Carla, because it was her phone.

"Give it here," Jeff demanded angrily.

Carla slowly reached into her bra and pulled it out. Jeff then reached out and snatched it from her hand, and threw it on the ground and stamped on it a few times. It was 6:25pm. He turned to Stanley and said, "They have probably tracked you by now, so follow me and stay close, you idiot! We've got to get out of here!"

❧

Meanwhile:

At an altitude of 500 feet, Agent Valdez turned to Brent and said, "I have lost one of the signals, and the second one is weak and intermittent. It is also no longer moving.

The pilot was also monitoring the same signal; he then turned to Brent and said, "We are five minutes away."

Shortly after the helicopter landed in the self-guided tour's brightly lit parking lot, Brent immediately spotted the two damaged phones as the helicopter was settling down. He looked back at one of the agents and said, "Glove up; we need prints from both of those phones and the history from Stanley Wilson's phone."

It was a bit ironic, because while Jeff had been all over Stanley about making mistakes, he had just made two costly mistakes when he left the two cell phones visibly lying in the parking lot. While Agent Ailes was bagging the phones, Brent was aimlessly looking around for other clues. Then, he quickly turned and ran back to the helicopter screaming, "Let's go!" While he was climbing in, he told the pilot, "Get back over the M25 and fly over the southeast traffic as low as you can possibly go! According to my calculations, they are at least 9 minutes ahead of us." Pointing his thumb up, he said, "Let's go!" Then he turned his head to look at the agents in the back and added, "Keep your eyes on the motorway, we are still looking for the black van, and we need the two spotlights on now!" Brent turned back to the pilot and said, "I need you to get five minutes flying time, southeast on the M25." The pilot immediately set the helicopter's time clock.

Brent also added, "From the time we discovered that the phones went out within one minute of each other, you said we were five minutes out." He looked at his watch as the pilot began flying over the M25 and said, "From then until now, it has been nine minutes, now it's ten." Brent looked back at the other agents, and exclaimed, "They are ten minutes ahead of us; their twenty minutes driving speed is equivalent to our five minutes flying time. They should be at average speed because they can't afford any unwanted attention. If we do not spot the van within our five-minute flying time, we must assume that they have reached their destination. If that is the case, we can box in the area from the self-guided tour's parking lot we left behind and a selected spot at our 5 minute call. Also, I want each of you to select a landmark when the pilot calls out, 'five minutes', and that includes you too Paul, my special agent."

Immediately, the pilot called out, "Five minutes."

Each agent called out their landmark—one said, "Motel," the other said, "Petrol station," and then Paul said, "Hillside!" All of the agents turned to him and asked in unison, "Hillside?"

Brent shook his head and said, "That's my special agent! Well guys, I'm looking at that motel and that petrol station also." Brent turned to the pilot and said, "Let's put it down on the far side of the empty parking area of the motel, and shut it down!"

As the helicopter's twin jet engine was winding down, Brent had already exited the helicopter and was walking away to get away from the engine's noise to call Sheila. The phone rang only twice before Sheila answered, "Agent Russell, give me some good news!"

Brent responded by saying, "They had carelessly ditched and destroyed the phones, but we were able to recover them both! Their discovery allowed me to strategically box out the area where they might be hiding. We landed and are shut down in a travel budget motel's parking lot off the M25 motorway, just outside Surrey. Boss, I'm thinking I need to set up a makeshift station here at the motel. I feel they are real close, so we need to carpet this area."

Sheila responded by saying, "There is a terror network connected to them, making this a matter of national security! Agent Russell, I trust your judgment. I will back whatever you feel you need to do."

"Thank you very much, but also, Boss, you need to get a search warrant for Stanley Wilson's flat, and send Derrick and a team to get on that!"

Sheila responded, "Agent Russell, I can think sometimes, you know! I'm already on that."

Brent then chuckled and said, "I'm sorry. "I'm leaving now to return there!"

"You need to get sufficient rooms for your agents," Sheila said as she rushed to get into another helicopter that was standing by.

Brent and his team had already settled into one of the motel rooms they had rented, and had also set up for the extra equipment they were expecting. It was now 7:00pm. Then came a knock on the door. When one of them opened it, Sheila walked in with three other agents who had the additional equipment with them.

Sheila turned to Brent and asked, "So where are we now?"

Brent turned to Paul, "You said there is a lot more to this number sequence! Can you break it down for us?"

Paul looked at Agent Williams, who had just arrived with Sheila, and said, "I need something to write on."

Agent Williams pulled out, and erected from a kit, a board and a marker as Brent nodded that it was okay to go on.

Paul walked over to the board and picked up the marker, turned to them all, and said, "Listen; before I go on I need to remind you that this information that I have obtained was given to me from a divine source, the Angel Raphael. Don't laugh, this is serious! I'm noticing your effort to hold back your smiles. If I were in your position, I probably would have felt the same way too. It was a little over four hours ago this revelation came to me, along with the affirmation to explain what I am about to tell you."

Brent jumped in immediately and said, "Hold up a second!" He turned to the agents who were sitting and standing around and said, "I know you guys are not privy to this information you are about to hear, but what he is about to say is important as it has gotten us to where we are right now in this room tonight! Now, I have to ask you all to restrain from calling family members and friends until we see our way through this. Need I remind you all that secrecy is protocol?" Brent turned to Paul again and nodded for him to go on.

Paul continued, "Now, you all probably should be familiar with the Bible story about the war that occurred among the angels in heaven. According to the biblical record, when Lucifer lost the war, he was cast down from heaven with a ⅓ of the angels that fought with him, into a black hole, commonly known as hell. 396 fallen angels, which included Lucifer and his determination to derail God's plan, manage to break away and took up residence here on earth."

He paused before continuing, "Now, I know you all are asking yourselves, why 396? Let me explain! There is one thing that seemed to be attached to Lucifer like an Achilles heel, and it is the fraction ⅓, which God had put on him; it is the very number or fraction he was cast out with. For his every thought and every move, we would have to include that factor in our calculations. Only he and six of his Generals retained most of their strength, he being the strongest of them all! But all the other dark angels were cursed as they only retained a ⅓ of their strength. Now this is where the two billion numbers comes in—the internet or social media is a tool that joins hands through cyberspace throughout the world. Unfortunately, there are a lot of agnostics and evil people in that mix! It's a perfect tool for ISIS and their recruiting methods. Russia is undermining democracy, and 'hell', and even child pornography, which is a gift to the Devil himself! And, do you know something? Even before I obtained this knowledge, I had no interest in social media. You would think someone my age would be all over it, right?"

Paul turned to the board and started to write, "Okay, here it is— two billion is the tipping point on the largest social media network. Go ahead, Google it! Last time I checked, the old data was right on the crust! Okay, alright, pay attention—let's subtract two-thirds (⅔) from the two billion, social media's turning point, that leaves us with a ⅓, right? This fraction represents 666,666,666.667. To reduce those decimal points we round it off at 666,000,000. The .7 after the series of sixes of that correct calculation, that is, at the seven level steps, we are to drop 10% on each step."

Continuing Paul said, "These steps represent the seven cardinal sins. Our first stage or cardinal sin is pride, which is 10% of 666,000,000; This leaves you with 66,600,000; the second stage or sin is greed, which is another 10% that gives you 6,660,000; the third stage or sin is lust, another 10%, which gives us 666,000; another 10% or sin is envy, that gives us 66,600, and another 10% or sin is gluttony, which gives us 6,660; and another is wrath, which gives us 666; and our last stage or sin is sloth, which represents 66.6. This represents 66 dark, fallen angels, who operate in each one of the six continents with one General as their head. They are separate, but equal in their tyranny over these continents, with the exception of Antarctica, because there is no constant stream of people living there. There are six populated continents, Asia, Africa, North America, South America, Europe and Australia. You have to multiply the remaining .6 by 66, which will give you the 396 earth surface fallen angels that are called demons. Remember that the two billion have to be reached to start that *trigger trip wire point*, for their world assault! Also, if you add up all of the social media followers, including those who are on Facebook, Twitter, Snapchat and others, you will find that those numbers are close to or they almost total ⅓ of the world's population. Do you see where I'm going with this?"

Paul went on to say, "Gentlemen and lady, turning to Sheila, "This information, which I have received clairvoyantly, is now telling me that there are 66 demonic angels in each of the six continents. In each continent there are 11 strategically selected heavily populated provinces or state of each country, 6 major populated cities of each of those 11 state or province, 6 multiplied by 11 is 66 demonic fallen angels of each continent. Paul paused for a moment to look at everyone's face, and then said softly and firmly, "They are what you would call clandestine fifth columnists that are buried in the very root of each and every country of this world; a world assault is coming on society's freedom."

At that moment you could hear a pin drop.

Brent then weighed in by asking, "Were you given any insight on their locations so that we can look for them? Are there any geographical maps in your head?"

"No, but I'm getting a sense that if we juggle and play with these numbers long enough, we will figure it out! I feel it! I feel it is our responsibility to figure it out, Agent Russell. Like I said before, our Angel will give us a window, but we will have to open the door."

Brent looked at Sheila and said, "We need the local police to put an APB out on that van and a look out for any strange behavior that would be of concern to national security in the Surrey area. I would like the local police motorway patrol to station a look out car in the boxed out area to alert us when they locate the black van, starting at the self-guided parking lot and ending at the petrol station across the street. We, along with our agents and the local police, should start a methodical combing of this area tonight. The use of the helicopter would not be 100% effective until tomorrow morning."

Sheila pulled out her phone and said, "I am going to call somebody to work on the local police right now! You go ahead and start your ground search."

$$\text{e\textc/o}$$

Meanwhile......

The time is 10:10pm, Russian time. 3,623.8 miles northeast of Russia, a cellphone rang out from the coat pocket of Veektor Sokol, who sat, after a dinner meeting, having cocktails with six Russian oligarchs in an exquisite restaurant in Moscow. He stood up, answering the phone as he walked over to the vestibule area.

The voice on the other end said, "We have her!"

As he looked at his reflection in the mirror by the check-in/coat area, his eyes turned a grayish yellow, "Very good, I will be there shortly."

⟨⁄⟩

Meanwhile....

Somewhere in Birmingham, Alabama, around 1:10pm, incarnated Gabriel, that is, Sam, sat high on a beam in an evangelical Baptist church. This time he was neatly dressed in a cream-colored suit. The church was empty, but on the outside, a luncheon was set up for the evangelical churchgoers and supporters of the underdog, the presidential candidate. Among these churchgoers and supporters there was a clearly pronounced racial divide because there was a confederate flag planted in the yard, and some of them were wearing confederate t-shirts. As incarnated Sam enjoyed his view of this so called, god-fearing church, a side door closing shut had sounded, and Pastor Alex Brown walked into the church, crossing over to the pulpit area. That is when Sam dropped a Bible. "Wham," it hit the floor with a loud thud.

"Pick it up!" Sam shouted.

Pastor Brown looked up and said, "Who are you, and what are you doing up there?"

Sam shouted again, "Pick it up!"

"I am calling the police," Pastor Brown cried out, reaching for his phone.

Right then Sam leapt from the ceiling's beam; his clothes flapped loudly as he touched down on the floor. He scooped up the Bible off the floor, stuck it in the pastor's face, and said, "Ephesians 6:5, read it!"

Pastor Brown looked directly into Sam's face, and trembling with fright cried out, "I know what it says!"

"Recite it," Sam persisted.

Pastor Brown said with trembling lips, "Slaves obey your masters."

Sam asked, "Did you write this?"

"Of course not!" Pastor Brown responded.

"Perhaps, your ancestors wrote it, or should I say a chain of your ancestors, or maybe it was just people who hold your twisted beliefs, who wrote it!"

Speechless, the pastor stood there staring at Sam.

Sam continued, "Do you and your members, who are outside and who are so jubilant in spirit, wish to reintroduce slavery? Why is this passage so convenient for you and your peers, and you do this in the name of God! Shame on you!" Gabriel's glowing image started to emerge from Sam.

The pastor's jaw dropped open and his eyes widened as a glowing Gabriel stood before him.

Gabriel said, "Try this on!"

Immediately the pastor's hands and feet were shackled.

Gabriel took one step back to get a full look at the pastor, and then he pointed towards the door and said, "Now, go, mix and mingle with your peers."

Pastor Brown stood there hesitating, not sure what to do next.

Gabriel angrily shouted at him, pointing towards the door, "GO!"

As Pastor Brown turned and walked toward the door, he started to cry, "Oh Lord, why?" He finally reached the church's front door, and after opening it, the on-looking crowd gasped as he cried out, "FREE ME!"

Gabriel said softly to himself, "Pride…. Message sent, message received."

Chapter 9

Detective Danny Stone was on his computer at his desk. He was going through more of the information in the Turner Diaries Report, including the information on the other White supremacists' behaviors he had received on the down low from his brother-in-law, Andrew Anderson.

Andrew was an FBI agent, and fortunately for Detective Stone, he was assigned to the team of FBI agents who were working on the warehouse carnage case. Agent Anderson, aged 43, and 5'11" tall, was a sandy blonde man with dark brown eyes. He worked out of the Riverside field office, and was married to Nancy Miller-Anderson, the sister of Debbie Miller-Stone, who was the wife of Detective Danny Stone. Agent Anderson, who was a thirteen-year veteran with the bureau, was assigned to work with a lot of White supremacists' cases in the past, but now they had just recently assigned him to Detective Danny's warehouse case, which he had found to be a unique and special one given the report he had read and the fact that his brother-in-law had worked the scene and had a special interest in it.

It was now 11:50am. Detective Danny was so deeply engrossed in the information on his computer screen that he didn't realize that his smartphone was ringing on vibrate and shifting position on his desk. Then he noticed it, and picking it up he said, "Hello, Detective Stone here. How can I help?"

"Detective Stone, this is James! I made that call you told me to make, and Mr. Davis wants me to meet somebody else at a location of his choosing. He said he will call me back with an address."

"That's great," Detective Danny said, "Call me the minute you get that meeting's address."

"Will do partner," James said and hung up.

As Detective Stone was straightening up his desk in preparation to leave the precinct, his phone rang again. This time it rang out because he had changed it back to its ringtone. He looked at his phone and saw that his brother-in-law, Andrew, had left him a message. He answered, "What's up bro? I was waiting on your call!"

Andrew replied, "I'm cool, Danny! I need to talk to you too! I was assigned to your warehouse case."

"According to your message, you seem to have something big for me!"

"Yes I do! Listen, I'm leaving my office now to go home for lunch, can you meet me at the house?"

"No problem, I can be there in 20 minutes," Andrew replied.

Both Debbie and Danny arranged to meet home for lunch—Debbie was picking up their take-out lunches to bring home with her. Danny lived only fifteen minutes away from the precinct. It was 12:15pm when a knock came at their door. Debbie walked over to open the door, and as she opened it she said, "Andrew, what a pleasant surprise!"

"Debbie, how are you?"

"I'm fine," she replied.

"Unfortunately, it's not a pleasurable one this time," Andrew said.

Danny walked up behind Debbie, eating shrimp fried rice from a Chinese takeout box. "Come on in! I hope you are hungry for we've got lots of food," Danny said.

After they had eaten, Danny excused himself and Andrew, not wanting to bring his wife in so early into his investigation. They went off to the den where Danny pulled out a flash drive and inserted it into his laptop to view the video clip.

"Who on earth, or should I say, what on earth did this?" Andrew asked, looking in awe at the video.

"It's funny that you should ask me that! That blurred vision of someone using that trashing strap is not of this world," Danny revealed.

Andrew turned to Danny, his eyes wide, "So what are you trying to tell me, that this is some kind of alien?"

Danny interlocked both hands behind his head and laid back in the couch they both were sitting on, and taking on a blowfish face to exhale, said, "This is difficult to explain to say the least! You and Nancy tend to go to church a lot more than Debbie and I! Hell, the last time I was in church was at grandma's funeral, and you know that was a while back! But I do confess that I'm a God-fearing man, ever since yesterday when I was introduced to this guy named Sam because I believe he is somehow responsible for this carnage."

Andrew jumped in, "Wait a minute, are you telling me you know who did this? Danny, did you hit your head?"

Danny sat up straight and turned to look directly at Andrew, "You got to understand that this is not your average case. This guy," Danny paused a moment, "Ooooh, how can I put this? He knows things and says things a normal person wouldn't know or say! He moves in mysterious ways, appears out of nowhere, is very knowledgeable and talks with a great deal of confidence. They say he is an Angel."

"They? Who are they?" Andrew asked, quite taken aback.

"I was getting to that!" Right then Danny's phone rang. He lifted one finger, gesturing to Andrew to give him a minute as he knew the caller because his number was saved in his phone. He answered,

"Go James!"

James, on the other end, said, "Okay, here is the address—there is a little Mom and Pop restaurant in Huntington Beach on the corner of Golden West Street and Beach Blvd." While Danny was writing down the address, James continued, "He said to be there 6:00pm sharp. Mr. Stone, I'm starting to feel a bit edgy about this now!"

Danny stopped what he was doing, and putting the pad and pen down, he asked James, "What's going on?"

"I don't know! This guy doesn't seem too friendly now! He was speaking with a different tone," James said.

Danny then said, "Listen James, I don't want to force you to do anything you are not comfortable with. If you are having a change of mind and heart, this is the time to tell me."

James responded, "I do feel deep down inside that it is my civic duty to protect the law abiding citizens of this country and the world, so I'm going to man up on this one! You guys will be watching over me right?"

"You bet my friend! You might not know it now but my latest understanding is that there is a greater Protector that's going to be watching over us all! Oh, I almost forgot, I need you to come over to my house to go over a few details in preparation for certain questions they will be asking you. Let's say 4:30pm. Here is my address." Danny's home was not too far from his precinct on Anaheim 425 South Harbor Boulevard.

As Danny rested his phone down, he looked over at Andrew and said, "Yes, you can say I have been a bit busy. I have formed a little team! That was James Carey, a reporter and journalist; he's the latest team member. There are two others, Christopher Rodgers, a journalist/reporter and Stephan Smith, one of the abductees. He is where it all began, and oh, there's also Sam, our mystery man. I would simply like to refer to him as our "thank God-send" Angel! You are going to meet him I hope, sooner than later! Listen Andrew, I know this is out of my jurisdiction and you are going to have to work this because it's a federal case, but these guys are comfortable with me, so allow us to work with you, incognito. I trust these guys, and I know that they will be a great asset to us."

Andrew sat there for a minute without saying a word, then he broke his silence and said, "Danny, I'm going to have to meet with my team on this as I have to discuss most of what you just told me with them first. I'm going to hold back on that mystery man until I meet him. I will be back for that 4:30pm rehearsal meeting as there are specific guidelines that you need to follow. See that your two other players are there also!"

"No problem," Danny said as they both stood up and walked towards the door.

Chris had called his boss earlier to request compassionate leave to assist Steve in his time of need. They were sitting around Steve's apartment making and receiving phone calls to and from family members. In between calls, Steve showed Chris a photo album with photos of their childhood and more recent ones of both families.

Sadly, Steve reminisced, "Her family is pretty small. I never had any children with her, but she has a son named Joey before our marriage. He lives in Nevada with family members. She always talked about when she died that she wanted to be cremated. I guess my next step is to call the funeral home."

Suddenly, Chris' phone rang, "Hello!"

"Hey Chris, my friend, Detective Stone here."

"Yes sir, I recognized your number. Danny, before you go on I have some bad news! Steve's wife passed."

"You're kidding me, right? When did that happen?" Danny asked.

"He got the call the minute we left the park. The doctor wanted him to return to the hospital immediately. I'm at his apartment now helping him with the funeral arrangements," Chris said.

"Put him on the phone please," Danny said.

"One second, Steve, Detective Stone would like to speak with you," Chris said, passing the phone to him.

"Hello Sir," Steve said.

"Hey buddy, I'm so sorry! Please accept my condolences," Danny said.

"Thank you very much," Steve replied and then went on to say, "But I want you to know I have been knocked down, but not knocked out; I'm still here with you guys to fight this case to the bitter end. I just got some personal stuff I need to take care of."

"You do that my friend, and take your time; the seat will be right here whenever you are ready to come back in," Danny said.

"Thank you," Steve said, as he passed the phone back to Chris.

Meanwhile.....

Back in Alabama it is 2:45pm. Sam, through Gabriel's guidance, had strangely been drawn into an unknown phenomena for he found himself walking up the dirt path of a hill that led to a little dilapidated church that was in desperate need of repair. As he got closer, he also noticed two guys working on the church's front door locks.

"Hello there," Sam shouted as he approached them.

The two guys stopped what they were doing and turned to look at Sam. Then both said in unison, "Good afternoon!"

"It looks like you've got a lot of work ahead of you. My name is Sam Watson and I'm just strolling by!"

The older of the two took the lead and said, "Hello, I am Dunstan Archer and I hope to become the preacher of this church one day. This is my helper and friend, Julian Bates." He nodded to his helper and extended his hand for a handshake. Dunstan was a fifty-three-year-old black man of a light brown complexion, brown eyes, and graying black hair. He was a muscular built, and 6' 3" tall. When they had gripped each other's hand, they both froze as a glowing flicker shone from them. It was followed by a warm feeling that emanated from them. There was recognition as Gabriel's voice spoke first from Sam, "Andrealphus..."

Dunstan replied in an all so soft voice, "Gabriel, is that you?

Please forgive me. I have waited so long for this moment to have the opportunity to return! I was so wrong."

Andrealphus was one of the fallen Angels that had been unjustly caught up in the politics with Lucifer, and had made the wrong choice. He had somehow stepped back shortly after a few of the other fallen Angels had become residents on the earth over the eons of time. After winning individual battles, he had managed to avoid being taken down by the demons that once were angels.

Incarnated Sam pulled Dunstan in towards him, and then kissed and embraced him. Then he said, "Andrealphus, my brother, my brother, of course, I forgive you! That is what we are all about, you know that. Come, let us walk in faith."

Dunstan turned to Julian, and with tears in his eyes, said, "My friend, you have no idea what meeting this man has done for me today. You can wrap this up as we are done here for now. I will meet you back at the house. I'm going to spend some time with my long, lost friend."

Julian Bates, a twenty-four-year-old Caucasian male, had long blonde hair, and blue eyes. A large man, he was 6'4" tall, and had had behavioral issues while in high school that had forced him to drop out. Soon after that he had ran away from home, and had become a drifter, getting by with odd jobs. Then he met Dunstan Archer, who took him in and became his mentor. As a result, he turned over a new leaf and literally became a gentle giant. He has since been in touch with his family, and they are very happy with the major changes he has made in his life working and living with Mr. Archer, they speak and visit often. He is also in night classes to finish up what he had mist in high school.

Dunstan himself was a caretaker at an old folk's home, which was one of the many jobs he had that positively impacted the lives of many troubled or hurting people. He was Andrealphus incarnated throughout his time on the earth.

Julian stood there with an ear to ear smile, not quite noticing the glowing flicker but yet he experienced that warm feeling that surprised him as he had not expected to have this type of experience with Dunstan. After a short pause he said, "Don't worry Mr. Archer, I got your back!"

Dunstan looked at Julian with a stern face and said, "What is it that I keep telling you about this Mr. Archer thing? Dunstan, Dunstan is my name!"

Julian shot back, laughing out loud, "Archer is your name too, Mr. Archer!"

They all chuckled a bit as Sam wrapped his arm around Dunstan, and as they started to walk away, Julian shouted out, "Aren't you taking the car?"

Dunstan turned back and shouted, "You know I can't drive and No, we don't need a car!" Then he mumbled to Sam, "Cars, I never liked them anyway! We can fly right?"

Sam looked at Dunstan and smiled. Then Gabriel's inner voice sounded out, "I can!" When they were out of view, Sam stopped and looked at Dunstan, and said as he clapped his hand, "Come with me!"

Immediately they both were standing on top of the Cheaha Mountain, 2,407 feet high, in Birmingham, Alabama. Dunstan shouted out, "Whoa, what are we doing here?"

Right then Gabriel emerged from Sam and said, "I like to be on top of things, and away from watchful eyes so that I can do what we are about to do!"

"And what are we about to do?" Dunstan asked.

Gabriel grabbed Dunstan's hand and started running with him down the snowy mountain slope. As they ran he bellowed out, "We're going to fly!" Gabriel took off with Dunstan in his grip. Suddenly, he let him go, and Dunstan dropped thirteen feet, and started rolling head over heels down the mountain slope for about forty feet. Then he came to a stop on a landing and, looking up at Gabriel hovering over him with a smile, he asked, "Are you trying to kill me?"

"Ha, ha, you have to be a living soul to be killed!" Gabriel quipped.

"Says who? I'm just an Angel at heart who is taking refuge in a human body. Gabriel, in case you didn't know, they do feel pain!" Dunstan said.

As Gabriel descended, he looked in shock at Dunstan, who was lying in the snow, flapping his arms and legs. Gabriel asked, "What are you doing?"

Dunstan smiled up at him and said, "See, you made me an Angel again, a snow Angel!" Dunstan then laughed heartily. Suddenly, and without warning, Dunstan's stopped laughing as he looked over Gabriel's shoulders at someone who was standing directly in front of him and looking down on him. He saw a massive image standing on the peak of the mountain. It was Michael. Dunstan muttered, "Uh, oh!"

At that very moment Gabriel turned and looked up to find Michael staring down at both of them. Michael stood silent for a moment, and then he looked down to his left and saw Sam sitting on a rock, shivering from the cold. With a gigantic flap of his wings, he took off with lightning speed and vanished into the blue skies.

"Is he angry?" asked Dunstan.

Gabriel responded, "No, no, he's not! If he were, he would have said something."

Quite surprised, they both looked up at Sam who was shouting from the top of the mountain, "Hey guys, are you done down there? I'm freezing up here! I'm too old for this cold!"

Gabriel reached out for Dunstan's hand, and suddenly, they appeared at Sam's side. Sam looked up at both of them and said, "Your boss appeared to be mad with you!"

Gabriel looked down on Sam and said, "Shhhh, say no more," as he once again joined in one with him.

Chapter 10

Gabriel and Dunstan sat on separate large mountain rocks. "What is it like? And what did you do over the eons of time?" Gabriel/Sam asked.

"Gabriel, I was running from capture the whole, entire time! No doubt, Lucifer was angry when I reversed my decision to follow him," Dunstan replied.

"How were you able to avoid being caught?" Gabriel asked.

Dunstan declared, "I would re-incarnate myself in dying human bodies whose age was compatible to mine and whose diseases could be cured. I would cure them, preferably loners, through my incarnated presence, to avoid being recognized by their loved ones. I moved from town to town, state to state and country to country. Gabriel, I had so many hearts that sometimes I felt that I was very close to having a soul."

Right then, Gabriel perked up, and with an alarming look on his face, said, "That is impossible!"

Dunstan looked directly into Gabriel's eyes, and with tears in them, said, "I know, but can't you see? I have cried so many times; I've felt sadness and I've felt pain, but I'm an angel!" Then Dunstan held his head down and whispered, "Or just remnants of one!"

"Don't you worry my brother, you are going to be fully back! I can guarantee that, and sooner than you think," Gabriel confidently declared. Then he added, "Don't you know this is what the war was all about? You had that favorable position which Lucifer was so jealous of, and fought so vehemently against! My brother, have you thought that maybe the fact that you are in this position is not so bad after all?"

"I do feel that way sometimes," Dunstan replied, "but the constant fights and the running to get away from him and his generals are making it so difficult for me to channel the truth of what our Father had intended for man," Dunstan said as he rubbed his head.

"Your church, does it have a name or is it a part of a denomination? You know why I'm asking, right? It's because there are so many of them!" Gabriel said with a smile.

Dunstan looked up, and staring up at the clouds in the sky, said, "Church, that's it, the sign would say *Direct Channel Church*." Dunstan looked at Gabriel with a look of wonder as if he was on to something, "What do you think?"

"Yes, you are definitely in for the fight of your life for Lucifer's flightless birds would surely tune in to that!"

"But Gabriel, do you know that our strength here on earth is nowhere close to that which we had in heaven?"

"Andrealphus, when a third of you and the others were cast down from heaven, our Father let you all have the exact same group size in measure to your strength. Come to think about it, how were you able to escape that black hell hole that you were cast into?" Gabriel asked.

"Lucifer, somehow, kept most of his strength. He was determined to derail God's plan here on earth. I guess I was lucky enough to be in the chosen group when he, including me and 394 others, managed to escape the black hole known as hell," Dunstan replied.

Suddenly Dunstan perked up as his angel's sense of alarm signaled that there was a problem. "Hold up a second Gabriel, they have located me again! Julian's in trouble! It's at the church! We have to go back."

"I'm picking up on the very same signal," Gabriel replied.

"Are you ready for this?" he added, placing his hand on Dunstan's shoulder to get his full attention.

"I better be," Dunstan exclaimed.

"Andrealphus, I'm talking directly to you this time," Gabriel/Sam said.

They held hands and disappeared. Then they reappeared fifty yards down the dirt drive to the church. Gabriel stepped out of Sam and into his angelic form, and turning to Sam said, "Sam, my friend, keep your distance from this church."

Earlier Dunstan had told Julian to wrap it up and go home, but when they had left, Julian had decided to stay on and surprise Dunstan by finishing up on other things they had planned to do that day. It was then Lucifer's dark demonic angels came to him in human form. It was Abaddon, Uzza and Shax. Abaddon was the ranking leader, who was assigned to track down Andrealphus. Abaddon was a sharp dresser in his human mutated form. Slender built, he was very cunning and manipulative. Like a chameleon, his eyes would change color to suit every mood and situation he found himself in. Now, his mood color was a grayish yellow.

Sam started to walk down the church's dirt path to keep a greater distance. Dunstan/Andrealphus, started to walk up the path with confidence as he quickly marched towards the church door. Gabriel, on the other hand, took flight and landed on the rooftop of the little church's steeple.

With the force of a battering ram, Dunstan/Andrealphus kicked the church's front door in. There was a table right beneath the church's pulpit, and Julian was lying on top of the table. On the right stood Abaddon, and on the left of the table was Uzza. They were preparing for some sought of sacrifice.

"I was expecting you a lot sooner, are you getting slower in your old age? Like the bodies you always seek to host, tell me whose poor soul are you in now?" Abaddon asked.

Dunstan/Andrealphus started walking slowly towards Abaddon, and said, "There is nothing poor about this soul. In fact, there is nothing poor about any of those souls at all! Isn't this why you are here? Isn't this why Lucifer started this quest to begin with, given your ongoing pathetic thirst for the blood of those good, poor human souls, like this one lying before you? Then Dunstan/Andrealphus shouted with a voice of authority, "Julian, get up!"

Julian was moaning as if he had been sedated with something, but was slowly coming out of it.

"I'm surprised Andrealphus! You seem to have a lot of confidence in yourself! You are not trying to run, and you are not trying to hide," Abaddon said as he unwrapped the cloth that held the dagger he was going to use to kill Julian, his sacrifice.

"So, am I to be concerned about this sudden level of confidence you are displaying?" Abaddon asked.

Dunstan had stopped five yards shy of Abaddon, and as he slightly turned his eyes to the left, he saw Uzza smiling and giggling as if he was on some type of illegal drugs. Then he said, "You tell me."

Shax had slipped out of the side door the minute Dunstan first entered the church; now he was about to slip back in through the front door. As he turned the corner of the church, he walked smack into Gabriel, and in shock, he slowly looked up to see Gabriel's face that shone with a dim glow.

Gabriel looked down at him and shouted, "BOO!" Immediately, Gabriel grabbed him by his neck with his left hand, lifting him up until he was on the same level with him. Then he shoved his right hand up through his lower rib cage and pulled his heart out. Before his mutated body expired, Gabriel whispered in his ears, "You are heartless!"

Abaddon began looking around with a curious look on his face because he had just noticed Shax was nowhere around. Then he shouted, "Shax, where are you?" Immediately, he looked over at Uzza and, nodding at him, he gestured that he should take care of Dunstan/Andrealphus. In response, Uzza leapt like a bullfrog towards Andrealphus.

With lightning speed, Andrealphus caught Uzza in mid-flight and with the angel strength that had remained, he body-slammed him to the church floor, and with a massive fist punch, he smashed his chest cavity and destroyed everything that was in it. Uzza quickly succumbed to his injuries.

Abaddon stepped forward to look down upon Uzza. Then looking back at Dunstan/Andrealphus, he said, "I'm impressed, but you know you are no match for me! You were my foot soldier!" He quickly reached out and grabbed Dunstan/Andrealphus by his neck, pulled him close and forced him to his knees. "You little weasel, you cost me so much time with your evasions and distractions! It is now my pleasure to…" as he lifted the dagger above his head.

Suddenly, the tables turned as Andrealphus slowly lost his angel's strength. Then without warning, it started to manifest itself within him. He rose to his feet again, reached up, and using his left hand, he grabbed Abaddon's right hand that held the dagger. He managed to stand up, and now face to face, he held Abaddon by the throat with his right hand.

All of a sudden, Shax's lifeless body came sliding and rolling down the church's aisle, stopping at both Andrealphus' and Abaddon's feet. "Last rites!" a voice shouted from the church's front entrance.

Abaddon quickly shoved Andrealphus away from him as they both looked towards the church's front door. There stood Gabriel, who started to walk slowly up the church's aisle. Then he said again, "Last rites! Abaddon, isn't that what you want before you leave this earth?"

"Gabriel, is that truly you? Does He know you are here?" Abaddon asked with a surprisingly frightened look on his face.

"He knows all things, you know that!" Gabriel replied.

"You know we've got this fight locked down here on earth. This is global! Nobody believes in God and angels anymore," Abaddon said. "Yeah, sure there are lots of churches and religions around, but isn't it ironic that so many are defeating their purpose? Free will, oh yes! That is what made it so easy for us to tap into their greed! You see, everything is skin deep here, there's a quest for beautiful women, fast cars and fancy homes, which most church leaders display, ergo they sell them!"

"Abaddon, you know full well that there are a lot more believers than you think, like this young man who is standing up behind you," Gabriel said.

At that very moment, Julian stood up from the table he was lying on. Dunstan/ Andrealphus had walked over to console him and then he escorted him to one of the church pews because he was still dazed from whatever spell they had put on him.

Gabriel slowly pulled out his sword, which he seldom used, and said, "Abaddon, I am not here to debate with you, but I have a message for you! We are here, and we know about your assaults on the world! We are triangulating every outpost and operations you have, as we speak. But I will give you this, a choice, you will, or I will…"

Abaddon stood there in silence, staring at Gabriel and weighing his options. Slowly, he stared at the dagger in his hand, and knowing that he was no match for Gabriel, he quickly plunged it through his heart. When his body hit the ground, simultaneously, all three of the human demonic mutants' clothing fell to the floor as their bodies turned to dust.

Dunstan walked over to Julian and sat down beside him. He reached for his hand and held it tightly as he said, "Listen, I know there is a lot I didn't tell you, and a lot I didn't show you, so I'm truly sorry you had to find out this way. A lot of things are going to change in the coming days, for my true duty is calling me. So don't be surprised if I leave you every now and then."

Julian, looking at Dunstan as if he knew about him all along, asked, "Can I be an angel?"

"You are an angel, one of God's special angels," Dunstan replied.

"But I can't fly," Julian said, looking up at the church's beams.

"Neither can I," Dunstan said with a smile. "Julian listen, you have a soul which some angels envy, but, most of all, you have a

99

big heart that will get you far down here, and eventually up there," Dunstan said as he pointed to the sky. Then he slapped him on his thigh and grabbed him in a single arm neck hug and said, "Come, help me clean up this mess!"

Gabriel took on an amazing glow as he stood there with an astonished look on his face. Watching Dunstan display this type of compassion as he comforted Julian, surprised him but somehow, it also made him feel a bit envious at how well Dunstan had handled the situation.

Meanwhile......

It was 4:30pm when a knock sounded at Detective Stone's door. Danny Stone opened his door to find James Carey standing before him. "James, my friend, come on in!"

James nodded and said hello as he walked in. Danny was home alone this time for his wife had long gone back to work. As Danny rested his hands lightly on James' shoulders, directing him to the den area, he asked, "Have you heard? Steve's wife passed away shortly after he left the park."

"No, you are kidding me, right?" James asked in shock at the unexpected news.

"Christopher called me a half an hour ago when he had a little time alone away from Steve to give me a little more details about her death. It wasn't something that was unexpected apparently. I was told she was hospitalized with recurring issues linked to a terrible stroke that she'd had several years ago. Christopher is there with him now. He's trying to console and help him make a number of personal decisions," Danny said as he directed James to a seat.

"I don't know them personally, but I do hope he can get through this," James replied.

"Would you like something to drink or perhaps something to eat? I have a lot of Chinese left over from lunch."

"No, I'm good, but a glass of water would be fine," James responded.

When Danny returned to the den, and while passing the glass of water to James, he began to say, "There is someone else coming to this meeting that I would like you to meet. He is my brother-in-law, and his name is Andrew Anderson."

Right then the doorbell rang.

"Oh, this must be him now," Danny said as he turned to walk to the front door. Suddenly, he stopped, turned to James and jokingly whispered, "Don't be alarm, he is F.B.I."

As soon as Agent Anderson entered the room, James leapt to his feet and enthusiastically greeted him. He knew that once the feds were involved, he would be given that extra cover he needed, which boosted his morale.

While shaking James' hand, Andrew turned to Danny and asked, "Didn't you say there were three of them?"

Danny responded, "I did, but unfortunately, Mr. Smith's wife passed away a few hours ago so he's unable to be here and Christopher is there with him, to console and help make personal decisions."

"I'm so sorry to hear that," Andrew replied as he took his seat. Then he stood up again, and taking out his side arm, he ejected the clip and slid back the chamber, simultaneously catching the ejected bullet. Sitting down again, he declared, "Mr. Carey, if this group is who we think they are, they would believe strongly in the second amendment—in short, they are a very militant group!"

Right then Andrew quickly tossed his weapon to James. Caught by surprise, James fumbled with the catch, and with his arm extended, he quickly placed it on the couch far away from him.

"Afraid of guns?" Andrew asked.

"No, I just don't care for them too much," James replied.

"Danny, these guys are going to read him and hurt him really bad, or perhaps, even kill him," Andrew said as he stood and picked up his gun from the couch and loaded the clip.

Right then James stood up and walked towards Andrew, and turning his back to him, said, "Go ahead, put the gun to my back!"

Andrew did as he was told.

James stepped back until he felt the gun at the center of his back, and with a quick sweeping motion, he turned to his left, and using his left arm in an upward motion, he bent Andrew's elbow, and stripped the gun away from his right hand. Immediately, he said, "Sorry," as he walked over to the bar. Then he said to Danny, "Time this!" James quickly started a field strip to disassemble Andrew's Glock 9mm, and then he reassembled it, slid the clip back in place, and spun the gun on his finger, and holding the nozzle, he passed it back to Andrew. He looked at Danny, waiting to hear how long it took him to do this.

Danny said, "19 seconds."

Andrew, pleasantly surprised, exclaimed, "Very cute! Do you think that was right for you to mislead me in that way?"

"I'm sorry if you took it the wrong way, but I wasn't trying to mislead you. I just told you I didn't care for them too much, meaning all guns," James replied. "Listen, when my father was in Special Forces, he was trained by Army Rangers. He was obsessed with his work, and since I was the only child, he forced his weapons and combat training on me. At first, I was really into it, being a child and all that! I learned everything he taught me, so there isn't a gun you can put before me that I won't know something about it! But as I grew older, life took on a different meaning for me. It started when I was in college; I was more for peace than war or violence, and my girlfriend at that time was responsible for that. She was just completing her Bachelor's degree in social work. We had only spent four months together when she was pressed to return home to Bosnia because she knew, as a qualified social worker, she was needed there. I decided to return home because I wanted to become an advocate for families of victims of gun and gang violence. Many of these innocents were unjustly forced from their homes and neighborhoods, and have received very little help from their governments. I decided to be their voice by helping out at community centers, and with my journalism degree, I tell their stories in newspapers and magazines to bring awareness of their plight. Someone has to do it, and why not me?

Right then both Andrew and Danny looked at each other, nodded and smiled in mutual understanding and approval.

Chapter 11

Pulling a chair towards himself, Agent Andrew Anderson asked James to take a seat on the couch. He positioned himself directly in front of him and said, "Now that we have seen that you are capable physically, and knowledgeable about weapons training for this particular infiltration, let's see if we can get you mentally acclimated with their way of thinking. James, there are certain things you must understand about these types of people! They don't care about anybody's problems but their own, and that's mainly their immediate families. They have known to be disloyal even to their peers! The only thing that keeps them tightly knitted as a group is their ideology. They lack empathy and walk in apathy. So when you are in their midst, try not to show compassion for others, especially when in a conversation with them. But being courteous occasionally, like opening doors for those outside of their group, is acceptable because blending in is important to them."

Andrew looked at Danny and asked, "Do you have anything you wish to add to this?"

Danny suddenly looked down at his watch and said, "Damn, it's five o'clock! I'm slipping as it takes at least 35 minutes to drive down to Huntington Beach from here, and that's with light traffic, and he has to be there for six! I should have held this meeting earlier! James, you've got to get going, and yes, there is something I want to add," Danny said as they hustled James to the door. "James, they are going to ask you about your racial experience after they tell you what they are all about. You need to have a similar story, even if you have to make it up, or tell them about somebody else's experience that you'd heard about. This first meeting will be short as they only want to feel you out! Oh, also your Dad can play an important role in this too—tell them about your weapons training. They may be interested in acquiring weapons, thinking you may have a possible connection," Danny added as he and Andrew walked James to his car.

As he got into the car, James looked up at Andrew and asked, "Aren't you guys supposed to wire me up with some listening device?"

Andrew chuckled a bit, and with a smile on his face said, "You watch too much TV! We can't do that on your first meeting. If these people are who we think they are, they will frisk you."

Passing the address to Andrew that James had given him earlier, Danny, with a sense of urgency said, "Okay kid, you got to get moving! There is going to be a traffic build up real soon! Use the surface streets, and don't worry because they will be following you," he added as he pointed towards the unmarked FBI car that was parked across the street. There was another agent sitting in it.

It was five minutes to six when Agent Anderson and his partner, Kenny Johnson, covertly pulled up alongside an 18-wheeler tractor trailer that was tucked away in the far right-hand corner of a Hess fuel station, located directly across the street from the mom and pop diner. It was there they observed James as he walked from his parked car towards the diner's entrance. Seconds after he entered, they heard the roaring sound of a supped up car pulling off from the traffic light's left turn green signal on a four way junction. It was a light blue late model Shelby mustang roaring east up the boulevard between the diner and the station.

"Damn Kenny, check out that Shelby mustang," Andrew said with excitement. All of a sudden, the mustang slowed down and made an illegal U turn and roared back up the opposite side of the street; it signaled to turn right to enter the parking lot of the diner.

Andrew quickly lifted his Sony digital zoom binoculars with

HD video capture to his eyes, and focally zoomed in on the mustang. Noticing two occupants in the vehicle, he said softly, "My guess is these are our guys!" He immediately zoomed in on the car and its license plate, and with its camera component he took pictures. Seconds later, the driver parked the car. The passenger door opened first, and Andrew zoomed in on the male who exited the vehicle. He was a middle-aged male Caucasian about six feet tall. He had collar length hair and was neatly dressed. When the subject faced him directly, he took a full body and facial close up shot of him.

Immediately after, Andrew trained his binocular's camera lens on the driver who exited the vehicle, locked his door with an alarm key, and started to walk quickly towards the diner's entrance. Andrew had to zoom in really quickly using video mode, and just before the second subject walked through the door, he was able to get a close face frame shot of him. The driver was also Caucasian, and roughly 5' 8" tall. In his early thirties, he was a skinhead, who was casually dressed.

As Kenny pulled out the laptop, Andrew pulled the memory card from the Sony's equipment, inserted the card, and started the process of downloading the photos. While the information was downloading, he thought out loud, "The driver and his passenger look familiar, and if memory serves me right, they were on an updated-wide bureau briefing list that another team was working on."

While Agent Anderson was trying to focus on the glass window of the diner, Agent Johnson said, "Here we go," as the information started to appear on the screen. "Our passenger is a Russian, Grigori Ovich, who is 46 years old. The Bureau is presently investigating him for campaign meddling, and our driver is Nathanial Parker, who is 31 years old."

Right then Andrew perked up and reached out for the laptop, "Let me see that! See, I told you these faces looked familiar! I know I knew that face, Parker, Nathanial Parker! Six years ago, I tracked him down because he was one of the leaders of a White Supremacist team that was trying to obtain an arsenal of weapons. But I guess he felt the heat and he and his team went underground. I would have to notify the agents who are working on Ovich's case and let them know our cases are tied in with each other."

Meanwhile:

When Nathanial and Grigori walked up to the booth, James was already sitting with Peter Davis, drinking beers and engaging him in light conversation. Nathanial looked down on both of them and said, "Follow me!" They both stood up to follow them as Nathanial turned to an older man behind the counter and said, "Uncle Ronnie, I need to use your office for a few minutes."

"Sure, go ahead," his Uncle responded. Ronnie Parker, aged 62, was very skinny, and even though he was balding, he still managed to wear his hair in a ponytail. He was one of the owners of the diner, and was the older brother of Nathanial's mother. Even though he knew and supported what his nephew was involved in, he stayed out of it.

As soon as Peter closed the door to the tiny office they had all piled into, Nathanial turned to James and said, "Take your shirt off!"

"What's going on? "James asked, as he looked to Peter for an answer.

Peter responded by repeating Nathanial's request, "Take your shirt off!"

Right then and there he experienced an eerie feeling and with a bit of chill in the air, he complied. Really slowly he started taking his shirt off.

After seeing no upper body attachments, Nathanial walked up to James and lightly ran his fingers around the inside of his pants' waist. When he was satisfied, he stood directly in the front of James and said, "Your glasses, let me see your glasses!"

James quickly took his glasses off and handed it to him.

After Nathanial was satisfied with his examination of the glasses, he handed them back.

"My name is Nathanial" Nathanial said as he reach out for a hand shake

"I'm James," James responded.

"Have a seat, James," Nathanial said as he walked around his Uncle's desk and sat down. "How old are you James?" Nathanial asked.

"29," replied James.

"I got you by two! Tell me James, do you know why we wanted to meet you here?" Nathanial asked as he pulled his chair closer to the desk.

"Peter here, told me earlier about being in the game, and me, being a blind adventurist and not having anything to do tonight, I decided to take him up on the invite. At that time he just gave me his card and told me to give him a call, and if I was interested, he said he would give me details on where and when! Well, I guess this game or whatever it is that you guys do, it is deep and covert so here I am meeting with you," James declared confidently.

While James was talking, Nathanial was secretly ejecting the clip from his gun underneath the desk. He was preparing to do the same test Agent Anderson had done on James earlier. Suddenly, Nathanial tosses his gun to James, who saw it coming, and caught it! Then he quickly ejected the round that was carelessly left in the chamber; he catches the round with flamboyance, and with a fancy finger spin, he stepped forward and passed the gun with the round back to Nathanial, saying, "You ought to be a little more careful about throwing a loaded gun around!"

"Impressive," Nathanial said with a smile, realizing that he had made a terrible mistake by forgetting to eject the round from the chamber after he had ejected the clip. Nathanial quickly changes the topic and asked, "James, what are your thoughts about migrants, you know Mexicans, Africans and a host of others? But my main focus is the Mexicans and Africans, especially Africans, those Blacks! For the past eight years, this country was in shambles under that Nigger leadership, do you agree?"

James paused for a few seconds as he nodded his head, looking in the faces of all three of the room's occupants. He gestured in agreement, and said, "I see where you are going with this, and I do agree that the last eight years was terrible! Hopefully, that is going to change soon!"

"No, it won't with hope! It will change if we support the right candidate! You are with our guy, right?" Nathanial asked.

"Oh definitely! I'm not going with her, with all that liberal agenda.

Nathanial responded, "That is exactly what I wanted to hear! James, you are in a unique position as far as your work is concerned. You can become a great asset in many ways for our little organization because you write columns and you also report the news, which can be a serious pivoting point for us, if you do it with consideration! Do you understand what I am saying?"

James nodded with understanding.

"Now back to this racial integration issue, you know, White guys, Black girls, White girls, Black guys—there is too much of a mix up! It's slowly eroding our superior color, that is, our White race, do you agree?"

James looked at Nathanial with a straight face and said, "Yes, I do."

"You know when you mix black with white, you get a shade of gray! Now I don't know, but you guys, I don't want gray skies! I want sunshiny days back again!" Nathaniel quipped.

Right then everybody started to laugh.

Suddenly Grigori's phone started to ring, and when he answered it, he spoke in Russian.

James' attention was quickly drawn to him for up until then, Grigori hadn't said a word the entire time. James knew it was Russian because he had done a thesis on Russia in his last year in college, and he had to study their language to complete it.

Grigori gestured with one finger to excuse himself and left the room. Nathanial looked at James when the door shut behind him and said, "He is a good guy, quiet but very smart! You know, he's assisting us with our gentle persuasion of getting people to understand and think, so that they can get on our path, the right path," Nathanial smiled. Then he added, "If you know what I mean! So tell me James, where did you get your weapons training? You seem to know your way around guns, with your fancy display! It looks as if you are a gun enthusiast? Where did you get your training? The Army, the Marines, tell me?

"My Dad," James answered. Then he went on to explain how his father trained him, exactly what he had told Agent Anderson and Detective Stone

"I like this guy Peter, good catch," Nathaniel grinned.

Peter smiled at his approval, glowing within himself, that he had made such a great choice.

"James, don't worry about our group's meeting tonight. There's no need to go there since we are going on a field trip tomorrow after I have voted." Then Nathanial pulled his phone out and asked James for his number. After he had entered the number in his phone, he asked James, "Going to the polls tomorrow?"

"Yes I plan to, at some point in the morning."

"Well, let's go together! Me and a couple of the guys are going to a polling station somewhere near here, not quite sure of the address, but I will give you a call! Ahhh, let's say 10:00am. I will have details on where we can meet."

"Okay, ten it is! I'll be waiting," James said as he reached out and shook Nathanial's hand.

Five minutes later James got into his car and drove off! As he drove he wondered whether or not his covert agents were going to call or show themselves. Then his phone rang. "Hello," he answered.

"James, my man, how did it go?" Andrew asked.

"I was convincingly believable, if I may say so myself," he responded.

"Good, that's what I like to here! But listen, do you have a similar pair of glasses?"

"Yes, why?" James answered with curiosity.

"Do you have it with you?" asked Andrew.

"Yes, I think I have a pair in the glove box—just a sec! Yep! Got a pair right here, what's going on?"

Andrew paused for a second, and then said, "Look, we are right behind you! There is a shell gas station coming up on your right, pull in there."

"Got it," James replied. Seconds later, he pulled into the station, and stopped alongside the station's dumpster. Agent Anderson and Johnson pulled up alongside him. Anderson got out, tapped on his passenger's door glass, gesturing him to open the door. Then he got in, and immediately asked, "So you said you are in, right? Did you get a follow up meeting?"

"Yes, I'm in, and I think they really like me. Nathanial is the guy who seems to be the leader of the pack! He came along with this Russian guy who didn't introduce himself, so I don't know his name. Well, Nathanial told me that he would give me a call 10:00am tomorrow. He wants me to go with him to the polling station. I guess it's to make sure I vote. Agent Anderson, these guys are dead set on this race divide, and it appears that this candidate (all suit, no man,) is sparking it," James said.

"I feel you James, but in this line of work we have to remain objective. On another note, we do know the players—Nathanial Parker and Grigori Ovich is the Russian. We got a hit on our photo recognition site when we took their photos before they entered the diner," Anderson said as he reached out to shake James' hand. "Congratulations, you passed your first covert infiltration mission, my F.B.I. agent," Anderson added with a humorous smile.

"Your glasses, let me have a look," Anderson said as James quickly passed them to him.

"My old back up pair," James exclaimed.

"I don't see much of a difference from the pair you have on," Anderson said as he quickly tried them on. "Damn, you are blind," he added as he quickly pulled them off. "Listen, I would like to take this pair in to see if we can outfit it with a James Bond style mini cam."

"By all means, I think that will be cool as Nathaniel already checked my glasses. I see no need for him to check it again," James said as he nodded his head in approval.

"Okay James, go home, get some rest for your big day tomorrow! I will give you a call around 9:00am," Anderson said as he stepped out of the vehicle.

Chapter 12

Meanwhile:

At the crack of dawn, around 6:45am, Brent hustled his group together in the work setup room of the Motel Lodge located just across the big pond of Surrey, England.

"Where is Paul? Anybody seen Paul, the kid? Where is he? Who was his roommate?" Brent asked, looking around at the group.

Hawk raised his head and said, "Me! We were together, but when I woke up this morning he was gone."

"Ah hell, somebody please go and see if you can find him," Brent said, showing his frustration.

Suddenly, there was a knock on the door. When Hawk opened the door, Paul was standing there with a cup of coffee and a bag of donuts in his hands.

"Hey guys, my cash was limited so I was only able to get a few donuts. You are on your own with the coffee! Besides, that petrol station across the street had a long line of early morning lodgers and travelers, and that's why it took me so long," Paul said as he placed the bag of donuts on the table.

Brent looked at him with relief because he was a key asset to their operations. "Paul, I appreciate your consideration. You will be reimbursed, but please let us know your every move. We have to work as a team in order to be successful with this operation. Oh, by the way guys, I have already arranged breakfast for you, which will be provided by the lodge's staff. They do offer continental breakfast you know, and they should be delivering it any minute now."

Then Paul walked over to Brent and said quietly, "May I see you outside for a minute?"

"Sure," Brent said as they both excused themselves and exited the room. "What's up buddy?" Brent asked as he closed the door behind him.

"Last night I got several strong clairvoyant messages from our divine interventionist. They had something to do with a location next to a hillside. I'm getting flashes of it, like I pictured a little farmhouse on a dirt path that's off a side road near a hillside or mountainside. I'm feeling that it's close by. Maybe that is the reason why I instinctively mentioned *hillside* last night when we were in the helicopter."

Looking excitedly at Paul, Brent said, "That is awesome! That is what I needed to hear for we are in the area!" Looking aimlessly at the neighboring hills nearby he asked, "Why aren't we able to get more details or information since we have an Angel as our assistant?"

Paul paused for a few seconds, and began staring aimlessly at the hills. Then he said, "Agent Russell, ever since this phenomenon, I've been gifted with incredible insight into many things. I have been able to answer questions that normally, I wouldn't have been able to answer. Now with that said, here is your answer: There are six populated continents, like I said last night, there are sixty-six fallen Angels operating in each of these continents. Here in Europe, we've got the United Kingdom, France, Germany, Spain and Russia Eurasia; these are the predominantly populated countries. Our Angel was able to foil the terror attack when it surfaced, but finding its root is where they have limitations. You have to keep in mind that they are Angels fighting fallen Angels, and there are only three God-sent Angels right here on earth!"

"Three," Brent said quite surprised.

"Yes, that's what I've been told. They are Michael, Gabriel and Raphael. Their main purpose is to take down Lucifer and the 395 fallen Angels that escaped the pit of hell and followed him here to derail God's plan. Even though these three Angels are vastly outnumbered, the fallen Angels are significantly weaker than they are as they are only left with a third of their strength. For a lack of a better word, they were stripped of their wings. But our only concern is running into one of the six generals who is located in each of the six continents of the world, not to mention Lucifer himself.

Using this 1/3 fraction again, and based on countries with greater influence and very large populations, there are at least twenty two dark Angels in the UK and France. Twenty two should work out to be a 1/3 of the 66 in Europe. That twenty two is in major populated cities posted throughout the UK and France. Their operations are spread out throughout a number of strategic areas, one for each major city throughout England, Wales, Scotland and Ireland, and so on with the remaining forty four throughout the very high populated countries and cities in Europe."

He paused as Agent Russell, who was listening intently, nodded his head in agreement.

"Agent Russell, even though they are fallen Angels and weaker, they are still clever enough to form a strategy such as this one, and they know that the Heavenly Father's watchful eyes will eventually reveal and unveil it. Remember our Angels will give us a window but we will have to open the door."

"Wait a minute," Brent said, reaching out and putting his hands on Paul's shoulders, "You said there are three Angels on earth, right? So if Raphael is here in the UK, working with us in our security services, there may be one or two of them working with the FBI in the United States."

"That is possible," Paul replied.

"With that, we would have to reach out to the FBI to see if they have had similar cases and have had some phenomena assistance," Brent added.

Suddenly a car horn sounded. When Brent looked up, it was a 2015 dark blue, 4-door Land Rover with tinted windows. Rolling down the driver's window, Agent Derrick Holder shouted from the car, "You need any help down here?" Agent Holder, a Caucasian, had brown hair, and was 6'1" tall. Physically fit, his rate of success with terrorist operations was very high, so you didn't want to take him on one on one.

"Park that car, and get in on some of this breakfast that should be coming soon," Brent shouted back.

Derrick worked under Brent when he first started in the security agency, and they worked well as a team. They were also regarded as two of the sharpest agents whose success rate was the highest in the agency.

When Derrick approached Brent, they both gave the other a hug and a fist bump.

"Tell me, did you get something good on that Stanley guy?" Brent asked.

"Oh yes! He's a character if I may say so myself! Do you want to do a briefing now? Is everybody here?" Derrick asked.

"Yeah, they are all right here in this room. I'm trying to get some grub in them, so we can brief over breakfast," Brent said as he opened the room door.

Right then a Motel Lodge's staff, rolling a cart, approached them with their breakfast. Brent walked into the room and said, "Gentlemen, the food's here, but we've got to hurry. Derrick wants to brief us on Stanley Wilson, the owner of the black van, and I also have a lead I wish to share with you."

While they were eating, Brent informed the agents, who had come with him, and also the ones who had arrived the night before, that there was a need for them to join him in his search on his lead. He reminded them about the Carla Wallace's matter, which was urgent. He did not want the trail to go cold. He also told the agents that they needed to check the side streets near the dirt path that led to a farm. He only wanted them to locate the residence, not enter it until they received further instructions. Then Brent turned to Derrick and gestured to him to give his briefing.

"Gentlemen," Derrick said, holding up a large mug shot of Stanley Wilson. "What we have learned about Mr. Wilson in the past 12 hours is shocking. He is heavily involved with the Russians and is deeply entrenched in their ideology. We came across materials and information that indicate that he is assisting the Russians by undermining the politics and democracy of the United States for a political one-sided gain. He's tapping into the largest social media service provider, and is spreading fake news and propaganda. However, he's not alone as we've seen a lot of heavy email traffic bouncing all over Europe, the United States and Russia, as well as we've found evidence of espionage as they are trying to hack into our government's and military's computers. Our tech is sensing their main hub is here in England. But what is interesting is the relationship between Stanley and the Russians has been going on for years. Lately however, it has been stepped up during the United States' election campaign, which, as we all should know by now, is a highly watched event on all of the major television news networks. Today is November 8th, their election day."

All of sudden, Hawk jumped up, and looking around at all of them, said, "Can somebody tell me, how on earth that clown got to be nominated for President of the United States?"

One of the agents, who was sitting on the bed, responded, "Maybe it's not the clown we should be mocking! I'm sorry to say but my main problem is with the clowns that support and follow him because they mirror his pathetic behavior to those who are unfortunate and broken. You see this is how I see it—that guy might have had a head injury as a teenager and has never been the same since. Fortunately for him, he had a father with an awful amount of cash who dumped a big heap of it on him, and then after that, he really went nuts. Now that is his excuse! There're at least 60 to 65 million of his followers out there, what is their excuse?"

The whole room lit up with laughter.

"Well gentlemen, that's their politics! We have our own; now we need to get to work," Brent said as his phone started to ring.

"Hello," Brent said, waving his hand in a downward gesture, indicating that he wanted them to be quiet.

"Agent Russell, this is Officer Green of the Metropolitan Police Service (MPS). We have found a partially burnt out black van on a dirt road, about two miles from where you are right now. Take down this street address."

Brent immediately beckoned for a pen and paper. "Okay, got it! I'll be there ASAP." He hung up his phone and then turned to his team, "Okay guys, MPS found the van. Derrick, you drive! Paul, I need you to come with us too, and also I need a dust team of two to follow us! Come on, inhale that grub, and let's go!"

As Brent was opening the door, he suddenly stopped and said, "Oh, and another thing guys, I'm sensing these guys are real close, so most likely they are using neighboring shops and even the petrol station across the street, so it's imperative that we remain inconspicuous. See them before they see you!"

"Got it," the agents said in unison.

"Nice car," Paul said as they drove off from the Motel Lodge. "Are these types of vehicles in the MI-5 motor pool?"

"Nah, this is my personal vehicle! It's funny though as driving through the Surrey hills is what I had in mind when I bought it. Now here, I'm mixing business with pleasure," Derrick said with a smile.

"Paul, I need you to study these hills as we drive, just in case something should pop up!" Brent said as he looked back at him in the back seat.

"Yes sir, I'm studying them!"

"Okay, here is the cross street that he mentioned to me! It's near a dirt road," Brent mumbled as he was barely being audible. Then he quickly said aloud, "Derrick, here it is! Take a right, right, right, right, RIGHT HERE!

"Calm down dude, I got it," Derrick said as he quickly glanced into his rearview mirror and turned right onto the dirt road. Suddenly, they heard the sound of Agents Ailes' and Valdez' squealing tires. They had been following them because they too had to make a quick turn.

"There it is! They said it was partially burnt, but it looks pretty fine to me. Oh, now I see their attempt. Derrick, park in front of the MPS' patrol car. These guys seem to be very incompetent, leaving the phones in the open last night, and now this botched attempt to burn this van!"

As Ailes and Valdez began walking around the van, Brent approached the officer and said, "Officer Green I imagine."

"Yes sir," the officer replied.

"I need you to immediately impound this vehicle in an enclosed area because of our untimely weather!"

"You got it," Officer Green replied, pulling out his cell phone.

There was a stench of burnt wires and seat fabric emanating from the vehicle as the team began gloving up to open the van's doors to gather forensic evidence from it.

While the team was going through the van, Paul, who was standing alongside Derrick's Land Rover, called out, "Agent Russell, I think we need to get back up into the helicopter. I'm getting a strong urge to get an aerial view of this general area in order to look around."

Immediately stopping what he was doing, Brent walked towards Paul and asked, "You mean right now?"

Paul answered, "Yes, right now!"

Brent immediately turned to Derrick and said, "Derrick, let's go! We have to go up in the chopper." He also told the forensic team, Ailes and Valdez, to gather as much evidence as they can at the scene, and then follow Officer Green, along with the impounding team, to the police's impound.

While they were driving away, Brent took his phone out to call Sheila. "Hello boss, we found the van! They tried to burn it but screwed that up too! Our forensic team is working on it right now. Paul said that he had gotten a number of clairvoyant messages last night, and urgently approached me a minute ago about getting up into the chopper for an aerial reconnaissance of the general area, so that we could focus on a particular hillside and a farmhouse he keeps seeing in the mix."

"That's wonderful! You keep following his lead as it's a blessing to have this divine intervention assisting us," Sheila said on the other end.

"Oh, by the way boss, how is Sandra doing? Through all of the excitement in working this case, I totally forgot about her, and I am also tremendously worried about Carla. I'm feeling guilty but I'm hoping they fed her because I pulled them out of that diner before they had a chance to eat."

"Yes, I could understand your concern, but don't worry about Sandra, she is being taken care of. I put her up in a hotel last night! Poor girl, she has no clothes to wear. But I have somebody right now helping her to gain access to Carla's condo." Sheila said.

"Okay, that's great! I have to go now, I've got to get the pilot to take us up! I will keep you posted! Take care," Brent said as they pulled into Motel Lodge's parking lot.

Chapter 13

The constant sound of dripping water echoed throughout the musky-smelling underground cave. That is what Carla was enduring as she stood holding the steel bars of a dungeon cell. There was a bucket that was about five feet away from her that had a little bit of urine in it because she had to use it. At least a half an hour had passed since she had awoken from the worse night of her life. "Hello, hello, can anybody hear me?" she frantically called out over and over again.

Five minutes later, she heard the sound of keys opening an outer door that was out of her view. It was followed by sounds of echoing footsteps that were slowly approaching her cell. Soon Carla was standing face to face with a blonde hair, blue-eyed man in his mid-thirties. He had a tray that had a sandwich and a cup of water on it. He also had an embroidered nametag o n the left chest of his shirt that had his name, Richard, inscribed on it.

Carla immediately gave him a fake smile as her eyes locked onto his nametag, "Richard, can you tell me what is going on and why am I here?"

Richard responded, "Step back please!" as he opened the pocket window door to slide the tray in to her.

Carla, ignoring the tray, asked, "I would like to speak to the person who is in charge?"

Richard said nothing as he turned and walked away.

Meanwhile:

Brent waited until the pilot had gone through his mandatory starting procedures and radio calls, to put on his voice-activated head set. Then he had turned his head to the back seat to instruct Paul and Derrick to do the same. Afterwards, he turned to the pilot when he saw that it was okay to give him instructions. "Can everyone hear me?" Brent asked.

The pilot nodded as the others gave a thumbs up and said, "Yep, you're good!"

Brent turned to the pilot, whose name was Vernon and said, "Vernon, I need you to get at least a thousand feet above this area. The reason for this is I need this chopper to appear to be in transition as though it is going somewhere else. I don't need anyone on the ground thinking this helicopter is looking for someone or something. We need to minimize blade flapping because from the ground that is an indication the helicopter is banking. I also need you to box in this area within a two mile radius. We're trying to find a farmhouse that is in close proximity to a hillside."

Vernon, the pilot, gave a thumbs up, and immediately pulled up on the vertical control collective to enter into a maximum performance take off. He had to elevate vertically from the ground to about 75ft in order to clear ground obstacles, and then he forwarded his cyclic for an effective translational lift. The pilot flew out of the general area in order to gain sufficient altitude, he climbed to 1500ft in order to get the effect Brent was looking for. He made a shallow left bank at 1500ft to fly a slow reconnaissance over their boxed area.

Brent looked back at Paul and asked, "Are you getting anything?"

Paul responded only with a hand gesture as if to say wait a minute.

There were many farmhouses next to a number of hillsides, but there was one that stood out, and Derrick calmly pointed out the likely reason for its unique location. "Vernon, there is something that does not look right to me! We just passed a farmhouse down there on our left that is now at our 7 o'clock position! Don't turn just yet, just make a wide turn and put it off to my left."

The helicopter flew another 1/8 of a mile, and then Vernon started a shallow one hundred and eighty degree left turn to avoid a noticeable sound of blade flapping.

Forty seconds elapsed before Derrick said, "Okay, that's great!"

Brent looked down at the farmhouse that was off to the left. It had a big shady tree that stood alongside the hill. "Now, what do you see that is different from the other farmhouses?"

"Next to the farmhouse, I see a well-worn dirt road that runs directly to that tree on the hillside," Brent said.

"That's what I'm talking about! Don't you find that odd?" Derrick asked with a grim look on his face. "We need coordinates on this area for a satellite feed!"

"You got it!" Brent said as he turned to the pilot and said, "Let's get a GPS lock for this area."

Vernon nodded as he started to push buttons on the helicopter's GPS system.

Brent also added, "Okay, let's fly back out and go wide around from the back to the motel."

Back at the motel's parking lot, and as the rotor blades' speed was decaying, Brent turned to Vernon and said, "I need you to write the coordinates down for me please!"

"You got it!" Vernon said, pulling his pen from his top pocket. Vernon Marshall, a forty-five year old, was a veteran helicopter pilot with twenty-seven years' experience in the field. 6'3" tall, and a fair-skinned black man of African descent, he was born in Sussex Brighton, England. At the age of twenty-seven, he trained instructors of the RAF for 10 years in the squirrel HT1 helicopter, and then joined the MI-5 team when he was thirty-seven, and was now flying the Euro copter EC-135 twin jet engine.

After Brent took the written coordinates from Vernon, he walked away to the far side of the parking lot, and speed-dialed Sheila on his cell phone. "Hello boss! I think we may or may not have something, but I need you to take down these coordinates, so that we can monitor satellite images of a farmhouse located near a large tree alongside a hill. I want to monitor your feed through our portable here at the motel."

"I'm on it," Sheila said and they both hung up.

While Brent was walking back to the Motel's room, he spotted Paul walking towards the Motel's office area. He shouted, "Paul, where are you going?"

"I have a sugar tooth, and was wondering if they have a vending machine here," Paul said, smiling at him.

"Let us both go! I can do with a candy bar too," Brent replied. As he closed in on Paul, he said, "You were quiet up there. There was no input from you!"

"There was no need because you got your window!" Paul said with a smile.

"I hope you have been checking in with your family," Brent said as he opened the door of the motel's office for Paul. "We'll soon be going on 24 hours since I met you," Brent said, patting Paul on his back.

"Yes, I called them last night," Paul said.

"You live home with your mom and dad?"

"Nahhh, my grandparents. I don't know my dad, and I'm estranged from my mom, and that was my choice," Paul responded.

"May I ask why?" Brent asked and then said, "I got this," as he put money in the vending machine, and turned and beckoned to Paul to select his choice.

"Her belief system is not aligned with mine! She is in the adult entertainment business. In short, she's a porn star."

"I can feel your pain," Brent said softly, as he slightly shook his head, left to right.

They both tore the wrappers off their candy bars and casually took a seat in the lounge area. Suddenly, Paul's face took on an angry look that was not characteristic of him, especially since he was the on and off host of the Angel Raphael. He turned to Brent and said, "Get this! Academically, she is brilliant, but irresponsible you know as she had me when she was eighteen. She finished school, despite her pregnancy, and then went on to college. I guess it was the money issue that made it easy for her to be convinced by friends and associates to become a strip tease dancer. Then she moved on to adult films. I could barely understand why she did it but I guess it was to take care of me and to finish school. But nooo, she's now engulfed in that world of burning flames, and is a one hundred percent believer in what she's doing."

Brent listened in silence as he continued.

"And get this, she is now thirty-eight, so really, she holds 'grandma's status' in an industry that has a very short shelf life in terms of holding a lot of viewers' attention! According to their cover advertisements, the high volume of skin deep beautiful women are canceling out each other's success. In fact, once you see one, you see them all. It's like shelving out milk under the sun. Now that we're in the internet age, how on earth do they still make money? She is probably working behind the cameras now. Seeing and knowing this, I could perhaps understand my father, who probably believed that he'd made an overnight mistake as he envisioned her future. So he got the hell out! Isn't it strange and ironic, in normal situations like this, one would be upset with one's father, but me? I would really like to meet him as I think that we might have a lot in common. I'm feeling too that he may be able to fill in the blanks of my cloudy life!" Paul said as he stood up to get a cup of water from the water dispenser. After he dumped the cup in the trash, he turned and asked Brent, "Would you like a cup?"

Brent said, "Please!" Then he went on to say, "My situation was somewhat similar to yours! But it was the total opposite as far as my parents were concerned. My mother was a striver and motivator! She became the very foundation on which I built to become what I am today."

"Lucky you!" Paul said.

"No, lucky you! The angel did not come to me! He came to you," Brent exclaimed.

Right then Brent's phone started to ring. It was about 9:50am. "Hello," Brent answered. It was Sheila.

"Agent Russell, I'm watching a satellite feed right now! Are you getting this?"

"No, I'm not in the room right now," Brent said.

"Well, get there!" Sheila said, urgency in her voice.

"Boss, stay on the line! I'm going there right now," Brent said as he beckoned to Paul to follow him.

"Agent Russell, I'm watching a vehicle that just drove from beneath that tree."

"You are kidding me, right?"

"Of course not! The vehicle just stopped at the farmhouse, and a man stepped out of it and is now walking towards the farmhouse," Sheila added.

As Brent started running across the parking lot with Paul right on his heels, he said, "Boss, I'm going to call you right back! Ailes and Valdez are working forensic on the burnt out van. They should be done, and hopefully are coming back through that area right now because that farmhouse is only a few miles from where the van was found. Is that the only vehicle at the residence?"

"Yes," Sheila replied.

"Please stay on it until I get a feed," Brent said and then he hung up. Immediately, he dialed Agent Ailes' number.

"Agent Ailes, are you guys done with that van?" Brent asked.

"Yep, we are on our way back! We're just passing the dirt road where the van was found," Agent Ailes said.

"Good, I need you to pull over and park somewhere until I get back to you with an address. Just stand by please," Brent said.

Brent immediately entered the GPS coordinates he had gotten from Vernon into his phone to obtain the address of the farmhouse. Soon after, he called Agent Ailes back to give him the address.

"Agent Ailes, here it is! Write this down........."

"Got it," Agent Ailes said.

"Agent Ailes, there is a vehicle that may be leaving that address real soon! I don't have the make and model, but it is the only vehicle at that residence. I need you and Valdez to observe it! Do not approach! I need you to observe and tail it from a great distance." Brent then looked down at Agent Brooks who was stationed at the makeshift high tech equipment center that was set up in the room. "Brooks, I need you to get that real time satellite feed they are sending us from headquarters."

"I'm on it," Brooks said. Brooks, who was one of the agents that had arrived with Sheila the night before, booted up the monitor's screen. It took less than a minute as suddenly, they were looking at the satellite feed.

"There it is!" Brent said, clapping his hands with delight. "Zoom in on that car Brooks! What kind of car would you say that is?"

"Looks like a black, four-door Lincoln," Brooks replied.

"And there is our driver! Can you zoom in closer?" Brent asked.

"That looks like our subject, Stanley Wilson. Wouldn't you say that he's wearing a ponytail, right?" Brent asked.

"Yeah, it does look like he's wearing a ponytail!" Brooks responded.

Brent immediately called Agent Ailes, "Agent Ailes, the car is on the move! Do you have it?"

"Yes, we got it! We're going to start to tail him right now," Agent Ailes said.

Agents Ailes and Valdez positioned themselves in the parking lot of a little strip mall that was elevated; it was located 1/8 of a mile from the farmhouse's road path that intersected the main public road. It was an advantage point that enabled them to use their binoculars to study the subject. They got onto the main road just in time to pick up the black Lincoln that had driven onto the main road from the farmhouse's entrance.

Agent Ailes called Brent right away to let him know their position. "Mr. Russell, we got a tail! We're three cars behind the subject. He just made a left turn, and if I'm not mistaken, it looks as if he's trying to get on the M25."

"Stay on him," Brent said as he covered the phone, and looked down on Hawk, who was sitting idly by. "Hawk, you and Agent Roberts go and find a vantage point from which you can watch that farmhouse. Watch it like the hawk that you are," Brent added with a smile.

"Mr. Russell," a voice was heard coming from Brent's phone.

"Yeah, I'm here! What is it?"

"Our subject is taking the ramp for the M25, northwest bound," Agent Ailes said on the other end of the line.

"Don't lose him," Brent said in a loud, excited voice. "He's headed back to London! I'm going to call ahead to get you some assistance. Derrick! Has anybody seen Derrick?" Brent asked out loud after hanging up his phone.

"Right here slick! What's your problem?" Derrick said as he opened the door of the room.

"Get in here! We've got a feed and vehicle movement on the dirt path of the farmhouse that you picked up out there in the chopper."

Brent and Derrick spoke to each other as if they had grown up together as children. 37 minutes passed before Ailes got back on his phone to call Brent.

"Mr. Russell, our subject is going to the airport. We are now on the off ramp, heading to Heathrow."

"Okay, keep your distance! Another team of two will liaise with you! You should be getting a call about now."

The timing was impeccable with Stanley Wilson on this run because just as he pulled up to terminal one, the arrival section, Victor Sokol and two of his assistants, Vera Petrov and Boris Ivanov, (the name Ivanov ironically means, God's grace, along with a lot of other derivatives), met him. All three stepped out onto the curb. When Stanley pulled to the curb, Boris step down from the curb and opened the car's rear door for Victor and Vera to step in. When they were all in the car, Stanley looked back at them and said, "Good morning, Mr. Sokol."

Without even reciprocating Stanley's good morning gesture, Victor Sokol's only response was, "Let's go! I want to see this girl."

Chapter 14

Thirty minutes later, Agent Ailes reported back to Brent about the three passengers Stanley had picked up at the airport. After tailing them back to the farmhouse, they returned to their positions at the northern end of the parking lot of the strip mall to once again give them a hilltop advantage to observe the farmhouse.

Stanley drove slowly passed on the right side of the dirt road between the farmhouse and the barn. He honked his horn and stopped as an elderly man named Winston Parker walked down a flight of stairs from the back kitchen door to him. Winston was the owner of the farmhouse. He lived there with his wife, Nancy. They were an eccentric couple, to say the least.

Stanley powered down his window and said, "Avoid all visitors for the next 24 hours." He did not wait for a response as he drove away, not even noticing Winston's nod who understood his message. The car drove slowly onto the adjoining dirt road to the very large tree near the hillside. When the car was completely covered by the tree, the camouflaged hillside opened like an elevator's door, and the car drove in. Then the hillside's door closed.

Meanwhile:

Back at headquarters, Sheila was trying to call Brent who was in the motel room also trying to call her. Both calls ended up canceling out each other. Then Brent was the first to connect when Sheila hung up her phone.

"Boss, what do you think we have here, a picnic brunch beneath a big shady tree?" he asked as he studied the satellite feed.

"Oh my God, that could be a secret hillside tunnel bunker, cleverly positioned using that tree for cover! I can't see the entrance, can you?" Sheila asked.

"No, no! I'm not seeing anything either, but still, that could be a picnic brunch taking place under that big tree where the four of them are doing who knows what," Brent said smiling. "Boss, this is your call! What do you want to do?" Brent asked.

"We wait! We don't know what's going on in there, and if it is what we think it is…." she added as her voice trailed off.

"What about the farmhouse's owners? Surely, they know what's going on! They're complicit!" Brent exclaimed.

"No, no! Don't approach them, for then you will trigger an alarm. They must have some alert system. We don't know what's back there, and if we go in now, we will be going in blind. I will find out who owns the farmhouse, and if it is being sublet, I will find out who is presently living there. That Stanley guy, he seems to be their runner! He will be coming out sooner or later, and when he does, we will hold his feet to the fire," Sheila said with confidence.

Meanwhile:

Carla was squatting in a bird-like perch in a corner at the back of the bunker's cell. Right then she heard the echoing sounds of keys opening the outer door, and footsteps approaching the cell. She quickly jumped to her feet, and there, once again, was Richard standing before her. But this time Richard was unlocking her cell's door. He beckoned her to follow him.

"Where are we going?" Carla asked.

Richard said nothing. He just waited for her to walk out of the cell, and without restraints, he walked her out to the outer door.

With a bit of humor and sarcasm, Carla asked, "Do you always talk this much?"

Richard suddenly stopped in front of a closed door, and turning toward her, stared at her for a few seconds, and then he opened the door and gestured with his head toward the inside of the room, and said, "You wait in there."

As he locked the door behind her, her eyes wandered around the room. There was a table with four chairs set up around it and an eight by four feet mirror that was directly in front of her. Carla knew right away that this was an interrogation room. On the other side of the glass, she was being observed.

Victor Sokol and his two assistants, Vera and Boris, stood silent as they observed her. Then Victor spoke, "I'm not seeing or feeling any of our adversaries hiding within her, do you?" turning to Vera and Boris. They both responded by shaking their heads left to right.

Victor Sokol was one of the six incarnated fallen angels' generals in the European continent, while Vera and Boris were low ranking incarnated fallen angels.

It was an unusual courtesy knock at the door of the room Carla was in. Vera, then Boris, walked in. Both of them sat down at the table.

"Hello, how are you?" Carla asked, as they both sat there staring at her and saying nothing.

Then Victor walked in, portraying a bubbly spirit. "Good morning, how are you doing?"

He asked as he reached out his hand to shake hers.

"It is very nice to meet you! You are the first one that greeted me with such pleasantries," Carla said.

"I'm the only one that matters, my little friend," he replied.

"Now, you are my friend? My, my, my, why so soon?" Carla asked, a look of cynicism on her face.

"You look as if you don't trust me," Victor said, staring at her.

"I don't know you," Carla responded.

"Well, let's get to know each other, then! My name is Victor," he said, smiling at her.

"Don't you think you would have had a better chance of being my friend if you had just come to my office or even just introduce yourself as a mutual friend like everybody else, other than physically dragging me down here and locking me up?" Carla asked angrily.

"Okay, okay, I apologize for the way my people treated you, but I recently watched a video that showed you releasing some extraordinary powers that I'm not convinced were from you. So tell me, what is your little secret?" Victor asked.

"What secret?" Carla asked.

"Mrs. Wallace, we can go back and forth with this all day, but neither you nor I have the luxury of wasting time," Victor said as he closed the file on her that he had been glancing through as he spoke to her. He slid it across the table to her to indicate that he knew a lot about her. Then he said, "If you haven't noticed by now, I am asking questions that I already know the answers to!" He began tapping his fingers on the table.

"And you say that it is me who is wasting your time?" Carla interjected sarcastically.

"So who was it? Gabriel? Raphael? I know it wasn't Michael for he goes solo; he's ruthless, and to engage in incarnation would be beneath him. I know you don't know what is going on here!" Victor said softly.

Carla sat back in her chair, and boldly staring Victor dead in his eyes, said, "I may know a lot more than you think!"

"Is that so? Well, why don't you enlighten me?"

"You first," Carla responded.

"Well, this is what I know—your friend, or should I say friends, don't like the underground! That is why you or your moralistic diggers and weepers have to personally open this door, and that I won't let happen. We are everywhere! Come, walk with me," Victor said as he walked behind her chair to assist her in moving it so that she could stand up.

Victor was an incarnated sixty-five year old, 5'9" bald-plated Russian. He was a general of the fallen angels. As they walked the floor of the enormous bunker, many techs, analysts and geeks were sitting behind scores of computers, busy at work.

"All of my workers are very good at what they do," Victor said as he gestured with his hands, pointing out the lit up screens of at least forty computers.

"What are they so busy working on?" Carla asked.

"They are reaching out and touching somebody," Victor said with a smile. "Isn't the internet's social media a gift? For me it is. You people can be so gullible for if something is said enough times, you will believe it."

"Speak for yourself, not everybody falls for that BS you are spooling out, or should I say fooling others with! And what do you mean by you people? You speak as if you are not a part of this human race!" Carla said as her eyes wandered around, looking at faces that seemed to be mesmerized and fixated on what they were doing.

"Ha, ha, ha! Your speculations are dead on! Very soon good behavior will be a distant memory of the past. For too long it has been controlling bad behavior," Victor rejoined, grinning in delight.

Carla whipped her head quickly towards Victor with a shocked look on her face when he confirmed her conjecture. Then she asked. "What exactly is it that you are doing?"

"I am merely desensitizing people to our truth. Freedom of speech does more for the bad, than it does for the good. I will give you a perfect example. You have heard and seen the election that is taking place in the United States today, yes? You have guessed it—that misfit, and whatever else your kind may want to call him, with his grandiose beliefs, will win."

"You've got to be kidding me! Are you personally engineering this?" Carla asked with a surprised look on her face.

Victor went silent for a moment, and while he was looking around, he marveled and then responded, "Personally no, this is the combined effort of many of us, and once and for all we will prove that your God is fallible." Victor's eyes suddenly locked onto Richard's, "Richard, come here."

When Richard got closer to him, Victor straddled one of his arms around his shoulder and walked away from Carla's listening ears. He spoke softly, "'Take her back to her cell. We can use her— she will be our sacrifice." Richard suddenly turned and walked towards Carla, held her by her arm and started to escort her off the floor.

While they were walking away, Victor shouted out, "Mrs. Wallace, there are too many leaders in this world! I'm merely trying to get it down to a few that will follow the dictates of our dark belief system. I call it divide and conquer."

Meanwhile:

It is 1:30pm in England. Back at headquarters, Sheila walked back onto the floor from a quick coffee break, and asked, "Any changes?"

"Nothing but the time," one of the agents said as he monitored the screens.

Back at the motel Derrick asked Brent, "Have you eaten yet?"

"No! What time is it?" Brent asked as he stood up from the computer. He was vigorously rubbing his eyes.

"1:33pm! I noticed when we were driving earlier that there was a Frankie's Fish and Chips not so far down the street. Are you down with that?" Derrick asked.

"Whatever, because I can eat anything right about now," Brent responded, holding his stomach.

"You got it!" Derrick said as he opened the door to leave.

Meanwhile:

Three hours later at 6:30pm in Syria, President Almasi, the host of a grand formal dinner party, was feeling confident that in the grand scheme of things everything was set in motion to reveal the results of the rigged elections in the United States of America that would favor him and Russia. In fact, at that very moment people were casting their votes. While he and his guests were popping champagne bottles, suddenly he noticed a beautiful, tall, young, shoulder length brunette, wearing a seductive, light blue formal dress. His eyes followed her across the room. It appeared that she was walking in slow motion, and he, and only he was watching her. Suddenly,his assistant Albadi touched him on his shoulder. President Almasi angrily spun around because of the distraction and asked, "What is it?"

Albadi eyes popped open with surprise as he immediately responded with an apology, "I'm so sorry I startled you. I was just wondering if everything was okay!"

"I'm fine," said Almasi. But when he turned back, the lady was gone! "Where did she go?"

"Sir, where did who go?" Albadi asked.

"Didn't you see her, that gorgeous, young lady in a light blue dress? She looks like a beautiful angel!"

"I'm sorry, Sir! I did not see her, but would you like for me to find her and bring her to you, or perhaps, check the guest list and find out whose guest she is?" said Albadi.

"No, that won't be necessary," Almasi replied as he curiously started looking around to see if his wife had been watching him. He then reached out for the glass of champagne that the waiter had brought for him.

Ahmad Almasi had graduated from Damascus University in 1988, and had become an ophthalmologist. Following the death of his father, and the untimely death of his older brother, he was catapulted into the leadership of Syria. Although he had promised to be a 21st century transformational leader, he continued to follow in his father's footsteps as a brutal dictator of Syria's secular government.

Five minutes later, President Almasi excused himself to go to the restroom. As he was leaving the restroom, he turned to his right, and there she was again. This time she was directly in front of him! His shock turned into relief as her stunning beauty engulfed his vision. His armed guards that always seemed to be in close proximity to him was momentarily startled, because it appeared as though she had come out of nowhere.

"Do I know you?" Almasi asked.

But she just stood there and smiled at him. Suddenly, her face took on a more serious and demanding look as she stared directly into his eyes. It was almost as if he had become hypnotized, because she only nodded her head and said nothing.

Almasi nodded in return as if he had made an agreement with her, one which they had both secretly agreed on. They both then turned and walked away, going their separate ways.

Ten minutes later, General Amena Nasser of Afis Air Force base in Syria hung up his phone. He had just received an airstrike order.

Chapter 15

High above sea level, approximately 9,232 feet, Michael, the Archangel, sat perched on the peak of Mt. Hermon in Syria. His muscles rippled as bright lightning flashed and loud thunders crashed against the sky. Suddenly, he stood up tall from his perched position because, finally, his sensors had picked up on the moment he was waiting for ever since the 396 fallen Angels had taken residence on the earth. He had waited for this moment. Is this for real? He had asked himself this a number of times as he stood with his head lifted to the sky. With a slow left to right turn, as if he was tracking a scent on the winds and trying to determine which direction to go in, he walked to the left and then quickly turned right, and with a gigantic flap of his wings, he took flight.

On the second floor terrace of President Ahmad Almasi's palace, there behind a pillar, a guard was hiding. He was taking a cigarette break while the jubilant sounds of music and singing could be heard in close proximity inside. A light breeze had picked up. The soldier lifted his head when he smelt the pretty scent of a perfume that floated with the breeze. The soldier slowly peeked around the pillar, and his heart almost stopped when he saw the stunning beauty in the blue dress. He quickly pulled himself back behind the pillar, and stood at attention as if he was trying to fuse himself with the pillar. Then he slowly turned to edge his way around the other side to get a better view.

The lady in blue was thirty-six year old Abigail Jones. She was born and educated in London, but spent her latter days living throughout the United States of America. She was the Devil's advocate in its truest sense. She used her beauty to attract wealthy men who owned large companies. She was very smart and cunning, for she blinded them with false love that weakened them. She used her business education to convince them to flip one of their successful companies to a prearranged bidder, always making sure she locked in her percentage. In short, she was a busy, manipulative woman. This time she was working with the Devil himself. She was Lucifer's favorite type of host. He walked with her, and many who were like her, had created some of his major catastrophes, like the one she had set in motion ten minutes ago.

Abigail started to turn slowly because both she and Lucifer, who was now inside of her, felt the soldier's presence. That light breeze suddenly turned into a 40 knots tropical storm wind. Abigail's hair blew like a wild fire as she clutched the cement railing of the second floor terrace. A beast of a roar sounded out from her—it was Lucifer frantically trying to shed her away like a snake's skin because he suddenly realized that he was under attack.

The guard fully revealed himself, and stood in horror when he witnessed what happened next! To him the creature appeared to be a gigantic bird who quickly swooped Abigail and Lucifer off the terrace. Suddenly, the wind subsided, and because of the beast's loud roar, along with the howling winds, a small number of the party's guests, who had become curious, walked out onto the terrace. The guard stood there, looking like a ghost as he stared at his cigarette and wondered about its contents.

In a dark, deserted alleyway in Damascus, Michael, the Archangel, held Abigail and Lucifer by the throat against the wall of a building as he stared them both down with a vicious, angry look.

"Long time no see, my brother," Abigail/Lucifer said.

"Show yourself!" Michael responded.

"Why the hostility against my host? Don't you appreciate this beautiful specimen your God created?"

"Why the hostility against your host? She is a willing participant! Show yourself! I have no feelings of remorse for her or you! You and your host will fall asunder by my hands!" Michael declared, obviously frustrated for his patience was running thin.

Right then, the roaring of fighter jets could be heard overhead. Abigail/Lucifer began to smile, and then giggled sinisterly. "My, my, my, soon many innocent children will suffer."

Michael suddenly looked up, slightly distracted but understanding what was about to happen. However, when he looked back down, Abigail alone was shouting profanities, "Get off me!

Then some distance away, Lucifer's voice could be heard echoing through the air, "Michael, to show compassion is my greatest sin!"

A soft smile came across Michael's face as he was reminded of the nature of the beast. But that was okay because he knew deep down inside that he would find him again, sooner or later.

Shouting profanities, Abigail was totally oblivious to what was going on as she flailed around under Michael's throat grip.

"Calm down, heathen," Michael shouted angrily. "That blind fool said you were a beautiful specimen, created by my Father, but you are his mutant, a mere alteration of my Father's creation! You are incredulous, lacking substance and grace! You're disingenuous, and for that I'm going to shed light on one of your greatest earthly fears."

Michael then slowly ran his fingers down her face, which aged her by thirty years. Yes, she was thirty-six, but was living in a sixty-six year old body. Michael held her head with both of his hands and said, "Lady, try and humble yourself, and if you succeed, this will change and I will see you when you get there! Now go, and right your wrongs!" Then Michael quickly turned and left her.

That simple act had a rippling effect around the world for it affected every woman who had similar traits as Abigail. Filled with a deep guilt, they experienced a thirty-year jump in age.

That dramatic change was sent from above!

Michael touched down and stood on the highest roof in Damascus. There his focus was directed to the fighter jets that had passed over three minutes ago. They were carrying a poison gas, and were attacking a rebel stronghold outside of one of the Syrian towns. Commander Asfour, squad leader of the fighters, called out to the other pilots, "Abort mission! Abort mission! I'm losing fuel fast!"

Then the other pilots started to crowd the radios as they stepped on one another's transmission. They cried out in unison, "I'm losing fuel too!"

"Let's go back! Flight's heading 270," Commander Asfour said and repeated, "Flight's heading 270!"

Just as they were flying over the same area they had just left a few minutes before, an explosion occurred on all four fighter jets. This released their chemical payload, forming black rain over the city of Damascus.

Chaos set in throughout the city of Damascus as people were running everywhere for cover from the fallen debris and chemical gases. When many people of the world consider the fact that most Syrians supported the president and his regime, it is easy to understand why they would call this disaster poetic justice.

Meanwhile:

7,127.7 miles away in California, at 9:00am, James Carey was shuffling around in his kitchen. He was preparing breakfast for the start of the big eventful day he was about to embark on. The timing was a little off because he had planned, before he had met with Danny Stone, and his now new agenda that he was going to cover some of the polling stations for the presidential election, after he had voted himself. But what he was now involved in was big. A brief thought ran across his mind that put a little smile on his face—he now had an 'S' on his chest.

Suddenly his phone rang, which startled him for a second because he was in deep thought. "Hello," he answered.

"How is my super hero doing this morning?" Agent Andrew Anderson said, obviously in jubilant spirits.

James immediately started to blush with embarrassment because somehow he felt for a moment that Agent Anderson was reading his private thoughts. Then he responded, "Ahhh, stop it now! Nothing has come out of my watch as yet."

"Stop being modest! You impress me, and I have a sneaking suspicion that I know the type of guys you sat down with! They even gave you a weapon's test! I know you razzle dazzled them. And do not tell me that I'm so wrong for that," Andrew said, smiling at him. He was tickled to death on the other end of the line, knowing fully well he was putting James at ease. Then he asked, "James, they didn't ask where you were staying, did they?"

"No, he just said he was going to call."

"That's great! Listen, shoot me a text on your address. I had put a rush on your eye glasses last night and it's ready. We got a judge's approval updated on Nathanial Parker and it's also a go on the infiltration. I need to stop by so we can conduct a quick test on your new glasses. You might be able to use it today. They didn't slip a tracking bug on you, did they?" Andrew asked, holding his breath because he knew that he had forgotten to mention it during their last briefing.

"No, I highly doubt that! My father taught me to always be aware of my surroundings and watch out for unusual physical contacts." James responded with confidence.

Andrew paused for a few seconds and then said, "Okay, it's 9:05am, go ahead and shoot the text to me. I will pick up my wife's car and come by alone, to be on the safe side; give me 15 minutes to load your address into her GPS, and then I'll call to give you my ETA. I'm a few minutes away from her office now. But I'll still have to run a bug test when I get there.

"No problem, I'll be waiting," James said, and then hung up.

Twenty minutes later, James' ring tone sounded off, "Hello," he answered.

"Okay James, the GPS is telling me I'm 10 minutes away. I'll see you then or shortly after my slow drive by reconnaissance."

"Gotcha!" James said.

James lived in Fountain Valley, so Agent Anderson was traveling just a little outside Irvine from his wife's office. A knock sounded at James' door, apartment #10 of the high-rise complex. He opened the door.

"All clear," Andrew said, as he cautiously stuck his head inside.

"Come on in," James said gesturing with a welcome hand.

"All seems to be okay on the outside as I didn't notice anybody sitting in a vehicle! Hey, what time is it?" Andrew asked. Then he answered himself, "9:38am! James, could you bring me the clothes you wore at last night's meeting, including your shoes?"

When James returned with the clothes and shoes, Andrew took them and went over them with a wand detector. A few seconds later he said, "No detection! Okay, let's do this, try this on!"

James reached out for his back up, his high tech hidden cam glasses. "Feels good, the correction hasn't changed!"

"James, we didn't do anything with your lens! We just fitted it with an almost microscopic audio video camera. Hold up a sec, let me connect it," Andrew said as he pulled out his laptop from its case. "Okay, we're up."

"I'm going into the kitchen, and you go out onto the balcony. Talk to yourself, and tell me what you are looking at."

"Okay," James said as he walked over to the balcony and began to describe what he was looking at. "That is good! I'm reading you loud and clear. It's working fine!"

"Okay, I better go, got to keep my distance!" Andrew said.

It was 10:03am when James' ring tone sounded off again. He allowed his phone to ring a few more times so that his excitement would not be detected by the caller. "Hello," James answered.

"James, my man, got a pen?"

"Yep!" James replied.

"Good, here it is, Sun View School, off Silver Lane and Hail Avenue, west of Beach Boulevard at 7723 Jules Low Drive. Leave now if you can."

"Okay," James replied.

James started scrambling about as he loaded up essentials in his work case. He quickly walked out of his apartment but then with a quick glance, he stopped and circled it, to double check the checklist that was in mind. As he reached for the door's handle, he stopped again in a makeshift vestibule to look into the mirror that hung on the wall. He checked the fit of the covert high tech glasses he was wearing. After locking the door behind him, he scurried down the stairs, as he made a quick speed dial call to Agent Anderson to give him the address Nathanial had just given to him.

Chapter 16

A t 10:35 am, James pulled into the parking lot of the school's polling station in his black 2014 Ford Ranger's double cab pickup truck. As he was stepping on and off his brakes for the occasional pedestrian that was scurrying across the parking lot to join the polling station lines, his eyes were scanning for a parking spot. Then in his mind he said, "there we go," when he saw a car's brake lights and then reverse lights, indicating a car was about to back out of a spot. He quickly jockeyed into position so that no one else could take that spot. While waiting, his phone rang, and when he looked down at it, he saw Agent Andrew Anderson's name. He quickly answered, "Hello."

"James, I'm going to make this quick! I see that you are there now! In fact, all of the agents that are assigned to this case are watching everything you are seeing, and listening to everything you are hearing right now. Listen up, there are important steps you need to follow. Do not try to communicate with us through your device. If you must, do it only if it's absolutely imperative and you know that it is okay to do so. Do not pan your head around like a video camera; try to forget you are wearing this high tech equipment, and remember, this is only a one way device, so we can only see what you see and hear what you hear. There is no earpiece, so there is no way for us to talk to you through it. But don't worry because we've got you covered! We will have a special surveillance group or an SSG set up within an hour. Oh, by the way, if you had put my name and number in your phone contacts, delete it, and commit my number to memory. Also, remember you are not working as a journalist, so try not to play one in that public arena. You are now a part of that White Supremacist group, so any information you need for your personal records will be recorded by us through you subtly trying to gain information from your conversations with them. Okay, that's it! Now go and be careful!"

As James was walking towards the polling station lines, he immediately saw the gathering of the White Supremacists who were wearing intimidating attire, including the distinctive red baseball caps that had been worn at all of the political rallies of the elected presidential candidate of the Republicans. Inscribed on them were the words, "Make America Great Again". They were also carrying picket signs. Right then an eerie feeling came upon James that made him think that the red caps were a subliminal hypnotic catch for angry paranoid White voters who lacked empathy. It was a dog whistle that cried out, "Make America White Again".

"James," a voice shouted out. He looked towards the voice, and realized it was Nathanial's. He was standing near the door of one of the school's polling station's lines, beckoning him to come over.

As James approached and got closer to him, Nathaniel said, "Go ahead of him! We've been here an hour and a half already." He was holding onto the shoulders of a young man, who was apparently a member of his group.

"Last night, you told me to wait for your call at 10 'o clock," James responded.

"You are right, but it came to me after you left that these polling station lines can be a bit stressful and time consuming, so I decided to step up the time to get out here a little earlier, so that I can put you here," said Nathanial.

"You want me to jump the line," James said under his breath with his hand over his mouth.

"You good, trust me," Nathanial said as he stared down at the people who were standing behind them. James stepped into the line with his head hung down because he was feeling a bit embarrassed for this was not the type of person he was. Then Nathanial gestured with his head towards Todd, the young man that was standing in line, and said," Let's go!" As he looked back at James, he added, "You didn't think I was that rude, did you? My boy here had to re-enter the line so that you wouldn't have to stand in line too long," Nathanial said as he straddled his arm around Todd's shoulders, giggling loudly as they walked away.

It took James 15 minutes, waiting in the line, to cast his votes. James was standing outside the polling station feeling relieved and thankful for the thoughtful gesture Nathanial had extended to him. As he stared around aimlessly, he reminded himself of what Agent Anderson had told him. His eyes then caught Nathanial, standing with the group of supremacists' picketers, waving him over. "You did the right thing, right?" Nathanial asked.

"Yes, of course," James said with a smile.

"Okay, let's go! We are going on a field trip," Nathanial said. As they were walking to their cars, he told another member, Richard, to drive with James to make sure he didn't get lost in traffic.

"Where are we going?" James asked.

"You will see when you get there," Nathanial said as the roaring sound of his muscle mustang came to life.

There were five cars, James' making the fifth one, and each of the supremacists filled them to capacity. After making a few right and left turns on the surface streets, with Nathanial roaring up ahead leading the pack, James turned to Richard and asked, "Is this a race?"

Richard response was short, "Keep up! Let's go!"

"Where are we going?" James asked again.

"Santa Ana," Richard said as he looked over at James through the corner of his eyes. Richard Harris was 6 feet tall. He had strikingly blue eyes, and one would think that by just looking into his eyes that he would be an angel, but it was quite the contrary. He was one

147

of the older members of Nathanial's group. A thirty-eight year old radical White Supremacist, he made a clear statement of who he was, as evidenced by his tattooed-filled body. There was no hiding what he believed. He was also known as having a short-fuse or a very hot temper.

When James first shook Richard's hand back at the polling station, he had an uneasy feeling about him. It also appeared that this feeling was mutual because he could feel Richard constantly staring at him, and whenever James turned his head to look at him, he would turn away.

The small caravan of five cars got onto the 405 and then onto the Costa Mesa. After a while, they turned on to the Silverado Canyon Road. A short while after that, the road became desolate. They were now in the Santa Ana Mountains.

James asked again, "Where the hell are we going?"

"He told you! You will see when you get there," Richard responded with a bit of tension in his tone.

James went quiet, focusing his attention on changing the dial tune on his stereo radio.

Ten minutes later they turned right onto a dirt road. The road had right and left curves, as well as valleys and hills as they drove down and then up, up and then down. Finally, they came to a landing on a mountainside. James started to exit his vehicle as he listened to the sounds of car doors slamming and the jubilant spirits of the wild group hooting and hollering, "Yee haa!" James stood alongside his truck, with a look of amazement on his face as he took in what he was looking at—it looked like a Hollywood movie set. There were makeshift shacks and two-story buildings along the dusty roads. In short, it had the look of a cowboy's western town in the middle of nowhere.

James jumped in fright when Nathanial walked up to him from behind and lightly rested his hand on his right shoulder.

"I know your mind must be buzzing with questions about all of this now. But James, we've got a lot going on here in order to protect ourselves and our country. I personally rushed you up the ladder to show you all of this, and I must say, I had a lot of push back from my most seasoned members. I see a lot in you, which they fail to see right now! I see that there is a lot more you have to offer, other than your journalistic background, and your ability to reach out to potential followers," Nathanial said as he looked out over the mountain range.

"How so?" James responded.

"Well, let's see! You appear to have an extensive background in weapons training and knowledge, and last night you mentioned that your father somehow had buried that seed deep within you, so that started from your early years."

James suddenly turned to Nathanial and asked, "Where are you going with this?"

Nathanial paused for a few seconds and then asked, "Your father, are you guys still close?"

"Ever since he divorced my mother and married his much younger sweetheart, I had somewhat distanced myself from him, but I do occasionally visit him from time to time," James replied.

"Does he still have connections inside the armed forces?" Nathanial asked.

Back in Orange County's FBI field office, Agent Andrew Anderson, who jumped up out of his chair while he and the other agents were listening and watching the feed from James' eye glasses, said, "I knew it was coming! He wants an inside to the military so he can get weapons! That's why he embraced James and showed him so much so early! Look at their set up—it's a training camp for a tactical force! They are forming a god damn militia."

Agent Anderson quickly turned to Agent Kenny Johnson, beckoning him to walk out of the room with him. Then he turned to Kenny, and to grab his undivided attention, he lightly gripped his shoulders and said softly, "Kenny, this is big! We can't be sure even with our own agents who they may have reached out to and persuaded with this radical ideology, so for now we need to be quiet about this! Hopefully, in that room we don't have a leak, but I will have a talk with them to deal with that. I need you to go through the proper procedures—go and get a GPS lock and satellite feed on that location."

"You got it boss," Agent Johnson said as he turned and hurriedly walked away.

While James and Nathanial walked towards a prop, that is, one of the two-story buildings, Nathanial unclipped a hand held radio he had attached to his belt and said, "Are we good to go in there?"

"Affirmative," a voice responded over the radio.

While Nathanial was waving over one of the group members to bring the bag he was holding, Nathanial stopped and turned to James and said, "Tactical training, have you been on one of these field workouts before?"

James paused for a moment as his eyes wandered over the properties set up and then turned back to Nathanial and answered, "No, not of this magnitude!"

"First time for everything, right?" Nathanial quipped as he knelt down to unzip the bag that was brought to him.

"For a tactical hostile's close quarter's entrance, what is your weapon of choice?" Nathanial asked as he looked up at James.

"For precision, aim, less kick, and one shot take down, give me a 9mm," James replied with confidence.

"Good choice for people who don't like to make a mess! Me, on the other hand, at close quarters, I am taking my pistol grip shotgun," Nathanial said with a smile as he stood up and handed James his weapon of choice.

James held the gun and then ejected the clip to physically see the rounds and their levels.

"Be careful, those are live rounds, and we've got spring loaded targets inside," Nathanial said as he wracked his shotgun.

James looked at him and chuckled.

"What are you laughing at?"

"You! I was thinking, you're not only going to make a mess with that, you're going to make an example of it," James said as they both started to advance toward the building.

Nathanial kicked the door in, and they were off! It sounded like the fourth of July as the barrage of bullets fired off.

Two minutes later, they shouted out, "Clear!" Sweating profusely, they walked down the front steps of the building.

James turned to Nathanial and asked, "So tell me, what is going to be the actual cost of all of this?"

"Cost? What are you talking about—cost for what?" Nathanial asked with a puzzled look in his eyes.

"The cost to rebuild what you just ripped up with that monster you are carrying with you," James said with a smile.

Chapter 17

Meanwhile in Cleburne County, Alabama, at 1:15 pm, Dunstan/Andrealphus, Sam/Gabriel and Julian sat in the living room of Dunstan's modest two-bedroom home. The house was bequeathed to him by a lovely, elderly lady, named Claire Saunders, nine months ago. She was a former patient in the home for the elderly, where Dunstan worked as a caretaker. She was very fond of Dunstan, as he was of her. Claire, aged 81, lived alone in her little home after her husband passed away five years ago, and between the two of them, they had no children. She was admitted into the homecare facility two years ago by concerned distant relatives. A year after her admittance, her health took a turn for the worse, and shortly afterwards, she passed away.

Earlier that morning, Dunstan had called in a favor from a colleague. He wanted him to take his shift at the care center. Immediately on arriving to work, he requested a leave of absence, effective immediately, for personal reasons. A favorite among the administrative staff, he had never missed a day of work since he had been working there for two years. He was always on time, and when he was asked to take his vacation, he would refuse until they stressed that they feared he would suffer diminished faculty if he didn't take it. "Everybody needs a break," his colleagues and the workers in the administration's office would say, so they insisted that he take it.

Reluctantly he did, and that was three months ago, which is when he first saw the chapel and had decided to take it on as his new project.

Dunstan had just finished explaining to Sam how he came into possession of the house, when a moment of silence enveloped all three. Sam then stood up and walked over to the fireplace's mantel that was built on the dividing wall from the kitchen. He picked up a photo of a lady and said, "Is this her?"

"Yes, that's her. She was a mother like no other. I guess that is mainly because she had no children," Dunstan answered.

"That is interesting," Sam said as he placed the photo back and walked over to the living room's main front window. In silence, he stood there looking out of the window. Then a car pulled into the driveway. He said, "You have a visitor."

Dunstan immediately stood up and walked over to the window. "Oh boy, I'm in trouble now. That's Angela! I didn't see her at work to explain my new plans, and I know she was trying to call me! Through the excitement of you being here, I forgot to charge my phone last night, so I left it charging in my room this morning. My guess is it has a bunch of missed calls from her. She's probably wondering why I wasn't at work today."

Angela Romano, aged 37, was 5'9" tall. She had brown eyes, olive skin and long, wavy, black hair. Her father was Italian, and her mother was African-American. Angela was also known as Angel by relatives, close friends and colleagues. That is what most people thought of her because of her empathetic, caring and giving attitude toward others, not to mention her stunning, natural beauty. She was unique among her kind. She had studied medicine and had gotten a four-year degree in Nursing at Phoenix University in Phoenix, Arizona, which was where she lived at the time. She worked as an RN at Arizona General Hospital for five years, but was not thrilled over the politics related to uninsured patients, so she quit her job to search for a position that would give her more direct contact with those who truly were in need. Angela decided to go back to medical school and then became a doctor, family practitioner. That still wasn't enough, she studied further and became a Neurosurgeon. In that field she work freelance, and tried to focus mainly on special cases by using donations from philanthropist, for those who could not afford their surgery. All through her life, she served as a community service animal care provider, and now with her practice, she had an on and off day to day commitment with a homecare facility provider for the elderly. She would work in the capacity of the administration and serve when needed as a medical doctor. Angela believed that her true purpose in life was to help others wherever and whenever she can.

Unlike many other beautiful women, who were mainly opportunists, she was not someone who used her beauty to open doors for her, or whenever she met people for the first time, judged them based on face value, thus, failing to see the true content of their character. In fact, she was flawless when it came to her beauty, but she ignored the fact that she was beautiful. She constantly reminded people, who complimented her on her beauty, that, "beauty was only skin deep". Angela had a special attraction for Dunstan because of something she felt and saw deep within him. So I guess you can say that she was like an angel who could read others well.

Julian sprung to his feet when he heard Angela's name. He ran to the door but just as he was about to open it, he turned to Sam and said, "Sam, you ought to tell your Angel that heaven has to be missing an Angel because she is right here with us!" Then, with a smile, he opened the door and asked, "Angel, how are you?" he opened his arms to receive her with a hug.

After their pleasantries, Angela asked, "Is Dunstan here?"

"I'm right here," Dunstan shouted out as he quickly walked out of his bedroom where he had gone to check his phone for messages. "I'm so sorry, my dear, that I was unable to answer your calls because my phone was charging," Dunstan said as he held her hand to walk her into the kitchen for a private moment.

"I was worried when I asked for you, and you were not at the office. The girls at the office said you came in to request a leave of absence effective immediately! What's going on?" Angela asked, looking concerned.

"Sweet girl, I've been hard-pressed to explain exactly what is going on right now. But I can assure you that it is nothing misleading, mischievous or anything other than the deep personal issues of that elderly man out there. I feel obligated to help him sought them out.

Angela, I'm going off for a short while. Julian is going to stay here to keep things together at the house, but I need you to check on him from time to time. It's not that I don't trust him because in light of all that is going on with me right now, I need us to be together on this. Angela, you need to trust me on this! In time, I'll explain everything."

"Dunstan, you know you are special to me, unlike any other male that I've met, and believe me, they're too few to mention. I know I never told you this before but given this sudden trip you are going on, I'm feeling compelled to tell you that I'm attracted to you. I know you know this but you seem to shy off from it, and it seems that you're turning a blind eye to it. Perhaps, it's our age difference that concerns you. But Dunstan, I'm an adult just like you, and that age stuff doesn't faze me at all! I'm all about substance—to me you are a phenomenon. Actually, since I've known you, you have built me up, brick by brick, filling me with confidence, and giving me the reassurance to move forward toward achieving my life's goals. Through your mere presence, you've helped me believe in myself when there were times I wondered about myself. Oh God, here I go again—bleeding out my emotions. What time is it? I have to get back to work especially since we're on half-staff given that they are taking turns to vote at the polls," Angela exclaimed, forgetting she had just arrived. She was feeling a little embarrassed too since she had revealed her true feelings to him.

"Sweet girl," Dunstan whispered in her ear as he pulled her closer to him and softly embraced her, "I feel you! I understand you, and yes, I know. But with me right now, it's a bit complicated! But you can rest assured that there is no one else. Although I will tell you this—as soon as I put behind me what I'm about to embark on, I promise you, I will be here for you! Together we will embrace our future, whether it be in the flesh or in the spirit."

"I hear you too, and thank you for understanding and seeing me like I see you. But that very last word you used concerns me. Dunstan, what is going on? Is it dangerous? What are you going to be doing?" Angela said as she held him with a tighter grip.

Dunstan stepped back as he held both of her hands in his so that he could look more fully at her, and then he said softly, "My, my, my, I'm not sure if it is possible for you to understand how much you amaze me right now!" Staring at the ceiling for a brief moment, he said with a smile, "Listen, I'll call you every day, and you can call me too. Angela, it's not like I'm leaving this planet." He stroked her hair, and then went silent because he felt a bit of guilt deep down inside since leaving the planet was a possibility. They both slowly started to walk to the door.

"Sam, my friend, come meet Angela. She is an extraordinary person, really an earth Angel inside and out!" Dunstan said as he turned her to face Sam.

Sam reached out for a handshake and said, "It is my pleasure to meet you, Angel!"

"It is also my pleasure. Sam, I'm not going to pry, but I trust you and Dunstan will take care of each other," Angela said as she headed to the front door, and then she stopped, turned and said in a high-pitched voice, "Julian, I'm eating alone tonight, but how about you joining me for dinner? How does Applebee's sound? My treat."

"Great, you are on girl," Julian said in jubilant spirits.

"Okay, I will pick you up at seven," Angela said as she opened the door.

All of a sudden thunder crashed, lightning flashed, and immediately buckets of rain came pouring down. Angela shouted in astonishment, "Oh my God, where did this come from? I'm stuck here! Dunstan, do you have an umbrella? I have to get back because there is so much to do."

"No, I'm sorry, I don't," Dunstan answered as he reached out and grabbed a coat that was hanging on a coat rack near the door. "Let's make a run for it," he said as he draped the coat over her and himself. The rain was coming down in sheets as they ran to the car. Angela quickly opened the door and jumped in. Dunstan helped her close the door and then tapped the glass with kissed fingers as he turned and ran back to the house.

Angela stepped on her brakes, and then pressed her start button. The engine came to life on the first spin. As she was reaching for her gear shift, she quickly stopped in shock and amazement! When she looked down at herself, there was not a drop of water on her. She slowly raised her head, and there was Sam standing at the window, smiling and looking back at her.

Dunstan ran inside and slammed the door, letting out a sigh of relief. "Woof, was there a tropical storm forecast?" he asked as he started brushing off his clothes with his hands in an attempt to dry himself. Then he realized that he was not wet. He turned to Sam and asked, "Gabriel, I'm speaking to you, is it not too soon for her right now?"

Sam just smiled, and suddenly that smile took on an expressionless look as Gabriel spoke, "Andrealphus, we have to go! There are messages that must be sent right away!"

"Okay, let's do this," Dunstan said. Then he turned to Julian and added, "Young man, watch the fort! I'm not sure how long we're going to be gone!"

"I got it Pops! Take your time as I got a date tonight," Julian said with a flamboyant dance spin.

"Yeah, and about that, you better be a gentleman," Dunstan said, waving his finger and staring cross-eyed at him.

Chapter 18

In Fairfax County, Virginia, time 2:45 pm temperature 20 degrees Fahrenheit. Rodger Drake, the top seat holder and advocate of the many groups throughout the country that support the second amendment rights to bear arms, was in the backyard of his prestigious lavish home. 74 years of age, he had white silver hair, green eyes and was 5'9" tall. There he sat on the indoor veranda, pool side, with three of his guests. They were in a meeting. They talked over light finger foods and soft drinks. Rodger was engaging in small conversation with them, which was a stalling tactic, because there was a fourth and most important guest that he was expecting.

Rodger's guests included, Daniel Pike, who was a 53 year old heavyset Caucasian with light, slightly greying hair. He was the named Director of a corporation that oversaw the music and entertainment industry; Mark Colebrook, who was a six feet slender 58 year old, had neatly cut dusty blonde hair. He was the named Director of a corporation that had ties with the Hollywood movies and adult film industries. He also had strong ties with White Nationalists and key personnel of the far right news stations; and the third guest was Fedorov Volkov, who was 56 years old. Gym fit built, he had black hair and a scar beneath his right eye. A Russian Oligarch, his soul interest was to swing the presidential elections so that sanctions could be lifted, and he, and others like him, could tap into the oil in Siberia.

Adam Moore, who was late, was the fourth guest, who carried the simple title of banker, (a world banker). Some would say he was the top leader behind the Illuminati's New World Order group. But our God had sent Angels down to take care of him as he was one of the six generals in North America that had been targeted to be taken down.

The three guests had their PSD protective services detail with them, and these men were being entertained by Kirk Woods in the foyer of the home. Kirk Woods was Rodger's personal bodyguard. Aged 42, he stood 6'4" tall, and was 245 pounds. He had dark brown eyes and dark brown hair, and was well trained in combat as he served with the army's Rangers.

This small group was a part of the plot of the New World Order. Rodger was pushing the second amendment to the hilt by putting weapons of war in the hands of shallow minded militia groups that were growing at a fast rate throughout the country. They were easily manipulated to rise and defend their supporters in the event of an up and coming new government overthrow. They held their allegiance to the ones that believed in them.

Social media followers, with their burning desire to be socially accepted, and their great dependence on social internet sites, were easy targets for these clandestine New World Order groups. In this world of glamour, these persons needed to be better looking than the others. Using subliminal, illicit messages, these groups force these individuals to engage in destructive, distractive and apathetic behaviors around the world. But where would we be, if people didn't care about each other?

Suddenly, lightning struck the metal frame of the indoor pool's glass roof structure, sending three shattered glass sheets splashing down into the center of the pool. It was followed by a thunderous sound. Rodger and his three guests, in fright, jolted back and fell over in their chairs. Kirk and the other three PSD's looked at each other in shock, surprised at the sudden change of weather. Kirk slowly walked over to the window to look out, but he saw no change just the snow-covered ground, and the trees that shook as a result of the high velocity winds. He turned, shaking his head as he brushed off the thought, and continued his billiard game with the others.

As Rodger and his three guests started to stand up from a knee-crawling position, all four of them simultaneously jumped back in fright again when they saw Dunstan Archer and Sam Watson standing before them in long trench coats that flapped slightly like flags because of the wind that was funneling through with a jet blast that came through the opened glass rooftop.

Sam/Gabriel waved his hand with a command for the wind to subside.

"Gentlemen, have a seat," Dunstan said in an all so smooth voice.

"Kirk!" Rodger shouted out for his bodyguard, fear and anger rolled into one on his face.

Dunstan took one step forward and smacked Rodger behind his turned head, like an abusive parent would do to a child. Then he said, "One more outburst like that, and I will put you back on your knees, and you will never stand upright again!"

"Kirk!" Rodger boldly shouted again. This time Sam/Gabriel stepped in front of Dunstan and put his hand on Rodger's forehead that suppressed his anger. Although he was assisted in gaining his composure, he still was looking around for Kirk, wondering why he had not responded.

Sam stepped back and in a circular motion, looked at the other three as they stood there surprisingly quiet and motionless. They were aware of a mystical presence and were feeling something deep down inside for what stood before them was someone or something that was not human.

"Gentlemen, please take a seat. I promise you, this won't take long. Oh, and need I warn you? Before you try to do or think about doing anything stupid, it will be met with a force beyond your wildest imagination. We are not your average guys," Sam said in a calm and convincing, but very friendly voice.

They complied with his request.

Kirk did not respond because he and the other PSDs had moved from the foyer to the recreational room, which was some distance away from them. This was a shift away from his protocol, but since he had been at many casual meetings such as this one, there was never a call or request for his presence or attention.

Fedorov was the first to regain his demeanor, that is, his well-known arrogance. In broken Russian, that feigned an English accent, he declared, "In my country these punks would be dead right now! That's it! I'm leaving," and started to stand.

Immediately Dunstan walked behind him, held his shoulders and shoved him down with a force that damn near broke the chair. Quickly he took on a friendly and calm composure as he squeezed Fedorov's shoulders as if he was a close friend, "Stick around, you'll want to hear this," Dunstan said as he slowly walked around and pulled a chair to sit directly in front of him.

"Look at me!" Dunstan demanded.

"What is it you want from me?" Fedorov asked.

Dunstan looked deep into Fedorov's eyes, and then turned to Sam and said, "It's not him!"

Sam moaned with curiosity as he slowly stared at each of the other three. He stepped forward and pulled a chair to sit directly in front of Daniel and Mark. He stared directly into both of their eyes and then turned to his right to make direct eye contact with Rodger. Sitting back in his chair, he asked all four of them, "Where is he?"

"Where is who?" Rodger responded with quivering lips, which was a mixture of his fright and the cold.

Sam sat there quietly observing him. He didn't say a word. At least 12 seconds elapsed before he broke his silence, "Is there even a scintilla of compassion within you all?

They all sat there in silence, staring at him with looks of not quite understanding the question.

"Okay, let me ask you this, do you have any concern or care for anyone outside of your immediate family?"

The silent mode continued.

"Do you appreciate the intricate work that created you all as human beings?" Sam added, and again there was no response.

"Now you see, what's bothering me is you all are so silent and dumb-founded by these simple questions. You have no understanding of what makes you tick, and yet you think you are geniuses because you are trying to form a world dictatorship. Whenever a decade passes, how often are you going to say, 'My, how time flies?' Sam asked, staring intently at each of them.

"What I'm getting at is not one of you have stopped to think of the amount of work it took to create you and every other species, including plants and this very atmosphere. Do you think it's going to blow over like a fleeting illusion? It should be obvious to you because here on earth it takes a great deal of time to build structures of such grand magnitude, and they have been built for a reason. So I ask, why are you so ignorant and unable to answer the questions I previously laid out for you? Is it because of your arrogance?"

Then Rodger took the lead and said, "I'm curious? You speak as if you are not of this world. What is it you want from us?"

"Curious? You should be! What is it I want from you?" Sam responded, repeating Rodger's question. "Other than the hope that I have that you would understand these things, there is nothing you can give me! Apparently, the one I'm looking for is not here, so really there is nothing your kind can do for me."

Sam paused as he looked at them with disgust. Then he said, "But there is something I can do for you, do for you all, and that is to give each of you ten minutes to figure out and answer a two-part then and now question, that you need to ask yourself, that is, "Why I am, who am I?' If you are successful in answering them for yourselves, you can repent and reverse that which would delay your ultimate demise. Responding appropriately to them would result in significant rewards for you. But if you fail to do so, or you choose not to do so, then I would suggest that you use your ten minutes to get your affairs in order. Using your medical terms, you will experience a series of vascular disorders, starting with a tingling sensation in your fingertips. So, what is it going to be?"

Both Sam and Dunstan stood up from their chairs as their eyes wondered about the place. Then Sam looked down at each of them again, and said, "If it helps, let me tell you that your two-part question will require a two-part answer, and it should have more than one interpretation. The answers are deeply-rooted in your God-given hearts and souls, so good luck. I am a messenger, and my message is for you. For your sake, I hope it has been received. Now, we will leave you to your own devices."

Note: *These questions have been asked throughout the world—in countries, states and cities—by innocent, intelligent children, the message senders.*

ले

It is 3:05pm in New York City, Queens, and in a modest suburban home, Mellissa, a beautiful blue-eyed blonde, who was twenty-seven years old, had just completed setting up her video camera that was mounted on her desk alongside her computer. She was an online streamer of live seductive pornography. For four years she had acquired a great number of weak-minded followers who were sexual addicts. She had made a great deal of money through her online payment plans.

Graduating college with honors, she chose to take an easier route by using her body. She had many job offers given her business credentials, but yet she chose to go this route, big mistake!

Just as Mellissa started to position herself for the seductive poses in her bed, her computer screen started to flicker on and off. Suddenly, a child's face appeared on the screen. She sucked her teeth in disgust, thinking it was a malfunction or a computer glitch. As she was getting up to correct it, the child on the screen spoke.

"Mellissa, you need to ask yourself, "Why I am, who am I?"

You and many like you are being simultaneously sorted out at this very moment because of your incredulous viewpoint. You have been allotted ten minutes to think about and respond to this two-part then and now question, and then, repent and believe. If you succeed, you will reverse and/or delay what will ultimately happen to you. You will be rewarded tremendously if you respond appropriately. Remember, it's a two-part question that requires a two-part answer, which carries with it more than one interpretation. You are a smart girl. Tick tock, tick tock!"

Sitting on her feet in the bed, Mellissa felt compelled to consider the mystical message, particularly given the manner in which it was sent. Then suddenly, she felt compelled to rub and massage her hands.

Note: *Throughout the world, this shocking message created a ripple effect as it reached other disingenuous people of all walks of life.*

Less than twelve hours from now the election results will roll in for the new president of the United States of America. Less than twelve hours from now the world will see a drastic shift in his behavior and his true colors will be revealed. Less than twelve hours from now all those who have deeply rooted empathetic beliefs, will see the true faces of their senators, congressmen, pastors, business partners, employers, next door neighbors, and, even sadly, their so called close friends.

Note: *It is my belief that if you support bad behavior, you are that behavior.*

Chapter 19

At 7:45am on Wednesday, November 9, 2016, in London, England, Sheila Hall was eating breakfast as she shuffled around her condo picking up her essentials to rush to the MI-5 headquarters. Ten minutes ago she had gotten a call from one of the overnight agents who had been monitoring the satellite feed of the farmhouse and hillside bunker. He reported that there was movement, which was the reason she was hurriedly preparing to leave for the office.

As she was simultaneously picking up her purse and her computer bag as well as holding a half-eaten cream cheese covered bagel in her mouth, she froze in her tracks when she overheard a news report on her bedroom TV—the news reporter announced who had become the new president of the United States of America. Shockingly surprised, her bagel dropped from her mouth and onto the floor. She stood there for a few seconds not even bothering to walk in the room to see the visual; she just quickly turned and ran to the front door. Scrambling down a short flight of stairs and stepping on the surface walkway path of the parking lot, she unarmed, unlocked and remotely started her BMW with her smart car key. She slipped and almost fell, accidently dropping her bag. Her cell phone slid out, and, apparently, it was on silent mode, but the face was flashing and ringing on vibrate. Sheila quickly picked it up, and realizing that it was Agent Russell, she answered.

"Agent Russell, yes, I got the news! In fact, I got too much news, bad and good, so I'm fumbling over myself. Look! Whatever movement you're observing right now, stay on it! I will call you when I get to headquarters. I have to compose myself before I get into a car wreck," Sheila said as her tires squealed when she backed out of her parking spot.

"Got it boss," Brent said and then they hung up.

Back in the makeshift motel room, Brent stood over Agent Brooks with both hands on his shoulders and said softly, "Brooks, I need you to zoom in close as you possibly can; I need to know the number of occupants in that vehicle."

Agent Brooks did just that, but this time the vehicle was a white panel van, with tinted door windows, which made his request impossible.

Brent began talking to himself, "I wonder where they are going?" Quickly he turned to Derrick, "Let's saddle up, and grab that portable uplink because we have to take him down whenever he stops. Brooks, I need you to accurately control our couple feed! Oh, and when Paul comes around, tell him I want him to sit this one out for safety reasons. Have him monitor the screens with you in case something pops up." Then both he and Derrick quickly walked out of the room.

As they drove out of the motel's parking lot, Brent immediately called Ailes on his two- way radio. He had had a shift change and was back at the high point strip mall with two other agents that were on the all night stand-by shift, watching for movement. "Ailes, are you and Valdez back in position?"

"Yep, about five minutes ago. Right now, we're tracking the van's movement—got a white van that pulled out from the farmhouse and it's traveling down 120th Street.

"Don't lose him! We are about five minutes away from the strip mall," Brent said as he looked over at Derrick who was waiting for confirmation. Derrick confirmed by nodding his head.

"We are rolling, and about to pick up his trail on the 120," Ailes added as he slapped the dashboard to get Valdez' attention, who was driving erratically. "Slow down! We need to be inconspicuous, remember!"

Five minutes passed as Ailes got back onto the two-way, "Agent Russell, he is turning right on A3."

"Copy that, we are closing in hot," Brent responded.

Three minutes on the A3, Ailes transmitted once again, "He is turning right into the parking lot of a wholesale distributor called Harro Foods," Ailes said as he looked up at the sign of the large parking area the van was pulling into.

"I know exactly where that is," Derrick exclaimed.

"Good, let's get there," Brent responded as he held up his two-way radio, keyed it and said softly and calmly, "Ailes, do you have an occupant count?"

"Negative! Tints are too dark!"

"Okay! Wait until the van parks, and allow the occupant or occupants to exit. I need you to do a swift take down. After you have patted him down, it is important that you immediately confiscate his phone, as we cannot afford it if he sends an alarm out to the others. Hold him until we get there."

Ailes and Valdez pulled directly behind the van, a parking row between them. They both put on their neck-hung badges and then exited their vehicle with guns drawn. They walked quietly, approaching the van from the rear, a blind side out of the van's rearview mirror. Valdez took the left passenger's side, while Ailes approached with caution on the driver's right side. The driver's door opened, and the driver stepped out—it was Stanley Wilson. Ailes immediately rushed up on him holding his gun to his side so as to remain inconspicuous and said, "Stanley, don't even think about doing anything stupid."

Completely caught off guard, Stanley immediately complied with Ailes' command to face the van. He quickly handcuffed him.

Then Valdez shouted, "Clear," from the passenger's side because Stanley was the only occupant in the van. Suddenly, the sound of squealing tires could be heard as another vehicle came to a stop. Ailes looked over his shoulder to see Agent Russell and Agent Holder, who had swiftly exited their vehicle and had begun approaching him and the subject.

"Phone! Phone! Where is his phone?" Brent exclaimed.

"Here you go," Ailes said as he passed Stanley's phone to Brent.

"Okay, good! We will take him from here. I need you to call Officer Green, and have him send a team to impound this van, and then, you and Valdez work this like you did the first one."

"Got it," said Ailes as he pulled out his phone to search for Officer Green's number.

Brent's phone rang as he was pushing Stanley's head down to put him in the back seat of Derrick's Land Rover.

"Hello," Brent answered.

"Great job, Agent Russell, saw it all," Sheila Hall said on the other end of the line.

"Thank you, Boss! It's our guy Stanley Wilson. We're going to take him down to Guildford Headquarters. I had to inform the guys down here to assist, since we knew that we were going to make an arrest," Brent said.

"That's great! But not in that vehicle—you know you can't transfer an arrestee in your private vehicle," Sheila said with a hint of sarcasm in her voice.

"Damn boss! You're like God watching over me," Brent said with a chuckle.

Brent quickly turned to Valdez. "Valdez, give me your keys! Where did you guys park?"

"What's going on Bro?" Derrick asked puzzled.

"One of these jokers got to drive your whip," he quipped.

"Ah shit! We need to use a car from the motor pool, right?" Derrick asked with a frown and then looked guilty.

"Okay boss, we're switching up now," Brent said as he held his hand up, thumbs up because he knew he was been watched from above.

"Okay Agent Russell, I'm getting ready to fly down there. See you at Guildford Headquarters," Sheila said and then hung up.

The police's main headquarters was located in Guildford Surrey, England. After arriving at the headquarters, Brent and Derrick stood silently observing Stanley Wilson's demeanor through the one-way glass window of the interrogation room. Stanley kept standing up, walking around, and sitting back down again. He was constantly looking at his watch.

"What do you think?" Brent asked as he turned to Derrick.

"Looks like the classic behavior of someone who is about to crack," he answered.

"My thoughts exactly," Brent responded as he nodded in agreement.

"Let's break him," Brent said as he turned to open the door, but paused in surprise when he looked up to see Sheila Hall standing before him.

"Jesus, boss, you frightened me! Didn't I just speak to you a short time ago when you were at London's headquarters?"

"The advantages of having a helicopter, my friend," Sheila said with a smile.

"Helicopter, right! I'm starting to wonder if you are an undercover God sent Angel," Brent said sarcastically as he took two steps back to look at her from head to toe.

"So that's our Stanley Wilson in the flesh," Sheila said as she looked passed Brent through the one-way glass window.

"Yep, that is Stanley our boy! His behavior is showing that he is vulnerable, which suggests that he is breakable. I was just about to go in and work him over," Brent said as he was adjusting his trousers as if he was going on a date.

"Where is Paul?" Sheila asked.

"He is back at the motel," Brent said as he started to walk toward the door of the interrogation room.

"Agent Russell, wait up! Why isn't he here?" Sheila exclaimed.

"Boss, we had to do a field take down so I didn't think it would be safe for him to be there. Besides, his mystical presence doesn't seem to be with him."

"You said it! Mystical, to me it's a mystery, so we are not sure when it will return. Russell, get him down here," Sheila ordered.

"Derrick, can you get one of those guys back there to bring Paul here?" Brent asked.

"No!"

"Derrick, be a darling and get him yourself as he is special," Sheila said as she straddled her arms around Derrick, walking him out the door.

"Boss, are you going to sit in with me?" Brent asked as he walked towards the door of the interrogation room.

"No, not yet, because I want to observe him for a while out here," Sheila answered.

Stanley Wilson was a high tech geek, but was mainly used as a gopher because he lacked leadership ability.

As Brent quickly opened the door to the interrogation room, Stanley immediately jumped up in fright, backing into the corner of the room.

"Settle down! Can I get you anything, OJ, a cup of coffee?" Brent asked.

"Coffee, coffee please," Stanley spluttered out with a nod.

Brent secretly gestured with his hands when Stanley wasn't looking, motioning for a cup of coffee at the one-way glass window. He knew Sheila would pick up on it.

"Stanley, have a seat." They both then sat as Brent asked, "Stanley, do you know why you are here?"

"No! Why am I here?" Stanley asked with a blank look on his face.

Brent dropped his head and struggled to hold back a chuckle. Flashing a quick smile, he quickly composed himself, and sternly looked back up at Stanley, "Carla Wallace! Do you know Carla Wallace?" He took her photo from his file and slid it to him. "She is a prominent lawyer and was last seen being thrown in the back of your van at Delmar's diner."

"I don't know any Carla Wallace, and I don't know where Delmar's diner is," Stanley responded as he turned his head away from Brent's deep stare.

"Stanley, if this was a declaration of war with Russia, you would have been charged with treason." He quickly started reading from the file, "A Russian ideologist, who subscribes to 'putinism', made fruitless attempts to tap into our Government representatives' and military's computers. You would be looking at life imprisonment. Some years ago this would have resulted in capital punishment. At best you surely would be outfitted with an orange jump suit and spend a considerable amount of time in jail."

"I want a lawyer," Stanley exclaimed.

"Stanley, this isn't shoplifting that we are talking about! This is a matter of national security and we have you *dead to rights*. Now, you can somehow save yourself, but that will depend on how well you can play ball."

Brent then threw his hands in the air with a fake ball throw and said, "Catch Stanley, the ball is in your court."

Suddenly there was a soft knock on the door, and Sheila quietly walked in with a cup of coffee. Apologizing, she said, "I'm so sorry it took so long; we had to brew a fresh pot."

Stanley quickly looked up in shock and asked, "How did she know I wanted coffee?"

Brent looked at him with his fingers on his lips and said, "Shhhh, that's our secret."

Brent waited until Sheila took her seat and said, "Stanley, meet my boss, Sheila Hall. She is the head of the MI-5 field operation."

"You have a woman running a predominantly male tactical squad?" Stanley asked as he looked disparagingly down on Sheila.

"What are you, a misogynist? She got there after being highly recommended by the Commissioner, and that by no small measure. In my personal opinion, she is very effective."

Sheila turned to Brent and smiled with a thank you and quickly turned back to face Stanley and with a straight face asked, "Mr. Wilson, how are you doing on this fine morning?"

"Yeah, fine for you," Stanley said, snapping at her.

Brent quickly jumped in and said, "Stanley, I'm about to take that ball back, bury you and move on with what we have."

Suddenly a strange cellphone's ringtone sounded off; its vibration startled Brent, who jumped as he realized it was coming from Stanley's phone that he had put in his pocket earlier. He quickly pulled it out and looked at its face.

"Jeff! Who is Jeff?" Brent asked, looking at Stanley.

Chapter 20

B rent let Stanley's phone ring until his voice mail picked up. He waited a few seconds; and then he asked Stanley what steps to take to open it. Stanley gave Brent his code, and when he entered it, he put the phone on speaker.

The voice mail sounded out, "Stanley, answer your phone, or just call Richard because there are some additional items that need to be added to the wholesale list."

"What is it you guys got—a restaurant in that underground cave?" Brent asked as he slowly slid the phone over for Sheila to visually examine and glance at his contacts.

Stanley was visually shocked when he heard Brent mentioned the cave.

"Oh! That's right, I didn't mention that we have been watching you driving in and out of that hillside cave. And, talking to Mr. Winston Parker, the farmhouse owner, who is he? Your landlord?" Brent asked as he pulled the still shots of the farmhouse and the driveway to the hillside from the file.

Both Brent and Sheila sat there reading his demeanor and waiting for his response.

Stanley tilted his head and thought a while, realizing that they did have him *dead to rights*. Then he looked up and asked, "What is it you want from me?"

"For starters, who is Jeff?" Brent asked.

"Jeff Stewart is his full name; they have him as coordinator, the overseer of the UK's branch," Stanley responded calmly.

"What is it that they are doing in there?" Brent asked.

"Well to start with, they wanted to alter the thoughts and perceptions of the opponents of their main candidate, who just won the Presidency of the United States of America. It worked," Stanley concluded with a smile.

"Oh my God! I totally forgot about that, being so engulfed with this case! That's right, this is Election Day! What is this world coming to?" Brent asked in a brief moment of thought as his eyes drifted across the room. "You are telling me we have British citizens working in underground caves, are somewhat bent on and dedicated to the politics of the United States?" Sheila chimed in, amused at such a notion.

Stanley turned to Sheila and said, "It's a lot more than that because from what I understand, there are eleven such fixed bases that are similar in each continent, which means that you have 10 more that you don't know about here in Europe."

"Do you have any information on their locations?" Brent asked.

"No! That's above my pay grade, but they are all connected. If you get to their main server and get the correct password, you should be able to track them. Time is of the essence because from what I understand, there is a much larger plot afoot! I don't have the full scope, but what I do know is it may be days or even hours away! The world that we've all become accustomed to is going to change drastically, and I do mean irreversibly so! To get further information on that Jeff would be your guy! Better yet, not Jeff as he spooks me."

"How so?" Brent asked.

"He gets that occasional blank stare that I have noticed with a few others in the bunker, like that guy, Victor Sokol, and his goons that I picked up from the airport yesterday."

"Yes, I was going to mention him—we did track you on that pick up, and also have still shots of it," Brent said as he shuffled through the file and slid the photos over to Stanley.

"You got that too? Huh!" Stanley said as he looked up at Brent with a guilty smile.

"Stanley, we are all over this case. Stanley, I'm beginning to see another side of you, a compassionate side. Is it that you feel that you are unjustly caught up in the politics of this mess that has been created?" Brent inquired, attempting to reach out to Stanley's better Angels.

"Listen, in the beginning it was the ideology I was sold on, but now I realize I was wrong because of this eerie evil presence that sits like a dark cloud just hanging over me. I'm feeling threatened and hopelessly boxed in," Stanley said as his voice softened.

"Threatened! How so?"

"You know it's like recently I have been approached and stared down by those inhumane goonies, who are always telling me, 'Mr. Wilson, you better do the right thing!' It's almost as if they sense my wavering belief in their fight. It is also funny when they say that I always seem to ask myself, what is so right about what we are doing?"

❧

Four and a half miles away, while in route to Guildford police headquarters, Derrick, who was driving, turned to Paul and asked, "Paul, about that number sequence, I don't want to appear to be slow, but as you know I wasn't there the night you drew the details on the board. I only got Brent and the other guy's rendition."

Paul looked at Derrick and rubbed his chin a little and said, "Let me see if I can simplify this a little—you are familiar with the Bible, right?"

"Oh yes, my mother always referred to the Bible in her teachings and disciplining."

"Okay, so this should not be too hard for you to follow then," Paul said and then began to explain it to him. "In heaven, after Lucifer's and his band of angels' uprising, God cast him and a third of them into the abyss that we all know as hell. Tens of thousands were cast down, all but 396, including Lucifer, who was able to slip onto our planet, Earth. Ever since then it was a waiting game for their numbers to link into the world's populated system. Although they were able to create havoc throughout time, this number link was important so that they could create a web throughout the entire world, which is now possible because of the internet. The largest social media company has given them that worldwide web reach. Two billion social media users had to be reached to trigger their labeled third fraction—two billion will give you a rounded off figure of 666,000,000. Now Derrick, you have to listen carefully because I can see you are wavering as you try to take in all of this information, especially all of these numbers. Now the next step is you need to take the seven from the seven cardinal sins, and subtract seven steps, that is, take 10% from your 666,000,000, which will bring you to the number or mark of the beast, 66.6, spoken of in Revelation. You got it?"

"Hell yeah, I see the break down," Derrick exclaimed.

"But hold on, there is more," Paul said. "Now in order for Satan to have a worldwide hold, he had to methodically place 396 of his angels throughout the world. There are seven continents, but only six are well-populated, so he has evenly distributed 66 fallen Angels in them. He used eleven of the most populated states, and provinces, and six of the highly populated cities in each state or province in countries like Canada. Note that 6 X 11 = 66 x 6 continents = 396. YOU GOT IT?"

"Yes I do," Derrick answered in excitement.

e/℗

Back at Guildford police headquarters, both Sheila and Brent were sitting before Stanley, in a brief moment of silence, thinking of their next strategic step.

All of a sudden, Stanley broke the silence by shouting out, "Patricia!"

"Patricia! Who is Patricia?" Brent asked.

"She is the young lady you need to talk to as she is brilliant. In secretly talking to her, she shared the same concerns I do. She's also feeling boxed in. The top bosses trust her, and also, she hasn't s said it, but I believe she found a way to tap into their global servers. You need to get to her!"

"And how do you propose we do that?" Sheila asked.

"Look, can I make a deal with you guys? I can get you in. Please give me a chance to right my wrongs."

Brent looked over at Sheila for her approval, and she, in turn, nodded her head, and then turned to Stanley and said, "Stanley, you have to call that guy Richard; they are probably wondering why you haven't called by now. Let's see, tell them you have a flat tire, and you would have to call in your order to save time."

Sheila slid Stanley's phone over to him, and he immediately hit a couple of keys to connect his call. "Richard, Stanley here! Jeff said you have an additional item for my list, what is it?"

"Orange juice, add a case of orange juice," Richard said.

"Orange juice, got it! Oh Richard, I got a flat tire out here, so I'm going to call the order in to save time. Can you pass that on to Jeff as he just called me before it happened," Stanley said as he stared at both Brent and Sheila to get a sense of approval from his now allotted responsibility from the MI-5.

"Hold up Stanley! Jeff is right here, and he wants to talk to you," Richard said as he passed the phone to Jeff.

"What's going on?" Jeff asked.

"Got a flat on the A3, a mile before Harro's."

"Stanley, you left almost an hour ago, how is it that you only got there?" Jeff asked with curiosity.

"Well for starters, I had to fuel up the van, and myself, took a quick breakfast bite, I was starving."

"Okay! Get back as soon as you can before we all starve as the kitchen needs that stuff," Jeff said as he hung up and passed Richard's phone to him.

The interrogation room took on a moment of silence. Suddenly, Sheila quickly reached into her bag for her phone to call Lieutenant Jeremy Ross of the MI-5 Air Task Force strike team. "Lieutenant Ross, I need an air strike team for briefing within the hour. I'm coming in now to speak with the Chief," she said as she quickly stood and then added, "Agent Russell, I trust that you, Derrick and Mr. Wilson here would coordinate a knock, knock! Open the door with a welcome mat for the strike force's arrival, and also coordinate with the local police to ensure there'll be substantial backups. There is going to be a lot of arrestees."

"I'm on it," Brent responded and immediately turned to Stanley and said, "Mr. Wilson, I'm starting to warm up to you, so I'm going to release your van and have them bring it to a certain location so that you can get loaded up with that order. Go ahead and call it in, and when you are done, we will have a chat about what to expect when we enter that bunker."

"Ready whenever you are," Stanley replied, a look of relief on his face. He was finally feeling that he would be able to break away from the hold that nefarious group had on him.

As Brent and Stanley were walking out of the interrogation room, Brent quickly speed-dialed Ailes. "Ailes, drop whatever you are doing with the van because I need you to drop it off at Harro's Wholesale parking lot. Leave it unlock and place the keys beneath the driver's car mat." Brent then turned to Stanley and said, "Come, let us talk in this conference room over there."

Just as they were about to enter the room, Derrick and Paul walked up on them.

"Derrick, we got a new friend here—he's Stanley and he has told me a lot and has a lot for us to go over and deal with right away," Brent said as he patted Stanley on his shoulder.

"Is that so?" Derrick said, looking at Stanley with a soft smile.

Suddenly, when Brent saw Paul, he was reminded of the talk they had had about there being a similar situation—that involved a divine presence—taking place somewhere in the United States.

He then waved to get Sheila's attention as she was walking out of the Commissioner's office. She had just explained their situation to Surrey's Commissioner. As she approached, Brent pulled her to the side to ask her if it were also possible for her to talk to the Director of the FBI.

Sheila pondered this request for a few seconds and then replied, "This will be difficult to explain, but I will get on it! Got to go as time is of the essence and the chopper is waiting. Agent Russell, do what you do best!" Then she quickly shuffled toward the headquarters' exit side door.

Brent turned and walked back over to the guys, gesturing to them to enter the private conference room. As they were walking into the room, Brent straddled his arm around Derrick and said, "Bro, we've got a lot to go over, but only a little time to do it."

They all then sat at the table. After discussing a few details of their next move, Brent quickly looked at Paul and said, "Paul, I don't see that halo."

Paul shook his head in agreement, and then held his head down feeling somewhat disappointed because there was nothing he had to contribute to the discussion. It was as if a burden had descended upon him.

"Hey bro," Brent exclaimed as he looked over at Paul, "We wouldn't have gotten to this point if it wasn't for you, so don't you feel bad. Oh guys, you have to excuse me for a moment, I will be right back! I just remember that I have to brief the Commissioner on a few things that I need his guys to be up to speed on." Brent quickly shuffled out of the room.

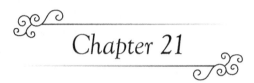

Chapter 21

Meanwhile in Raqqa, a city of Syria, in its main square called Nine & Heaven Square, seven men were lined off and forced to kneel to be executed by beheading because they did not follow the Islamic state's literal teachings of Sharia law. While kneeling, one of the seven men managed to secretly untie himself. He slipped out from the others and ran away as the executioner and four appointed executioners were somewhat distracted by their leader's rants on Sharia law's 7th and 8th century punishments for onlookers. However, they quickly turned and spotted him running towards the square's fence. In no time he was over it, running, ducking and dodging through the thick, timid-crowded streets.

The leader, Ghada, turned to two of the four executioners, and gestured with his hand to retrieve the escapee. They quickly turned, shooting their guns in the air in order to separate the crowd in pursuit of the escapee.

The escapee ran into an alley and quickly turned right, pushing his way through an iron door that opened into a miniature courtyard's cul-de-sac. There he spun around in a circle looking at the many doors that surrounded him. Then he stopped when his eyes locked onto a door that was slightly ajar. He ran and practically dove into it, crashing through it. Inside he rolled head over heels, jumped up immediately, and ran back to the door slamming and locking it. Very frightened, he panted loudly as he stared at the door.

Walking backwards into the dark room, he suddenly bumped into something, and shouted out, "Isa (Jesus)."

A voice responded, "Close, but not quite."

In fright, the escapee turned slowly to find Michael the Archangel standing before him. Michael's image took on a glow that lit up the room.

"What is your name?" Michael asked in Arabic.

"Ruzgar," he answered.

"That name means 'wind', and you run like the wind," Michael said with a soft smile and a touch of humor.

"Who are you?" Ruzgar asked in a whisper.

"Shush!" That was the sound Michael made when he heard the sounds of one of the radical IS soldiers outside the door. He quickly walked to the door and opened it, and with lightning speed, he pulled the soldier inside, throwing him like a rag doll so hard against the wall, that his skull crushed on impact.

Michael then leaned over the soldier's body, which was seconds away from total expiration. It was lying in a bit of blood that started to form a pool. He picked up the IS radicalized soldier's AK-47 machine gun and stripped away his side arm. He then turned and passed them both to Ruzgar and said, "I am a soldier too, God's soldier! This is your personal fight for if I intervene at this magnitude, it will upset humanity's balance. I will guide and protect you, but it is important that you muster up the courage to physically take back what they have taken from you, that is, your pride and dignity. Your actions will send a rippling effect among all God-fearing idle bystanders. It will unearth the courage buried deep within them, the true believers."

Holding Ruzgar's head in both of his hands, and staring directly into his eyes, Michael said, "You have that courage! In fact, you all have that courage so fear not that evil that is out there! They are less than you as they are Satan's version of human beings—men who have been stripped of their souls. They are like clones. Now go! Another one is approaching the door." He turned Ruzgar to face the door, and pointing at it said in a low bass voice, "Go! Take back what is yours."

Ruzgar looked down at the moving shadow that was outside the bottom of the door. A cold look came across his face because he knew right then what had to be done. He pointed the machine gun that was set on semi-automatic, and squeezed the trigger four times. It sent four precision shots through the door. Then he reached out and opened the door, stepping out over the lifeless soldier's body. He quickly took on a bold, purposeful demeanor. As he was about to leave, he stopped realizing that he needed to carry as many weapons as he could, so he reached down over the dead radical soldier, and gathered up his weapons. He knew now that he was about to go into battle.

As Ruzger approached the iron door that led to the outside of the courtyard, his peripheral vision caught a young man, who was standing in his doorway, watching him. He had seen what had just happened. They briefly looked at each other, and as if they were communicating through telepathy, they both nodded in agreement as the young man quickly ran up to him. Ruzgar immediately tossed the AK-47 machine gun he had just picked up at him, and looking at him with a commanding stare, said in Arabic, "Young blood, let's do this."

As luck would have it, they both had had short-lived careers in the Syrian army, so their training took over as they ran in stealth mode seeking out their enemies.

Ruzgar ran right back to the spot he had ran from. Along the way they took precision kill shots at unsuspecting enemies, the IS radical soldiers. And just as Michael had said, a rippling effect of courage took over all of the on-looking males that were hopelessly under siege. They started picking up the weapons of their dead enemies. It seemed as if they all understood what had to be done because they collectively formed a little army and followed Ruzgar, their team captain. Ruzgar covered 200 yards down the main street of Raqqa before he made a left turn into the alley where he had escaped previously. On his return, he collected weapons and emboldened other followers. Suddenly, he turned quickly to face his little army that now totaled seven. He realized that they would have to wing it if they wanted to take down as many of their enemies as they possibly could. He quickly picked out two sniper rifles from the weapons his followers had picked up, and turned to exchange them with the young man he'd called, 'young blood', and another follower. Then he directed them both by finger pointing to a rooftop, so that they could gain a high above ground advantage overlooking Nine & Heaven Square. As they turned, Ruzgar stopped and held 'young blood' by his shoulders and then motioned to the other, and said, "I hope you guys are good. Get on point for a clear view of the square! GO!" The others knew exactly what needed to be done. Before long Ruzgar was standing before Ghada inside the square.

Ruzgar Akalia, a thirty-eight year old Syrian, was thinly bearded and 5'11" tall. He was recruited in the Syrian army at the age of 19 and served until he was 27 when he moved from Damascus to Raqqa. He had gotten married and started a family. Six years later it was discovered that his wife Adela had leukemia. Two years later, she died. Then one year ago he met Aliya, and while courting her she became pregnant. Islamic State radicals found out from an unworthy informant that she was unwed and pregnant. They questioned her, but when she failed to tell them the truth, she was publicly stoned to death. Soon after however, they linked Ruzgar to the pregnancy, and decided to execute him with several others.

Ruzgar stood confidently before Ghada and then spoke with conviction, "Ghada, you stand before many to strike fear in them! You are demented, but you have no idea what fear is."

"I see you seemed to have grown a spine! I'm surprised. Were those gunshots I heard coming from you?" Ghada asked. Visibly ruffled and confused, he looked around, wondering if this man who stood before him was responsible for the lack of response from the other IS soldiers. Then he saw among the crowd five emerging civilian men who had just become soldiers, carrying weapons in their hands. Ghada stood there, along with the remaining two of his so called executioners, who were still standing over the kneeling, frightened men that were supposed to be executed. To answer his own question, Ghada looked left and then to his right at both of his men that stood beside him and said, "I guess it was your shots that were fired! You are good, six against three. Is that fair to you?"

"I'm confused, which fair/fear are we talking about now?" Ruzgar asked without blinking an eye.

"You may have controlling numbers now, but on the south side of Raqqa we have many, and they just got the message," shouted Ghada as he held up his two-way radio, his thumb keying in on the button so that the other side could hear the conversation.

"Get up!" Ruzgar shouted at the men that were kneeling at Ghada's feet. The men rose slowly and gingerly to their feet. "Snap out of it as we need to move! Get their keys, we need their vehicles."

Immediately the two radicals that stood beside Ghada pointed their weapons at the men that had just stood up. Suddenly, there was a sound—'puff', which was instantly followed by a 'pap'. They were the delayed sounds of shots from two distant snipers' rifles. Without warning, Ghada's two men's heads burst open and their bodies flopped to the ground. The two accurate precision sniper shots had come from 'young blood' and his assistant, from the rooftop where they were positioned. It so happened that they were both highly trained snipers who were in their comfort zone.

Shocked and amazed, Ghada looked down at his men's lifeless bodies, and then quickly grabbed one of the men who had stood up. He swiftly pulled his side arm, and putting it to his head, shouted, "You value human life too much! That is your weakness! Now, I'm going to walk away, and your compassionate belief system will only allow you to watch me do it." Then he started walking backwards to exit the square's gate.

"I'm not at all surprised, knowing that a simple-minded person like you would think life is that simple. I bid you farewell for now for you will go to a place where you will experience eternal regrets,"

Ruzgar said as he casually turned to walk off, looking up in the direction of 'young blood'. As if on cue, an echoing, cracking sound of another sniper's precision shot rang out.

Ruzgar quickly got into a rallying mode, not even looking back to confirm Ghada was dead with that kill shot. He started screaming instructions to the people of Raqqa that were standing by. "All of you who feel that you have been unjustly caught up in this radical system, you need to leave now! Their friends, who are on the other side, are 10-15 minutes away. We have control for only that time, so we will use their trucks. Load up now! Women and children first."

Ruzgar then started giving subtle orders to the men who chose to follow him. Showing his appreciation he said, "I don't know your names, but there will be plenty of time for that. You," he said as he pointed to one of the men, "take him and try to get a little more assistance as we need a few more vehicles. Bring them to this square! GO! GO!"

Ruzgar then started running through the streets, shouting and pointing to the square where most of the cars and trucks were waiting to be loaded. "Quickly! Quickly! Load up, we have to leave now!"

The people were scurrying through the streets of Raqqa as they gathered up their personal belongings, kissing and hugging loved ones who had decided to give the weaker and fearful ones the opportunity to leave.

It took about 12 minutes to fill the trucks and cars. Ruzgar chose to send the bigger trucks ahead. They were heading northwest along the Euphrates River, bound for Aleppo. He decided to pull up the rear with his little army of street fighters that had now grown to twenty strong.

The caravan of vehicles sounded like a train as they drove in single file out of the city, fleeing to Aleppo. As the dust cleared, one drivers noticed in his rearview mirror a young lady, who was seated on the back of his truck, holding her child in her hands. With tears in her eyes, she was looking back from the growing distance of the Nine & Heaven Square and visioning in her memory the gory sight of the heads that had been severed and placed on the fence's rod spikes that circled the square. That is what Ghada had the women and children watch to instill fear in them.

Before long a reinforcement fleet of IS soldiers started to fill the square, and when they saw their dead comrades lying in the streets, like an angry mob they immediately started terrorizing the citizens that had been left behind. Suddenly one of the IS soldiers, who was holding a pair of binoculars in his hands, ran up to the leader of the reinforcement fleet, and shouted, "I see them! They are running; they are running." He pointed in the direction towards Aleppo.

As they were gathering their men together to pursue the fleeing citizens, a blinding light that tripled the light of day flashed like a strobe light in the center of the square. Then a ghostly image slowly appeared. Everybody turned and stood still in shock and awe. Immediately there was a true divide of those who believe and those who didn't. Nonbelievers turned and scurried like rats, running for the cover of darkness. They included IS soldiers and a few of the citizens. As they ran, their bodies' temperatures increased resulting in spontaneous combustion.

All of the wicked non-believers died an atrocious death. It was poetic justice given the life they led. Yes, Michael was responsible for this turn of events, and as he would always say, he said, "The wicked will be destroyed, but all who believe and muster up the courage to live right will be protected."

There is a mystical thing that always follows people who are kind-hearted, morally upright and have a strong and steadfast faith in their Creator, God Almighty. At the end of it all, if anyone commits a wrongdoing against them, whether physically or otherwise such as slander their reputation, he or she will be no match for God's wrath, no, not even by tenfold. In short, their enemies will surely fall at their feet.

To tip the scale of justice, God's wrath is necessary.

Chapter 22

M eanwhile back in Surrey, England, Brent, on walking back into the conference room, apologized, "Sorry guys, it took so long because the Commissioner wanted me to meet his top guys and brief them personally." Brent then sat down with Derrick, Paul and Stanley so that they could discuss what they needed to do to obtain vital information to breach the underground bunker. "Stanley, tell me, what is the security level like there?" Brent asked.

"Well, the main entrance opens like an elevator door, but I guess you already know that because of your surveillance. There are first and secondary security checkpoints. When the door closes, identification is confirmed, and then the vehicle is checked for any devices that might have been placed on it. When driving through the secondary checkpoint, the vehicle is thoroughly inspected and the contents are matched with the purchase order list. There are two heavily armed inspectors at the first and secondary checkpoints."

"Are there any drive-thru doors between the first and secondary checkpoints?" Brent asked.

"No! There are ground workers that take care of the offloading, and then there are unarmed techs on the work-station floor."

"Stanley, do you have a total count of everyone in there now?" Brent inquired.

"A total of 50 personnel can be found in that underground bunker, ten are armed, but you have to remember six of the ten that I had mentioned earlier, have that stone cold demeanor. Agent Russell, their eyes…" Stanley said as he paused, staring at the ceiling.

"What, what about their eyes?" Brent asked in excitement.

Stanley continued, "It's just a little strange because whenever they are flustered in any way, their eyes turn a milky, grayish yellow. Now, I have only been able to catch a glimpse of this on a few or rare occasions."

"Huh, that's gross! You call that a little strange?" Derrick cried out, shaking his head.

Brent then jumped in, "That is sick! Aren't there others in there who feel the same way you do?"

"Yeah, of course! Genevieve, you know the young lady I'd told you about when we were in the interrogation room. We both would talk secretly about it. Most of the others seem to obey their every request, even if it only a hint of a demand, and they do it without question, almost as if they worship them like some do a dark god. I kind of think it has something to do with their every sixth day celebration."

"Every sixth day celebration? What are they celebrating?" Brent asked, quite curious.

"It's a poll that they conduct on social media worldwide. They show a weekly graph of their success in changing people's perceptions about life. They also display a global screen map of the countries that are turning in their favor. Oh, and there is that awful cocktail drink they offer up, and drink every sixth day. It's almost like what they serve at a manager's cocktail party. A herbal-based beverage, it has a tint of alcohol in it. I always thought it was just a cultural thing for the Russians and Romanians, who seemed to be on a higher pay grade than the others. It appears that Genevieve and I are allergic to one of its contents because an itchy redness appears on our arms whenever we drink it. I'm not sure what it is, but I had experienced that itchy feeling and redness before, a long time ago! But I don't remember when it occurred, and I'm not sure what caused it. So Genevieve and I stay away from it. We kept our thoughts and opinions to ourselves. Agent Russell, you have to single her out, please! She can be very helpful."

"That's not a problem! Derrick, take note of that," Brent responded, turning to Derrick, and then he asked, "Stanley, you said that there are six of them with that strange demeanor?"

"Yes," Stanley answered.

Immediately Brent turned to Paul and asked, "Paul, you said that there are twenty two of those dark angels in the UK and France, am I correct?"

"Yes, that's right," Paul answered.

"So we should have close to sixteen more, with France being the exception with the balance, that are spread throughout the autonomous regions of the UK, including Wales, Scotland and Northern Ireland."

"That's right," Paul answered again.

"Are their stations similar in nature to this one?" Brent asked.

"They would have to be if those dark angels are in the mix! Agent Russell, they are like vampires! They lurk in the dark, and travel by night! That's why bunkers such as this one are suitable for their deep-seeded covert operations. But there are some exceptions as those among the higher ranks often engage in day travel. But they will still find the darkest corner of a room, or when in vehicles, the windows have to be deeply tinted."

Brent pondered for a few seconds, and then quickly looked at his watch and said, "Stanley, we have to get going! Derrick, you think we can outfit him with a tiny camera? We need a floor plan of the bunker, so that we won't be blind going in."

"Yeah, sure we can, but didn't he say they inspect for electronics?" Derrick questioned in response.

"Yes, yes, yes," Brent said as he held his head down in deep thought. He realized that he had been thinking in haste because he had missed that vital piece of inspection information.

Stanley chimed in by raising his hand as if he were in a classroom, "May I make a suggestion? I'm known to wear a baseball cap! In fact,

I have one in the van! You can rig the cap's embroidery with your mini-camera clip for I'm sure if it is a super-mini cam, it would just blend in with the other electronics that are assembled in the van. I can slip it between or under the van's seat, and after the van and I have been cleared, I would just put it on and walk around casually as I normally do."

"That's it," Brent said, snapping his fingers as he turned to Derrick. "Get Ailes on the phone! He should have the camera equipment in their kit! Tell him what we want to do before he drops the van off! Tell him find and rig the baseball cap that's in the van. We're running out of time! They would probably be calling Stanley soon."

"Agent Russell," Paul called out as he raised his hand to also chime in.

"Yes Paul, what you got? Is our angel back?" Brent asked in hopeful excitement.

"No, I'm not feeling him! I'm just getting residual information that is just now coming to me."

"What is it?" Brent asked.

"You have to get Carla out of there now! Because of their quest to grow and blend in as much as they can, they need to sacrifice her; it's imperative to get her out of there! Like me, she too is our angel Raphael incarnate. Her blood would empower them to withstand day travel, and achieve their ultimate goal. Also, if and when you do get in there, you have to remember a head shot is a kill shot for each of the six dark angels you need to find in there!"

"Duly noted," Brent said as he looked Derrick directly in his eyes—to translate, there was no room for error.

Suddenly, Brent's cellphone's ringtone sounded off. "Hello," Brent answered.

"Agent Russell, Sheila Hall here. I spoke with the chief, and he just called me back saying it's a go! It was handed down directly from the prime minister. I'm here now with Lieutenant Ross, who wants to go over a strategy brief with you via video conferencing."

"Boss, I would love to, but right now we are trying to set Stanley up with a surveillance mini-cam. What I'm going to do is send him in early so that we can get a layout of the underground cave bunker. In this way we'll also get to identify our armed threat targets."

"Okay, I got you! I will tell Lieutenant Ross who is here with me right now," Sheila said, and was about to hang up when she barely heard Brent's urgent voice.

"Hold up, hold up boss! Let me speak with him."

"Just a sec," Sheila said as she handed the phone to Lieutenant Ross.

"Jeremy, how is it going my distant friend?" Brent asked as his face took on a glowing smile.

"It's going! I'm just here holding my ground as usual," Lieutenant Ross said with a reciprocating smile.

"How are Becky and the kids?"

"They are great, and you?" Jeremy asked.

"Oh, you know, it's the same old being single lifestyle, work, work, work. Our paths haven't crossed in a while, same department, just a different level. But Jeremy you know there is no love lost here. Listen, I wanted to talk to you one on one because of this unique case. We've been closing in for two days now, and I'm still finding it hard to rap my head around it. Jeremy, it feels like I'm caught up in the middle of a sci-fi and a spooky movie all rolled into one! With that said, this case is not to be taken lightly."

"I hear you," Jeremy said, listening intently.

Lieutenant Jeremy Ross was a thirty-eight year old short, handsome, blonde Caucasian. He joined the Royal Air Force at the age of eighteen, and was trained in all categories related to flying a helicopter. He was highly trained to fly the Apache Attack MK-1. He flew sorties during the invasion of Iraq in 2003. He then left the Royal Air Force in 2005, and joined MI-5—he was in charge of the Rotor Craft Air Wing section.

Brent then said, "It's imperative that your team does not make the mistake of taking what I'm about to say lightly. It appears that what we are up against is somewhat supernatural. I'm sure Mrs. Hall has given you or would be giving you her version of events based on what she has experienced. But based on new information I have just recently obtained, once we've breached this underground cave bunker, we immediately have to seek out six subjects that are instant death threats to us. To distinguish them from the others we would need to be extremely aggressive. So far we know that a strange, sick, grayish-yellow tint appears in their eyes when they are excited or flustered." Brent paused to allow what he had said to sink in.

Continuing, Brent added, "Oh, and this part is very important, the only kill shot is a head shot. Okay, what I need you to do now is to put your team on standby and full alert regarding what I have just told you. I'm working with a guy who was working with them on the inside. He's now working with us, and his name is Stanley Wilson. I just need to get him back in there with a hidden mini-cam, which we are working on as we speak. My plan is to get him back in there, which is no problem, because they are expecting him. In that way I can get video footage on what to expect from them. Okay, I've got to go to set this thing up. Jeremy, try to explain to your team the best way you can regarding what to expect from all of this! We'll talk soon."

"I'm on it Brent," Lieutenant Ross said, and then he passed the phone to Sheila, who wished them good luck before she hung up.

"Okay Mr. Wilson, tell me, do you have access to where they are holding Carla?" Brent asked as he turned towards Stanley, and quickly pocketed his phone.

"Me, personally no! Richard, on the other hand, does! He is like the shopkeeper as he has keys for almost everything," Stanley said as he fiddled with a pen that was on the table.

"How would we recognize this Richard?" Brent asked.

"By his embroidered nametag—all of the workers have coats and shirts with embroidered nametags. But those with nametags on their coats don't always wear their coats, so you would have to ask them who they are."

"Okay, we have to get you back in there before they start calling, wondering why you are taking so long."

Brent quickly reached for his phone to speed-dial Ailes. The call was picked up on the first ring.

"Ailes, give me some good news! We don't have much time. Please tell me you have a suitable mini-cam for what we have to do?"

"Yep! We lucked out because I thought I had left it back at headquarters as I almost couldn't find it, but it was just a case of misplacement. Look, I'm working on the baseball cap with it right now, and it's perfect. The color scheme and the embroidery pattern make it next to impossible to pick up."

"That's super! Now I need you to take the van back to Harro's parking lot. Park it where you took it from, so we won't have a problem finding it," Brent said as he lip-synced, 'we've got to move' to the guys who were sitting before him! At the same time he beckoned to them to get up quickly.

The time was 9:18am. Brent was sitting in the passenger seat of the van which was still parked in Harro's parking lot. He was giving Stanley last minute instructions on what he needed to do, and how he needed to do it.

"Stanley, don't forget to keep the cap stashed under your seat. This mini-camera system is a video and audio recording one, so we can see and hear you but you cannot see or hear us. You can talk, but Stanley please be discreet. We just need video footage on the layout of their floor and a path to where they are holding Carla. We also need footage on all of the personnel that are armed, especially the six supernatural subjects. Stanley, please try not to be obvious while obtaining footage of them. Okay, I guess that's it! Now go pick up your order, and get back in there, and then get out after you have done a complete sweep of the floor and all that I had mentioned. When you are done, and have been given clearance, give whatever excuse you wish to leave, just simply and softly say, you are done. That would be our signal to go in when you come out. When the outer door opens for you to leave, we will come in. Now go!" Brent ordered as he opened the van's door, and on exiting, he waved Stanley off.

With a nod, Stanley pulled off, determined to make amends for the part he had played in his enemies' diabolical plans and activities over the years.

Chapter 23

The time is now 9:45am. Brent, Derrick and the other agents sat in the motel room watching the screen of a video call they were on with Lieutenant Ross, who was in his briefing room.

"Lieutenant Ross," Brent addressed Ross after poking a little subtle fun to lighten the atmosphere, which was a good technique for agents who were preparing to go on a unique, intense mission such as this one. Slowly panning the room, he looked at all of the faces that came up on the screen in Lieutenant Ross' briefing room, and then he continued, "Can you guys hear and see me?"

"Loud and clear Mr. Russell, and it looks like you need a haircut," Lieutenant Jeremy Ross responded with a smile as the room lit up with laughter.

"Okay, very funny! I see you got jokes," Brent said as he consciously looked into the motel room's mirror. "Lieutenant Ross, like I said earlier, that's how it is living a single lifestyle—there's no one there to cross-check you," Brent said as he thought he'd better quickly change the subject as he was feeling a tad bit embarrassed because of the blasting he'd gotten in the front of the entire squad. Then he said, "But it's great to see that your team's morale is high. Now let's get down to business. Lieutenant, I hope you briefed your team on what we had spoken about earlier."

"Yes I did, and they all appear to have an open mind on this, particularly since they understand the world's climate concerning people's radical behaviors; so it comes as no shocking surprise to them that we would be at this juncture in life," Lieutenant Ross responded as he gracefully and confidently panned the faces of his team.

Right then Sheila handed out copies of the still shots of the farmhouse, including the camouflaged big tree that stood before the camouflaged main entrance door.

Brent quickly chimed in, giving further instructions, "Gentlemen, those still shots are photos of your destination—that large tree is in the direct path of the camouflaged main automatic hillside door. Lieutenant, when that hillside door opens and our guy, Stanley, drives out, you should designate someone who has the rocket launcher to disable the door immediately before it closes again."

"Got it," Lieutenant Ross responded.

Everybody went silent when Brooks shouted out from his computer post in the motel room, "He is in!"

"Okay guys, show time—lights, camera, and action!" Brent said as he rubbed his hands together and peered at the split screen of Lieutenant's Ross briefing room and Stanley's hidden camera walk through the underground bunker.

"Okay gentlemen, pay attention for even though we are recording, I need everyone to focus and memorize everything our inside man, Mr. Wilson, is showing us." Brent said as he sat and pulled his chair closer to the screen. Suddenly, he stood up and clapped his hands and said, "No! No! No! Better yet Lieutenant, go mobile with the video, and study the footage in flight because we are running out of time! Stanley might be sent out or find a way to leave after his walk-through. It's going to take you at least 18 minutes flying time, so get airborne!"

"You got it! Gentlemen, let's rock and roll," Lieutenant Ross said with a loud hand clap. Two to three minutes later the sounds of two helicopters' jet engines began spooling up for lift off.

Just as Brent instructed, Stanley casually made his walk-through so that he could intercept every one of the armed guards to show the breaching team where they were posted. He then started to seek out the six dark angels. Seconds later, he spotted one of them and whispered under his breath, "Here is one," hoping Agent Russell could hear him through the mini-cam's one way audio. He then intercepted the dark angel's path. "Good morning," Stanley said with a smile.

The supernatural suited up subject, incarnated in human form, just turned and nodded, but as he casually walked by, he quickly turned back to face Stanley as if he was alerted to something. Stanley's body took on an instant chill as he struggled deep inside to keep his composure. He quickly deflected whatever thought the primal subject had, by asking, "Oh sir, have you seen Richard? I got his order out front. I know he was concerned about it because I took so long."

The subject just shook his head, turned and walked away. Stanley silently exhaled in a sigh of relief, and then turned to continue his sweep.

Carla felt a chill run up and down her spine when she asked Richard, "Where are you taking me now?"

"Just taking you on the second part of your extended tour. Relax yourself! Aren't you happy to get out of that cell for a while?" Richard said as he walked her through a dimly-lit curving corridor of a tunnel.

"Yeah, but the question is, why was I even in that cell? Furthermore, there is nobody around, and this is spooking me more than the cell itself! Listen, I'm not up for this tour. I want to go back to the cell now! Please!" Carla said in a demanding voice.

Right then Richard stopped at a door, and as he opened it, he turned to her and said, "You will be fine." Then he beckoned to her to walk in before him.

"My, my, my! You are a beautiful girl! What a shame and a waste," Victor Sokol said, staring at her as she walked into the room.

Shocked, Carla stopped in her tracks, as she stared frantically at the room's décor and furniture. The room was a little over 500 square feet and filled with lit torches and candles. It was set up for human sacrifices. There was a large table with a black cloth draped over it, and on each side there were six candles sitting in extended floor-standing candleholders. There was also a chalice that was sitting on a separate table. Eight large flame torches were also sitting in a semi-circle on the table.

With an eerie feeling overcoming her, Carla slowly panned the room, taking in the scary site. She also thought for a moment that she was in a sauna bath because the room was dreadfully hot. Just as she was about to open her mouth to speak, Vera Petrov stepped quickly behind her holding a cloth filled with chloroform, which she placed over Carla's nose and mouth to render her weak and too defenseless to fight. Carla flailed for a few seconds until Boris stepped in to hold her down so that Petrov could inject a drug into her to completely render her unconscious.

"Quickly, bring her and put her on the table," Victor said urgently as his intuition told him something that he couldn't quite figure out. He just felt right then that time was of the essence. There were many chants they had to go through before they sacrificed Carla. Victor, Raleigh, Boris and Petrov, along with three other clan members, began their chants.

A quiet knock was heard at Mr. and Mrs. Winston Parker's front door. They were sitting in their living room watching game shows on television. Putting down his newspaper that he was reading off and on during commercial ads, Winston walked to the door and looked through the peep hole. A young man stood on the other side of the door with a parcel in his hand. Even though he and his wife lived like hermits, and weren't expecting anything, he thought it was safe enough to open the door.

Immediately when the door opened, the young man dropped the fake parcel and pulled out a writ which stated that he was a Surrey police officer with a court order to conduct a search and seizure. The officer, along with two others who were standing on each side of the door, invited themselves in. Shirley Parker quickly got up and reached down to press a buzzer that was five feet away on the wall by the hanging phone. The young officer, Patrick Scott, aggressively shouted, "Ma'am, I wouldn't do that if I were you! SIT DOWN!" Just as quickly, Patrick's demeanor changed to a quieter one as he lightly rested his hand on Winston's shoulder and steered him back over to the chair. Then he said, "Now, I need you both to have a seat and don't move."

e/®

Meanwhile, back in the bunker, Stanley was diligently doing the undercover job he was assigned to do. After showing, via video, the second primal subject, he swept the bunker for a few more minutes, and then quietly slipped behind a wall where he couldn't be seen so that he could talk quietly to Brent. "Agent Russell, I only could find two so far; I have no idea where the others are! I'll try another sweep, but I'm getting strange looks that are spooking me. I think it's time for me to get out of here."

Just as Stanley walked from behind the wall, he saw Richard walking out of an open door that he closed behind him. Stanley hailed out, "Richard, man, you are a hard man to find! Listen, the guys are stocking your order now. Oh, by the way, what is going on with that girl Carla we brought in yesterday?"

"What's it to you?" Richard responded snobbishly.

"Just curious," Stanley replied as he tried to get the hidden cam to get a direct shot of Richard.

"Well, don't be!" Richard shot back as he reached into his

pocket and pulled out another list. "Here Stanley, there are several electronics I need you to get for me."

"I'll be glad too," Stanley replied as he took the list. He felt a sudden relief deep down inside as he realized that he could finally put this nightmare behind him. He quickly walked away, intentionally holding the list so that it would be visible to anybody who might be watching him and wondering what he was up to. As soon as he closed the van's door, he said softly, "I'm done."

Brent and his team were already in position at the back of the farmhouse when he heard Stanley's signal to go. It was perfect timing because he looked two farmhouses over to the left, and saw Lieutenant Ross and his team in the two helicopters they were about to set down. They were awaiting further instructions. Brent quickly picked his radio up and said, "Ross, it's a go! Move in!"

With GPS accuracy, the choppers started to advance quickly towards the hillside. Brent smashed his gas pedal to the floor as he shouted over the radio to the others, "Move in, move in!" The choppers and the ground units converged with high speed towards the tree. Suddenly, the camouflaged doors began to open as Stanley sped out, wasting no time. Brent got back on the radio and shouted out, "Ross, disable the doors, now!"

Ross then nodded at one of his team members, who was holding a rocket launcher and who had also heard the order. He jumped from one of the settling helicopters, advanced quickly forward and then took a knee-stand position and fired.

A loud explosion was heard, and Brent quickly shouted over the radio, "Go! Go," as both Brent's and Lieutenant Ross' heavily armed squads quickly advanced through the smoke-filled main bunker door. Brent, as the anchor, quickly turned to Brooks and Paul who were sitting in the back seat of his vehicle, "Brooks, I need you to stay here with Paul. Don't engage, I repeat don't engage! Stay low until this is over." Brent quickly switched from his hand-held radio to his headset communication, and then tapped his team mate, who was sitting upfront with him. They both quickly exited the vehicle.

As Brent, along with five heavily armed agents who made up the third wave to enter, quickly advanced towards the smoke-filled entrance of the bunker. Then he heard the fire fight grew louder. He ran through the entrance, holding his tech-9 in a safety off position to engage any attacker. His secondary weapon's side arm remained holstered. He slowed his running to a brisk walk, and looking down, he saw the two armed guards' lifeless bodies that were the first to be taken down on the initial breach. As Brent walked onto the floor, he saw that the teams had systematically split up into three groups. One group was corralling the floor tech computer workers in a safe corner of the floor, while the others split up to look diligently for the six primal subjects and any other threatening targets. Brent immediately spotted Derrick across the floor, but as he started to approach him, he spotted on Derrick's blindside, a dark angelic subject who leapt out like a frog from a dark corner. Brent shouted, "Derrick, look out!" as he simultaneously shot at him. It was an accurate, mid-flight head shot. The subject's flying force knocked Derrick to the floor.

Derrick yelled out, "Aahh" as he shoved the lifeless dark angel's body off of his. Suddenly and simultaneously, two doors immediately opened from both sides of the room, and with unhuman super speed, two primal subjects shot out from either side—one blindsided a team member. With flailing arms, he ripped away at the agent as he took him down. Hawk quickly advanced over to the subject, putting his Glock 17 9mm to his head, and blew his brains out. On the other side, Derrick rolled over and took a knee stand position, aimed and again with head-shot accuracy, the second subject fell.

Brent shouted out, "That's three!" He then raised his hand, holding up three fingers to rally their attention, and with the other hand, he pointed out areas and doors that had not been checked. Then he said, "Three more!" Brent quickly looked down at the wounded agent and called out on his communicating head set radio, "Brooks, is Surrey's stand by medic team there?"

"Yes!" Brooks responded.

"Send them in on full alert! Tell them to take every precaution!" Brent exclaimed.

As planned, Surrey's police and medical emergency teams were on standby immediately after the breach.

Chapter 24

B rent panned the corner of the room where the personnel workers were standing, and then his eyes locked onto an embroidered nametag that read, 'Richard'. Brent immediately started to walk in Richard's direction, and with one finger he beckoned to him and said, "Richard, come here!"

Dumbfounded, Richard looked at Brent as he placed both hands on his chest and asked, "Me?"

Brent sarcastically mocked him as he pointed at a random girl that stood in the group, "No her! Of course, you!" He stopped two feet before Richard, tilted his head and asked, "You are the shopkeeper, aren't you?"

"I don't understand," Richard stammered.

"You have the keys to every room in this facility, right?" Brent queried.

"Why would you say that?" Richard asked.

"Let's say my guardian angel told me so, and also the fact that you are wearing many keys on your belt's loop. Come on, let's go! I'm going to be your new best friend, but you're going to have to take me to Carla Wallace right now!" Brent rejoined as he straddled his arms around Richard and walked him towards the door he saw him leaving earlier on Stanley's hidden cam. At that very moment Brent looked up and around, and noticed that there were cameras covering the floor. He then looked over at Hawk as he pointed up and said, "We are being watched! Take them out!"

Hawk immediately began seeking and taking precision shots at the CCTV cameras in the bunker.

ℰ∕◎

Meanwhile:

Back in the secret room where the ritual was being held, Carla, who was unconscious, was sleeping quietly like a baby on the human sacrificial table. Victor, Boris, Vera, and the three remaining Surrey primal subjects that included Jeff Stewart, who was covertly one of them, suddenly stopped their ritual ceremony because of the breach. They were staring intensely at the monitors, which were set up in the room, when they suddenly snowed out one by one. Victor angrily disrobed his ritual robe and ordered Jeff and the two others to defend them.

Shaking feverishly, Richard sorted through the keys to open the door he was seen coming out of earlier. Brent beckoned to Derrick and two other agents, Scott and Mike, to come with him. While they were approaching the entry of the open door, Brent told the remaining teams to cover the remaining areas of the bunker. After Richard opened the door, he led Brent and his selected team down a lit corridor. It was a fifty foot walk that came to a sharp right turn. All of a sudden, the lights went out.

Brent shouted out, "Richard, what's going on?

There was no response, just the sound of Richard's footsteps scrambling down the dark corridor. Because Agent Russell and his team were highly trained professionals, they quickly went into dark room mode by simultaneously clicking on their gun mounted lights, along with their pin-point accuracy laser beams. The group began aiming blindly in defense of a sudden attack.

"There, there! Up ahead, there is light coming from that room's doorway," Brent said softly as the door was quickly slammed shut. The team started to advance quickly in the direction of the door.

"Derrick, watch our rear," Brent ordered as his brisk walk picked up to a trot. All of a sudden, Brent exclaimed, "What the......" as he saw what appeared to be glowing cat eyes rapidly approaching them. Without a second thought, he came to a quick stop, took aim and fired! Tap, tap was heard, followed by the thud of a body hitting the floor. "Jesus!" Brent said as he shone the light that was mounted on his weapon down on the expired primal subject.

Moments after they started to proceed, Derrick shouted out from the rear of the team, "Woe! Woe! Woe," as he defended himself from the second subject that leapt on him from the darkness. He gave him no time to fire a shot. A fight ensued, the dark angel subject fighting ferociously like a wild animal. For a while Derrick was holding his own, given his combat skills, trading blow after blow. The other team members shone their gun-lights frantically, trying to get a fix on the subject that was in the scuffle behind them. Then both Brent and Scott got a double light hit directly in the subject's face, which startled and distracted him, forcing him to freeze momentarily. They both shot at him with a direct close range hit. The subject fell, expiring immediately.

Brent knelt down beside Derrick and asked, "Buddy, you okay?" He shone his light up, down and around Derrick looking for visible signs of injury.

"I'm okay! I'm okay!" Derrick said as he shuffled to his feet. "My ears are ringing though! Hey Brent, is everything still intact?" Derrick asked as he shone his gun-light to the right side of his face.

"You'll live! Looks as if you had a minor shaving accident! Let's go!" Brent replied as he patted Derrick on his back.

As the team closed in on the door, Richard had ran through. Brent said softly, "Two down, one more to go! Hope we can find some light before these unwanted surprises jump us again."

"Tell me about it! I know I'm a grown man, but this shit is

spooking me now," Derrick said as he swatted at his shoulder, thinking a bug was crawling on him.

Now they were standing at the door, but what they didn't notice until now was there were two doors side by side. Brent quietly put his finger lightly on his lips, "Shhhhh." He pointed down at the bottom of one of the doors, where there was a faint glow of light and a tainted light burning smell that had risen to their noses.

Derrick looked at Brent, who was now a silhouette, and asked in a whisper, "Do you smell that?"

"Yeah," Brent answered, and now curious and with a sixth sense, he immediately ordered his team to step back a few feet from the door. As they stood in a line behind him, and with his back to the wall beside the door, he reached out for the door's handle. Upon touching it, he felt it was warm. Right then and there, Brent knew what was happening. He turned to his team and with his hands he beckoned them to move further back. The door was an outer open one. Brent then got as far away, an arm's length, from the door with his face shielded against the wall. He then turned the knob and with a quick pull the door burst open with a ball of flames that leapt out and panned up a few feet on each side of the doorway. In unison, the team dove to the floor, and just as quickly as the flames came, they went. It was what firefighters called a backdraft. A sealed room that has a small fire and burns a large number of torches and candles, soon depletes itself of oxygen, and when oxygen is released into the room, small flames turning into a ball of flames, will leap out like a gigantic beast who is feeding.

Unbeknown to Victor and his crew, it was the first time this ritual was taking place in this underground environment. For them it was more of a surprise than it was for Brent and his team for they had been caught up in the moment performing their ritual and watching the monitors.

With guns drawn, Brent and his team got to their feet and proceeded to enter the smoke-filled room. While they were standing in the center of the room, that is, in the ritual's circle, the door suddenly slammed shut and a wall of flames circled them. A voice then shouted out, "Welcome to hell!"

Then the door was intentionally opened by Vera. Brent and his team were at a disadvantage because they were now facing Victor, Boris and Vera, who were high ranking members of the fallen angels, who had supernatural strength. Brent and his team were spinning blindly, trying to find a target in the smoke-filled, hot room. Suddenly, a cry rang out as one of the team members was viciously pulled from the circle. Derrick and Brent frantically stared at one another, trying to determine who was missing.

Then Scott screamed out, "Mike! Mike!" All they heard was Mike's gurgling cry. Then as quickly as Agent Mike was pulled away, Scott was pulled away. Brent and Derrick immediately placed their backs against each other and started randomly firing their weapons as they swept the room in a circle. Loud laughter echoed down the halls.

Suddenly, a big blast of wind circled the room like a tornado filled with fine ice particles that stung like a sand storm. The room became deafeningly quiet. Both Derrick and Brent curled up in the middle of the floor.

"Stand up!" a voice ordered.

Brent lifted his head to find Paul levitating two feet above him in the doorway. When Paul smiled, his cheeks took on a rosy glow as he looked down at Derrick and Brent, who were looking up at him from a kneeling position.

Brent slowly turned to Derrick with an awesome look of relief on his face, and said, "He is back!"

The room then took on a bright white glow, which revealed all three dark angels, Victor, Boris and Vera, each cowering in a corner of the room. They were foaming from their mouths, and squirming as if they were rats trapped in a raging fire.

As Paul descended, Angel Raphael emerged, dazzling with a great splendor that engulfed the room with a warm feeling of comfort. In raising his hands, Raphael said with an all so pleasant voice, "Fear no evil, for I am with you."

The radiating light from Raphael's appearance was vibrant because the gamma rays were at the highest level imaginable. They were only receptive to evil itself. It started to peel away skin, layer by layer, from the primal dark angels' mutated bodies. There were cries and screams like those from the pits of hell as their bodies slowly burnt out like a smoldering fire.

As the room slowly returned to its ambient light, Raphael stepped forward and blew air onto the dying agents, Scott and Mike. Immediately, the two underwent rapid recovery. Seconds later, Derrick and Brent sprung to their aid when they heard them call out. When Paul and Raphael became one again, he stood over Carla's unconscious body lying on the sacrificial table. He slowly placed his right hand over her forehead, and she immediately opened her eyes. While Paul was helping her to a sitting position, he said, "Welcome back! You are going to be fine now!" As he looked around at the agents, he hugged her. As Raphael's host, he smiled and said, "As I said, we will open that window of opportunity, but you would have to open the door."

While Carla, Agent Russell, Agent Holder and Paul were helping the two recovering agents to the underground bunker's floor, Agent Russell keyed into his mic, "We got two down back here, and the three that flew in yesterday, so there has to be one more out there! What you guys got?"

Hawk responded, "We checked this place high and low, but there're no further surprises, just a few more harmless workers that were hiding."

By this time Brent and his team were a few feet away from the initial door they first entered to walk down the corridor. Suddenly, Brent tripped over something, and fell to the floor. "Goddamn it! What the hell?" Brent exclaimed as he quickly got up and opened the door that led to the bunker's workstation floor. Suddenly, a welcoming bright light appeared on the bunker's workstation floor.

"What is that?" Derrick asked as they stared down at the floor.

"It's a damn body—that's what it is!" Brent said sarcastically.

"Is it one of those spooks?" Derrick asked.

"Not sure as he's dressed a little differently from the others," Brent replied as he knelt down and began digging through the unknown subject's pockets for some form of identification. When he found and opened his wallet, he said, "Jeffrey Stewart, this is the Jeff Stewart Stanley spoke about. He had talked with him on the phone back at Surrey's headquarters."

"Is he dead?" Derrick asked.

"Give me a second! Yep!" Brent said as he checked for a pulse.

"But he's not our kill!" Derrick exclaimed.

"I know! What the hell happened to him?" Brent asked quite curious.

Chapter 25

After pulling Jeff's body onto the main floor, paramedics made final ditched efforts to revive him. Brent immediately speed-dialed Sheila Hall, "Hello boss, you've got to see this!"

"I'm walking in right now," Sheila said. Then she shouted across the floor, "What do we have here?"

Brent quickly rushed to her side, and then spoke quietly, "We have ten aggressive subjects confirmed dead."

Then Brent quickly looked over at one of the paramedics, who indicated that Jeff was dead. Using an indicating gesture by slashing his neck with his hand. Brent turned back to Sheila and said, "Correction, now it's eleven; the eleventh one is considered a mysterious death. It was a rather strange one."

"How so?" Sheila asked, looking puzzled.

"We are trying to figure it out right now," Brent said as they walked over to Jeff Stewart's lifeless body.

"And I guess all of these people here are civilian tech workers, who now would probably plead ignorance?" Sheila quipped as her eyes wandered across the many faces that stood and sat in the far corner of the room. "So where is our friend, Stanley?" Sheila asked?

"He took off!" Brent responded.

"What do you mean he took off? He is still an arrestee, right?" Sheila inquired as she looked at Brent in astonishment.

"Boss chill out! He was our only way in! Furthermore, we have a drone locked on him," Brent said as he patted her on her back.

"Agent Russell, get him back here please," Sheila said as her eyes wandered over to the computer stations.

Brent paused for a second, rested his hands lightly on Sheila's shoulder and then softly asked her, "Do you really want to bring him back here to face his colleagues so that they would find out that he was the snitch? He was our CI, so let's keep it confidential. What do you say?"

"Well, okay, but this one's on you," Sheila replied as her eyes continued to wander about the place.

Suddenly, Brent remembered the name, Genevieve, which Stanley had spoken of as his 'trusty' friend. He immediately looked feverishly at all of the females' faces, and then his eyes locked onto a young female whose demeanor appeared to be reaching out to him. Brent walked slowly in her general direction so that he wouldn't startle her and make her clam up. As he got closer to her, he whispered, "Genevieve!" She nodded as Brent put his hand lightly on her shoulders and asked, "Can you take a walk with me?"

She again nodded as they both started to walk away from the crowded corner. When they were a comfortable distance away Brent asked, "Are you a friend of Stanley Wilson?"

"Do you know Stanley?" she asked, quite surprised.

"Oh yes! Standup guy, isn't he?" Brent rejoined.

"You just missed him! He left, I would say about a minute before you guys came in. You didn't see him?" she asked.

"Oh yes, we saw him as he was the reason we were able to get in here."

"How so?" she asked.

Let's say he met some new friends—very highly trained professional friends."

Genevieve Martin, 31, was born in Sussex, England. She was of French descent as her father was French, and her mother was English. 5'5" tall, she was a pretty brunette, and a simple home girl but she never really dated much, despite her gorgeous looks. She received her education through a government scholarship. After all of her schooling, she became a computer programmer. It was expected that she would do well because she was a book worm, and her family and friends always addressed her as a 'smart cookie'.

Brent and Genevieve walked behind the floor's computer stations. He then found an office cubicle that was situated in the far back, which is where both he and Genevieve sat.

"So Genevieve, tell me what was going on here?" Brent asked as he spun the office swivel chair she sat in to face him, "We need to get to the bottom of this. Genevieve, Stanley told me straight up that we have to find you because you have knowledge of the grand scheme of things."

Genevieve paused a few seconds and said, "I guess you can say I know my way around this cyberspace mess they created to alter people's minds. Listen, I hacked their main server, and it showed me all of their twisted conspiracy links. Sir, I didn't get your name."

"Brent, Agent Brent Russell, MI-5," Brent answered.

"Okay, Agent Russell, you have to get to the mother server, and when you do, we all would have to leave this place immediately because it is rigged to self-destruct when tampered with if you don't use the password code."

"So now that you told me this, time is of the essence! Where can we find this server?"

Genevieve got up and with a head gesture indicated to Brent to follow her. She then walked over to her cubicle and said, "Agent Russell, better yet, don't worry about that server. When I said I hacked into their main server, I had also downloaded the information." She stopped at her station, picked up her large carry bag, and pulled out and showed Brent her laptop, adding, "This is all you need from here." Suddenly, Genevieve looked around at Brent and asked. "What are they doing?"

Brent quickly turned around and saw that Sheila had ordered

the team to break down the essential computers to take them back to the headquarters' lab.

Brent quickly ran over shouting for them to stop immediately. Sheila then responded, "Agent Russell, what's going on? We need these stuff."

"Boss, this place is rigged to blow! We have to get everybody out of here now! Trust me, I have what we need," Brent exclaimed in excitement.

As Brent was addressing Sheila, Genevieve shut down the computer she had tapped into a few seconds ago. Then she ran to Brent's side and said, "We have 3 minutes!"

Brent immediately started barking orders, "Derrick, Hawk, and all team members, get everyone out of here NOW!"

Both Paul and Carla sprang into action to assist both teams in evacuating the bunker. Suddenly, Carla was drawn to a young female staff worker. "Come young lady, we have to get out of here! Is there anyone you notice that is missing here?"

The young female said nothing, but a male staff worker overheard her and said, "Yes, Richard, he's not here. I saw him went back there with the agents, but he didn't come back out."

"Do you have his number? Does anybody have Richard's number? Call him now! Go, Go, Go! We have to get out now."

Sheila Hall thought she was the last one standing at the bunker's opening, so she was about to use the captain of the ship's methodology when she heard Brent's voice screaming out orders inside. He was trying to complete a final sweep, looking for anybody who was stuck or hiding inside.

"Agent Russell, you have no time! Get out of there NOW! That's an order!"

Brent quickly ran to the exit, grabbing his boss by her arm. They both ran like sprinters and then, a big explosion was heard. The blast sent them tumbling to the ground. Brent immediately rolled over, and getting to his knees, he looked down at Sheila and said, "Boss are you okay?"

"Jesus that was hell on earth! What the hell is this world coming to?" Sheila responded, as she rolled over on her knees and stood up.

ـe/ف

It is now 12:45pm. The bunker's explosion occurred at 10:35am. It took that amount of time for Sheila and the Surrey police department to coordinate and arrange for the transfer of all of the detainees from the bunker to MI-5's main headquarters. There they were all split up into three groups and held in the headquarters' very large briefing room and one of their conference rooms. Soon they were simultaneously conducting individual interrogation interviews with them.

Somehow Carla continued to latch onto the young lady that she had assisted during the evacuation of the bunker. Her name, she later found out, was Caroline Boles. Caroline was a 24 year old pretty lady with shoulder length black hair. She was a new recruit of the underground bunker, and had similar attributes as Genevieve.

Both Sheila and Brent took Genevieve and Stanley into Sheila's main office. Stanley, who was pulled in off the streets of London, willingly came in with no problems. Sheila also asked Paul and Carla to sit in with them, since she believed that this all started with them, so it was most likely that it would end with them. Suddenly, she decided to exclude Carla from the interrogations as she felt that she had experienced enough trauma. She pulled her aside and said, "Carla, I need you to sit this one out. We need you to have a medical check-up."

"I'm fine," Carla responded, giving her a confident look.

"I'm sure you feel that way, but this is protocol. Please!" Sheila said as she looked directly into Carla's eyes, while lightly stroking the hair on top of her head. She then beckoned to a desk worker to take her down to the medical center.

Sheila then looked at Genevieve and said, "Genevieve, I hear that you have information pertaining to this case. Can we see it?"

Genevieve nodded as she pulled out her laptop from her large carry bag.

"Agent Russell, be a gentleman and pull those chairs together for you and our guest so that we could all evaluate what shows up on this screen," Sheila politely asked as she pulled out her desk drawer for the long computer cord to which Genevieve connected her laptop. Then she turned her computer screen towards the arranged seating.

Sheila quickly looked over at Paul and asked, "Paul, how are you doing? Is our friend here with us?"

"I'm fine, and no, I'm sorry he's not! He's a busy Angel!" Paul replied as he pulled his chair to sit next to Brent.

"Oh well, I must say his timing has been great, but he'll be back," Sheila said as she nodded at Genevieve to begin.

Genevieve started tapping a few of the keys of her laptop that soon made Sheila's much larger screen come to life. At first, nonsensical gibberish appeared on the screen until Genevieve separated it into departmental segments.

Strict guidelines appeared on the screen, sent via email to a Cambridge British political consulting firm. An ongoing communications network group had asked the consulting firm to provide and combine data mining, data brokerage, and data analysis information on voters. This clandestine operation, who were planning to take over through a world's plot, used social media's fake news, geographically and demographically, to manipulate and alter their voters' mindset.

"So what is this telling me? Are these the results of the United States elections? Then it's somewhat fraudulent right?" Brent asked.

"You can say fraudulent through manipulation! The people have voted already, so the question is, is it a crime? It's not as if somebody physically held a gun to their heads," Stanley said cavalierly.

"Is that so, Mr. Wilson?" Sheila asked with a striking look of curiosity, and then she went on to say, "It seems convenient for you to make that statement, seeing that you were a part of this manipulation.

Stanley slumped back into his chair, and quite embarrassed said, "I'm just saying," realizing that he had just been checked.

Sheila looked down over her reading glasses at Stanley and said, "I'm keeping my eyes on you."

Genevieve quickly chimed in to divert attention from Stanley, "Look, this was simply done through a combination of altering social media news with subliminal messages."

"Subliminal messages?" Brent asked, knowing the word but was dumbfounded by the way Genevieve had laid it out.

Suddenly, Stanley jumped to his feet in an attempt to redeem himself. "Yes! Subliminal messages, let me show you. It is common in the movies whenever you need to trigger an appetite." Then he turned to Sheila and asked, "May I?"

On sliding her keyboard to face him, he pulled up a random theater movie clip. On running the ad, he slowed it down to a point where they could see the subliminal flashes of food items that were sold in that theater. "You see, the subliminal messages targets the subconscious mind to trigger a thought. Now, let's look at it from another perspective as far as social media is concerned. The collusion between Cambridge and this misguided operation uses these types of messages during elections. For example, let's use our female candidate who just lost."

Stanley started tapping a few keys on the keyboard to pull up a common well known scandal, and then went on to say, "Now, I guess we all heard about this ridiculous claim about the losing presidential candidate being involved in this child sex slave scandal. Or, to say the least, I'm even embarrassed to say that I was a part of this mind manipulation. With that said, we all can agree that this is a ridiculous claim on its face. I personally feel that anybody with common sense would ask him or herself, why would she do this when all eyes were on her as a major public figure?" Stanley asked as he stared at each of them that sat before him.

They in turn all nodded in agreement.

"Okay, here we go," Stanley said as he began running a social media news clip of the losing presidential female candidate. "Now, I'm going to run this clip the normal way the public saw it." The clip ran for thirty seconds. "Okay, what did you guys see?" Stanley asked as he again stared at them.

Brent quickly chimed in, "I see a ridiculous claim of a sex slave scandal that allegedly a prominent public figure was involved in."

The others nodded and said in unison, "I agree!"

"What that tells me is that every one of you are not that deep into, or are not at all fans of, social media, Facebook and any of the other social media stuff. Now check this out, this is what those who are deeply involved in social media see because they would be looking at repetitive clips of this very same ad and/or similar messages," Stanley responded. Then he ran the clip a second time, but this time a lot slower as he had done with the movie clip.

"Whooooaa!" everybody cried out in amazement when they saw the slowed down clip with super imposed images of chained up kids in the cellar of a video photo shop of this candidate in the mix.

Genevieve sat quietly through the demonstration, knowing all of the technical techniques Stanley was revealing to them because she was the one who brought it to his attention from the very beginning. Now she decided to speak and weigh in, "The bunker you have discovered, and what has been revealed, are merely the tip of the iceberg. This is worldwide for the information that I have here is showing me there are eleven similar setups in each continent. Having presidents and prime ministers don't sit well with them, so one of their main goals is to replace them with monarchs who shares the same belief system rooted deep within them. Guys, they are trying to destroy democracy worldwide. "

Suddenly, there was a quiet knock at the door.

"Yes," Sheila responded. The door slowly opened, and Pamela, Sheila's assistant, stuck her head in and said, "Mrs. Hall, sorry to disturb you, but I was trying to reach you through the phone call on hold system. Sheila immediately looked over at her phone that was somewhat obscured beneath the reshuffled papers and files on her desk, and saw the flashing holding call on her phone.

"Who is it?" Sheila asked in a fruitless attempt to whisper.

"Andrew Anderson, FBI agent! He's calling from the field office in California!"

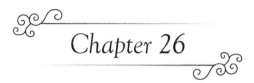

Chapter 26

S heila immediately turned to everyone that sat before her, and
said, "Excuse me, I have to take this call." She walked over to
the far corner of her office and picked up the phone on the side-table
near the couch. "Sheila Hall, how can I help?"

"Mrs. Hall, I'm FBI special agent Andrew Anderson from the
Riverside field office in California. I have just gotten off a conference
call at headquarters with the director. He'd said that you had called
him to talk about a case you are dealing with that may have some
connection with the very case I'm working on now."

"Yes! Yes! Thanks for calling! I called your director about
two and half hours ago about a case we are working on, and just
recently, we've shut down one of the regional-based operations of the
perpetrators. Special agent Anderson, my hunch is, and I'm sure you
may feel the same way, that this is a strange case to say the least. It's
highly unorthodox and somewhat of a mystery to us," Sheila said as
she paused for his response.

"Oh my God, you're getting that there too?" Andrew exclaimed
as he fumbled with his phone, almost dropping it.

"So I take it we are on the same page?" Sheila asked, feeling a
bit relieved that they appeared to be getting somewhere with their
connection.

"Mrs. Hall, for some months now we have been investigating a
possible conspiracy plot perpetrated by Russians who appear to be

undermining our democracy as they appeared to have been tapping into several of our political agencies. I'm presently working a case that seems to have a mystical presence too. It's a case based on a racial divide that has ties to this Russian interference."

"Special agent Anderson, I'm also getting information that this is a global initiative, so we're going to have to work together on this. Presently, we're conducting interviews with suspects of our recent takedown. Listen, this is big! Give me some time to complete them! I'll have my leading agent, Brent Russell, contact you by the end of the business day."

"Thank you, Mrs. Hall, I'll be looking forward to it," Andrew replied and then hung up.

After being medically cleared, Carla, who was putting on her blouse, turned to the doctor and said, "I emphatically apologize for my personal hygiene. It's been too long since I had a shower, so I can't wait to have one."

"It's not a problem! I totally understand," the female doctor said with a warm smile.

"So you say I'm good to go?"

"Yep! You're good to go," the doctor said as she opened the door for Carla to leave.

Carla walked out, but to her surprise found the young lady, who was assigned to assist her, sitting outside the door waiting patiently for her.

Looking down at the young lady, Carla exclaimed, "You're still here?"

"Yes, Ms. Wallace. Oh, Mrs. Hall just called and wanted me to bring you back to her office the minute you were done."

"Okay.... I'm right behind you," Carla replied as she tried to keep a little distance from her because she was so conscious of her lack of personal hygiene.

It took a total of three minutes for them to get to Sheila's office from the medical center. The assistant knocked lightly on the door.

"Come in," Sheila's voice was heard from the inside.

"There you are Ms. Wallace! How are you feeling?" Sheila asked with a welcoming smile as she thanked the office assistant for taking care of her.

"I'm fine! The doctor said I'm good to go, and that's exactly what I want to do right now! Mrs. Hall, I badly need a shower."

"I'm sure you do," Sheila said with a softer smile. Then she added, "Oh! I took the liberty of calling your cousin, Sandra Wright. She was very pleased and happy to know that you were alright. Here is my phone, give her a call. I'm going to arrange for someone to take you home right now."

Carla took the phone, thanked her and then called Sandra to reassure her that she was okay. After speaking to her, she returned the phone and then paused to ask a question, "By the way, Mrs. Hall…"

Sheila quickly jumped in and said, "Stop! You can call me Sheila."

"Okay Sheila, thank you! But do you remember the young lady, Caroline Boles, who had latched onto me during the entire ride from Surrey?"

"Yes, yes, I remember! She is still downstairs being interviewed by our agents. What about her?" Sheila asked.

"She is a loner! They had just recruited her yesterday, so she said, but I'm just thinking she may have been one of their unwilling participants. Can you check in on her for me?"

"Okay, I'll get on it right away," Sheila replied as she walked behind her desk and picked up her phone.

Before Carla left Sheila's office, both Paul and Brent stood up and gave her a confident hug.

Gently pushing them away, she said, "No! No! Get back, get back, I'm icky and embarrassed."

Brent burst out laughing and said, "Okay, chill out girl! Go home and nourish yourself! We've got a lot going on right now! But don't worry, we'll keep you posted."

Right then Sheila hung up her phone and said, "Carla, Caroline is with two of our agents right now. I told them what you told me, but they still have to question her on several other matters, so as soon as they are done, they will bring her straight up to me. I will then conduct my own evaluation and get her personal contact, and give her yours so you both can stay in touch with one another."

"Thank you, I appreciate that! Oh, why don't you just give her one of my cards? Here you go," Carla said as she passed her business card to Sheila.

Then there was another knock at the door. "I think that is your ride, Carla! You take care, and get some rest! Talk to you soon! Bye, bye," Sheila said as she walked Carla to the door.

ero

Meanwhile, at 6:15 am in Riverside, California, in a three bedroom two bath modest home located on a hillside alongside a golf course, an old school bell ringtone sounded. It was barely heard by a middle-aged man, who was scrambling out of the shower, and wrapping a towel around him. He wanted to catch the phone before the other side hung up. "Hello," the man answered.

"Hello Dad," the caller responded.

"James, my boy, long time no hear!"

"Sorry dad for calling so early, and I also apologize for taking such a long time to call you."

"No worries my son, I know you are a busy man! But I sense some urgency in this call given that it's so early," James' father said as his eyes started to wander over to the TV set.

"There is no problem with me, but there is some serious stuff that I got involved in recently, and I wonder if it is possible for us to meet up."

"Meet up? No problem…. Hey James, are you watching the news? That crazy dude won! Oh, my God!" his father exclaimed as he divided his attention between listening to James and watching the TV.

"Funny you should mention that because that is what I want to talk to you about!"

"How so son?"

"Dad, I'd rather not talk about it over the phone. Let's just meet, okay?"

"Okay, but I won't be free until after one. I'm working my bodyguard detail shift this morning! Well, you know what I do, and in fact, I'm going to be late if I don't get out of the door in the next five minutes," his father said, multi-tasking as he hopped on one leg to put on a pair of pants as he talked on the phone.

"No problem, I will call you before I come then," James said and then hung up.

Frank Carey, a well-trained gun enthusiast, who got his basic training with the Army Rangers, worked as a detail bodyguard for high end clients. He was a fifty year old well-built, 6" tall, handsome man, unlike his son, James, who had a smaller frame like his mother.

It had been two weeks since they had spoken with each other.

e/⊚

Meanwhile, at1:15pm in New York City, on an unknown high rise building, Sam and Dunstan stood on its very edge looking down on the crowded streets. Suddenly, a flock of white doves flocked around Dunstan's feet. Then some flew up and perched on both of his shoulders and the top of his head.

Sam, who was standing at least 10 feet across from him, turned and said with a smile, "You are the fallen Angel of birds, aren't you? It's as if you're their king. It's funny! I thought you were supposed to be more in line with the peacock, an attractive bird of splendor, but we are too high for peacocks right now."

Suddenly, Dunstan's phone started to ring! Shooing off the birds, he shuffled through his coat pocket to find his phone. "Hello!"

"Hi!"

"Angela, sweet girl, how are you?"

"I'm fine! Where are you?" Angela asked as her voice crackled to indicate her emotional sensitivity.

"Sweet girl, I'm standing on the edge of a very tall building in New York City! Thinking about jumping.... No, no, no, just kidding," Dunstan quickly said as he turned to Sam with a smile.

Sam just shook his head and said, "I say no more."

"Sweet girl don't worry, it isn't long now! We are big boys doing big things! Trust me, what we are doing is going to make a world of difference," Dunstan said as he tried to share his smile through the phone.

"You sure you can't tell me what you are doing as it will make me feel a whole lot better," Angela said as she held hope, listening for his response on the other end.

"It's a little too complicated to explain now, so let's just say we are turning prayers."

"Okay, I trust you! I'll leave you be," she replied in an all so soft whisper. "Dunstan, I need you! Bye."

Pocketing his phone, Dunstan turned to Sam and said, "Oh, what a lady! You know what is so amazing? Through the eons of time that I have spent in this world, it has been rare that I would meet women with such substance. Why would our Father allow so few women with substance? They are so hard to find even though they are the very tool that can fix broken men and make them great?"

"It's free will, you know! But it was derailed by the Angel you decided to follow! But you just said it, they are the tool to fix and make men great! Lucifer had keyed in on that very tool and used them to undo what God had done. He tapped into the very weakness of man," Gabriel/Sam said, looking at the clouds in the sky. "Andrealphus, I have very little time here on earth to send key-point messages, so that they can manifest in order to right this ship we call the world. Look down there, what do you see?"

Dunstan began to gaze wildly down from the edge of the building. Then he asked, "What am I looking for?"

"Focus, use your angel's sense."

"I see many people going about their daily business."

"Can't you see what I see? They are close but yet they are some distance away? Why?" Gabriel/Sam asked with a tad bit of frustration.

"Okay, I see they all seemed to be focusing on their mobile phones," Dunstan said with a bit of excitement as he looked over at Sam.

"That's right! That is the distance, and it's one of the key problems or major distractions of our times. Many of them do not know half the time what's going on around them."

"So where is our next assignment?" Dunstan asked.

Turning to him, Sam smiled and said, "I'm going to let you take the lead on this one! It's easy. Haven't you notice that there is something else about the crowd down there?"

"What did I miss?"

"You know this is a significant day for many people down there in this country. I can even go as far as to say it's significant even throughout the world. Before you ask why, think about it for a moment."

Dunstan stepped forward, looked down at the people, and then around at each of the buildings. He thought for a moment and then said, "I give up," as he scratched his head.

Sam looked back at him and said, "Stop! Think like Andrealphus, the angel that you are. Okay, here is a hint for our next assignment— it starts with the letter T and rhymes with dump."

Dunstan looked over at Sam as he shook his head and snickered. Then he asked, "Gabriel, is that coming from you? Hold up! I don't want to know! I see it and I also get it, so let's take the trash out. "

"No Dunstan, this trash is going to end up taking itself out."

Chapter 27

Gabriel/Sam walked over slowly to Dunstan, rested both of his hands on each of his shoulders and said softly, "Not so fast, this is both a message and a delivery. Do you know what just happened? Do you know now what the blind failed to see?"

"No, I don't!" Dunstan answered as he shook his head and stared aimlessly down and around him.

Sam nudged his shoulders so that he could turn to face him, "This is all by our Father's design. Through ignorance and arrogance, the wicked have boldly unmasked themselves. By carelessly voicing their decision to follow a known deceiver, who is destined to become a tyrant, they have unveiled their personal nefarious agenda and their hidden or deceptive character. Don't you see? Metaphorically speaking, the bad have decided to wear brightly-colored and very noticeable uniforms. Now, in most cases, those with morals will be surprised to find out just who their so called friends and colleagues truly are. No Dunstan, we don't have to take the trash out because the trash is going to take itself out. Let's go!"

On one of the top floors in the boardroom of a well-known tower that stood high above other towers in New York City, family members, associates and friends were jubilant after manipulating the electoral voting system to win the seat of the highest office in the land. In a celebrative mood, they wasted no time holding a meeting with key government players of an adversarial country.

"Is everybody here?" A young man asked in a commanding and confident voice.

Another voice responded from the midst of a high-spirited small group of eight, who were still giving handshakes and bear hugs, "Yes, we are all here!"

"Well, close the damn door," the young man replied. He was apparently in charge of the meeting. "Everybody, have a seat please," he said as he pulled his chair to sit down.

The room then came to order with the exception of a few who continued to whisper in light conversations with one another.

Suddenly, there was a light knock on the door. But before anyone on the inside could respond, the door slowly opened.

It was Dunstan, who stuck his head in with a foolish looking smile on his face and gave a childish wave, "Hi! Can we come in?" Without waiting for an invitation both he and Sam walked in.

"And who may you be? This is a private meeting! You have the wrong room," the young man at the head of the table said angrily as he stood to usher them out.

"Hey, calm down! We are messengers," Dunstan said as he looked back at Sam, who then turned to close and lock the door.

"If you are messengers, you should know better! Messages are not given from the street level to this high office! Now leave and do it the right way before I call security," the young man said angrily as he quickly walked towards the door to throw them out.

Dunstan's demeanor quickly changed as he stepped into the young man's path and stopped him with a shove. Dunstan angrily started poking him in the chest and walking him backwards on his heels. Scolding him, he said, "We are not your average bicycle riding messengers! Idiot, sit down!"

"That's it! I'm calling security," the young man said. Apparently, he was the son of the newly elected President of the United States of America. He quickly ran towards a side table to grab the phone, but to his surprise in a mystical move, Dunstan got there before him. Dunstan picked up the phone and smashed it on the floor. With a ferocious look, he stared the young man down, who then got the message, stood down and humbly walked back to his seat.

(Note: Ever since Andrealphus/Dunstan split from the band of fallen angels that had started this seismic wave of evil doings, he had bottled up contempt throughout time for all humans who knowingly refused to do the right thing. They knew that God had given them the insight to know the difference between good and evil, yet they conveniently chose the latter because it was the easy way out. This sickened him because he had to live with and around it for so long. Now being emboldened because Gabriel was present and had forgiven him, he lashed out).

Gabriel/Sam casually stepped forward and when he quickly waved his hand, a gush of wind like that experienced in a tornado blew loose paper documents from the board's table, scattering them throughout the room. Then the wind quickly subsided. While sheets of paper were floating to the floor, Sam asked, "Do I have your attention now?" He wasted no time waiting for someone to respond, "It behooves you to listen very carefully, and don't take what I am about to say lightly. Like my friend said we are messengers, and this message is now a delivery. Right here, right now is the beginning phase of your slow demise."

Suddenly, the young man, who was leading the meeting, jumped up from his seat, apparently suffering from a memory lapse as he seemed to have forgotten the display of the shocking mystical wind. With his well-known arrogance, he again spoke out, "You have no idea what you have just done—coming in here unannounced and making threats! Do you know who my father is?"

"Unfortunately I do, and I don't care to know any more about him that I already know," Sam replied softly as he stopped momentarily to entertain the arrogant young man

"My father is now the most powerful man in this world."

"Oh, is he now? Can he make the world spin? If and when he is able to do so, you and I can sit, and perhaps have a sensible conversation! Until then, SIT DOWN and SHUT UP," Sam bellowed out with an intimidating stare, which compelled the young man to take his seat once again. He continued staring at them that sat before him, challenging any of the others to interrupt him.

Then he said as he looked down at the only woman in the room, "Now, lady and gentlemen, unlike my previous meetings with you so called surface thinkers, all of you get to stay a while, yes? You get to reign supreme for a while at least, but there is a method to what you are probably now looking at as madness. Oddly so however, there is a silver lining within this mess you have created. With that said, your message has been given, and I do hope it is received. I see that you all were in a jubilant mood, so I want you to continue your festivity. Oh, what a joyous moment! I'm going to leave you with a gift, just a little one. An ember of guilt will be buried deep within each of you, and it's going to burn like a tiny piece of molten laver, which in turn will not only force you to clash with your moral sensibility, but it will make you deliberate on every decision you make from this day forward. There is another thing, when we leave here, this will all appear to you as an illusion, like a dream, which will nag or haunt you with feelings of guilt as you try to put the pieces of this so called dream together."

Sam slowly walked over to the plated-glass window, glancing off for a moment at New York City's forest-like concrete jungle. Then he turned and looked over his left shoulder at the now quiet and timid group that sat like kids sitting in a daycare center, who had just been warned that they would get no treats if they don't behave. Sam sarcastically whispered, "Nice view!" As he walked towards the door he added, "We will leave you now! Sweet dreams."

Sam walked out of the room. Dunstan stopped and turned to look down on the now quiet onlookers and said, "Here is a little something that will act as a confusing reminder." He quickly opened his trench coat like an eagle spreading his wings, and like a magician, seven white doves, representing each of their cardinal sins, flew out and around the room. Then he quickly turned and left the room.

The room was filled with chaos as the eight occupants scrambled around, wondering how the birds got in there.

℘

Two and a half hours later, around 1:00pm, California time, in Riverside California, James parked in a Dunkin' Donuts' parking lot. He began tapping his phone, burning off a few more minutes as he waited patiently before calling his father once again. At 1:05pm, he redialed his father's number. "Hey dad, what's up? Are you free?"

"Yes, I am James! Meet me at the house in ten minutes."

"Great, on my way!" James said as he turned the key to his Ford Ranger. James purposely parked in Dunkin' Donuts' parking lot because it was in the vicinity of his father's home, and he thought he might want to meet somewhere nearby. James was a lot closer than ten minutes, but because of unexpected traffic, it took just that, so they ended up pulling up to the house at the same time.

Both James and his father Frank shook hands and embraced each other before walking inside. Once inside, Frank made a beeline for his TV remote to turn the TV on. Ever since he saw the news coverage that morning on the new President of the United States of America, he couldn't stop thinking about it. "James, this shit is mind boggling!"

Tell me about it! That news is directly linked to what I wanted to talk about!"

"Oh, is it now? That's interesting! You've got my attention," Frank said as he walked into the kitchen, and opened the fridge door. "Son, you want something to drink? Are you hungry? Got some leftover pizza from last night! It'll take a few seconds to nook it."

"Water would be fine for now, thanks! The coffee and sugar donut I got at Dunkin' Donuts got me water thirsty."

Frank placed a glass of water down for James as they both pulled up their bar stool chairs to the island bar's kitchen table. As Frank popped the lid of an orange soda can and took a sip, he said, "Come on, talk to me! I'm dying to hear this!"

"Dad, you won't believe this! I'm working for the FBI," James whispered as if they were in a crowded room.

"Speak up son! What are you whispering for? Did you say the FBI as in the Federal Bureau of Investigation?"

"Yep!"

"You've got to be kidding me," Frank said as he stood up to get the remote to turn the TV down.

"Dad, you were right! Years ago you told me about your fears regarding Russian aggression. I thought then you were just being paranoid, but now my most recent encounters are telling me different. Dad, you really have to keep this between us because the bureau's main agent on this case, Andrew Anderson, swore me to secrecy."

"Shoot, what exactly are you doing?"

"It's about the forming of white supremacist militia groups, and I'm in one of them."

"What do you mean you are in one of them?" Frank asked with a look of surprise on his face.

"I'm in! I have secretly infiltrated one of them, and now I'm a member."

"What are you telling me? You are posing as a white supremacist? Jesus James, you couldn't come to me before you did something so stupid and dangerous! I thought I brought you up better than that!"

"I had a feeling you would feel this way, but Dad it came on me so fast. In the beginning I was given a card, and suddenly, I was looped in with this homicide detective, Danny Stone, who had worked the case that involved that mysterious slaughter in that warehouse that the news stations have been blaring about since Saturday. Then I met with his brother in-law, Agent Anderson, because it became a Federal case. Luckily for Detective Stone, it was passed to his brother in-law's department. Stone met with me at his house because of the short time frame. Agent Anderson immediately gave me an aptitude and weapons familiarity test, and because of you I passed it. I was supposed to meet a few hours later with this group. I was only given a small window to respond to get in. Dad, I know if you were in my shoes you would have done the very same thing."

Frank slumped down into his chair, and his head flopped back as he stared blindly at the ceiling. It was then that he realized that his son was right, and was not a boy anymore. A few seconds went by before Frank pulled himself to an upright position, looked his son dead in the eyes and said, "Okay, you're in! What can I do to help?"

"Well for starters, you will need to meet Agent Andrew Anderson. I would much rather he explain what we need to do next," James said as he sighed with relief.

Chapter 28

Meanwhile, in Riverside, California at the FBI field office, Agent Anderson was just about to step away from his cubical when his desk phone rang, "Hello, Agent Anderson here."

"Agent Andrew Anderson?" a voice with a British accent responded.

"Yes, it is! How may I help?"

"Agent Anderson, this is Special Agent Brent Russell of the MI-5 London office. How are you today?"

"I'm fine! I was expecting your call, but I thought it would come much later," Andrew said as he pulled his office desk chair to sit back down.

Brent quickly responded, "Oh no, had it been any later I would have been stone cold asleep! It's 9:30pm here."

Andrew slapped his head, "Ah hell! Pardon me Agent Russell, my head is so jammed up right now that I'm forgetting the time difference! I'm so sorry!"

Brent quickly responded, "No need to be! My field boss, Mrs. Hall, said she spoke with you and gave you somewhat of a breakdown of what we have been experiencing here."

"Yes, she did! She also mentioned that some mysterious encounters occurred in your case that have some striking similarities to what I faced in the case I'm working on right now," Agent Anderson said as he fished his cellphone out of his pocket because it was ringing. He saw James' name on the screen, and abruptly said, "Agent Russell, give me a second please!"

"James, what's going on?" Agent Anderson asked, holding his breath and thinking that there was a problem.

"Everything is good! I thought you would like to know that I connected with my father. I'm sitting with him right now."

"James, you are one amazing creature! How did you know I wanted you to do just that?" Agent Anderson asked with a sigh of relief.

"Intuition my friend! I knew this was where Nathanial was going with his questioning, so I decided to step it up a bit."

"Good job James! Listen, I got to call you right back to set up a meeting! I'm on the phone with Britain's MI-5! There's a connection. James, this is a lot bigger than we both imagined! Anyway, I'll call you back soon, bye."

Agent Anderson hung up and then pocketed his phone. While picking up the landline's holding call, he quickly adjusted his tie as if he was about to go somewhere. He returned to his conversation with Agent Russell.

"Agent Russell, I do apologize but I had to take that quick call! Where were we?"

"I think it was about our case being similar," Brent responded.

"Right, right! Agent Russell, through soft talks I have been told that there was a divine intervention at the beginning of my case, that is, before it was handed to me."

"Agent Anderson, your soft talks is an understatement when compared to my direct link that strangely enough, came through two unrelated civilians. It started with one of them taking down a terrorist cell at Heathrow Airport. Mysteriously enough, the person that was caught via CCTV footage was responsible for the terrorist cell takedown. I was assigned to look for that individual, and guess what? It was a female, and she found me. After meeting with her and two others… Agent Anderson, to put it briefly, had I been an atheist, I would have completely reversed my beliefs because of the mystical inside knowledge and tips that we received, and shortly afterwards, helped us takedown two terrorist cells."

"Is that so?" Andrew replied, rubbing his chin with curiosity as he wanted to learn more about Agent Russell's encounters.

Brent pondered for a few seconds, and then asked, almost in a whisper, "Agent Anderson, can I call you Andrew?"

Andrew perked up quickly and said with a chuckle, "Sure, you can! I have no problem with that Brent!" They both chuckled, sensing the other's smile.

"Andrew, but seriously speaking, our information is that this is a clandestine global operation, all in an effort to rid the world of democracy. The results of your elections hinge on what we are working with at this time. From our latest major takedown, which took place in Surrey England, we have gathered a great deal of Intel from a bright, young female, who was an inside and well-connected employee. Andrew, social media plays an extremely important role in this too. If you see what I have been looking at, it would baffle you, and when I say important, I mean worldwide mind-altering work of art importance. Given this new age of social media, you can truly say that we're in a World Wide Web."

"I hear you partner," Andrew said as he struggled to find words to match Brent's colorful ones. "Well Brent, to tell you the truth, in the beginning I have not personally witnessed anything here, but talk has it that some strange ET non-human like thing, something in angelic form, appeared to several people. My CI's and in-laws are now calling it an angel, whom they believe was responsible for the warehouse slaughter. But listen, that part is so confusing to me! So if you are right that this is a clandestine world assault, and we're major players in the world, let us work this together. Let's exchange our findings and see where there are connections, and where there are, we'll consolidate them."

"I agree. Listen, Interpol is all over this as we speak, and I understand Madrid, Spain is showing similar activity. Okay, let's do just that! I'm going to see where this Madrid thing is going and lend my assistance where it is needed. I hope our better angels are assisting them also," Brent said and then added, "Look, I better go and get some sleep! I have a big day tomorrow."

"You do that, and we'll talk soon," Andrew said and then hung up.

Meanwhile, at that very same time, at an undisclosed vineyard located adjacent to a farmhouse in Orange County, California, near Newport Beach, Nathanial and Richard stood in an underground specially-built bunker assessing the cachet of weapons they had been stockpiling.

"What do you think, Richard?" Nathanial asked.

"I think we are good to go," Richard responded.

Nathanial quickly turned to Richard, shaking his head, "No, no, no! That's not the right answer! Richard, you know better than that! You know we are no way near to where we need to be. That kind of haste will cause us all to fall on our faces!"

"With all due respect Nathanial, now that you've mentioned haste, why are you embracing this guy James so quickly, and involving him in our operations?" Richard asked hesitantly.

Nathanial paused for a few seconds to calm down and collect his thoughts. Then he rested his hands on Richard's shoulders and replied, "Yes, I know, it was rather a quick evaluation of him, but it was my call, and it was a call I had to make. Richard, here is what you seem to somehow fail to see—our guy has won. We have one of the strongest advocates that support our movement. He is now going to be sitting not only in the highest office of this land, but of this world. Obviously, the other side is not going to like this! They are going to push back, and they are going to try to take back what we are about to take from them, so we have to be prepared for that."

Nathanial stood alongside Richard as he draped one of his arms around his shoulders. He looked up and around at the stockpile of weapons and said, "Richard, my boy, this and the other two stockpiles here in the west are miniscule to what we really need. Now, are you with me?"

Richard shook his head lightly as he stared at the fifteen feet high cachet of weapons.

Nathanial vigorously rocked Richard back and forth with a one arm bear hug and said,

"Okay, let's go find our guy Jimmy."

"Jimmy?" Richard turned to Nathanial with a shocked look on his face, "Who is Jimmy?"

Nathanial started to laugh, "You don't know that the name James is also called Jimmy? It's like your name Richard, which is also known as Dick, and that is fitting because you are a Dick." After locking the storage's bunker door, and on turning to walk away, Nathanial said with a smile, "Come on Dick, let's go find Jimmy."

Richard physically shoved Nathanial and said, "Stop it! I'm no damn Dick!"

Nathanial's loud laughter engulfed the quiet vineyard as they walked towards their vehicle.

As Nathanial and Richard drove back to Newport Beach, Nathanial pulled out his phone, swiped his screen, touched contacts, and began scrolling through the J's, "Jimmy, Jimmy, Jimmy, Jimmy, James! Here we go!"

James picked up his phone on the third ring, "Hello!"

"Jimmy, my boy, how are you doing? Oh, by the way, our boy just won the president's seat, and if it's okay with you, Mr. Carey, I'm going to start calling you Jimmy."

"Personally, I much rather James, but if it floats your boat, Jimmy is my name," James said as they both laughed out loud at his rapping flow.

"Jimmy, I would like to meet your Dad! Can you make it happen?"

"Nathanial, I'm a bit ahead of you on that. After reading through your questions, I got the message, and I'm sitting with him as we speak," James replied. Gesturing and pointing his finger at his phone, he mouthed in silence to his Dad, "This is the guy."

James' father quickly picked up his soda can, stood up and took a few steps back as he did not want to distract his son while they spoke. James' wheels started to turn real fast in his head as he took control of the conversation. He gained the upper hand by setting up the meeting's time and place.

By using the power of suggestion James said, "Listen Nathanial, knowing my father's very busy schedule, let's say a good time would be 6:00pm and the place, ah, ah…." James then turned to his father and asked, "Dad, where would you like to eat tonight?"

"Steak," Frank answered.

"Dad, I didn't ask what you would like to eat, but where would you like to eat?"

Frank again responded but this time with a stupid grin, "Okay, steak, Outback Steakhouse."

James looked at his father from the corner of his eyes, sarcastically shaking his head at him. "Nathanial, looks like dinner's on me. I hope Outback Steakhouse is one of your favorites, because it is his. Oh, let me get back to you with a suitable address for us."

"Sounds good to me! I'll be waiting," Nathanial replied and then hung up.

James hung up his phone, turned to his father and said, "Dad, that's the guy, Nathanial Parker. He's a notorious white supremacist who is leading a fast growing militia group in this region. His interest in me is purely because of you."

"Me! Why me?" Frank asked with an eye-widening stare.

"Because of your service in the armed forces. You are a senior and have clout with the higher ranks," James replied as he held back a moment before springing the real reason on him.

"Son, where are you going with this?"

"Weapons Dad, weapons! Remember, it's a growing militia group, and they need weapons."

Frank immediately reached for the TV remote to shut the TV

off. The house became deafeningly silent. "You are telling me I am supposed to secretly go into a military base to make deals with my former counterparts, so I can bring out a truckload of weapons. Son, are you nuts? How do you propose I do that?"

"Dad, remember I'm working with the FBI! It's a government agency, so they can stage this. All Nathanial's group need to know is that you are onboard with them like me," James said as he watched his father pace back and forth.

"So when are we going to meet this agent of yours?" Frank asked as he stood there staring at his son with his hands on both sides of his waist.

"He said he will call me right back, and it has been….." Before James completed his response, his cellphone rang. James raised his hand to his father with a just a moment gesture,

"Hello, hey, I was waiting for your call! I just got off the phone with Nathanial. He now wants my father to join me. I stalled for time, with a six Oclock dinner meeting. We need to meet fast."

"Where are you?" Agent Anderson asked.

"At my father's house here in Riverside."

"Good, I'm in Riverside. Give me the address," responded Anderson.

Chapter 29

Andrew hung up his phone, and quickly opened the door to the neighboring coffee shop that was a block down the street from the Riverside FBI's field office. All the agents often met or gathered in there for morning coffee, breakfast and lunch. Once inside, he stopped abruptly when he noticed his partner, Kenny Johnson. He had told him that he would meet him there twenty minutes ago as he was looking into a few things pertaining to their case. Kenny was sitting with another agent, Mark Green, on the far left in a rear window booth. Mark was Kenny's cousin on his father side. He was a flamboyant thirty-two year old FBI agent who worked on white collar crimes. He was based in New York and was working the stock exchange market, investigating insider trading.

Andrew abruptly stopped because he was curious about Mark being there, given that he was considered a questionable character among the agents within the bureau. Mark Green was known to voice his views of, and involvement with politics. FBI agents were supposed to be impartial, and Kenny knew this. Perhaps that was the reason he was nervously looking around and over his shoulders all the time.

Andrew decided to quickly make himself known to him to break up any discussion that may involve his covert operations. "Kenny, my boy, I'm sorry I took so long," Andrew said as he pulled a chair up to the booth's table as he did not want to squeeze himself on either side of them.

"No, no, you are just in time! I just ordered. Oh, Andrew call that waitress over there as she's our waitress! Let her add your order to ours." Kenny said, relieved that Andrew arrived when he did as he did not want to be seen alone with his cousin for fear of being labeled because of his controversial political views.

Andrew gave his order to the waitress, and after she had turned and walked away, Mark looked over at Andrew with a childish grin and said, "Agent Anderson, what do you think?"

"What do you mean, what do I think?" Andrew asked, knowing quite well where he was going with the question because of his stupid grin.

Mark quickly followed up by saying, "Come on, you know what I'm talking about, our new President! What do you think?"

"You seem to be delighted, but I guess it worked out for you. Mark, before you go on and make a mockery of yourself, we, as FBI agents, are not supposed to care either way who sits in that seat. So if you wish to climb the ladder in this bureau, I suggest you cease voicing your political opinions."

"Ahhh, come on, lighten up! Kenny, are you going to allow your partner to talk to me this way?"

Kenny sat there looking morosely at him because of the negative energy he always seemed to bring to the table! Then he shook his head and said, "Mark, he is right! You have to keep your personal opinions to yourself! It's not going to do you any good."

"Ha! I see you both seem to be sore losers! I like that guy! Some big changes are going to be made, you'll see," Mark responded with a light chuckle.

Andrew flopped back into his seat, exhaled with disgust and said sarcastically, "This is going to be a long lunch!" Then he looked over at Mark and asked, "Mark, aren't you supposed to be working white collar crimes in New York, at the stock exchange?"

"Yeah, but I decided to take a little time off to get away from the cold."

"Yeah right! And you decided to bring the coldness here to antagonize us! Thanks," Andrew said with a soft smile.

All and all it took about twenty minutes before their order came. In haste, Andrew shoveled down his light lunch because of a sudden desire to leave Mark's presence.

"Got to go!" Andrew said as he threw the used table napkin in his plate.

"Where are you going?" Kenny asked looking surprised.

"It's something personal I've got to deal with! It won't take long. Listen Kenny, I left some written instructions concerning our case on your desk for you. I will call you when I'm done, so we can meet up later," Andrew said as he stood up, and then added, "Mark, I hope you enjoy your time off here, and please don't take what I said lightly! You know, impartiality is important."

Andrew purposefully set Kenny on another agenda so that he could meet James and his father alone. Knowing the very sensitive nature of the case, he had to be very careful to avoid any leaks. Earlier he felt a little awkward about not trusting his partner, that is, in wanting to meet James and his father alone, but now that he had seen his surprise visitor, Mark Green, he realized that he had made the right decision.

Twenty minutes later, back at the home of Frank Cary, James' father, James shouted out, "Dad, turn the TV down—I think I heard the doorbell." He had just stepped out of the bathroom. He made his way to the door, and on looking through the peephole, he suddenly jumped back, turned to his father and excitedly said, "It's him!" Frank flopped his hands to his side, looking at his son as if he were a moron, "Son, don't just stand there! Open the damn door!"

James quickly composed himself, and then turned to open the door, "Agent Anderson, that was fast! Glad you could make it!"

"Damn James, for as important as this is, I'm surprised I wasn't able to make it here any sooner," Andrew replied as he walked through the door.

Frank stood before him with a shining expression on his face and a warm welcome on his lips. "Mr. Andrew Anderson, for the past hour I have been hearing a lot about you. You are a company guy, and I'm glad to meet you," Frank said as he reached out his hand to shake Andrew's hand.

"Come on in! What can I get you? Are you thirsty?" Frank railed off with his welcoming hospitality.

"I'm good! Okay, maybe a glass of water," Andrew replied.

"You got it! James, get our friend here a glass of water, please. Come on have a seat."

Frank walked Andrew to his cozy living room, which he hardly used; it was clean like a showroom in a furniture store.

"This is a lovely house! It looks as if I'm the first guest to sit in here," Andrew said, looking around and admiring the furniture.

Frank was smiling as he absorbed the compliment. "I would like to say it's my wife's doing, but it's not! It's all me as I'm a neat freak! It was handed down from my father and then the military, which solidified my cleaning habits."

"I wish I could say that for myself, but I'm not that bad! However, I've been known to leave my bed unmade at times, but I blame it on the job," Andrew said as he reached out for the glass of water James was handing to him.

"Ha, ha, sure it is," Frank said with a chuckle and then added, "Okay, Agent Anderson, James gave me the basic rundown, but didn't want to go too deep until you arrive. Now from what I understand, the Russians are involved. I told James a long time ago that those guys spooked me! They have you constantly looking over your shoulders and wondering about any guy whose demeanor is strange, and who may be sitting next to you in a restaurant.

They are everywhere; they're control freaks. But don't get me wrong, because it's not the entire nation for I have met great people from Russia! It's just those at the top, who are monarch seeking dictators—oligarch tyrants." "I agree with your sentiments, but sitting in the bureau, my views go a lot deeper than you think, which is why I'm here. I understand that both you and James set up a dinner meeting for 6:00. Where are you going to eat and what's the address?" Andrew asked as he looked over at James.

James heard the question but was caught off guard because he was deep in thought.

Because of the delayed response, both Andrew and Frank looked at him. Then Andrew asked, "James, are you with us?"

"Yes, yes! Sorry, my mind was so engulfed with all that's been going on.... We're going to meet at Outback Steakhouse, 151 N McKinley Street, Corona. Damn! Almost forgot, I have to call Nathanial back with the address."

"Go ahead, and call him now! James please, I need you to focus! Don't fold up on me now."

"Sorry," James said as he bit his lip and redialed the number Nathanial had called him on.

"Hello, Nathanial, the address is 151 N McKinley Street, Corona! See you there at six."

"Got it," Nathanial said on the other end and then hung up.

Andrew took another sip of his water, rested it down and said, "Guys, I guess it's fair to say that Nathanial Parker embraced James here mainly because of you, Frank. Now that their guy is in the White House, they have to ramp up their operations in the event of a military retaliation. Weapons! Having as many weapons as possible is imperative. This President has been given nods and winks, which White supremacists see as a go! In their delusional minds they want to take back what they believe to be their country! We have to do whatever is necessary to stop their fast track gain towards equal strength that they seem to want so badly."

Frank turned to his son and said, "Son, for quite some time now, and from the onset, we've had folks in our White race who are doing, and have been doing atrocious things! That's not to say that there weren't others who have done some good things, given the many creative inventions around us! But from our race pool, certain groups have sought out the fine and brilliant ones among us to invent or create a number of things for the agnostically-minded bad ones. James, it's all by design! They limit capitalism so that they can become monarchs and remain at the top. But because of their arrogant behavior, there is one thing they had not envisioned or bargained for, and guys this is the funny part—you see out there, there is a dominant gene, and this was all of their own making, that is slowly erasing that supreme pure white dream of theirs, and that frightens them."

James turned to his father and asked, "So what is this dominant gene?"

James' father looked at him with an astonishing look and said, "James, are you kidding me? You don't get it!" Then he looked over at Andrew and said with a smile, "You don't see them calling Tiger Woods an Asian Black American! No, he is simply African American. Listen, here is my message for those egotistical, self-centered White supremacists—get used to it, and try to embrace it. Based on anthropologists' findings, we started out with one color, so we may simply just end up with that color, and that should bring us to the realization that there is only one human race."

"Dad, are you serious?" James asked because he had never seen his dad so passionate about this particular subject.

"Serious! I'm serious as a heart attack," Frank responded and then went on to say, "Think about it! You mix the White and Black races together, or should I say Caucasian and African American or African! Whatever! Regardless of gender, the offspring tends to identify more with the Black race more than the other."

Frank then stood up, looked down at both of them and added, "It's poetic justice when one considers how White supremacists look at it! Oh, what a tangled web we weave when at first we try to deceive."

Both James and Andrew sat silent for a few seconds nodding in agreement over what Frank had just told them.

Andrew broke the silence as he looked at his watch and said, "Hey guys, its 3:10pm! We better start going over some stuff. Okay, Frank, do you know any high official at the military base here in California, someone you can trust with our secret?"

"Lieutenant General Ronald Woods!" Frank replied without hesitation. "We're still close! Ever since James told me about this infiltration thing, my mind popped on him."

"And he is someone you feel you can trust?" Agent Anderson asked again.

"You bet! He is also a good man," Frank replied with a confident stare.

Andrew again stared down at his watch and said, "It would have been super if we'd had the opportunity to meet up with him before this meeting, but that's wishful thinking. Look, we all know what they want, so in the meeting you have to be realistic. Frank, don't let them think that this is a walk in the park for you to pull this off. In fact, go in with a bit of apprehension. Let them do a bit of coaxing to win you over. If you go in with open arms and agree to everything they say, they may sense something is wrong. Oh, and Frank, don't give them your guy, Lieutenant Woods' name."

"I hear you! You got it," Frank responded with enthusiasm as if he was following orders back in the military.

Andrew quickly sat up to reach for his Mackenzie leather briefcase as he asked Frank, "Is there a table top I can use?"

"Sure, over there," Frank replied as they all got up to walk over to Frank's dining room table.

"What you got?" Frank asked as he was clearing away plates and cutlery from a section of the table.

Andrew opened his bag to pull out a map, and as he was spreading it on the table, he said, "I was thinking we should start scoping out suitable safe areas for the weapons exchange takedown. It is good for us to familiarize ourselves with our chosen area, which we have to convince them to use. We also have to be prepared in case they force last minute changes."

They all sat there looking down at the map when suddenly, James' phone rang. "Hello!" he said as he raised his hand to gesture silence. "Hello, hello," James repeated, but there was no response on the other end. Then he suddenly cuffed his phone to his chest and with a loud whisper said, "Hold up guys, this is a pocket dial." He then quickly put the phone on speaker. There were sounds of vehicular traffic and a faint conversation between Nathanial and Richard.

They heard Nathanial say, "Richard, I understand your concerns, but I'm not going to take meeting these guys lightly. Look, if it makes you a little more at ease, I have already decided to do another electronics wand check on James, and of course, on his father."

Hearing what they needed to hear, Andrew began waving his hands vigorously as he whispered loudly, "Hang it up! Hang it up!"

James immediately complied.

"Damn James, had we not picked up that pocket dial, you would have walked into a trap. I was going to send you back in there with the mini-cam glasses."

They all went silent as they pondered that thought.

Chapter 30

Meanwhile, back in Cleburne, Alabama, in the Sipsey wilderness area of the Bankhead National Forest in Northern Alabama at 5:25pm, Dunstan/Andrealphus and Sam/Gabriel stood on a tree branch of a very large water hickory tree that was 115 feet tall.

Resting his hand on Dunstan's shoulders, Sam as Gabriel turned to him and said, "Andrealphus, even though you only have a third of your angelic powers, I need to know how agile you are, and whether you've experienced any changes in your body. I need to see what has manifested in you. You need to believe in our Father's grand intentions. Do you believe?"

"Gabriel, I never stopped believing, which is the prime reason I ran away from the dark side. But if you are talking about flying again, need I remind you about our first attempt?" Andrealphus responded as he began looking down and around from the very tall tree.

"Who said anything about flying? I only want to know how agile you are," Gabriel said, simultaneously shoving Dunstan back, and causing him to lose his balance.

Andrealphus shouted out, "Hey…" as he leapt and caught another branch, swinging on it like a gymnast on an uneven bar. He looked down at Gabriel with a straight face, and then he smiled and said, "I see you like to play games!"

"And I see you are afraid of heights!"

"Not really, but ever since the great fall, I should be. Gabriel, do you really want to play games up here?" Andrealphus asked as he side-stepped him and casually leaned against the tree's trunk.

"If you want to call it that, try and keep up," Gabriel replied as he ran out to the edge of one of the branches and began jumping with frog-like leaps from limb to limb. Soon he was standing on the branch of another tree, twenty feet away.

Andrealphus looked down at Gabriel, who was now thirty feet away, at a ten foot drop. He smiled again and ran out to the end of his branch, and leaped off. Seconds later, he was standing next to Gabriel once again.

Gabriel frog leaped again and again, with Andrealphus in tow. Before long they were both jumping and swinging from trees as if they were flying red Colobus monkeys.

At the end of what some would call a training exercise, both of them stood alongside a pond in the wilderness. Gabriel stared at Andrealphus, looking at him from head to toe. He marveled as he noticed Andrealphus' rapid climb on becoming a part of God's band of Angels once again.

"Andrealphus, I have to leave you for a short while. I will take you back to town for it is time for you to see and reassure people that have concerns, and perhaps, are worried that you have left them."

"But don't we have work to do?" Andrealphus asked with a disappointing look on his face.

"Yes, we do, but there is something I have to do that I can do alone. Don't worry, you are going to be made whole once again! I will be back! You can believe that! Besides Andrealphus, as Dunstan you have a life down here; people are counting on you; they believe in you, and believe it or not, somehow deep inside, I envy you."

Then they both embraced. Shortly afterwards, Andrealphus found himself sitting on a park bench in Cleburne County's town area. Then he shared a sad moment with Dunstan, his incarnated counterpart. With his head hung low, and his feet three feet apart, he sat on the park bench. His feet were separated by the water that had pooled up from an earlier rain shower. A single teardrop fell from his eye into the water and its ripple revealed his reflection that was staring back at him. He reflected on his past experiences, including the difficulties true believers face on earth, and wondered whether life was really fair for someone like himself who was partly human with feelings. He quickly shook that doubtful thought from his mind, convincing himself that there was a reason for it all. But then he thought that certain things on the earth might have gone a bit too far. After all, didn't his Father send his Angels to right the wrong?

As he stared at his reflection in the puddle of water, to his surprise another face appeared.

"Why are you so sad?" asked the voice of a blonde little girl who was about five or six years old.

Dunstan quickly looked up in surprise as he had not noticed her approach. He quickly deflected her question because he did not want to explain his concerns. "Hello, what is your name?"

"My name is Michelle."

"Michelle, what a lovely name! My name is Dunstan."

"Dunstan, are you an angel?" She climbed up on the bench to sit beside him.

"Why would you ask me that?" Dunstan asked as he began looking around for her parents or an adult who may be looking for her. She smiled and answered with an all so sweet voice, "That little birdie told me so," as she pointed to another park bench by the children's play pit. Dunstan looked over at the bench and sure enough there was a little bird perched on it.

"Oh, is that so?" Dunstan replied softly as he stared at the bird on the bench. It was close to where a group of teenagers were playing and dancing to music that was playing on a CD player.

All of a sudden, a teenaged girl started running towards them and shouting, "Michelle, Michelle, what are you doing? Get over here!"

Michelle started to giggle as she jumped off the bench, looked up at Dunstan and said, "That's my sister!"

The teenager took Michelle by the hand. "I'm so sorry, Sir! Is she bothering you?"

"No, no, of course not! She is a very intelligent and a sweet kid. Is she your sister?"

"Yes, she is, but she is also a wandering, mischievous little one," She replied as she lifted Michelle as if she were her own child.

"That's my friend Dunstan, and he is an angel," Michelle said, glancing over her sister's shoulders to look for the bird on the other park bench, but it had already flown away.

The teenaged girl reached out her hand to shake Dunstan's hand and said, "Hello, Angel Dunstan, I'm Gina, Michelle's oldest sister. Aren't angels supposed to have wings?" Gina asked as she looked down at Dunstan with a soft smile.

Dunstan sat back, straddled his arms along the bench's back rest, and squinting his eyes from the setting sun, he looked up at Gina and said, "I'm being punished."

"Okay, bad angel, I'm sorry to hear that, but we have to leave now before my mom gets back and both of us are punished for talking to a stranger. She is just across the street getting us ice cream."

"I understand! Yes, you better go now," Dunstan said, as he waved goodbye to Michelle as they turned and walked away.

Dunstan sat there for another five minutes, watching Gina near the park's play pit and the group of teenagers who were dancing to a dance song. He then decided to leave.

As he walked pass the dancing group, Gina shouted out, "Mr. Dunstan, can you dance?"

Dunstan stopped abruptly, and pointing both hands at his chest, he shouted back, "Me?"

"Yes you!" Gina shouted, pointing at him.

Dunstan then smiled and walked briskly over to the group. "Okay, I think I can show you a little move I learnt a little while back." Dunstan stood before the group, and then instructed them to form a half circle. Clipping his fingers, he said, "Play the music, then listen and watch closely! He lifted his hands and started rhyming out words to a hip hop beat. "Interlock your thumbs, put your palms to your chest, pop your shoulders, and let your hands do the rest." Dunstan started bouncing to the beat, popping his shoulders, and flapping his hands that imitated an angel bird's wings.

Gina's eyes popped open as she repeated the words and the steps over and over again. Then looking at the rest of the group, she shouted, "This is so cool! Mr. Dunstan, you are the Rocking Robin! Does this dance have a name?"

"I don't think so, but let's call it the Angelic stance."

They all started laughing and dancing as they repeated the angelic stance steps and words over and over again.

Dunstan quickly stopped and turned to the teen who was playing the CD music box. Lowering his hand to direct him to lower the music, he formally introduced himself as Dunstan Archer. It was his way of creating a friendly bond with them as they appeared to be a group of aspiring teenagers. Then he stepped back as if he were a coach, and they were members of his team, "Listen up, I'm just curious! I want you to tell me what are your aspirations for your lives? What I mean is, what do you hope to become when you finish high school?"

All of the kids chimed in, shouting out what they wanted to become once they graduated high school. Some said that they were going to college, while others said that they wanted to become an airline pilot, a doctor, a lawyer, or they plan to join the armed forces. They also called out other professions teenagers their age aspire to become.

"That's good, that's very good," Dunstan said as he nodded his head. Then he said, "You can do that! Of course, you can become that. But what I want to know is do you have the formula to achieve your goals?" He paused awhile as they stared at him, looking clueless. "Okay, I guess you don't know the formula. The formula is called the Triple A, (AAA), and no, I'm not talking about roadside automobile assistance."

Puzzled, the group of teens looked at each other.

Dunstan stared at each of them, and then said, "Triple A stands for *'Ascendant, Assiduous,* and *Asunder'.* Become *'ascendant,* and *assiduous,* so that you won't go *asunder'. Ascendant* means, *'Lift yourself up, and rise to prosperity'. Assiduous* means *'Become diligent, careful, meticulous, and learn to persevere'.* You need the first two, so that you don't go *'asunder, or break apart, or fall to pieces'.* You have to become *ascendant* and *assiduous,* so that you don't go *asunder."*

Dunstan stood quiet for a few seconds so that what he had just said could sink in. Not wanting to lose his audience by coming off or looking like a Bible beating fanatical Christian, he just kept it simple! He used strong, substantive words that rang truth, and caught their attention. In closing, he added, "There is one last thing I need to say. Yes, I'm a God- fearing person, and you ought to be too, but there is one simple word you need to carry with you at all times!" Then he pointed to the sky, and simply said, "Believe!"

Suddenly, Dunstan looked down at his watch and exclaimed, "Uh oh, got to go! Got to run!" He waved goodbye as he quickly turned and walked away.

꿯

It was 6:15pm so he thought it was a good time to call Angela. But just as he shoved his hand in his pocket for his phone to call her, his phone rang. He quickly answered it without looking at its face, "Hello!"

"Dunstan, where are you?" It was Angela and she was frantic.

"What's going on sweet girl? Are you okay?" Dunstan blurted out as he froze in his tracks and a tense look appeared on his face.

"Why are they following me?"

"Who is following you?"

"I don't know! I just dropped Stacy home." Stacy was her co-worker. "Dunstan, I'm scared because everywhere I turn, they are right behind me."

"What street are you on?" Dunstan asked.

"I'm travelling south on Pelham Road! It's not too far from the hardware store where our maintenance guy shops!"

"Okay Angela, try to stay visible in heavily populated areas! Slow down, and if you come across a police station, pull in and repeatedly sound your horn. Since he wasn't too far away, he added, "Do not turn off on any of the side streets that are dead ends! Don't worry, I'll find you!"

Using his angelic senses and strength, which was seemingly at 60%, Dunstan/ Andrealphus honed in on her location like a pigeon. "Damn, these primal fallen angels were on to him again," he said to himself! With his nose pointing to the skies, he took a deep breath as if he was trying to track a scent on the wind. He quickly turned left and then right, and like a track star, he took off with the swiftness of a bird in flight. Down the main street he ran, and then into a side street that brought him to a dead end. He leapt over fences, and ran through backyards. The loud sounds of dogs barking could be heard but instantly faded away in the distance he created. Before long, he ran out onto Pelham Road, turned south, and there she was twenty yards up ahead.

Angela had just been forced over to the curb by a black SUV that had two primal fallen subjects in it. In a flash Dunstan ran towards her vehicle, and with the technique of an Olympic triple long jumper, he hopped, skipped and leapt from the rear of her vehicle over the top to the front and landed directly alongside the SUV driver's door. The driver flinched at his sudden appearance! Dunstan casually tapped his fingers on the window. Then without warning, he quickly punched his fist through the glass, and with both hands, he pulled the driver through the window's opening. Slamming him to the pavement about a feet away from Angela's front bumper, he punched the primal subject in the chest with so much force that he crushed his chest cavity. Then he quickly pulled him up to a sitting position, gripped his jaw from behind, and viciously snapped his neck.

The second subject jumped out of the passenger's side of the vehicle and came around to assist his partner, but quickly changed his mind when he saw what Dunstan had done, using the enormous strength that Andrealphus, the incarnated angel, had given him. He retreated and ran across the street and smashed the front glass door of a closed Mom and Pop hardware store. Dashing inside, he began desperately looking around for a suitable tool to defend himself.

Across the street, Dunstan stood up from the lifeless primal subject's body, and immediately caught Angela's eyes, who was staring in shock at him. He slammed the palms of his hands on the hood of her car and shouted, "GO! Get out of here!" Then he quickly turned and crossed the street to pursue the second subject. Suddenly, he stopped, turned back and saw that Angela was still in shock, frozen to the spot. He stared directly at her as he pointed aimlessly, and with a whispered mouth gesture, instructed her to "GO NOW!"

Angela quickly hit reverse, slammed her gear shift into drive, and with the tires squealing, she was out of there!

Dunstan quickly ran towards the hardware store in pursuit of the dark fallen angel. Hearing the blaring sounds of the store's alarm, he knew he had to move quickly because a police patrol car would be arriving in a matter of minutes. He kicked away the excess broken door glass, and on entering, he noticed right away the broken lock of a display case containing edge tools. He saw a little tag sign that read, 'scythe', that indicated that this antique tool was missing from the rack. Dunstan immediately reached into the display case and pulled out a machete because he realized that he was no longer the prey but the hunter. He walked down the store's aisle, spanking the shelves and making a racket to heighten his prey's fear.

"So tell me, which one are you?" Dunstan fearlessly shouted out. "I'm not surprised at your choice of weapon for how fitting it is for you! A scythe is a typical edge weapon or tool for the grim reaper that you are!"

Without warning, and like a cornered rat, the primal subject sprung out of hiding, took the offence and charged at Dunstan, swinging the scythe. Doubling his speed, Dunstan closed the distance between them by advancing quickly towards his aggressor. With tremendous agility, he swung the machete up and with a downward thrust, like a hot knife through butter, he hit the scythe and cut its extended wooden handle in two! Then Dunstan turned back on him, flailing him with multiple slashes, and then with one last roundhouse swing, he beheaded him. He quickly kneeled down beside the headless body, then he wiped the machete's handle off on the expired primal subject suit jacket, dropped it, and, pulling a canvas off a shelf, he draped the bloody mess even though he knew that the mangled body would dissipate in minutes. Dunstan quickly ran to the emergency exit at the back of the store, and using his hips to open the door, he ran off into the dusk.

Chapter 31

Loud sounds of banging was heard on Dunstan's door. Startled, Julian ran to the front window, and saw Angela's car parked out front. He quickly ran to open the door.

As Angela pushed her way in, she was shaking, quivering and crying, "Please lock the doors! They are coming!"

"Calm down! What's going on?" Julian asked, holding and hugging her in order to restrain her erratic behavior.

She quickly turned to lock the front door, and then ran to the back door to ensure that it was locked. Mumbling inaudibly, she feverishly ran through the house checking and securing all of the windows.

"Angela, will you stop and please tell me what's going on?" Julian exclaimed with a tint of anger in his voice.

Suddenly, there was another knock on the door. Angela jumped in fright and quickly turned to run to one of the bedrooms. But a comforting voice followed the knock; it was Dunstan crying out, "Open the door, please!"

Julian quickly opened the door, and before Dunstan completely passed the threshold, Angela, still frightened, ran up to him and began hugging, holding and passionately kissing him. Quivering and crying she asked, "Dunstan, what is going on? What are you? Who are you?"

Dunstan, in return, hugged her, and then quickly stepped back.

Holding both of her arms, he said, "I'm sorry!" He once again pulled her back into him, and while cradling her head on his chest, he said, "Close your eyes, relax, and this should explain everything."

Suddenly, a preponderance of feelings and a vision engulfed her mind, body and soul. Yes, Angela experienced the vision of the glory of the heavens in all of its splendor. She also saw flashes of significant battles, past and present, initiated by the world. She received the answers to all of her unanswered questions, and even though she was a bit confused, she looked at Dunstan with glowing eyes. She shook her head, understanding now, and feeling a new sense of comfort and trust, she embraced him once again.

Unexpectedly, and to everyone's surprise and shock, they heard a voice say, "You have to go south." They all turned to find Sam/ Gabriel standing there.

"Gabriel, thank God you are here," Dunstan said with a sigh of relief. "Gabriel, they came at me once again, but this time they targeted Angela. Somehow they tied her to me!"

"I know!" Gabriel responded.

"If you knew, where were you?"

"It's a big world, and furthermore, you are quite capable of taking care of yourself, just as I thought! Like me, you would find a way! All is well, that ends well." Gabriel paused a while and then went on to say, "Andrealphus, you have to physically take them south, to the great Angel Falls in Venezuela."

Dunstan started to ask a question, but Sam quickly stopped him, "No questions, this is very important! You will find a way, and I'll be around! Go now!"

Dunstan turned once again to Angela, and looking directly in her eyes asked, "Are you with me?"

Feeling more confident about their relationship, Angela nodded her head as she now trusted and believed in him.

He then pulled her close and kissed her lightly on her forehead. Suddenly, her knees buckled, and Dunstan quickly held her weight, "Are you okay?"

She just smiled and said, "I'm sorry!"

"It's no problem! Angela, we have to go now! If you have personal items here, get them now! We will call and alert the necessary people concerning us leaving! Also, we can pick up clothing and other personal items along the way."

"Where are we going?"

"Have you ever been to Venezuela?" he asked.

"No, I haven't!"

"You'll like it there!" As he stepped away from her, he turned to where Gabriel was standing but noticed that he had left them. He instantly shrugged it off for he knew his style. Then he quickly called out to Julian, who had seconds ago walked to his room. "Julian, we are going on a trip! Pack a bag as you have four minutes tops!" Dunstan quickly glance at his watch, saw that it was 7:40pm, then he rushed to his room to pack.

℮∕℮

In Riverside, California, at 5:40pm, 2 hours and 10 minutes from 3:30pm, Frank, James and Agent Anderson ended their meeting. As James and Frank headed to Outback Steakhouse for their dinner meeting with Nathaniel, James' phone rang. He looked down at the phone and saw that it was Nathanial calling. He immediately answered, "Hello!"

"James, my friend, we should be there in 20 minutes, on time. Listen, if you get there before us, I need you to wait in the parking lot until we get there."

"Not a problem," James responded, and then hung up. James turned to his father and repeated Nathanial's request and then added, "Expect an electronic search and a pat down."

Smiling, Frank looked at James and said, "Oh, I kind of like this excitement, but truly I'm hungry for that steak dinner, so hurry up, let's get there."

When they arrived at the parking lot of Outback Steakhouse,

James backed into a parking spot, so that he could see when Nathanial arrived. Three minutes later, they heard the roaring sound of Nathanial's Shelby mustang and then they saw it. James quickly flashed his head lamps to indicate where they were. Nathanial saw the flash, headed towards it and aggressively pulled into the empty spot alongside them.

"James, you are a punctual guy," Nathanial shouted over the loud roaring sound of his muscle car's engine to James, who was literally only 4 feet away, and staring directly at him through his rolled down window. After shutting down the motor, Nathanial added, "And I like that!"

Simultaneously, they all quickly exited their vehicles. Nathanial walked quickly and directly towards James' father and said as he held out his hands to shake his, "Mr. Carey, I'm so pleased to meet you. James, I see the resemblance." Then looking Frank directly in his eyes, Nathanial flamboyantly added, "Sir, she didn't lie on you."

With a puzzled expression on his face, Frank looked at Nathanial and said, "Excuse me, she?"

"Yeah, James' mother! She didn't lie on you being his father! You get it?" Nathanial declared, not realizing that he had a sick sense of humor.

Frank smiled and chuckled a bit, "Mr. Parker, I thank you for your flattery! It is also nice to meet you."

Suddenly, they heard the sound of Nathanial's car trunk been slammed shut, so they all turned to find Richard standing behind them with a metal detector in his hand.

Nathanial quickly looked over at James and said, "Sorry James, I know we have been through this before, but I've got to check you again, and of course, your Dad. You never can be too careful."

When they entered the restaurant, took their seats, placed their order, and began the meeting, they heard the sounds of two unruly children playing and eating two booths down from them. They were a distraction to the meeting. The parents seemed to be having a difficulty calming their kids down. Nathanial, tired of repeating himself in the meeting, quickly stood up, caught the eyes of the two kids, unbeknown to their parents who had their backs to him, and gave them a nasty stare. Surprisingly, they quieted down immediately. Nathanial sat back down and asked, "Okay, where was I?"

"You were saying that we need to have the same underlying principles to work as a team," Frank responded as he recaptured the conversation.

"That's right! Frank, your son here seems to share the same beliefs we share," Nathanial added, holding Frank with his intense stare.

Looking over at his son, Frank, with a quick grin, responded, "Being my only son, we seem to see a lot of things the same way, despite the fact that we don't see much of each other anymore lately. I guess I get to blame myself for that! He loves his mother, so I'll just leave it at that."

Nathanial sat quietly at that moment because the waitress had just brought their ordered drinks. As she turned to walk away, Nathanial said, "I understand, so I won't pry. Frank, share your views on the outcome of the Presidential elections! I know I heard your son's opinion, and need I say, that I was pleased. But I need to hear your personal thoughts?"

While sipping on the draft imported mug beer he had ordered, Frank leaned forward and started shuffling around the salt and pepper shakers, and then said, "My personal thoughts... I believe the country is on the right track. But listen, being a company man at one time, I don't wish to discuss politics. My son already briefed me on the basic principles you live by, but if it is all the same to you, I wish to remain anonymous. I'll be the guy in the dark you can go to." Then he turned to his son for a bit of approval. Slowly pushing the salt shaker towards Nathanial as if he was playing a game of chess, he added, "It's your move! What exactly is it you need from me, and when do you need it?"

Nathanial leaned forward, turned his head to the left to look at

Richard and then turned back to Frank. He whispered, "I respect that! I respect your privacy and you being straight up with us." Pushing the salt shaker back towards Frank, he said, "Okay, let's move from the salad and go straight to the main course. Weapons! I need lots of them."

"Any particular type?" Frank asked.

"The type you use in war because that is exactly what we are preparing for," Nathanial said as his eyes stared aimlessly around for he was concerned about maintaining their secrecy.

"You must have deep pockets because that's not going to be cheap!" Frank replied.

"I know that! Listen Frank, this country is pretty much divided, and there is a large fraction on our side of that division, that shares our views, and are committed to supporting us to no end."

"That's a lot of support, but you do know you can purchase weapons of war over the counter these days? The NRA has secured that right for you for a long time now, haven't they?" Frank asked as he admired the big porter steak he had ordered, coming his way.

"Yes, you are right, but they are also limited. If you can tell me or show me in this world where I can buy a grenade and a rocket launcher over the counter, then you have the right to ask me, why on earth are we sitting here?"

"You've got a point, but I'm going to need some time," Frank said softly because the waitress was placing their food on the table.

The four of them quickly went quiet as they focused on their food. Nathanial looked at Frank's large porter steak, and asked, "Dude, are you able to eat all of that?"

While Frank was diving into his plate like a diver at a swimming pool, he looked up but did not lift his head, and said, "Watch me!"

✧

On Thursday, November 10th at 8:00am in London, England, Sandra heard Carla's bedroom door open as she was pouring herself a cup of coffee. Sandra looked over her shoulder and said, "Good morning, do you want me to pour you a cup of coffee?"

"That would be wonderful, thank you very much," Carla replied as she walked towards the balcony's French door to open it.

"Sandra, you don't know how pleased I am to be out of that hell hole! I see now how much we take for granted! We're so cavalier when we throw our moral fortitude to the wind," Carla declared as she stretched, and took advantage of her balcony's view.

Sandra walked up to Carla and passed her the signature mug of coffee. Weighing in, she said, "You're so right as these past few days have completely turned my life around. It's no longer how I once saw it! I called my mother yesterday morning around the same time you were still missing. I was pretty hesitant in doing so, but I did it anyway. Carla, I found it hard to explain to her what was happening, so I lied and told her everything was fine. I was hoping that things would turn out for the better, but I hated doing that!"

Carla sipped her coffee, tilted her head to look at Sandra and said, "Girl, don't worry yourself about that as what you did is commonly looked at as being justified. Some would call it a necessary white lie! I would have done the same, had I been in your shoes! You would have only worried her, especially since you did not know what was going to happen to me. Now, you can call her again and engage her in small talk to erase your guilt. And if I were you, I would do just that, engage her in small talk. Don't even try to explain what we had experienced." Carla then looked across the living room at the clock that was near the kitchen. It showed 8:08am. "Damn! I have to get ready! I've got to meet Sheila Hall at their headquarters at 9:30, for a debriefing. I wonder why she used that word. She probably momentarily confused me with one of her agents. Sandra, check this out, Agent Carla Wallace 007! How does that sound?" Carla asked as she stood clowning in the living room mirror, mimicking James Bond with a finger gun.

"You crazy girl, you better get ready before you miss your first assignment," Sandra said as she blew her off with a hand wave.

Sandra then asked, "Carla, on your way, can you drop me to the mall?"

"No problem, but you better hurry up and get ready for if I'm late because of you, I may have to shoot you," Carla replied as they both chuckled and walked to their rooms.

9:30am London time at the MI-5 headquarters, Sheila Hall, and Agent Russell, along with Stanley, Carla and Genevieve, were on the main work floor with a team of technical Intel agents who were linking various countries throughout the six continents, and diligently deciphering the information that was downloaded from Genevieve's software.

Madrid, Spain was the first to liaise with London's MI-5 office when they took down a similar operation like the one found in Surrey, England. Before long, secret intelligence agencies throughout the G7 countries were working on the down low, seeking out work stations throughout the world, that were changing human behavioral patterns to advance their agenda through cyberspace and social media. Sheila was approached with an array of disturbing information that linked the Russians to a lot of nefarious acts, including their heavy involvement with the New World Order movement. The information also indicated that the Russians were using their military Intel to dump or disseminate information on social media websites to tip the scales of the elections towards their selected candidates who would work in their favor within the major G7 countries.

"My God, this is heart wrenching to say the least," Sheila said as she read through hard copies of the briefs. Then she quickly rushed to a nearby phone, dialed her secretary's extension, and exclaimed, "Pamela, I need you to set up a conference call meeting with the director of the FBI immediately." She started looking feverishly around the room, "Where is Paul? Agent Russell, where is Paul?"

"He told me he needed to go home because he hadn't seen his grandparents since this all began," Brent replied.

"Couldn't he just call them? Sheila asked with a touch of insensitivity.

"Seriously boss, we all get to go home, so why shouldn't he? I know you are concerned about our national security, and that he has an inside connection with our guardian angel, but a big part of him is also human! Do you remember the main part of the angel's message? "When they open the window for us, we would open the door." And yes, when they opened the window, we did open the door."

Sheila stood quietly for a moment, and then said softly, "I guess you are right! Please keep him on speed dial." She immediately went back to the phone that she had previously hung up because she realized that she had to inform Director Buckley of their findings and their upcoming conference meeting with the FBI director.

Meanwhile, at the mall Sandra stood in the mirror of a women's department shoe store, modeling a new pair of winter knee high boots. She smiled her personal approval and looked over at the female store assistant for hers. The young lady nodded with a smile and a thumbs up gesture. Smiling, she walked out of the store with her bagged new pair of boots. As she stared around thinking about where to go next, her eyes suddenly became fixed on a web café. She sensed an urgent need to check her emails and social media contacts because her phone wasn't allowing her that capability since she was in another country.

Sandra sat down at a computer post, with a purchased latte. She tapped a few keys, entered her password, and seconds later she was looking at her account. While she was going through her emails, she couldn't help but notice a young Caucasian male three chairs down from her, excitedly cheering out loud about the candidate who had won the presidency of the United States of America. Sandra couldn't help but notice him because he was an annoying distraction.

Normally, it would have been a case of her thinking that ignorance is bliss and, thus, would have just ignored him and mind her own business. But what immediately captured her attention was when a sassy, short, bleached blonde, wearing dark sunglasses, and who appeared to be in her early twenties, approached the young male. She was carrying over her shoulder a designer bag that Sandra had seen in a catalogue and would have loved to buy, but was never able to find. The young lady's demeanor was the complete opposite of the young man's. She struck Sandra as being more reserved and deliberate.

The young lady sat in the chair next to the young man and started a conversation, which Sandra was feverishly trying to eavesdrop on. At first it appeared that the young man didn't hear a word she was saying, but that was mainly because of his arrogance and the fact that he was gawking at and flirting with her. The sassy blonde ignored the obvious as suggested by his shallow character, and continued with her reason for being there. It sounded as if she was giving him information on a particular website that his type might be interested in. She then stood up, got directly behind him to gain his full attention, and lightly rested her hands on his shoulders to tell him how to pull up that particular site. That was when Sandra noticed that her sassy, bleached blonde hair was a wig. This peaked her curiosity—mmm, she thought, why the disguise? Why the dark sunglasses, and blonde wig? This girl was incognito.

When it was clear that he had found the site, she sat down again, looked at him and smiled. Then she reached out to put one of her hands on his hand, which was obviously a manipulative move, and said, "I'm with that group! You need to follow their instructions."

The young man took his eyes off the screen, turned to her, placed his hand on top of hers, and asked, "And if I do this, can I get your number?"

She immediately stood up and said, "I will be back here tomorrow at the same time, and then we will see."

Chapter 32

As soon as the mystery lady left the web café, Sandra signed out of her account, picked up her bag and quickly walked out, sensing a strange urge to follow the young lady. As she exited the café, she quickly looked left and then right, and spotted her walking among other shoppers. Keeping some distance away, Sandra, very curious, followed her. She soon realized that the girl was heading towards the mall's exit.

Suddenly, a strange cellphone's ringtone sounded from Sandra's bag. It was a tone she wasn't used to because it was the phone Sheila Hall had given her so that she could keep her informed about Carla's kidnapping. Sandra's mind was so engulfed and focused on following the mystery lady that she questioned herself, wondering when her curiosity would subside. Because she was not used to the ringtone, she did not pick up on it right away. As the mystery lady approached one of the mall's exit doors, Sandra realized it was the phone that Sheila Hall had loaned her. As she followed the young lady out of the door, she answered the phone. "Hello!" It was Carla.

"What's up girl? Why you took so long to answer the phone?" Carla asked on the other end.

"Sorry, I didn't hear it right away! Where are you?" Sandra asked as she feverishly looked up and down the sidewalk because she had momentarily lost sight of the girl.

"I'm turning in the mall's entrance right now. Where are you?"

Carla asked as she quickly stepped on her brakes for a crossing pedestrian.

"Right out front, where you dropped me," Sandra answered with a bit of relief because she finally spotted the girl climbing into a black four door SUV/GMC Yukon with tinted windows.

Seconds later, Carla pulled up. "Hurry up and get in, I got an urgent call to use the restroom," Carla exclaimed as she looked around frantically as though she expected one to conveniently pop up for her. "There we go! TGI Fridays, thank God, what a fitting name!" Carla said as she made a beeline for the restaurant she had spotted in the far corner of the mall's parking lot. Carla quickly pulled up to a vacant spot. Opening her door, she turned to Sandra, and with a head gesture said, "Come on in! We might as well have an early lunch." It was 11:45am.

"Sounds good to me," Sandra responded being somewhat of a big girl with a hearty appetite.

Sandra was seated at a table for two. While waiting for Carla to join her, she couldn't help thinking about the mystery lady.

There were three male occupants in the black Yukon. The male occupant, who sat in the front passenger seat, turned to the young lady and asked, "How did it go?"

The mystery lady took off her sunglasses, and ripped off her wig. It was Caroline Boles, Carla's newly found innocent friend. Yes, she was the Caroline Boles, who Carla befriended back in the Surrey bunker's takedown. She responded, "Great! We need more of those web cafés as they can be very useful to use and recruit new, potential workers."

The three males in the Yukon were fallen angels or primal subjects that were selected from various outposts in Europe. The driver, Moloch's earth name was Edward Knowles, back seat passenger, Chemosh's earth name was Mario King and the front seat passenger, Dagon's earth name was Wesley Wright. He was the appointed group leader of the three males.

"Those fallen angels are destroying our coalition by revealing our plot," Wesley said, looking back at Caroline who was sitting in the back seat. He added, "Miss Boles, great plan! I see where you are going with this—subcontract freelancing. With that we can structure a pyramid with built-in rewards for individuals who are self-motivated and want to move up in the ranks to achieve their and our ultimate goals."

"I'm impressed," Caroline exclaimed. "You thought of that all on your own? Very good! You're spot on for that is exactly the plan," Caroline added, smiling at Dagon/Wesley. "Now, we have to complete what we started with this Carla Wallace because she is our link to regaining the earthly strength we lost following that unfortunate physical touch of that first incarnated fallen angel," Caroline lamented as she searched in her bag for Carla's business card that Sheila Hall had given her.

Note: Caroline Boles was one of the most recent, and one of the few human beings, who was incarnated by dark fallen angels. She was taken over by Belial, one of the six top generals of the fallen angels. Only the top generals of the fallen angels were able to achieve this as it was a very rare occurrence.

After using the restroom, Carla sat down with Sandra, fanning herself with her hands. Feeling relieved, she gestured and cried out, "Woof, I truly thank God for TGIF restaurant for I damn near wet myself!"

They both chuckled, not even noticing the waitress who had quietly approached and was standing over them.

"May I take your order, please?" she asked.

Suddenly, Carla's phone rang. While she dug into her bag for the phone, she said to Sandra, "Whatever you are having, I will have," and then she answered, "Hello!" A pleasant glowing smile appeared on her face because she recognized the voice on the other end. "Caroline, what a pleasant surprise!"

"Hello Miss Wallace, I'm calling to thank you for taking me

under your wings and being so nice to me. I was wondering, is there any possible way I can repay you?" Caroline asked in an all so innocent tone.

"Are you kidding me? Don't even mention it," Carla replied, changing her mind on wanting Sandra to order for her. She feverishly pointed out on the menu what she wanted to the waitress.

"Well, I thank you anyway, Miss Wallace."

"Hold on Caroline, don't go just yet. How about you joining me and my cousin, Sandra, for dinner tonight?"

Caroline paused for a while not wanting to appear too eager, and then with a bit of excitement she responded, "I would love to, what time and place?"

"Is seven o'clock okay with you?" Carla asked.

"Seven is fine as I have nothing to do. I must tell you, I'm not too familiar with London."

"You shouldn't have a problem finding me. Are you driving?"

"No, but a few of my family members have given me some contacts in London that should be able to assist me," Caroline responded.

"Great! Here is the address! Got a pen?"

"Yes! Got one, shoot," Caroline said smiling but had a sinister look on her face.

"Pond Mills, 151 West, 34th Street, Unit 4, #16."

"Got it! Miss Wallace, I would like to say once again, thank you for reaching out to me in that situation I was in. You are what most people would call an angel sent from heaven."

"You are so sweet! Again, don't mention it! Oh, Caroline, enough of this Miss Wallace business! It's Carla, Carla is my name. Okay, don't forget, dinner's at seven o'clock! Bye, bye!" Carla said, smiling as they both hung up.

"Who is that?" Sandra asked with a look of overwhelming curiosity on her face.

"Caroline! Oh, that's right, I forgot to even mention her to you, with the back and forth last night after what we both went through. I met her during the bunker takedown. Sandra, you have to meet her."

"By the look on your face, she seems to be an extraordinary, young lady," Sandra replied, rather astonished as she slowly rubbed her chin.

"Sandra, I don't know why I was so drawn to her, but I guess it was because she had this somewhat of a lost child's demeanor about her," Carla said, looking aimlessly at the ceiling and appearing to have an array of thoughts on the subject.

"Carla, I think you just stole my thunder!"

"Girl, what are you talking about?" Carla asked as the waitress placed their drink order on the table.

"Well... if you have to know! I was playing a bit of detective myself! I was also observing a young lady with a strange demeanor in the web café of the mall."

"How so?" Carla asked.

"Well, she approached this young man and befriended him. At the time I thought he was a total idiot, and before you ask why, I think he was and is an idiot because he got all loopy and jubilant when he found out who had won the presidency of the United States. I'm so sorry Carla, if you don't share the same sentiments as I do, but I do feel that he is also an idiot. Hear me, and hear me good, all those who support that man's behavior truly and secretly believe in that behavior," Sandra said, gripping her butter knife, pretending to be angry even though she had an annoyed look on her face. Then she added, "Carla, I pray you don't throw me for a loop by saying some dumb shit right now, like believing in that BS."

"Calm down girl, I agree," Carla replied, quickly changing the subject by returning to their initial topic. "So Sandra, tell me more about this girl."

"Okay! Where was I? Right! She seemed to be giving him instructions, which I found rather strange, and get this, I know she was wearing a disguise because that was a damn wig she was wearing, and to top it all off, she was wearing dark sunglasses indoors. Well anyway, after she had sold him on whatever she was selling, and wooed him into falling for her, she got up and left. Then I did too, and started following her."

"Why did you follow her?" Carla asked, looking at her wide-eyed.

"I wanted her bag! Just kidding, but really that bag she had—I was looking for that type and style for a long time now. But seriously, I somehow felt compelled to follow her. Long story short, you called, I answered, and then I saw her jumped into the back seat of a black SUV Yukon and they left. That's all and now we are here. That's it!" Sandra said as she started to clear her side of the table for her food order that was been placed in front of her.

"That's it? That's your thunder? You didn't get a license plate number? Sandra, what kind of detective work was that?" Carla snapped sarcastically but jokingly as she draped her table napkin across her lap.

"Ah, shut up and eat!" Sandra shot back with a snarl. She then asked, "By the way, how was your so called debriefing?"

"Great! I have been given another assignment, and don't ask me anything about it, because I'm not allowed to say! MI-5 secret stuff, you understand?" Carla said jokingly, cracking a smile.

"Yeah right!" Sandra responded, shaking her head.

They both went silent as they ate their food. Two minutes later, Sandra broke the silence, "Carla, about our friend Paul and our guardian angel—Have you seen or heard anything from either of them?"

"Yes, but only Paul. I asked Mrs. Hall, who told me he had to go home to see his grandparents. God, they must have been worried, but I miss him already, and not because of the divine presence, but they have both made drastic changes in my belief system and my way of thinking. Sandra, you know, we are truly bless! Hey, I have to ask, why the deep contempt for this new President?"

"Carla, it's different with me than it is with you. I live there, in Deep South, Georgia. You would be amazed to see how many bigots are crawling out of the woodwork. The federate flags seem to be planted in every ten houses I pass. Carla, I don't think you really get it—when the United States sneezes, the world catches the cold, and trust me it's not the common cold I'm concerned about!"

Chapter 33

Meanwhile, back at MI-5 headquarters, Sheila hand-picked a few other tech agents to work with Agent Brooks. As a team, they began dissecting information on this worldwide conglomerate situation. Stanley and Genevieve also sat in their meetings to give them key information on it. Following the bunker takedown in Surrey, England, Sheila and the MI-5 team reached out to all of the intelligence agencies within the G7 countries. Their covert instructions warned them to tread carefully as they sought and weeded out those who were working within the New World Order takedown within their own governments.

Sheila quietly walked behind Brent who was looking down on the team that was feverishly hacking information from a number of linked outposts. She tapped him on his shoulder and said, "I need you and Genevieve to meet me in my office in five minutes."

Brent turned to Genevieve, who was looking in his direction, caught her eyes and nodded her over.

Stanley also caught the secret move, and when Brent saw him, he finger-beckoned him over, "Listen Stanley, the boss wants Genevieve and me in her office in five to discuss some other matter, so I need you to stay with these guys because you know this operation, and you are a tech guy yourself. Oh, and Stanley, I want to thank you for coming through for me! You did and are doing the right thing," Brent added as he patted him on his back.

Five minutes later, Genevieve and Brent were standing in the doorway of Sheila Hall's office.

"Hey guys, come on in! Agent Russell, close the door, will you please?" Sheila added as she gestured to Genevieve to have a seat.

Suddenly, Sheila's intercom sounded. When she picked up the line, it was Pamela, her secretary, "Mrs. Hall, the call you were expecting is on line three."

"Thank you Pam! Oh, and Pam, please take the message on any other call."

Before Sheila switched over to the call, which was a video conference call, she quickly briefed Genevieve and Brent as she turned her desktop's screen towards them, "This is Madrid. They took down a similar operation, but this time they were able to collect some interesting material." Then she quickly pushed the button to connect the call.

"Mr. Pardo, how are you doing today?"

"I'm doing very well, thank you," he answered.

"It's great of you to share this information with us. I have invited two of my colleagues to sit in on this meeting since time is of the essence," Sheila stated as she looked over, and nodded at both Genevieve and Brent. She threw a soft smile at Genevieve even though she knew she wasn't a colleague.

Pardo decided to skip the small talk and immediately went on to his findings, "We have collected quite a bit of material, but I think you may find this one quite interesting," Pardo said, lifting up a bottle.

"Isn't it too early for cocktails, Mr. Pardo," Sheila rejoined, injecting her dry sense of humor in the conversation.

"Very funny, Mrs. Hall, but I don't drink, and I'm glad I don't! I won't be the one tricked into drinking this, now that I know its contents," Pardo replied with a bit of humor that was void of a smile.

Pablo Pardo was a fifty year old veteran who had served his country for thirty years. A distinguished, no nonsense individual, he was the Deputy Director of Spain's National Intelligence Centre.

Pardo turned to his department's chemist, Leonardo Andrada, who took the bottle and explained in detail its contents, "This bottle and its compound's base alcohol were made in Russia. Now upon testing, we also found traces of triazolam halcion and eszopiclone in it; these are drugs to induce hypnosis! In short, they can alter one's way of thinking and behavior." Leonardo looked directly into the camera and unconsciously panned his head left to right as if he had a live audience sitting in front of him. "These drugs affect the cerebral cortex of the brain. Coupled with indoctrination, they will ultimately alter one's subconscious thoughts," Leonardo explained.

Because of his broken English, Sheila interjected, "Sorry sir, I'm not quite understanding you! Can you repeat the last sentence?"

Leonardo turned to Pardo with a faint look of frustration on his face. Pardo, in turn, nodded him on. He turned back to the phone's camera and simply said, "Mrs. Hall, they are using drug enhancement liquids to assist them in the indoctrination of their people in order to get them to do their unscrupulous work for them."

The room became deafeningly silent as Sheila and Brent turned to look at Genevieve. Then Brent suddenly remembered the discussion he had had with Stanley on that very subject in the interrogation room. He immediately reached out and placed his hand on Genevieve's shoulder, and was casually about to ask her a question, "Genevieve..."

But Sheila quickly interrupted by rejoining the conversation with the deputy director, "Mr. Pardo, now I understand clearly! This is crazy stuff, but excellent work executed by your office. Listen, if it's not a problem, can you please send me information on the other material that you found, so that we can work jointly on this?"

"Not a problem, you got it!" he replied.

As Sheila gave him a thumbs up, and signed off, the screen went blank.

ᥫᩢ

At 6:00pm, Brent and Derick met at their favorite local pub to discuss the materials they had gathered from their operation. They ordered two lite beers.

Twenty-five minutes later, the waitress approached their table for the third time, "Are you guys okay?" she asked.

Suddenly, Brent's phone rang, and shaking his head to indicate that they were fine, he answered, "Hello!"

"Agent Russell, Patricia Taylor here! Look, I need you to come down to the lab right away!"

"On my way," Brent replied as he quickly hung up. "Yo Champ, let's go! That was Patricia, the medical examiner. She wants to see me right away."

While lightly scratching his cheek, Derick abruptly replied, "No rest for the weary! My guess is it's about the mysterious death of our Mr. Jeff Stewart. Okay, let's go," he added as he quickly swilled down the last mouthful of his Amstel Lite.

On London's busy streets, Brent was weaving in and out of traffic when his phone sounded off once again. "Hello," Brent quickly answered.

"Dude, what's up with the erratic driving? The man is dead, so I'm sure he can wait," Derick said with some sarcasm. Driving behind Brent, he was trying to keep up with him.

"Sorry bro, I just got this strange sense of urgency."

"Gee, that was fast! It felt like I just hung up my phone from you," Patricia quipped as she pushed open the two way swing door to the examination room. "Come on in here guys," beckoning Brent and Derick to follow her. As they were entering, a diener was rolling out a sheeted corpse. Derick jumped back with a bit of fright.

"What's up buddy? You scared of dead bodies?" Brent asked, giggling and staring at Derick with a sly grin.

"Dude, I just don't like morgues, okay! Furthermore, I'm going to wait out here."

Brent suddenly stopped, slowly turned to face his retreating buddy, and with a half-smile asked, "You what? Dude, man up! Get your ass in here. You need to hear this stuff too!"

Reluctantly, Derick followed him into the examinations room.

Picking up her chart, Patricia turned to Derick and exclaimed, "Big, muscular, gun-carrying man like you are afraid of the dead?"

"Look, it's just that I don't like this cold, icy feel that this place gives me. Now, can you both just leave it at that, and let's get on with it?"

"Alright, alright guys, let's get down to business," Patricia said as she flipped through her paperwork. "Agent Russell, this case is strange, to say the least. Upon my examination, I found no cause of death! It's as if this gentleman had fallen asleep, and strangely enough, just stopped breathing. Okay, let's set that aside as being a mystery, but check this out—when they brought him in here yesterday, he had a clenched right fist. Luckily, rigor mortis had not set in, so I simply unclenched his fist and bingo, your mystery death became a puzzle," Patricia said, holding up a female's necklace that had a charm attached to it.

"Does it have an inscription?" Brent asked as he reached out for the necklace with a gloved hand. On closely examining it, he saw the initials, CB. "CB, CB, does that mean anything to you?" Brent asked as he turned to Derick.

"Commonwealth Bank comes to mind, but that's because I bank there," Derick replied frivolously, knowing that that explanation didn't help.

Brent quickly pulled his phone out of his pocket, and a few seconds later mumbled, "I'm getting something, but I'm not quite sure..." Speed dialing Sheila Hall, he asked, "Hello boss, does the initials CB mean anything to you?"

"What do you mean?" Sheila asked on the other end.

"I'm down here with Patricia Taylor in the examination room where our mysterious dead guy, Jeff Stewart is. He had a necklace in his closed fist, and it has a charm that has inscribed on it, CB."

"CB, CB," Sheila repeated, thinking out loud. "Oh my God, Caroline Boles, could that possibly belong to her? Agent Russell, Caroline Boles is the young lady Carla befriended at the Surrey takedown. If that is truly hers, how did he get it?"

"I don't know, but I can do with a bit of divine intervention right about now." 'Where is Paul?' he thought to himself as he rejoined the conversation. "Boss, I've got to go! I'll call you right back." When he hung up, he quickly searched for Paul's number in his phone. Upon finding it, he quickly pressed the call feature.

On the third ring, Paul answered, "Hello!"

"Paul, my friend, how are you?"

"I'm fine! How about you?"

"Work, work, you know, it never stops! But listen Paul, we need your help here. Derick and I are down here with our pathologist and we're examining the mysterious death of Jeff Stewart. He had a necklace in his closed fist. Its inscription is CB, and now, we're thinking it belongs to Caroline Boles, the new, young tech worker Carla befriended in Surrey. What do you think about that?"

Pondering the information he had just heard, and receiving confirmation via his divine intervention connection, Paul replied, "It's a body jump! You have to find that girl, but be careful because one of the primal subjects has taken her over."

Suddenly, a beeping sound came over Brent's phone. It was an incoming call. "Paul, I hope you and your friend can join us. I've got to go, got an incoming call. Hello!"

"Agent Russell, I think that girl and Carla are going to meet up. Find Carla, and you will find her," Sheila said, unaware of Brent's call to Paul.

"Boss, it's worse than we thought! I just spoke to Paul, and he claims that a primal subject has taken her over! I'm going to call Carla right now. Boss, we need to get a team over to Carla's right now!"

"I'm on it," Sheila said and then hung up.

Brent quickly looked at his phone's time—it was 6:53pm. He immediately dialed Carla's number.

ه/פ

Back at Carla's condo, Carla shouted from the shower, "Sandra, check the pasta for me please! Caroline should be here any minute now."

"I'm on it," Sandra responded.

With the sounds of the shower and the music playing in the living room, no one heard Carla's phone ringing in her bedroom.

Back at the lab, as Brent continued redialing Carla's number, he tapped Derick on his shoulder and said, "No one's answering! We've got to go!" It was 6:57pm. Then Brent's phone rang again! It was Sheila.

"Agent Russell, I have diverted a team to you. They were engaged in a live fire training session, so they are in full gear, and should be there in thirteen minutes."

"Good! Link me up with the lead tactical agent using our three-way feed. We have to be prepared because if Caroline Boles is who we think she is, we will have a situation that involves primal subjects, similar to the one we had in Surrey."

"I hear you! Give me a second," Sheila replied. Twenty seconds later, she returned to line, "Agent Russell, go ahead!"

"Hello, hello, to whom am I speaking?"

"Bruce Thompson, lead tactical training agent."

"Agent Thompson, are you up to speed with this unique situation we have been dealing with?" Brent asked as he and Derick ran out to their cars.

"It was our priority during our training session this afternoon," Agent Thompson calmly replied.

"Good, you got the address, right?"

"Got it, and we are heading there as we speak," Agent Thompson said, blasting through the traffic with their wailing sirens and revolving lights.

"Agent Thompson, I need you to take it down a notch! Go in stealth! Be silent! On your arrival, park outside the security gate at the compound, and wait for us as we're just a few minutes away. Set up a checkpoint for exiting vehicles, and prepare to enter the grounds on foot. Her unit is probably very close to the security gate! I will dispatch an air stand by unit for air recon. It will be some distance away so as not to cause an alarm."

Meanwhile, a strange gust of wind blew viciously but briefly outside of Carla's condo. It came as if out of nowhere. It had blown down a single high stand potted plant Carla had out on her balcony. Sandra jumped with fright when she heard the crash! Immediately she saw what had happened and ran out onto the balcony to pick it up. While doing so, she glanced off to her left, for she had a clear view of the parking lot of the complex, and noticed the black Yukon she had seen earlier that day at the mall. It was backing up into an empty parking spot. Sandra stood up immediately and began walking backwards into the condo, her mind racing with curiosity. She was startled when she heard the doorbell rang. She mumbled under her breath, "I got it!"

Chapter 34

Sandra turned and walked slowly towards the front door, her mind riddled with red flags. Squinting one eye, she peeped through the peephole. As she looked through the convex fish-eyed peephole, there stood Caroline Boles on the other side. Bells immediately sounded off in her head. She stepped back and then forward once again. It wasn't so much the girl that caught her attention, but it was the handbag she was carrying that triggered in her mind somewhat of a strange connection. Yes, the mystery lady was carrying the same handbag she had wanted to buy back at the mall. She recognized her even though she was not wearing the wig and sunglasses.

Sandra quickly turned and ran to Carla's bedroom. When she got to her door, Carla quickly pulled her in, closed and locked the door. Holding her phone to her ear with one hand, Carla beckoned her to be quiet with the other. Carla had already gotten the information about Caroline Boles. Brent Russell was on the phone with her right then, giving her further instructions. "Okay, okay," Carla said as she ran to her bedroom window, and pulled the drapes shut. She ran over to Sandra, grabbed her by the arm, and quickly pulled her into the walk-in closet, quietly closing the door behind them.

Highly stressed, Sandra frantically whispered, "Carla, that's the girl in the mall that I had told you about! She's at the door!"

"That's the girl?" Carla blurted out as she held the phone to her ear, listening to Brent's open call.

"Carla, she is not alone because that black Yukon I told you I saw back at the mall is parked in the complex's parking lot!"

"What's going on? What are you guys talking about?" Brent excitingly asked over the phone as he quickly approached the compound of Carla's condo, which was just up ahead.

"Agent Russell, Sandra just told me that Caroline is not alone. They are in a black Yukon parked on the compound!"

"Stay in your room! We're coming in right now!" Brent replied as his car squealed to a stop, alongside the tactical team's van.

The doorbell rang a few more times and then stopped. Then there was loud knocking on Carla's door.

Brent, Derick and the team, which were seven in total, quickly advanced towards Carla's unit. As he ran over a grassy knoll, Brent spotted the black Yukon, and quickly signaled three team members over and whispered, "That's the subjects' vehicle! Occupants may be inside, count unknown! Go!"

All of a sudden, three of the Yukon doors opened simultaneously, and three primal subjects stepped out, Moloch, Chemosh and Dagon.

The general order was shoot to kill on sight. Immediately the three tactical agents took their positions and silently voiced out their targets over their headset radios—"I got the left!" "I got the right!" "I got the center!" Three silent suppressor shots were fired in unison so that they sounded like one single shot! They were followed by the flopping, muffled sounds of three fallen primal subjects, who hit the ground hard! There you had it—three head shots, resulting in a flawless takedown.

Seconds later, Brent heard aggressive banging on Carla's door as his eyes immediately caught a bright flash of light, like a lightning glow, on Carla's balcony. Suddenly, there was a loud boom—it was the sound of a complete breach of the front door.

In the walk-in closet, Carla and Sandra hit the floor, holding and wrapping each other in a tight ball.

Caroline walked through the open doorway with an angry,

ghostly look on her face. She casually stepped on and over the broken front door. Her attention was quickly drawn to a rocking lazy boy chair in Carla's living room; its back was facing her. She silently approached the chair. Suddenly, the chair swung a one eighty, and to her surprise Angel Raphael was sitting there facing her. (The bright flash of light that Brent had seen moments ago had emanated from Raphael).

"Are you that stupid to think your prey would be sitting here, after hearing the racket you just made?" Raphael asked softly as he casually stood up.

"What are you doing here?" a deep voice from Caroline asked.

"What am I doing here? I'm a guardian angel! But the question is, what are you doing here?" Raphael's eyes piqued with curiosity as he stared intensely at Caroline.

"Belial, is that you?"

"Yes, it is!"

"I thought I recognized that voice!"

"Good for you! Now you can go back to where you came from because this is our world now!" Belial angrily exclaimed.

"My! Look at what you have become—using the cover of this child to do your dirty work for you!" Raphael declared as he stood, towering over Belial/Caroline.

Belial was one of the top ranking members of the dark, fallen angels. These angels were determined to capture Carla so that they could hold their sacrificial ritual to drain the remnants of purity which had been left behind by Raphael when he first incarnated her. This would increase their strength to what they had had before when they were in heaven. This, in turn, would enable them to reign supreme over the strongholds of true, God-fearing, empathetic Christian believers. Raphael knew that this was their plan, but had to slip away after Carla's abduction. Now however, his senses had alerted him of Carla's and Paul's dilemma.

"Step out," Raphael demanded. "You are one of the generals, right? Come on, step out because I'm thinking this incarnation thing may be beneath you! Come on, give me a hug, angel to angel!" Raphael taunted, flamboyantly sarcastic.

"Get out of my way! Go back to where you came from! This is not your world anymore!" Belial cried out, obviously frustrated and extremely angry.

Raphael took one step back and asked, "Is that so? Listen, I have no time for these childish games you are playing here. But I know one thing, neither you nor she is leaving here!"

Suddenly, a greyish beast-like creature started to emerge from Caroline. When the manifestation was completed, there stood before Raphael an awful looking, torn remnant of a fallen angel. He had a drooping, broken wing. Frightened and crying uncontrollably, Caroline quickly separated herself from the two and ran to a corner of the living room.

Without taking his eyes off Belial, Raphael said softly, "Have no fear my dear! You are safe now." Turning to Belial, he exclaimed, "You look awful! What are you in? Denial? Through the eons of time, you haven't figured things out yet? Given your arrogance, I guess that's impossible! Evil sure paints an ugly picture! The immorality in this world is a definite reflection of you. If it is any consolation to you, you have done a great job in tearing this world apart. I am sending you back!"

With astonishing speed, Raphael reached out with one hand and gripped Belial by the throat. After asserting tremendous pressure on it, Belial slowly went down on one knee, fruitlessly attempting to muscle back in defense. Soon afterwards, there was a gurgling roar, followed by whimpering sounds. This puzzled Raphael because he didn't know why it was so easy to take Belial down. Was it that Belial had already started to fall to the grips of the pits of hell? Raphael pulled out his sword, and held it high. He looked down at Belial, whose labored breathing was like that of a fish out of water. As he wondered whether this slaying was really a mercy killing, he held his sword with both hands, and came down hard, swiftly plunging it into Belial's chest. Belial expired immediately. Raphael then quickly turned and walked over to Caroline, who had now become herself again. He reached out his hand for hers, and she responded, looking up at him with teary eyes as a soft smile came upon her face. A feeling of comfort engulfed her.

Unbeknown to Raphael at the time was the fact that Belial's rapid drain of strength was because he had incarnated Caroline Boles who was truly a blessed individual. She was just lost and confused at that stage of her life. Some call this God's fail safe mechanism. After simply touching Caroline, Raphael figured out why he was able to take down Belial so easily.

Suddenly, Raphael perked up on hearing the MI-5 tactical team, who were positioning themselves outside the breached doorway. He looked down at Caroline, and on stroking her head, and nodding at her, he quickly turned and walked onto the balcony, disappearing into the night.

Caroline looked towards the door to find Brent standing there in awe. Between the quick glance he had of Raphael's disappearance, and the beast-like angel on the floor that finally collapsed and quickly became a pile of ashes and dust, he shook his head, caught himself and started shouting for Carla.

Sounds of scrambling was coming from Carla's bedroom when all of a sudden a boom was heard—both Sandra and Carla had ran into the bedroom door in their haste to get out. Carla ran directly towards Brent, almost knocking him down with the force she ran on him with.

"It's okay! It's okay!" Brent said over and over again as he struggled to keep both of them from falling.

Sandra let out a scream when she saw Caroline standing in the far corner of the living room.

Brent quickly jumped in, in her defense, "She is alright now! What was in her is no more!"

Then they both followed his eyes, looking down at the smoldering ashes and dust on the floor.

⁄◌

It was 1:30pm in Southern Georgia, not far from Florida's border, on a Thursday afternoon, six hours from London's time of 7:30pm. In an unknown, high level racist town in Valdosta, Georgia, Dunstan had just slipped his bank card into an ATM machine. He decided to check his balance before making a withdrawal. All of a sudden, his head snapped back when he saw the figure that appeared on his balance receipt slip—it was a seven figure amount, a lot more than his salary allowed. He smiled and quickly looked up to the bank's ceiling and quietly gave thanks to God for this was clearly His work.

Dunstan, Angela and Julian had left Dunstan's home in Birmingham, Alabama yesterday evening. They drove south until 10:30pm when they decided to check into a motel in Valdosta, Georgia to get some sleep. They were only able to rent two rooms that night, one for both he and Julian, and being the gentleman that he was, the other for Carla, so that she could have her personal privacy.

Their destination was Miami, Florida because that is where Copa Airlines had flights to Venezuela. Dunstan quickly pulled his money, receipt, and card out of the machine, and then turned to open the door of the bank's vestibule area. A Caucasian man, who looked to be in his middle thirties, stood on the outside of the glass door looking strangely at him. Dunstan opened the door, and held it for him out of common courtesy. The man accepted the gesture, but snarled at him in response. Dunstan quickly ran across the street to the motel. He was feeling a bit uneasy about the racial tension that was deeply seeded in this little town. Yes, this town was filled with alt right groups, and White Supremacists.

At the room's door, Dunstan slipped his key card into the lock, and quickly looked left and right, and then over his shoulder to ensure that their rooms were not being watched by members of any of these groups given the racial tensions evident in the town. When he opened the door, Angela and Julian were sitting there doing their own thing. Julian was watching TV, and Angela was calling family and friends to reassure them that she was doing fine. She was trying to convince them that she had decided to take an early vacation because of an overlooked time factor at work.

Chapter 35

When Dunstan entered the room, both Julian and Angela looked up. "Yo Julian, you're going to get square eyes watching too much of that TV! Turn that down a bit for me please," Dunstan quipped as he lowered his hand. "Listen Julian, this town is not friendly towards Angela and me as Negros!" Smiling softly and taking a few hundred dollars from his wallet, he added, "I need you to go to the office and pay for another night. We're going to leave tonight, but tell them we will be checking out tomorrow morning at 11:00 am. We will use the drop box for the room keys."

"What's going on? Why the covert operation?" Angela asked.

"I'm uncomfortable with this high level racial tension I sense here! I'd much rather avoid a physical altercation, and furthermore, we don't need the distraction or the attention. What we do need is to get to Caracas, Venezuela as soon as possible. We will leave tonight, under the cover of darkness. So both of you get as much sleep as possible because you know I can't drive. We need to get out of this town and state. I would like to be in South Florida as soon as possible. There are lots of friendlier people there."

"Oh, Angela, how are we looking on the flights?"

"Right, right! Okay, Copa has a 10:00am tomorrow from Miami to Caracas, Venezuela, and a 3:00pm from Miami via Havana to Caracas, Venezuela. I'm just waiting on you to decide. Oh, and also, we're going to have to take a small commuter airline from Caracas to Canaima National Park, and then from the national park to Canaima town. Because there are no roads between the two, we'll have to fly again to access Angel Falls. Then there's the hard part, the boat ride, and the hike to the falls."

"10:00am—lock it in, and use my card," Dunstan said, quickly pulling out his credit card and handing it to her.

"Are you sure about this?" Angela asked as she hesitantly took his card.

"It's a lot of money, but I can cover this! You know that, right?" she added with a smile. Angela was concerned because Dunstan's job didn't pay much.

"Angela, everything we have been experiencing lately has been rather shocking, wouldn't you say?"

Angela nodded slowly.

"Well, you should have seen my face ten minutes ago, when I saw my balance." And with a sly smile, Dunstan said, "Use the card."

Five minutes later, Angela stood up and said, "Okay, 10:00am it is! We're locked in, but we have to be at the airport at 8:00am. Okay guys, I'm going over to my room and try to force myself to sleep," Angela said, stretching her hands and almost hitting the overhead ceiling fan. "Oops!" she quipped, quickly pulling down her arms to her side. She looked down at Dunstan, who was sitting at the table.

"Can I see you a moment?" she asked as she started to walk towards the door.

"Okayyy...." Dunstan said as he got up to follow her. Two doors down, at room 205, Angela quietly opened her door. Walking inside, she pointed to one of the double beds in her room.

"Have a seat Mr. Archer, we have to talk!"

"Oh boy, am I in trouble?" Dunstan asked with a boyish demeanor.

Angela sat down facing him on the opposite bed, "No, of course not! Give me your hands."

Dunstan extended his hands to hers, and Angela held and squeezed them tight. "I'm not feeling or receiving anything!"

With a soft smile, Dunstan looked at her and said, "I'm not sending out anything."

Angela was struggling very hard to hold back her emotions, but it showed anyway on her face because she was blushing.

"Listen, I'm trying to be serious here! Stop making it difficult," she said as she shook his hands, and began rocking from side to side.

A warm smile flashed across Dunstan's face, and laughing softly he exclaimed, "Ha, ha, I'm not doing anything! Girl, you crazy, you know that?"

"Yeah, it's because you're making me crazy! Dunstan, you said very little in the car when we were driving from Alabama, why was that? I need to know more! Look, it's obvious! I believe in you right, but it's only natural for me to want to know much more, in light of what's been going on around us," Angela declared as her voice trailed off into a whisper.

"Listen," Dunstan started to say, but was distracted by the sounds of children's laughter as they ran passed the room. "Look, there's a lot I want to tell you for it's literally out of this world! Angela, you believe in angels, don't you?"

"All my life, and it's because I believe in our Father above too," Angela replied, pointing her finger to the ceiling of the room.

Dunstan chuckled a bit and said, "I like that!" Then he reached out for her hands and went on, "In the beginning I came from far away, right from where you just pointed! I fell out of our Father's grace. Angela, I've been here a very long time, trying to work myself back into His grace. During my stay I was not just Dunstan Archer! I was here long before cars were invented! There were many others during my time too."

"Wow, so why is it you've been around them so long and haven't learned how to drive?"

"I don't know! I guess I just wasn't that drawn to them! Perhaps, you can teach me some day. Okay, with all that said, I guess I'm now your Guardian Angel."

Suddenly, a knock came at the door, and both Dunstan and

Angela looked up at the same time. Dunstan got up, walked over to the adjacent window, and pulled the drape, "its Sam," he said as he quickly opened the door. "Sam, my friend, come on in!"

Sam just stuck his head in the door, nodded at Angela, and then said to Dunstan with a head gesture, "Let's take a walk!"

Dunstan turned to Angela with a quick glance and said, "Sweet girl, get some rest! I'll see you later."

Just as Dunstan was about to close the door, Angela called out, "Dunstan!"

He turned back to face her.

She then lip-whispered, "I want to be more!"

Dunstan paused for a few seconds to take in what she had just said, and staring directly in her eyes, said, "We'll talk about it soon."

Both Dunstan and Sam casually walked east, up from the motel. They walked up the dual lane, two-way main street to the traffic light, when they saw a park on the other side of the junction. They then turned left to cross a pedestrian crosswalk located on a two-way street that made an easier path to the park. Two minutes later, they sat down on a park bench under a big oak tree.

"How are you holding up?" Sam asked.

"I'm holding, but I must admit, I'm a bit shaky crossing the streets around here."

"How is that? You are a full-fledged angel! How is it you don't sense the arrogance and ignorance that sit over this town like a dark cloud?" Sam asked and then smiled at him. "You're just now figuring this out even though you've been down here so long? Dunstan, arrogance and ignorance sit over this world like a dark cloud! Remember, that's why we are here!"

Dunstan threw his head back and exhaled like a blow fish, "Okay, you got me there, so why the walk?"

"I'm going to be a bit busy, and so are you. We all need to be at certain points on this globe. I'm going west and then north, to the Great Falls. You will be guided by your instincts, so follow them!

And oh, take this," Sam said as he reached into his pocket and handed Dunstan a little pouch that had a drawstring.

"What is it?" Dunstan asked as he started to open it, and then he answered himself, "Oh! My, my, it's a heaven stone." He held a crystal stone that was an inch in diameter. He marveled at the mere sight of it. "Thank you, Gabriel! This is the closest to home I have ever been. You know this is special to me!"

"I hope so, because you cannot lose it," Gabriel/Sam said. "Andrealphus, massive changes are going to take place, and arrogant people will suffer if they choose not to see the light in time. There will be a slow meltdown through painful sickness that will be directed at the evil fools of this world. It will affect some quicker than others, for there are a lot of lost, misguided souls out there, but we can only help those who are trying to help themselves."

Suddenly Gabriel's/Sam's attention was caught by a middle-aged woman who was walking pass the bench about fifteen feet away. He had caught her looking at him as she walked by. Her appearance was odd—her hair was jet black, and her face was pale. Her mascara had drained down her face as if she had been crying. She wore a black dress that was below her knees but it did not match the sneakers she was wearing. Gabriel/Sam took a double look for yes, he was very observant; but then, he decided to dismiss the strange thoughts he'd have of her and rejoin the conversation.

"What's up?" Dunstan asked, not noticing the lady, but just the blank stare that Sam momentarily had.

Sam said nothing but just nodded to him, indicating that he should continue with what he was saying.

Dunstan continued, "Gabriel, do you know what always bothered me throughout my stay here? There are so many people who sit back and do not see the obvious! They blindly believe in heresy."

"Andrealphus, they are the exact mirror image of Lucifer, who is narcissistic, and conceited. His vision is limited, and he is shallow-minded. Those who are led by him think and believe what they see from their heads and not from their hearts." Gabriel replied as his eyes caught sight of a flock of birds flying overhead. He quickly pointed up to them and said, "Look! Now that is freedom! Using common bird sense, they fly away from bad weather but Lucifer's doctrine is to have his people simply and blindly walk into it. His people are more convinced that it is best to follow what they see, or what they consider to be tangible. If it is something they can't touch, they won't believe in it. So it is obvious that they need to understand the intricacies of this world and every creature that walks the face of it! This in itself should tell them that there is a lot more to this world than meets the eye."

Dunstan reached out and softly touched Sam's hand and said, "Don't look now, but off to your right there is a patrol car that's pulled up to the curb, and that cop is watching us. I was watching! He circled twice before, and now he's watching us. It's been at least two minutes now."

Sam heard Dunstan, but his only response was, "Lake Rabun."

"What? Lake Rabun! Sam, you weren't listening to what I just said about the patrol car!" Dunstan exclaimed.

"Lake Rabun! You and that stone need to go into Lake Rabun. That is the lake beneath Angel Falls. About that car—I have seen you swing through trees one hundred and fifty feet high, and you are worried about that little puppy!"

"Of course I'm not worried! It's just that I thought I need to be a little more discreet while on this trip."

Sam just got up and said, "I'll see you soon!" Then he started to walk off.

"Wait, wait, aren't you going to at least walk me across the street?" Dunstan asked with the demeanor of a child.

As he walked away, Sam just turned to him, smiled and shook his head.

Just for fun, Dunstan decided to push on with his clowning behavior as Sam got farther and farther away. He stood up from the bench and started to rant and rave, "Okay, okay, that's just fine, and you call yourself an angel! You're just going to leave me hanging here! Well, I hope it hurts you real bad when you find me hanging somewhere else!" Then he turned aimlessly in a circle, and looking up at the tree they had been sitting under, said, "Yeah, maybe from this tree! Yeah, you go ahead! I'll be right here, hanging!" Dunstan quickly caught himself when he remembered the cop, who was still there, staring at him. Then, all of a sudden, the police car took off.

Chapter 36

Dunstan finally mustered up the courage to cross the street as he was jokingly thinking that a lynch mob would soon be running after him. The thought was quickly interrupted when he saw Julian and Angela walking up the sidewalk from the motel directly towards him. As their distance closed, Angela shouted out, "I tried to call you!" And as they got closer, she added, "I asked Julian to walk me to the store that he'd seen earlier as it may have what I need. I need more stuff."

Dunstan quickly looked at his phone and saw the missed call that somehow had dropped. "Angela, I'm not comfortable with that. I thought you had gotten your go kit from the store when we were leaving Alabama."

"I'm so sorry babes, but in haste, I forgot a few things. I'm a female, so I need more stuff," Angela quipped as her smile trailed to a giggle.

Dunstan just stood there in shallow thought, but couldn't help smiling back because of how cute she looked when she said, "I need more stuff." Then he cleared his smile, and declared, "Angela, just because Julian is white, doesn't *change* things! In fact, it will only compound them all the more, because now, you're going to have hatred mixed with jealousy."

"Stop worrying! We'll be fine," Angela replied as she reached out and pinched Dunstan on his cheek.

Then they parted ways. As Dunstan walked away, he stopped to look back at them, thinking maybe he should go with them. But then, he quickly waved it off as he knew his senses would alert him should anything happen.

℮∕©

It was now 7:40pm. Dunstan picked up the motel's phone to call Angela's room.

"You up?" he asked.

"You just woke me!"

"Good, we need to leave, how much time do you need?"

"Ahhhh, I need to shower, so give me twenty-five minutes."

"You got it," Dunstan said and then hung up.

Thirty minutes later, when Dunstan had just finished putting their bags into the trunk of the car, and was closing the trunk, he noticed a patrol car coming up the side street of the motel, its side door spotlight on. The light, beaming throughout the parking lot, stopped on Angela's car and momentarily on Dunstan's face, and then it was turned off as the police officer pulled away.

Travis Jones was the officer who appeared to be stalking Dunstan. Yes, he was the officer at the park earlier that day. Officer Jones, aged thirty-three, served thirteen of those years on the force. He was also a member of an Alt right group, who mixed himself up with any and everything that pertained to white supremacists' activities. It was a terrible combination for a police officer. Officer Jones constantly engaged in unsavory acts, and was, at this time, plotting yet another. He was forced to work day shifts because he had been reprimanded many times before, given the many complaints about him with regard to profiling black motorists. He had been known to intentionally leave his body and vehicle video cameras off to avoid recording his nefarious acts. Now he was elated because he had to work overtime since one of his colleagues was ill.

Officer Jones quickly gunned his car to cross the dual lane

two-way main street that put him on the other side and into the parking lot of a strip mall, directly across from the motel. He backed up his car into the slot across from a pharmacy as it gave him a clear view of the in and out traffic of the motel.

All three of the doors closed almost simultaneously on Angela's Acura. She started the motor, and then quickly pulled out her phone. On her phone's GPS, she requested the quickest route to Florida from their starting point.

The phone's GPS came alive when a female's voice began giving street directions. Angela pulled up to the side street and turned left as the GPS' voice sounded, "At one hundred feet, turn left on Franklin."

Angela waited for the traffic to clear, and then quickly gunned the car, turning left to join the traffic lane on the right.

Across the street, in the strip mall's parking lot, Officer Jones slammed his patrol car into drive and took off after them.

"Ah shucks," Dunstan sounded out with disgust as he glimpsed over his right shoulder, which his eyes barely caught, the officer in pursuit of them.

"Angela, don't look back, and please don't panic, just drive at the speed limit," Dunstan quietly said as he slouched a little and leaned back into his seat to get a better view from his side mirror.

Angela couldn't help tensing up as she nervously asked, "What's going on?"

Suddenly, the GPS sounded, "In 1/8 of a mile, turn right onto 12th Street."

Angela quickly flipped on her right signal, and then started to cross over to the right lane. Because she was nervous, she proceeded to turn through a corner road that was just before 12th Street.

"No, no, no, wrong turn," Dunstan whispered. But it was too late, she was already committed. Suddenly, their back glass lit up like a Christmas tree! It was coming from the patrol car's blue and red flashing lights.

"Damn!" Dunstan said as he kissed his teeth.

"I'm so sorry," Angela said as her face drooped into a harsh-looking sulk.

"Don't worry about it, but I think you need to get your driver's license and credentials out."

Angela started to reach over to the glove box when Dunstan quickly stopped her. "Not now! Wait until he asks for it!"

Then without looking back, Dunstan said, "Julian, no sudden moves, please!"

Officer Jones was smiling to himself because he knew that this unfortunate turn for them was a twisted and ungodly blessing for him. How fortunate can he be to order a stop in a dark, dead-end alleyway? It was perfect for him to perform his untamed urges of nefarious acts.

It was 8:16pm. Travis Jones intentionally placed a clipboard between the video camera's mounted lens and the windshield of the patrol car, so if he needed to explain, he could claim he had placed it there by accident. He pulled out his side arm to double check that it was loaded, and then he quickly opened the car door, stepped out, and proceeded to walk to Angela's side door. As he walked over, he turned off his newly issued body camera.

Even though Angela knew he would be approaching any second, she still jumped with fright when he tapped his Glock 22 on her window. This gun drawn procedure was only supposed to be used in heightened awareness situation, but Officer Jones used it all the time when he profiled black motorists, to heighten their fear.

Angela quickly powered her window down.

"Mam, I need your driver's license, registration and proof of insurance," Officer Jones quickly spewed out.

"Just a moment," Angela said as she reached over to her glove box and pulled out her registration and insurance. Then she reached into her handbag for her driver's license.

"Here you go," Angela said as she passed her credentials to Officer Jones. She quickly glanced over at Dunstan, who was looking at his watch.

Officer Jones quickly glossed over her registration and insurance, and handed them back, but he kept her license. He then proceeded to walk around the car to Dunstan's side. He beckoned Dunstan to power his window down.

"Boy, step out of the car."

"What is the problem, Officer?" Dunstan asked as he looked at him with his eyes staring cross at him.

Officer Jones took one step back, and placing his hand on his weapon, he repeated, "I said, step out of the car!"

Dunstan disgruntled, slowly opened the door and said, "Where do you get off calling me boy? I'm old enough to be your father, you disrespectful young man! You should be ashamed of yourself!"

"Just shut up, and let me show you why I stopped you," Officer Jones said as he walked Dunstan to the rear of the vehicle.

"So what is the problem?" Dunstan asked.

"Broken taillight!"

"Where?"

The Officer quickly smashed the rear right lamp with his night stick, and said, "There!"

Both Angela and Julian jumped as they looked back in fright.

"Are you serious?" Dunstan exclaimed as he took one step towards the Officer.

"Step back," the Officer ordered, thrusting the night stick into Dunstan's chest that caught him in his solo plexus. Dunstan keeled over from the shock and pain. Then he quickly regained his composure and posture, and said, "I guess that's why you shut your vehicle and body cameras off!"

Officer Jones paused for a second, slanted his head and slyly asked, "How did you know that?"

Dunstan casually put both of his hands on his waist and said, "I didn't! You just told me!"

As he rushed to write the ticket, Officer Jones quickly attempted to brush it off by saying, "Yeah, I'm having glitches with my system!"

Three minutes had gone by since the officer lit up their vehicle.

Dunstan then started a purposeful dialogue, "I imagine you have probably responded to a few traffic accidents, and you probably know about the five minutes' memory loss that occurs before and up to an accident when the occupant of the vehicle suffers a concussion."

When Officer Jones finished writing the ticket, he ripped off a copy of it, and handing it and Angela's license to Dunstan, asked, "Who are you? A doctor or something?"

"No, no, not a doctor, but I'm going to need your copy also."

"What do you need my copy for?"

All of a sudden, and with lightning speed, Dunstan punched the officer with such a force that the impact immediately knocked him out. Dunstan quickly kneeled down over his unconscious body, casually took his ticket book out of his hand, ripped away his copy, tossed the book on his chest, and quietly said, "Because she is not paying for this!" Dunstan separated the two tickets, kept Angela's copy on hand in case they were stopped again for their now broken taillight, and then he stood up, and stared down at Officer Jones for three seconds. Finally, he quickly flipped his wrist to look at his watch and whispered, "Five minutes." Then he turned and walked away.

Twenty one miles outside of the little town that Dunstan, Angela and Julian had just left, an early model tarnished pickup truck sped up to the barn of a farmhouse that sat on a large acreage in the countryside, It was the dusk of the day. The truck's driver quickly locked on its breaks fifty feet from the barn. As the dust settled, two of the three occupants exited the truck from the driver and passenger side. The third passenger, who was sitting in the middle of the bench seat, followed several seconds later. A distinctive pair of sneakers, followed by the tail of a black dress, stepped down onto the dusty ground.

Bess Addison was the lady at the park, who had locked eyes with

Gabriel/Sam. Bess, thirty-eight years of age, was born and raised in that little town outside of Valdosta in Southern Georgia. She was heavily involved with the evangelical church, and that was mainly in the beginning because of her parents. At the age of twenty-three, she married twenty-four year old Hank Addison. A year into their marriage they had a baby boy, whom they called Beau.

Three years ago Hank and eleven year old Beau were killed in a car accident—a drunk driver was to blame. Even being known as somewhat of a prescient, for this accident, she had not vision. Ever since then, Bess was not the same. She closed herself in, and was often heard by others asking the question, why would God allow that to happen to my family, when all my life I worshipped Him, the Almighty? Eventually, she turned away from the church, and went into seclusion.

However, two weeks ago, she joined a satanic cult. She hadn't mentioned anything to her immediate family, but they all shared their concern about her because her attire had changed to this Goth-type appearance.

Bess closed the door of the truck and walked slowly behind the two other occupants that had ran ahead of her.

Billy, the young driver, began banging on the barn's gigantic door, "Bam, bam, bam!" Bess stared left and then right at the many vehicles that were parked outside the barn as she slowly approached the large door.

A shuttered window of the barn's door quickly slid open. Then Billy, the truck driver, said, "She is here."

Chapter 37

They heard an iron bar clanked on the inside of the barn's gigantic door, and then sounds of the rollers as the door slowly opened. A head stuck out! It was that of a bouncer type looking white male, who looked to be in his forties. He quickly looked left, then right, and beckoning with his hand, he quickly said, "Come in, come in."

On the inside there were at least forty people performing some sought of weird, ceremonial ritual. Thomas, the big guy, quickly walked the three of them over to the far right corner of the barn, where a gentleman, who wore a rolled up sleeved dress shirt, stood alone. He had loosened his tie and was also wearing a black dress trousers. I guess you can say he was half-suited. He was the fallen Angel, Amazarak, and a teacher of sorcery whose earth name was Frank Smith. Frank stood in silence for a few seconds staring at the three. Then he reached out his hand to Bess, immediately pulling her close. He began inhaling deep breaths through his nose as if he was trying to pick up a scent that was unknown to humans. Frank quickly waved to get the attention of a man that stood with the others at the ceremonial table.

The man leaned over and whispered to a female, "I'll be right back!" Buford Dixon was the owner of the farm. He was one of the few large property owners within this cult that hosts these large rituals three nights per week. Becky, his wife, whom he had just whispered to, stood there as she blindly watched him walk away, deeply curious about what was going on. She was a subservient wife, even though she often disagreed with her husband, and found herself feeling uncomfortable about many of the decisions he made, but she tended to be dismissive. But anyone, who is both passive and dismissive tend to also be biased, and is often looked at as being complicit.

"What's up?" Buford asked.

"Need to get into your house," Frank responded, as he pulled his phone out to place a call. As he pushed the barn's back door open, he asked over the phone, "How soon will you be here?"

Before the other side responded, Frank heard a roaring and flapping sound. He quickly looked up and saw an incoming helicopter. "Okay, I'll see you soon," he said, and then hung up.

The helicopter touched down off to the side of the main house's driveway. When the blade speed and the dust subsided, the rear door of a bell 407 opened. Out stepped a well-dressed male, a primal human clone subject, who was another high ranking fallen Angel, called Apollyon. He was the angel of death, whose earth name was Ben Shaw.

Ben, along with his mate Elizabeth, approached Buford, Frank and Bess, and together they walked up the steps to the veranda of the main house. Buford took the lead as he opened the front door to his house. Once inside, he took no time in pointing at Bess, and in a demanding tone, beckoned to her as he pointed to a chair, "Have a seat!" He quickly slid another chair over to face her, and then sat. Looking Bess directly in her eyes, he asked, "You have something to tell me?"

Earlier that day, after the visual encounter Bess had had with Sam/Gabriel, she met up with Billy and Anne, the pickup truck driver and his girlfriend. Billy had driven her to the farmhouse's barn. She told them she had seen an angel. Bess and her special ability allowed her to obtain information that Sam and Dunstan revealed in their conversation, which they had had at the little town's park. Bess didn't disclose any details about this information to Anne and Billy, only the fact that she had seen an angel. Bess just sat quietly before Ben.

Then he asked her again, "What is it you have to tell me?"

"I think I saw an angel," Bess responded.

"Is that it? Did this angel say anything to you?" Ben asked in a tone that showed that his patience was running thin.

Bess just sat there, noticeably upset but passive. She said nothing.

Ben quickly stood up and demanded that she do the same. He silently beckoned her over with a two-handed, four-fingered silent gesture that said, 'Come here'.

Bess quickly responded, "I don't think I'm comfortable doing that!"

Ben took two quick steps towards her, and then he reached out, held her head in both of his hands and said, "I don't give a shit about your comfort level! Just stand still!" He then slowly pulled her into his chest and cradled her as if she was his lover. Then he quipped, "Yes, yes I see, I see!" Immediately his mind began downloading all of the information Bess observed in the park. Suddenly, he stopped and pushed her away.

Bess just stood there with a humble look on her face, hands to her side, and her head hanging low.

Ben slowly looked over at Frank, and waved him over to join him so that he could accompany him to the adjacent room.

"Good job! I think we're on to something. When I held her in there, I saw a lot as there was very little resistance. But there is something about her," Ben said as he pulled out his phone to make a call. Suddenly, he held his thought.

"What are you thinking?" Frank asked.

"Not sure, it's just something about her," Ben replied as his voice trailed off into a whisper.

Frank quickly chimed in, "When I first met her, she did seem to be harmless and distraught. She just recently joined this cult. I would say, it's been two weeks now."

"Wait a minute," Ben said, rubbing his chin. "I remember this lady! We had broken her three years ago, and singled her out because of her special abilities, and then we had taken her family. She is in religious remission."

"But she's stronger than you think, and she was special to him upstairs. She still appears to have the traits of a special one, but her prescient ability was in question because she was not able to envision the demise of her husband and son. That had diminished her beliefs, which in turn placed her in religious remission. There is a lot of strength we can gain from her sacrifice," Ben added as he continued to make his call.

The phone call was answered on the second ring. "Hey, this is me! I have great news," Ben continued the conversation as he walked away from Frank. He explained to the listener on the other end, the details of his encounter and the information he had obtained. Ben told the listener everything, except the part about Bess being clairvoyant and special, not to mention that she was also very ripe as a sacrifice.

"Hey, you didn't tell him that she was also special," Frank said as he had managed to eavesdrop on the conversation.

Ben just snapped at him, "This is our take! You want capable wings, don't you?"

Before Frank could respond, Ben said, "Come, let's go gut this lamb."

Ben quickly walked back into the foyer of the house, reached out for his mate Elizabeth, and while stroking her hair he said, "I have a surprise for you!" Then he looked over at Bess and repeated, "I have a surprise for you too! Frank, lead the way!"

Buford stood there completely clueless, and then followed. He asked, "What's going on?"

"Come, come," Ben said in response.

As soon as Buford opened the back door to the barn, chants were heard from the people inside, who were continuing with their ceremony.

Ben quickly walked up the steps onto the makeshift platform, and simultaneously taking his suit jacket off, he handed it to the main speaker in exchange for the mic. He introduced himself, "Hi! My name is Ben Shaw. I know most of you don't know me, and some of you may have heard about me. Anyway, let's cut to the chase. I'm sorry to interrupt your ceremony." He quickly looked down at the side of the stage, and catching Bess' eyes, he waved to her to join him. Then he said, "Ladies and gentlemen, I am proud and delighted to introduce to you this courageous, young lady. Some of you may know her, Bess Addison. Come on up Bess," beckoning to her as he tucked the mic under his arm to lead off with the applause.

Frank ushered Bess forward, who reluctantly walked up the steps.

As the small crowd cheered her on Ben continued, "Bess here has volunteered to share her soul by offering herself as a sacrifice."

Bess quickly turned to Ben with a shocked look on her face as he pulled her close and whispered in her right ear. "Why are you so shocked? Isn't this what you wanted, to go and be with your family that we took from you?"

With her head hung low, and a mild-mannered demeanor, she slowly rose to the occasion. Reaching out and beckoning for the mic from Ben, she said softly, "If this is to be my demise, may I at least have a few words in closing?"

With the mic in hand, Ben turned to the crowd and said, "Bess here wants to have a few words. Would you like her to give us a few closing words?"

The crowd moaned, and went on chanting meaningless words. Then suddenly, a single voice shouted out, "Quickly! Get on with it!"

"Here you go, you've got the floor," Ben said, passing Bess the mic.

"Hello everybody," Bess said in a slow, calculated, passive start, "Three years ago, March 23, I suffered a very significant blow," her voice trailed off almost to a whisper. Then she continued, "I lost my husband and my eleven year old son, Beau, in a car accident."

306

Since this was an apathetic crowd, another cold voice shouted out, "Boo hoo! Let's finish this already!"

Bess just nodded at the cold gesture, and went on, but this time she took on a much more confident demeanor, and came off sounding like a professor giving a lecture.

"I thought my life was over! In fact, it was over! I clamed up, and there were many times I rolled myself into a ball and cried. You see, I was a strong Christian woman with special attributes. They called me clairvoyant as I'm able to see things before they happen. But I did not see that accident coming? How ironic? That compounded the blow even more. Through so many unanswered prayers, my faith slowly eroded away, and then I joined up with you guys. I guess you can say I was looking for answers on the other side. Then there was a major seismic shift in me that made a change again. It happened on a quiet afternoon, when I was sitting on a park bench in town. I was still pondering my dilemma when an elderly man approached me. At that time it seemed as if he had come out of nowhere. He even knew my name. Then he asked with a smile, 'Bess, how are you doing today?'"

"I was taken aback, as I nodded okay to him, but I didn't recognize him as someone I should know. I wasn't angry, no, not at all because of his innocuous demeanor. Oh! I'm sorry for using such big words. I meant his appearance appeared to be harmless. He then sat down beside me, and asked, "Have you ever heard the expression, 'disappointments are for the best?' People tend to use it loosely, not knowing there is absolute truth to what it says. Bess, your loss, as tragic as it may be, is your gain. Disappointment also changes a person. Some people have to change to gain. Yes, before the accident, you weren't all that good, but yet you thought you were, because you were involved with the church. The majority of churchgoers get involved with the church, thinking it will give them an easy pass for their closet or bad behavior. Then he turned to me and said, 'Thinking is the operative word. People tend to think and rely on their minds and not on their hearts and souls.'"

Bess then went quiet for a few seconds, as she looked out over the on-looking crowd. "Look, look at yourselves, now! What are you thinking about? Look at you, you are standing there waiting on a sacrifice to drink someone's blood because someone had this masterful thought and said this is what you ought to do. How stupid is that?"

The crowd became disenchanted as sounds of boos could be heard.

Bess then quickly jumped back in and said, "Okay, okay, this is my closing! The man then said that he had a two-part question that required a two-part answer even though it was an ambiguous one and a strange way it was worded. He added that it would be a rather simple one, once I used the right application to answer it. He hoped that I would be successful in responding to it."

"He then held my hand and said softly, 'Bess, what I am trying to say is use your basic God-given, heart-rooted instinct, that which will trigger your mind. People often make mistakes by relying on their mind, and their mind alone, which is pure arrogance. They think they are gods, and this is their world. Now Bess, ask yourself and answer this two-part question.'"

Bess went quiet for a few seconds and then went on. "Needless to say, with the right application, I successfully answered the question. Now in my closing, I will ask it and then tell you the answer. It is 'Why I am?' 'Who I am?' Answer: 'I was created by God and given the will to fulfill my Father's wishes. Now I am who I am, for I have not. The second part means you can change.'"

Bess stood there, looking over the crowd's clueless faces, and then she said, "Let's see how much common sense you all have left. I see there are two exits in this barn; you have very little time, so I suggest you use them."

Suddenly, a strange deafening quietness came over the barn, and then the sounds of rumbling thunder, that was slowly growing louder. Bess quickly turned and walked up to Ben, thumped him in the chest with the mic, and boldly said, "You didn't break me, you just made me!" She quickly turned, faced the crowd once again, and looking at them with disgust, threw her hands into the air and shouted, "Lord, let thy will be done!"

Immediately, a lightning bolt hit the joist of the right corner ceiling like a missile projectile. It was followed by a thunder crash. Instantly that corner of the ceiling burst into flames, and came crashing down. A few seconds later, two more strategic lightning strikes caused 90% of the ceiling to come crashing down on the gathered crowd.

Screams and cries could be heard from a distance as people, who were on fire, ran around aimlessly. Then a bright light lit up the skies like daylight. There was also a humming sound like a hawk diving for its prey. It was Gabriel in his full angelic form. He quickly swept Bess off the stage and away from the turmoil.

Chapter 38

About 400 yards away from the barn in a nearby creek, Gabriel gently sat Bess down on a large stone five feet away from the running stream.

"You stay here! I'll be back," Gabriel said as he turned and flew away.

Bess sat there listening to the distant screams of farm and wild animals, including the sounds of wild birds, and then she heard a voice.

"Don't worry, he won't take long!"

"Jesus! You frightened me, old man! What are you doing here?" Bess exclaimed as she turned to see Sam approaching her. He had a warm, welcoming smile on his face.

"I'd much rather you call me Sam, than to remind me of my age," Sam said casually as he sat down beside her.

"Sorry Sam, didn't mean to fluster you, but did you see that? I was carried by an angel."

"You ought to get used to it as you are in like me. There is going to be a lot more, you'll see."

Bess just sat there in amazement as she mulled over her now newfound life. Then she quickly looked over at Sam, "Sam, you were right, because everything you'd said would happen, did happen. So how did I do?"

"I wasn't there. Now that you are here, my guess is that you did well," Sam replied as he stood up and saw that the barn was completely engulfed in flames.

Earlier Sam had met with Bess, prior to her walking passed both he and Dunstan on the park bench. Her visit to the barn was all intentionally planned and prearranged. Sam/Gabriel had left Dunstan out of this plan for a good reason.

"Let's go!" Ben shouted to the pilot of the helicopter as both he and Frank ran full speed from the burning barn. They had managed to escape the destruction of the barn. But it was not the same for his mate, Elizabeth as she was trapped, along with the others. Ben Shaw did not care! He was heartless. He would just simply find another.

The rotor blades of the helicopter were already at full speed for lift off, but suddenly, there was a flame out in the jet's turbine engines. A gust of wind picked up, and then quickly died down— both Ben and Frank stopped in their tracks because of Gabriel's sudden appearance before them. Immediately, they shed their human clone bodies to reveal their true identities, evil looking monsters with unfeathered wings.

Gabriel stood there in full, angelic glowing form as he slowly pulled out and raised his sword. From a faraway distance, way beyond space, a lightning bolt flashed and left its trace. From the tip of Gabriel's sword, down to its base, a white heat glowed brightly, revealing their monstrous faces. "Amazarak, and Apollyon, I can barely recognize either of you. Is it because of the fall you took on such a beastly look? To send you back would be doing you both a favor, wouldn't you say?" Gabriel asked as he took on a warrior's stand.

"We have a lot more control than you think, and yes, we know about your rediscovered friend, Andrealphus!" Apollyon spoke out in a loud baritone voice.

"Trusting him will be your biggest mistake! He ran from us, so he'll surely run from you. He is what these humans call a lone ranger. He likes it here, and will not be going back!"

Swiftly, Gabriel pulled back and held his sword with both hands as he declared, "Apollyon, by the looks of both of you, I would run too! I'm not particularly concerned about whether he goes or stays! It's not my decision. But I know for sure who is going back, and that is both of you; and it's certainly not going to be up there," Gabriel added as he nudged his head up at the moonlit sky.

"I know you, Gabriel, you're not that fast! You can't take the two of us with that one sword."

Suddenly, Gabriel took somewhat of a relaxing stand, and then took a step back to casually say, "Would you be so kind as to allow me to entertain that thought for a while? That's rather interesting! Let's say that that will be so, then one of you gets to go." Gabriel quickly took the offensive stand once again, and asked, "The question is, which one?"

The pilot of the helicopter managed to restart the engines with sufficient rotor speed for he had decided that it was his time to go. He pulled up on his collective control. With a maximum performance lift off, the trust blew down, blindly blowing dust all around.

Gabriel launched forward with his sword, slashed left and then right, and quickly walked over to the headless monstrous bodies, looked down at them, and then flew off into the moonlit night.

While both Sam and Bess sat quietly waiting, a light breeze blew, followed by a gentle voice, "Come, you two! It's time to go for we have so much to do, and so little time to do it." Gabriel reached out both of his hands to help them stand.

At 12:10 pm in one of Washington DC's prestigious lounge's VIP rooms, four of the top far right senators sat in a private meeting.

Smoking a large Cuban cigar, senior senator Richard Wilson, blew out a cloud of smoke, turned to Senator Robert Johnson, a forty-eight year old, slender male with light brown hair, who had just sat down, and said to him, "Ethan here has mixed feelings about what we are doing to change the course of this country. Before you got here, he was expressing his dissatisfaction with our gun control laws, and, I'm sorry Ethan, what was the other?"

"Seating biased Supreme court judges," Ethan replied, finishing Senator Wilson's lapse in memory. Ethan, the youngest of the four, was forty-three years old, of average height, with jet black well-groomed hair.

"Yeah, that's right! Go ahead Ethan, enlighten us more on this fairy tale world you wish to live in. Robert, I thought you said your guy here was on board, but I'm telling you, I'm not feeling comfortable."

"Ethan, what's up? What's going on? You don't like being on a winning team?" Robert asked as his voice quickly trailed off into a whisper because the waitress was approaching him with the drink he had ordered when he first walked into the lounge.

While waiting a few seconds for the waitress to leave, Ethan pulled his chair closer to the table to respond, "Look! I'm all about winning, and I'm also all about tax reduction for large corporations. What I'm not about is having bulls run through china shops, which is a metaphor for having weapons of war on the streets, which any crackpot of legal age can purchase over the counter. The Sandy Hook Elementary School's shootings comes to mind. Come on! Are you all just heartless, or even devils, minus the horns and the tails? Oh! Oh, not to mention the list of buffoon judges you want to select from, to be seated in the Supreme Court. They will simply just turn a blind eye to the truth."

Sitting back and crossing his legs, Richard stuck the cigar in his mouth. Surrounded by a silhouette image of his cloud of smoke, he began mockingly clapping his hands in a shallow round of applause.

"Bravo, bravo, a senator with a conscience, how about that!" Richard declared sarcastically.

"Hey, Richard, you can make light of that all you want, but the President won because he scaled through with the electoral votes. The majority of the country still thinks he is an idiot, and there is going to come a time, as he continues to have diarrhea of the mouth, he will remove all doubt."

Richard slowly sat back in his chair, and with a sinister smirk on his face, carefully crafted his words, "That may be so, young man! Yes, we all can agree that he is conceited, he is a narcissist, and easily manipulated, that is, if you carefully pull the right strings. So, how about it Ethan? Can you be a puppeteer? The president is suiting up his own army and will show force if need be, using just a simple dog whistle, and their cemented belief of making America great again. And get this, because of our gun laws he doesn't have to bear the cost of weaponizing them! Ha, ha!" Continuing to chuckle sinisterly he added, "Millions of his followers are already locked and loaded."

"That is truly dangerous talk, and you know that; yet you find that to be funny? I don't know Richard, but I'm sensing something sinister about the way you put that! If this is true, one may see you as being complicit."

Richard leaned back in his chair, and taking a puff from his cigar, he smiled, "You tell me Ethan, am I being funny or am I complicit? You don't have to answer that!" Suddenly, he changed the subject. "But, he likes to be downstage on every play, so let him shine! Let him do what he does best. Listen, we are on the right side of politics because of our party. I just like to be on the right side of history. There is no harm in that, is there?"

Ethan just shook his head as he looked towards Robert.

"So Robert, this is all a play to you too?"

"Ethan, it's like being on the right side of capitalism."

"Yeah, limited capitalism," Ethan responded as he quickly looked over at Hank.

Hank Smith, the fourth senator, had sat quietly throughout the whole dialogue.

"So Hank, I take it, this sits well with you too? Wait, don't answer that as your silence speaks volumes. Listen guys, I'm sorry if I'm making you all feel a bit on edge and uncomfortable. Yes, my conscience has been sending alarming signals ever since they found Daniel, the other two guys and Rodger Drake at his house, all dead a few days ago."

Suddenly, Richard's head lifted in shock and surprise.

"Wait a minute, you didn't hear anything about that?" Ethan quipped shockingly, looking astonished.

Then Hank suddenly broke his silence and chimed in, "I heard it was some home invasion of some sought."

"Of some sought? You must be kidding me!" Ethan shot back alarmed.

"It was cardiac arrest, all four of them—but what are the odds?" Ethan exclaimed as he ran his eyes over their faces. He added, "And strangely enough it was kept quiet—the news stations failed to mention the manner of death."

Richard quickly jumped back in, and this time with a less aggressive demeanor, "Ever since the elections, I try to stay away from the bad news and the negative and misleading press. But I'm surprised no one told me!" Richard responded in a guilty tone because he had been a mutual acquaintance of Rodger Drake.

"Something weird is going on," Ethan said. "I'd gotten a strange call from Daniel that day, but he didn't make much sense. He said that they were visited by two strange men, who gave them some strange or weird options. His voice started to trail off because his words sounded garbled, barely inaudible. Then the phone went dead."

After hearing Ethan's account, they all just sat there staring at each other.

On Saturday, November 12th, at 1:35 pm, a cloud of burnt rubber smoke clouded the under carriage of Copa Airlines, Boeing 737- 800 series, when it touched down on the runway in Caracas, Venezuela. Holding Angela's hand, Dunstan suddenly squeezed it in a nervous reaction as the jet landed hard on the runway. Angela turned to Dunstan with a soft smile, and giggling said, "An angel afraid of flying? How is that possible?"

Dunstan quickly released her hand, patted her on her thigh and said, "In this day and age, I'm skeptical about these machines and the hands that made them! You would be too, if you could see what I've seen in some humans' minds throughout time. Oh, and furthermore, it wasn't me that I tensed up for, it was for you and your safety."

"Ahh… that is so sweet," Angela replied as she leaned over and kissed him on his cheek.

While inside Caracas International Airport, Dunstan pulled Angela close, "Okay, sweet cakes, where do we go from here?"

Angela quickly pulled out the itinerary, and replied, "Aserca Aeropostal is the airline we are looking for, and oh, babes, through all the education I've obtained and languages I've learnt, I'm sorry, although I regret it, Spanish wasn't priority at the time. I was staging myself more for a European setting."

Julian was quiet during their walk, and then suddenly, he decided to jump in, "I know a bit of Spanish!"

"Okay Julian," Dunstan smiled and said, "Let me hear you speak Spanish! Go and ask that beautiful, young lady over there where we can find Aserca Aeropostal Airline."

Julian quickly turned to see where Dunstan was pointing, and sure enough, there was a young lady standing and looking through the airport department store's window. Surprisingly, for he was such an outspoken person, he froze for a second.

"Go on, you said you know Spanish."

Julian hesitantly walked over and quietly said, "Hola."

The girl turned and responded, "Hola."

Suddenly, Julian started to stammer in English.

Dunstan quickly walked up from behind and spewed out, "Donde puedo encontrar Aserca Aeropostal Airline?"

The young lady smiled at Julian, turned to Dunstan, pointed and gave him the directions.

Thanking her, they walked off. Unexpectedly, Angela ran up from behind, jumped up on Dunstan's back, and jokingly said, "Superman, I didn't know you spoke Spanish!"

"I'm Superman! Right! I speak all languages!"

They all broke out into laughter as they walked through the terminal toward Aserca Aeropostal Airline.

Chapter 39

They were walking about four minutes when Julian suddenly shouted out, "I see it!"

"Where?"

"Are you blind? Right there!" Julian shouted back, and then quickly flashed a smile at Dunstan.

Dunstan looked at Julian cross-eyed and with a soft smile said, "You are a nut, you know that?" Then he turned to Angela, "Sweet girl, let me see the itinerary." He walked up to the airline counter, and began conversing with the agent in Spanish. Both Angela's and Julian's heads turned when they overheard his Spanish suddenly turned to English for in a polite but disgusted tone he exclaimed, "You kidding me! No more flights today!"

The conversation went back to Spanish, and five minutes later, Dunstan walked over to Angela and Julian, three tickets in his hand. "Sorry guys, no more flights today. We are booked for the 9:00 am flight tomorrow."

Angela clasped her hands, and in jubilant spirits shouted out, "Yippee!"

"Why are you so happy?" Dunstan asked.

"This is my first time in Caracas, or even in Venezuela. Come, come, let's go; let's go downtown."

"Whoa, whoa, slow your roll, girl. Why are you so eager to go downtown?"

"You kidding me, right? Shops, shops! It'll be my first time. Come, let's GO!"

"You can't speak Spanish, so you'll take the entire day in one shop," Dunstan grinned, shaking his head.

Angela slowly walked up to Dunstan, looked up at him with a childish, beady-eyed look, straddled his arm with both of hers, and said, "No, it won't take any time at all, not while I have my big, strong superman translating for me, and he won't refuse because of his angel inside."

"That may be so, but don't you think it would be wise to get a couple of rooms first? In that way, we can dump these bags, and then you can go on your much needed excursion."

Although a well reserved person, Angela was eager to see the world, but she realized that Dunstan was right!

Moments later, they were standing outside the terminal hailing a cab. While they were jumping into the cab, Dunstan asked the driver to find a hotel that was close to the airport.

The cab driver immediately suggested Marriott Venezuela Playa Grande.

Ten minutes later they were jumping out of the cab at the hotel. As Dunstan was about to close the cab door, the driver shouted out in Spanish, "Aqui esta mi tarjeta, llama me si me necesitas!" ("Here is my card, call if you need me!")

Dunstan turned and reached out for it as he said, "Gracias, lo hare!" ("Thank you, I will!") But just as the cab was about to pull off, Dunstan shouted out, "WAIT, WAIT!" Waving him back, he quickly ran up to car, "¿Puede esparar uno's minutos para que nosregistremos, para que pod Amos dejar nuestra maletas? Entonces puede llevar a la ciundad." ("Can you wait a few minutes for us to check in, so we can leave our bags? Then you can take us to the city.")

They quickly checked in, put their bags in their rooms, and fifteen minutes tops, they were back in the cab. Twenty minutes later they were in the city. As they were hopping out of the cab, Angela suddenly grabbed Dunstan's hand, and led him like a child who was excitingly trying to establish a B line to a candy shop.

"Oh boy! Here we go," Dunstan exclaimed as he quickly followed her, Julian in tow.

"Slowdown!" said Dunstan, "Do you know where you're going?"

"Can we go eat?" Julian interjected.

"Yeah, in a little bit," Angela quickly responded.

"Come on, I'm a big guy and I'm starving! I'm telling you, if I don't eat, I'm going to pass out, right here on these streets."

Dunstan pulled back on Angela's metaphoric reins, and said, "Angela, Angela slow down! He's right! I've seen it happen before. Let's find a restaurant for big guys need fuel!"

"Okay! Okay!" Angela replied, biting her lips. "Let's eat!"

Dunstan quickly gestured a passing Venezuelan woman over, and asked, "¿Dónde está un buen lugar para comer?" ("Where is a nice place to eat?")

"Si, El restaurante Alto es muy agradable. No lejos," she said as she pointed up the street. ("Yes! Alto restaurant is very nice. Not far.")

"Gracias, gracias," he replied and quickly turned to Angela and Julian, "Come, come guys, there's a very nice place, she said that is not far."

They headed down the path, the woman had shown them.

"This is nice….." Angela marveled as they walked through the restaurant.

Alto was one of Caracas' upscale well-known restaurants. Soon they were seated, and a waiter came over to fill their water glasses. The second he turned to walk away, Dunstan lightly rested his hands on Angela's hands, nodded at Julian for his attention, and said softly, "Major political unrest is brewing in this country, with no end in sight. We have to be very careful about what we say, what we do, and where we go."

"What's going on here?" Julian asked.

Angela jumped in and whispered, 'It's an authoritarian

government with limited political freedom, and even individual freedom is subordinate to the state. And get this, it is ranking third in the world for homicides."

Dunstan quickly chimed in, "You forgot to mention that kidnapping has skyrocketed, ever since Hugo Chavez freed thousands of violent prisoners."

"That's right," Angela again quickly jumped in to address Julian. "It's supposed to be part of his controversial quote on quote, criminal justice system reform."

"Shush," Dunstan quickly whispered, and gestured by slightly lowering his hands because the waiter was approaching.

While handing out menus, the waiter, who spoke perfect English, asked, "Would you like anything to drink?"

"I don't need anything to drink, but I want something to eat," Julian whined quietly like a spoiled child.

Immediately, Angela kicked him under the table.

Julian responded, "What? I'm hungry!"

Angela quickly whispered, "Behave yourself."

While they were glossing through the menu, Dunstan turned to Angela, "Angela, how is it that you know so much about the political climate, but yet you feel comfortable about driving like the wind through the city with no concern about safety."

Angela dropped her head, sulked and with a touch of guilt confessed, "I guess it was selfish of me to think you would protect us should anything happen. For that I apologize to both of you for my childish and selfish behavior."

"I'm good with that, but how about you, Pops?"

"Of course, I'm good with that; and stop calling me, Pops."

Both Angela and Julian started laughing at Dunstan.

"Okay, okay, are you done now? Are you both done laughing at my expense?" Dunstan jokingly said as he tried to hold a straight face. "Are you guys ready to eat? Do you know what you want?" he asked as he waved the waiter over.

About eighteen minutes later, they were all happily eating. All of a sudden, Dunstan's alert system triggered off, so he immediately looked up and through the plated glass window of the restaurant, he noticed Diego, their cab driver, sitting in his cab across the street. He knew the name because it was on the card he was given earlier. "Did you tell our driver to come back for us?" Dunstan asked as he turned to Angela.

"No, but we should have! Why?" Angela responded.

"He is out there waiting," Dunstan said as he nodded in the direction of the window. "Wait a minute! He didn't drop us here," Dunstan said with a questionable look.

"What do you think—that he followed us here? Or perhaps, it's a mere coincidence as he may be waiting on a fare. There are quite a few bars and restaurants around here," Angela said as she waved off his curiosity.

Right then a dark blue van pulled up alongside the cab, stayed for a few seconds, and then sped off. Shortly afterwards, Diego, the cab driver pulled away.

Seconds later, the van drove back down the street, slowly passing the restaurant. Dunstan quickly picked up his table napkin, wiped his hands and mouth, threw it down on his plate, and said, "You two stay here, and don't you leave this restaurant. When you're done, you can wait in the lounge." Then he turned to Angela, "Angela, in the event, God forbid, I don't return, have them call the police, but neither of you leave this restaurant."

Dunstan got up, and casually walked to and exited the restaurant.

Angela looked over at Julian and said, "God, I hate these tense moments!"

On the outside, Dunstan looked down the street, in the direction the van drove. He just caught its tail turning left on a traffic light. He then walked to the side of the building so that he could not be seen from the streets. There he waited for a few minutes to see if the van would return. He began thinking that they were being set up for a robbery or a kidnapping by Diego, their cab driver. Five minutes later, he walked back into the restaurant.

When Angela lifted her head and saw him, she immediately shot out of her chair and ran to him almost knocking him off his feet with her huge, passionate hug. Yes, she was attracted to him, but for the past few days, she had become a lot more dependent on and drawn to him. There was a bond that was building between them that would soon be impossible to break.

Right then the waiter walked up to them as they were returning to their table, and asked, "Is there anything else I can get you all?"

"No, we are good, just the check would be fine."

Just as they were walking out of the door, a cab pulled up with a white couple. It appeared as if they were also tourists because they were struggling with the little Spanish they knew as they conversed with the cab driver.

Dunstan turned to Angela and asked, "Are you still up for shopping?"

"Nahh, let's just go back to the hotel."

Dunstan then quickly decided to hire the same cab that just let the couple off, to take them back to the hotel. When they got there, the cab driver offered his card, Dunstan took it, and agreed to call if he needed him. They had gotten two rooms at the hotel, one for Dunstan and Julian, and again, the other for Angela.

It was 4:10 pm, so they all decided to take a nap because they were tired after the long flight, and sluggish from their late lunch.

At 6:10 pm, Angela suddenly pitched up out of her sleep from a bad dream. She quickly sat up in bed, and ran her hands through her hair. She collected herself, got out of bed, and walked into the bathroom to wash her face and brush her teeth. Still feeling a bit frantic, she looked around, and suddenly decided to leave the room.

Seconds later, she was standing in front of Dunstan's and Julian's room knocking on their door.

Within a few seconds, Dunstan unlatched and opened the door.

"Are you okay?" he asked, with a concerned look on his face because of her disheveled appearance.

"I'm fine, just a bad dream. Can I come in?"

"Yeah, sure, but we have to be quiet because Julian is still asleep," Dunstan said as he reached out for her.

Angela quickly said, "Better yet, why don't you come over to my room, because the bad dream I had have me a bit spooked."

"Sure, no problem, just a second," he said as he turned back to put on his shirt and shoes.

While in Angela's room, they decided to walk onto the balcony. They stood there watching the sun set between the buildings of the city. Dunstan reached out and held Angela's hand. Angela slowly turned to him, and then gently hugged him with both arms. She looked up at him, and staring him directly in his eyes, said, "Kiss me."

Dunstan immediately complied as he slowly leaned forward and kissed her gently on her lips.

Angela smiled softly and said, "Wait a minute, is that what you call a kiss?" Suddenly, she pulled him in, and then passionately started kissing him. The sun had completely disappeared beyond the buildings as dusk came upon the city. Then a soft breeze began blowing as a sudden glow of light quickly engulfed them. Right then and there, they both became one. It was special, it was magnificent, and yes, it was from God. (What God has joined together, let no man put asunder.)

They stood there for a while embracing each other, both not wanting to let go because of the special feeling of warmth that engulfed them. The feeling was so astonishing that they both began to shed tears.

A moment later, Dunstan opened his eyes, which wondered down at the traffic below that was turning in and out of the hotel. Suddenly, he saw the van that he had seen earlier at the restaurant. It was across the street from the hotel, parked under a streetlight. While holding Angela, he lightly patted her on her back, and said, "Listen, there is something I need to do, but I need to do it alone. It won't take long, I promise."

"Do you have to, babes?" she asked.

"It's a now or never! I'm sorry!"

"Is that up for a vote? Because you know I'm voting never," Angela replied as she looked up at him with a wide smile.

"Julian should be up by now! I'll leave you two together. How does that sound?"

"Okay…if you must," she moaned as they turned and walked to the door.

Seconds later, they were back in Julian's and Dunstan's room. Julian was up watching TV when they walked in. Dunstan quickly open his clothing bag, pulled out a set of clothes, and then ran into the shower.

"Where are you going?" Julian asked.

"He's going on a date," Angela answered for him, and then smiled.

"Yeah, right!" Julian quickly responded, and added, "I think he knows people here, perhaps other angels."

They both chuckled, and continued watching television.

Twenty-two minutes later, downstairs in the lobby, Dunstan walked up to the front desk and asked, "Where can I make a local call?"

The clerk pointed over to the concierge desk, and said, "Marlene over there can help you."

Dunstan walked over to her desk, and looked down at the face of a smiling, beautiful, young lady.

"How can I help you?" Marlene asked.

"I would like to make a local call," Dunstan replied as he pulled out Diego's, the cab driver's card from his wallet.

"Would you like me to dial the number for you?"

"Sure, that would be very kind of you," Dunstan said with a smile.

When she had dialed the number, she handed the card back and nodded him to a phone over 10ft away that was in a lounge.

"Gracias," Dunstan said, as he walked over to the phone. When he picked it up, Diego was already on the other end, saying, "Hola, hola!"

"Hola mi amigoeste, es el tipo que recogiste del aeropuerto hace unas horas." ("Hello my friend, this is the guy you picked up from the airport a few hours ago.")

"Si, si," Diego responded.

"¿Diego, puedes recoerme del hotel?" ("Diego, can you pick me up from the hotel?")

"Si, si, no problema! ¿A que hora?" ("Yes, yes, no problem! What time?")

"Ahara si puedes!" ("Right now, if you can!")

"¿Me puedes dar 20 minutos?" ("Can you give me 20 minutes?")

"Esta' bien estare' esperando." ("That's fine, I will be waiting.")

Twenty minutes later, Diego pulled up to the front of the hotel, and shouted out from his window to Dunstan, who was standing outside the hotel's main entrance, "How are you my friend?"

Dunstan immediately walked up to the car and asked, "Diego, do you speak English?"

"Yes, yes, I do!" Diego replied.

Dunstan walked around the car, jumped into the front seat, and closing the door, asked, "Why didn't you tell me?"

"You didn't ask, besides, I thought you were Brazilian because you speak Spanish so well."

Dunstan, turned, looked at him, smiled, and said, "No, no, I'm American. So how about we speak English from now on? Is that okay?"

"Si! Oh, so sorry, yes. So tell me, where would you like to go?" asked Diego.

"You tell me, this is your town. Take me to the hot spots."

"No problema," Diego replied as he zoomed off in his four door Nissan stick shift.

While they were driving, Diego broke the silence, "I see your two friends did not want to go out tonight?"

"Yeah, one wasn't feeling well, and the other was really tired. How ironic is that, given that I'm the oldest?"

They both chuckled at the irony.

Dunstan began a purposeful dialogue with Diego, in order to stage his own kidnapping. He told Diego about a fictitious successful business he had in Alabama. He intentionally pulled out his wallet and slipped out a hundred dollar bill, passing it to Diego. "Diego, I'm a very wealthy man. You take care of me, and I'll take care of you."

"Gracias, gracias, sorry English right? Thank you, thank you," Diego said filled with gratitude as he looked over at Dunstan's wallet and saw a wad of cash stuffed in it that Dunstan intentionally kept opened so that he could see it.

Ten minutes later, they pulled up at a club called *Juan Sabastian.*

"My friend, this is a nice spot! Many people come here; it's a hot spot with a live band playing great jazz music! Hope you like," Diego said, and then added, "My friend, you know my name, but I don't know yours."

Dunstan quickly turned to him with apologies, "I'm so sorry, Dunstan, Dunstan Archer."

"Dunstan, very nice name. Mr. Archer I will leave you here and come back. You see, when you first called me, I was taking my sister to the food store, where I'd dropped her, so now, I need to go back to pick her up. No worries, I'll be back in an hour. You go in and have a good time, okay?"

"Yes, I will have a good time, and when you come back, you come in, and we both could have a good time. I'll take care of you as I've got lots of money," Dunstan said as he opened the door to step out.

Diego had driven a mile up the street when he pulled into a fueling station. While getting his gas, he pulled out his cellphone to make a call. The person picked up on the first ring, "Esta' bien, esta'Juan Sabastian; esparo que lo recoja en una hora. Tienes que estar alli." ("He is at *Juan Sabastian*. He is expecting me to pick him up in one hour. You have to be there.")

Yes, Dunstan was right all along. It was a set up from the beginning. They thought Dunstan was playing into their hands, but they had made a big mistake because they were playing into his.

Chapter 40

It was coming up on an hour, Dunstan noted on his watch as looked on and tapped his feet to the music of the Jazz live band that was playing in Juan Sabastian's. The band was very impressive. In fact, the establishment and the staff were very, very, outstanding. Ten minutes had gone by when Dunstan looked down on his watch again, and over his shoulders. He was thinking that Diego would be walking up on him any second. He was not really a drinker, but would just have an occasional glass of wine. However, he decided to go local in Venezuela. He quickly forced down the second virgin La Tizana, a tropical drink. As he looked again over his shoulder, he reached into his back pocket to pull out his wallet, and then waved the waiter over.

The waiter graciously smiled when Dunstan gave him a large tip after paying the tab.

"Thank you, I had a very nice time, and I hope I can return someday real soon," Dunstan said as he reached out and shook his hand.

On the outside, Dunstan stood alone, looking casually up and down the street for Diego to pull up, or perhaps, the van, whose driver would somehow find a way to sneak up on him. He started thinking about the type of approach they would have, whether it would be a kidnapping, or just a straight up robbery.

Suddenly, he saw the van on his right; it was pulling up to a stop sign on a side street. To convince them that he was oblivious about what was going on, he decided to walk in the van's direction. Then he turned down the same side street and began strolling slowly down it. He knew that walking down that side street would make him an easy target, and he played the role of an unsuspected prey well. Not looking back, he heard the van back up and turn around.

As he walked he kept thinking, here it comes, here it comes. Then suddenly, he heard the squealing sound of tires coming to a stop, and the sound of the rollers from the side panel door of the van being ripped open. Quickly he was grabbed from behind, and thrown in the back of the van by two thuggish looking, young Venezuelan males.

Dunstan pretended to resist by shrugging his shoulders and throwing his arms about but doing so with very little fight in him. He shouted, "What's going on? Where're you guys taking me?"

Without warning, one of the abductors smacked Dunstan on the side of his face with a riot shotgun, racked the chamber, and with a cold, mean look said, "No te muevas, cierra la boca!" ("Don't move, shut your mouth!")

But with all that, Dunstan's heart rate probably didn't even rise above 82 beats p/minute.

Cesar, the passenger in the front seat, looked back and shouted out, "Enssell, injector la droga, la droga!" ("Enssell, inject the drug, the drug!") Enssell had frozen for some reason. Suddenly, Alberto, the one with the shotgun quickly exchanged his gun for Enssell's needle, and then he stuck it in Dunstan's thigh, right after he turned to Enssell, and looked frustratingly at him.

As an angel incarnate however, Dunstan was immune to whatever was in that needle, but he played along anyway by slowly slumping down and rolling on the floor of the van. His abductors were ones of the most notorious groups of kidnappers that were responsible for the most recent kidnappings and murders in the city. Enssell was new at this game, which was why he had frozen and could not administer the drug.

Cesar Rodriquez, a twenty-eight year old, who was 5' 9" tall, with a dark brown short crew cut, was the leader of the group. He sat in the passenger front seat with the driver, Carlos. He was considered ruthless among his peers for even though he was small in stature, he would kill someone in an instant.

After fifteen minutes of driving, Cesar looked back and instructed Enssell to put the hood over Dunstan's head. Then he mumbled under his breath as he looked at Carlos, "Me pregunto si es capaz de hacelo bien!" ("I wonder if he is capable of doing that right!")

Twenty minutes later, Dunstan, who pretended to be unconscious, was still being tossed around. He understood everything they were saying, and realized that they were driving on a dirt road that appeared to be filled with a lot of holes because of the constant swaying to and fro. Then the van came to a stop. Right away Dunstan knew that they were near the sea, given the scent of the salty air, and the close sounds of rolling waves. The panel door of the van quickly opened as Cesar started barking out orders to the crew to take him inside. They had a makeshift stretcher, which they rolled Dunstan onto, and then they hustled him inside.

The kidnappers had an abandoned four bedroom beach house that was powered by a portable generator. On the inside they threw Dunstan in a back bedroom that was sealed up with reinforced boarded windows. They took his wallet, stripped him of his shoes, but left his pants on. Then they sat him in a chair and tied him up. After that, they closed and locked the door, leaving him because they thought he needed the time for the drug to wear off.

(Note: Their conversation was a mixture of Spanish, and an occasional English.)

Sitting in the front section of the house that had a veranda style porch and an ocean view, Cesar went through Dunstan's wallet as he talked to Diego on the phone.

"What do you mean he didn't have a phone on him? I'm pretty sure I saw a phone on him at one point," Diego spewed out in Spanish, quite curious.

"Look, we stripped him and searched his clothes, and I'm pretty sure there was no phone," Cesar said as he waved Alberto over, and then cuffing the phone and said, "Alberto, go back there and check that guy once again for a phone."

"But Cesar we stripped him, and checked for a phone, but didn't find one."

Frustrated and angry, Cesar looked at Alberto and said, "I don't care! Check again, because you know those phones carry GPS. He probably has it hidden in his ass." Cesar then went back to his conversation with Diego.

As he turned away, Alberto secretly instructed Enssell to check for the phone again.

Meanwhile, back in the room, Dunstan had already freed himself from the restraints, and redressed himself. Suddenly, he heard the unlocking sound of the door, which had a reverse lock. He quickly stood behind the door.

When Enssell entered the room, Dunstan came from behind, put him in a vicious headlock, and quietly said in Spanish, "You want to live, or you want to die? Simple question, because I would take you out in a second."

Because Enssell was not cut out for this type of operation, he quickly complied and said, "Si si, I want to live."

"Good," Dunstan replied as he turned him around slowly. "Why are you doing this? I can see you are not the type."

Enssell just stood there and started to shake. Knowing he had very little time, Dunstan pulled him in close, and then held his head so he could envision what he was all about. He then quietly asked, "How many are out there?"

"Three," Enssell answered.

"Is that all? Are you sure?"

"Si, si, three!"

"Okay, you stay here, and do not leave this room!" Dunstan then gingerly opened the door and quietly walked out.

Outfront, Cesar had hung up the phone, and when he turned around, he saw Alberto still standing there. He angrily spat out, "I thought I asked you to double check for the phone!"

"I sent Enssell!"

"You sent who? You know that boy is not cut out for this shit! I don't know why you brought him in any way! I should have known better," Cesar exclaimed as he shouted for Carlos, and all three began walking back to the room.

While they were converging, Dunstan noticed a machete that was carelessly left standing in the corner of the hallway. He immediately picked it up just seconds before Cesar turned the corner to the hallway. Without warning, Dunstan smacked Cesar on the face with the machete, spun him around and pulled him in. While holding the machete to his neck, he shouted to the others, "Back up, back up, or I'll cut his head clean off!" As he stared viciously at them, he followed up with, "Trust me, I can do it!"

"Kill this fool for he doesn't have the nerve!" Cesar shouted.

"You really want to test me on that?" Dunstan asked as he started to edge over to the table where he'd noticed the shotgun. He immediately picked it up and quickly shoved Cesar over to the other two. He took aim, shot Alberto in the leg, and said, "That's for what you did to me in the van!" 'BAM,' was the sound of the second blast that went into the ceiling. It was to increase the fear of the unscathed, remaining two.

"Please, please, take me to the hospital," Alberto cried out as he squirmed on the floor.

"Shut up you dumb shit, and man up," Cesar shouted as he nodded to Carlos to go over and help him.

"There is only one of us leaving here tonight, and I'm damn sure it isn't one of you. So you could forget the hospital," Dunstan rejoined.

Suddenly, they heard a door being slammed. It was Enssell, taking the opportunity to leave.

"Oops! I guess there will be two. You were right about Enssell, he is not cut out for this," Dunstan said as he flashed a quick smile. Then he ordered them to go to the back room. Abruptly, Dunstan quickly paused. "Wait up! Where is my wallet?"

Cesar nodded over to the side table where he had been sitting.

Dunstan quickly maneuvered himself across the room without taking his eyes off them, and picked it up. "Go, go, get to the back room, and carry him," he motioned with the shotgun once again. It was a standard 12' by 12' room that they used to hold abductees. The door opened from the outside in, which made breaking out twice as hard as breaking in.

Dunstan ordered the three of them to go into the room. They were somewhat reluctant, so once again he shot into the ceiling, and all three quickly scampered in. Dunstan pulled the door close and locked it. He walked back into the living room to get a chair to reinforce it, wedging it beneath the door knob. Then he walked out onto the veranda's deck that circled the house, and noticed a gasoline container. Guessing it was for the generator that was roaring in the background, he quickly picked it up, and walked back into the house. Walking backwards, he started dousing the gasoline throughout the house, starting in the living room. A trail of gasoline was left throughout the house, and picking up a lighter from the dining room table, he went out onto the veranda's deck. He placed the container down and walked over to the reinforced window of the holding room, and with Andrealphus' angelic strength, he ripped away one of the reinforced boards, and punched his fist through the inner window.

"How does it feel to be in a table-turned situation? The hunter becomes the prey! What do they call it? Poetic justice?" Dunstan asked as he peered through the hole he had created. "Listen, I'm not going to waste my time with you guys, since I know some of my people may be worried about me right now."

"We have a lot of friends out there, so how far do you think you are going to get? Oh! And don't forget our friend Enssell is probably out there right now, calling and telling them what is going on here."

"I doubt that very much for your friend is a changed man, and furthermore, there is a lot of miles to cover by foot because your van is still parked out there," Dunstan replied as he started testing the lighter he had picked up. He then stood up straight and started a monologue about how disappointed he was with them. "You know what I never quite understood throughout my stay here in this world? People tend to take shortcuts to become criminals or involve themselves in nefarious and criminal behavior. It has been documented repeatedly throughout history that it does not end well for the bad, no matter the color of the collar on the type of crime they commit. You just don't get it, don't you? Too much work has been put into this world for you to put so little into it, and yet expect to get a lot out of it. Okay, I'm done spoon feeding you. I guess by now you are smelling the gasoline fumes reeking through this house, and yes, your guess is right, you know where it goes from here. But don't worry, everybody will get a fighting chance, even you and your worthless crew."

Suddenly, Cesar shouted from the room, "Hold up, hold up! Don't do what I think you are going to do right now. Let's make a deal."

"Make a deal? What deal can you make with me?"

"Listen, you let us out of here, and we could forget this whole thing ever happened! How about it?"

"Yeah, right! My friend, I have already given you a leg up by weakening your reinforced window," Dunstan said as he picked up the rag that was used as a makeshift cap for the gasoline container. "If you want to make a deal, you need to make it with God. Repent, and I suggest you mean it because if you sincerely repent, He will hear you, and then you would be able to muster the strength to power yourself out. That is for all of you. You have ten minutes,"

Dunstan declared. Then he turned and continued to douse the remaining fuel on the deck to the stairs.

(Note: The conversation was a mixture of Spanish and English.)

Dunstan stood there a few seconds as he looked at the house and its surroundings. Then he lit the rag and threw it. As he quickly walked down the stairs, he heard the woofing sounds of the flames as they chased the path of the doused gasoline. He didn't even turn to look. Suddenly however, he realized that he was faced with another dilemma, and being alone, and not having his full angelic strength, he was not able to drive, so he had to travel in the conventional way—in this case, he had to walk.

All of a sudden, Enssell appeared out of the bushes.

Dunstan looked at him and asked, "Are you with me?"

Enssell nodded.

"Can you drive?"

Enssell nodded once again.

"Let's go!" Dunstan shouted.

Enssell quickly jumped into the driver's seat of the van, and started it as he knew that they never took the keys out of it.

Back at the hotel, Dunstan lightly knocked on Angela's room door. In a matter of seconds she opened it, almost as if she was standing there waiting on him. She swiftly reached out and pulled him inside, and her first words were, "Were you drinking gasoline?" She quickly smiled, putting her fingers on his lips. "Shhh… wait! I don't want to know."

Dunstan then smiled and kissed her on the forehead. "I need to clean up! Can I do it here?"

Without responding, she grabbed his hand, marched him into the bathroom, and helped him out of his clothes.

At 7:00 o' clock the following morning, both of them were lying face to face a feet away from each other. Angela stared at Dunstan for at least five minutes as he slept. She strummed his face real lightly, marveling as if she was looking on something that was lovely, extraordinary, foreign and new.

Suddenly Dunstan's eyes opened, and smiling he whispered, "What are you doing? Were you staring at me?"

Angela giggled, nodded her head and said, "I have never seen a sleeping angel before. In fact, I had never seen you asleep before. Your breathing was so light, and you looked so peaceful. Is that how it is when you have an angel inside?"

Dunstan slowly rolled over on his back, and quickly pulled the sheets over his head.

Somewhat embarrassed about what he was about to say, he pulled the sheets back down, and asked, "Did you ever thought that my angel inside had nothing to do with it?"

Angela smiled with a confidence she had never had before, and quickly rolled over on top of him, launching an assault of peck kisses all over his face and body.

Dunstan retreated, pulling back for cover, using the pillars and sheets. They both became engulfed with laughter and giggles. But Angela was being relentless with her assault, until she heard his muffled voice crying out, "Stop, stop, we've got a plane to catch. What time is it?"

"Let's catch another one, please...." Angela cried as she whined and moaned.

"Angela, it's the only one. Besides, we will have lots of time to ourselves later because I'm not going anywhere. We just have to put what I have to do behind us," Dunstan replied as he got up out of the bed.

Angela quickly shot up from the bed, and ran over to him and hugged him tightly. Looking up at him, she said, "Promise me, promise me, you're not going anywhere!"

Dunstan looked down on her and paused for a second because again he was taken aback, amazed at how beautiful she was to him. Then he kissed her gently and whispered, "I promise!"

Chapter 41

I t's November 14th, Monday morning, at 8:10 am, in London, England. Brent Russell sat with Sheila Hall in her office. Tapping her pen on the desk, Sheila opened the conversation of their meeting, "We have been getting a series of reports from the MI-6 department on similar takedowns like the one in Madrid, Spain. Unlike the hillside bunker we discovered, reports indicate that they are using commercial lofts to set up their computer work stations. Some are even mixed with legitimate businesses. Agent Russell, this has gone deep as South America."

"Boss, they did say it was going to be a global assault," Brent replied as he listened intensely to her.

"Based on Carla's cousin, Sandra's findings, when she stumbled on the then incarnated Caroline Boles, who was using street level recruiting methods, in that web café. That urged me to set up a team that included the local city police throughout selective cities of Great Britain. They would be able to cover the street level web cafés, and other similar web outposts to look out for individuals using that level to recruit others."

Sheila then quickly leaned in towards Brent to determine how he felt about it. She decided to call him by his first name, "Brent, through all the technology we have, we are limited to what we can do as far as this social media cyberspace warfare is concerned. What I'm really trying to say is I would like to get more into this divine intervention side of things, but this office only allows me certain limits, that are bound by law. You know, individual privacy is attached. Do you have any suggestions?" Sheila ended as she leaned back into her chair, waiting for a response.

Brent remained silent as he leaned back in his chair with both hands on his head, staring intensely at the ceiling, deep in thought, searching for an answer. "Okay!" he quickly said as he sat up, "We should look at this from the angle of divine intervention. Let's start with the 1/3 fraction—from the biblical standpoint, a 1/3 of the angels was cast out of heaven. So would it be safe to say that a 1/3 of the world's population probably already has evil baked into it? No, let me retract that as it's a bit harsh. Let just say, easily persuaded, a 1/3 would be subject to the rhetoric they have already been spooling out. Now let's say if we can use the balance of the remaining 2/3 as the social media population, we can turn the 1/3 on its face."

"How do you propose we do that?"

"Boss?"

Sheila immediately raised her hand and quickly stopped him, "Brent, I know you are just showing respect, but I wish you would stop calling me that! Right now, you and I, what we are going through, this unusual phenomenon we are facing is serious, so we can drop that superior/ subordinate stuff. Wouldn't you agree?"

"Okay.... Sheila," Brent said hesitantly, "These guys, given their diabolical rhetoric, can tap into the heads of social media followers and change their way of thinking. But what I'm trying to say is with the right tech workers we can too. We can reverse the effects, and redirect, or reroute their messages to those who cannot be fooled to bite into their BS, and those who can spot people like that coming a mile away—yes, these are the two-thirds that are willing to live by God's original plan. If you give it to one person, of course, he might say, how do you expect me alone to change the world? But now, if you reroute these messages to the masses of the 2/3 or billions of social media followers that are on the right track, every individual from that pool would see him or herself as a team member. They then would join hands with each other. Imagine that, billions of whistleblowers that cannot be desensitized will end up doing the work for you. See where I'm going with this? There would be a worldwide unified uproar that cannot be challenged."

"Brent, I don't know, but my main concern is with the legality of the entire thing," Sheila said softly.

"The legality you say? Do you think what they are doing is right? We can't just sit idly by while they force down our throats this New World order. Sheila, the world is on the precipice of losing the democracy, which it had fought so hard for decades ago. To steal from that kind of thief, God would smile."

"I hear you," Sheila replied as she rocked back and forth in her chair.

Suddenly, Brent's phone rang. "Hello," Brent answered.

It was Paul on the other end.

"Paul, young man, how are you?"

"I'm fine, but if we don't act now the world won't be!"

"What's going on? Talk to me," Brent said, as he quickly put his phone on speaker to bring Sheila in on the conversation.

"You remember the 2 billion social media trigger point?"

"Yeah! Go ahead," Brent responded, but now with an intense alert look on his face.

"I'm getting word it is closing in. It was lingering for a while but now it has started to pick up again. We need to do something fast. You think those election results were bizarre, and people are being desensitized to obvious bad behavior, which they tell their children to avoid, just imagine that on a global scale."

"Paul, Mrs. Hall and I are talking about this subject matter as we speak. Give me five minutes and I'll call you right back." Brent quickly hung up, and then rubbed his head a few times as he gave Sheila a questioning look as if he was asking, what should we do?

"Brent, Brent! Don't get all flustered on me right now! There is something we can do. What you were talking about a few minutes ago, it makes sense. But we need to put a team together on the down low, as I can't do it from this department. Let's see...... Okay, I got it. Call Carla Wallace, we need to go private."

Brent immediately pulled Carla's number up and dialed it. The phone rang for quite a while, but just before Brent thought the answering service would pick up, Carla answered, "Hello, hello," thinking she might have missed it.

"Carla, this is Brent!"

"Brent, how are you? What a pleasant surprise," Carla responded, with a hint of flirting in her voice. Yes, Carla couldn't help feeling a bit attracted to Brent as he was her knight in shining armor. After all, he had saved her life.

"Carla, you talk as if we hadn't seen each other in a long time," Brent said with a quick smile.

"Brent, if it was ten minutes ago we had seen each other, and you'd now call, it would have been too long! You are my knight in shining armor, so it would be impossible for me not to think about you."

"Well, if that's the way you feel, I guess this is perfect timing because I do need to see you. In fact, we need to see you, that is, my boss and I," Brent said as he turned to Sheila with a wink and a smile.

"Carla, it is a pressing matter, and if I may add, also urgent."

"Not a problem, when do you want me to come over?" Carla asked.

"No, no, we would much rather visit you."

"Great, great, come on by whenever you like! I'm home all day."

"Super! We're coming right now," Brent said, hung up, and gave Sheila a thumbs up.

Both Sheila and Brent decided to use Brent's car. As they drove, Sheila said, "I'm going to put a small team together that will include Ailes and Brooks because we need them as they are computer geeks. On the outside, we're going to need Genevieve Martin, Stanley Wilson and Caroline Boles, that is, if she is up to it. If Carla goes along with us, I'm hoping we can set up a makeshift computer tech floor in her condo, which will give us a great cover and privacy. You know I won't be able to stay to supervise, so that is on you. So when we get there, and get her permission, we can go ahead and call the guys over."

"Sounds like a plan to me," Brent said as he powered down his window at the security gate of Carla's condo complex.

"Good, let's do this," Sheila said in response.

Inside Carla's condo, Sheila and Brent made their proposal pitch. Carla willing accepted it without batting an eye. Maybe it was because she would get to play a 007 agent once again.

◦◦

A few hours later, eight people were milling around in Carla's condo. An hour before they had arrived, Carla made it known to her immediate neighbors that she was having a little get together with a few friends. She had also ordered pizza and soft drinks to host the tech workers.

Ailes and Brooks completed the final and necessary wiring and hook ups for the additional servers, so that they would have the functionality for the other programs, devices or clients. Ailes then looked at Brent and gave him a thumbs up, indicating that they were good to go.

Brent called Carla over, and to quietly reassure again, asked, "Are you good with this?"

"You saved my life, of course I am!"

"Okay, can you close the balcony doors and pull the drapes, just half way will be fine. Oh, and turn up the AC as it's getting rather hot in here," Brent said with a wink and a smile. Carla just blushed and complied.

"Okay, boys and girls, listen up," Brent said as he beckoned for their attention with a handclap. "I know some of you are not up to speed with the internal part of the Surrey takedown. Ailes, and Brooks I'm talking to both of you." As he reached out for Genevieve, he said, "I would like to introduce to you both," Genevieve Martin,

Stanley Wilson and Caroline Boles. They are working with us as they have extraordinary information that goes deep down into the worldwide veins, that are connected to and from that bunker operation we took down in Surrey. Now what I need for you all to do is work like professionals with one another. Ailes, when I breakdown on what needs to be done, I need both you and Brooks to follow Genevieve's lead on this. Is that understood?"

"Not a problem," Ailes responded.

"Good! So here is the deal. We're on the clock with the rising tide of social media followers. If we don't reverse what is happening before it reaches those 2 billion media followers' trip wire, we are going to have a lot of people walking around the world as if they are on some sought of hypnotic drug! They are functional, yet desensitized, and have no empathy whatsoever. Imagine that you are seeing this type of behavior already— emboldened people who think that doing wrong is better than doing right. Is that a world you want to live in? Good! Now let's get working!" Brent ended, and then turned to Genevieve.

There was a faint sound from Genevieve, who was clearing her throat. Not much of a speaker, she attempted anyway, "Agent Russell is right! This is a cyberspace cat and mouse chase, and we're going to start by being the cat." She then walked up to a large screen they had set up, and pointing at the map on the screen, she continued, "All the red dots are what we are going to call the mouse, all the blue ones are neutral-minded people like we are, empathetic, the untouchables. Now all the green lines in between those red dotted mice indicate that they are conversing with one another via chit chatting emails and other means of social media correspondence. Unfortunately, I was a part of this social media dissemination, which was designed to produce algorithms on the way people think and feel. This is mainly done to segregate and then colonize those that have been desensitized so that they can march to the drumbeat of their puppeteers, all in an effort to establish a New World Order movement. I was blindly caught up on the wrong side of politics on this matter. Fortunately,

I was stopped in time, and was given the opportunity to reverse this mess that has been created."

Suddenly, there was a knock at the door. The room went silent as all eyes turned to the door. Carla immediately walked to it. When she looked through the peephole, she quickly and jubilantly unlocked it. "It's Paul! Paul, come on in," Carla reached out and hugged him.

Brent walked up to Paul and quipped, "You're late! Just kidding, come on in! You know the party can't start without you, but it has! But I'm damn glad to see you."

After everyone had settled down once again, all eyes went back on Genevieve, "Okay, our goal is to throw them off their game, and that is, to reroute their conversations to the blues in a mass way. What this would do is make the unsuspected blues aware of their nefarious plans and schemes. There would be thousands upon millions of reports to the authorities. Hence, radio and TV news stations would pick up their stories and carry them even further." Genevieve ended by looking directly at Brooks and Ailes, hoping that they understood as they were just as highly skilled and knowledgeable about the computer hacking world.

Forty minutes went by as all of their heads faced their computer screens, disseminating messages. Brent turned to Genevieve, who had a curious look on her face that showed she was struggling with something. "What's going on?" Brent asked.

She looked up at him, and then waved him over. "They have divided the world, that is, the east from the west. Where we are right now, we are able to cover the whole of Europe and Africa, north to south. But I can't seem to reach North and South America without accessing a passcode, and right now, I haven't a clue what it is."

Brent immediately started to pan the room, and then his eyes locked on Paul, "Paul come here please!"

"What's up?" Paul asked.

"We need a password because we can't access the United States, or anywhere in the Western world for that matter. We have to play with numbers, and I think we should start with the '396 dark Angels'."

"No, it has to be at least six characters or more," Genevieve interjected.

Paul immediately said, "Calculate a 1/3 of the 396."

Genevieve paused for a few seconds, and with her swift mathematical mind, she said, "132." She quickly entered 396132. "Got it!" she said without looking up. Her fingers began to make quick tapping sounds on her keyboard.

Brent then excused himself, walked into the kitchen area, pulled out his phone and dialed an overseas number that connected him to Andrew Anderson in Riverside, California.

"Hello! Andrew, my friend, Brent Russell here."

"What's going on there, Agent Russell?"

"Are you alone?" Brent asked.

"Yes, I'm what's happening!"

"What I'm about to tell you, please, you have to keep it on the down low."

"You got it, my friend," Andrew responded.

"Very soon, you're going to get a series of reports throughout your country from the general public that will be giving information that will lead you and other authorities like you to the doors of people who are cooking up sinister illegal plots throughout your country."

"You are kidding me! Wow, this is huge!" Andrew said in amazement.

"Believe it, this is also worldwide, and it's being done through social media. I'm working privately with a selected few. So in general, our MI-5 department has no knowledge of this, and please, for now, we have to keep it that way."

"I understand, not a problem. I'll keep you posted," Andrew said, and then they both hung up.

❧

It was 8:00 pm in Riverside, California. Seconds after Andrew had hung up his phone from Brent Russell, it rang again. It was Frank Carey, James' father. Without exchanging pleasantries, Andrew immediately answered, "Frank! Give me good news! Is it a go?"

"Yes, it is! Ronald called me a few minutes ago as he is very much in on this. In fact, he insisted on pushing up the clock on this because he feels the present administration will soon be getting rid of your director, and you would soon be pulled from this case. Mr. Anderson, like I was saying all along, these guys don't care about white supremacy enhancement on their militia groups. In my personal opinion that is what they are calling for as suggested by their hints and winks. They want to reign supreme, have 100% control, stop migration and prevent race mixing. Got it? Make America great again, by force if necessary. So with that, let's do this, and let's do it fast."

Back at Frank's home, after taking the last swill of beer he was drinking, he quickly dialed James', his son's, number. "James, it's a go! Call your boy, Nathanial, and have him meet us at the same outback steakhouse within an hour. We need to go over the cost of the package my guy gave me."

"I'm on it," James replied and then quickly hung up.

An hour later the four were sitting opposite each other, like they had done a few days ago at their first meeting. In fact, and coincidently, they sat at the same booth. They engaged in a little small talk because the waiter was taking their order. This time they had only ordered a few beers, with James opting out by just asking for water.

"That was fast! I thought you said this might take at least two weeks?" Nathaniel queried.

"I truly did thought it would take that long. But surprisingly enough, he got back to me and said an opportunity had presented itself, and he took it."

"Okay, okay, let me see it! I was a bit anxious as I was thinking we may have to rob this place to pay your guy," Nathaniel said as they all begin to chuckle at his humor.

Frank quickly pulled out a pen and then slid over a cocktail napkin. He wrote a few numbers down on the napkin, then slid it over to Nathaniel.

Nathaniel again injected some humor when he asked, "Is that all? Hey Frank, you're not setting me up with this number are you?" Then Nathaniel quickly retracted by saying, "Just kidding," as he reached out to shake Frank's hand.

Although Nathaniel was flamboyant and humorous, both James' and Frank's hearts picked up at an erratic pace.

All of a sudden, Nathaniel got serious and beckoned for the pen. He quickly wrote on another cocktail napkin, slid it over to Frank and said, "That address will have the package there by 9:30 tomorrow night. It's a legitimate warehouse."

Nathaniel looked over at Richard, and they both hurriedly swilled down the last of their beer. Nathaniel slapped the table, stood up and said, "I'll be waiting there."

Chapter 42

Immediately after leaving the outback steakhouse restaurant, Frank pulled out his phone to call Ronald Woods at Fort Irwin. "Ronald, Frank here! It's on! He is going for it."

"Super," said Ronald.

"It's a 9:30 pm rendezvous! I will text the address the minute I hang up. Ronald, what's the size of the containers being used?"

"We're going to use one 20 footer container. It is sufficient for what is needed. I'm sending two of the best undercover army rangers that can assist, should anything goes wrong with the exchange."

"Wonderful! I will call in the morning so that we can meet with Agent Andrew Anderson to go over the particulars."

"Sounds good, see you then."

Meanwhile, back at Andrews Anderson's home, his phone rang. It was Frank calling to tell him the same thing he had just told Ronald Woods. Andrew agreed it was a good idea to have the meeting, but as he was hanging up, a thought of his brother-in-law came to mind. He quickly dialed Danny Stones' number. "Hello, my favorite brother in-law," he said, cracking a smile.

"Andrew, I'm your only brother in-law!"

"Oh! That's right, I forgot!"

"What's going on? Why are you so jubilant? It's not like you with your tight ass FBI demeanor?"

"Funny! Listen, we've got a lockdown on an arms deal we made with Nathaniel Parker."

"You're kidding me! You got him to bite?" Danny excitingly responded.

"Yep, he bit. It's going down tomorrow night. I'll keep you posted."

The following morning at 7:00 am, James began his morning routine, which started with brewing coffee. His mind raced over all of the things he had embarked on in the strange world of white supremacy. Suddenly, he started to think about journalism—'This is a big story, to get in on covering it would be huge,' he thought. He abruptly stopped what he was doing, and quickly walked to his room to retrieve his wallet. He pulled out multiple cards, and the one he was looking for popped up—Christopher Rogers' number, who was a fellow journalist. While the phone rang, James poured his coffee.

"Christopher, I hope I didn't wake you."

'Yes, you did wake me,' Christopher thought as he rolled over. Trying to clear his mind, he feverishly looked for the time. "Who is this?" he asked.

"James, James Carey! You are a journalist, so you should be up by now," James said as he sat at his kitchen bar, sipping his coffee.

"Right, right, James! How are you?"

"I'm great, and you are going to be too."

"What are you talking about?" Christopher asked.

"I'm going to give you a lead on a huge story. Can't give you any details now, but it's going down tonight! I'll call you. Be prepared."

⁊

At 9:00 pm, Frank was sitting in his car outside of James' apartment when his phone rang. It was Ronald Woods.

"Frank, everything is on schedule! The package will be there by 9:30 pm."

"Great! I'm on my way," Frank said as he honked his horn once again, frustrated because James was falling behind time. Just as he was about to call him on his phone, he looked up and saw James scrambling out of his apartment.

"What took you so long?" Frank asked as he hit the gas, and the tires squealed away.

James did not respond.

Everything was set in motion. Earlier that morning they were methodical as they went through everything that was needed and completed all that needed to be done. Andrew Anderson and his team had scoped out the legitimate warehouse earlier that day, and factored in the surface streets to be used, when to switch unmarked vehicles that would be used to tail the perpetrators because they knew that the legitimate warehouse would not be used as a storage facility for the weapons and ammunition. The plan was to get most of their crew in their safe storage area.

On schedule at 9:30 pm, Frank and James pulled into the warehouse. They noticed three vehicles parked in front of a loading dock.

"Where is the Shelby mustang?" James asked, thinking Nathaniel hadn't arrived as yet.

"He's not going to use that car! It's too loud, and I'm not talking about the exhaust kit."

As they were pulling in alongside the other cars, they heard the loud roaring sound of a tractor trailer gearing down and turning in. Suddenly, all six doors of the three vehicles opened.

"Bravo, bravo," Nathaniel shouted, clapping his hands, "I just love it because you guys are so punctual."

Frank was not surprised to see that all six of the guys were heavily strapped, although both his and James' weapons were concealed. This is not to take this type of situation lightly.

The rig made a wide turn so that the rear would be facing the bay. The hissing sounds of the air brakes were heard when the rig came to a stop. Two well fit, looking young men believed to be in their early thirties or late twenties, jumped out from both side of the monstrous looking rig.

"Who is Frank?" one shouted out.

"That would be me," Frank said, stepping forward.

The driver waved him over as he walked to the rear of the container. Nathaniel and two of the other guys followed.

The man took keys out his pocket, unlocked the padlock, pulled out and then pushed up on the handle. A clanking sound was heard, and then the door popped open.

Looking at cases on top of cases, Nathaniel and the two guys gave one another high fives. The driver of the rig pulled out and opened one of the cases. Nathaniel stepped up and looked down –it was an M60 machine gun. Nathaniel shook his head with approval, and looking side to side at both of his boys, said, "Okay, okay! Let me see the other one."

The driver opened another case that revealed a rocket launcher.

Nathaniel immediately clasped his hands and jubilantly said, "Now, that's what I'm talking about!" Then he stepped back, whistled for one of the other three, who, in turn, popped the trunk, lifted out a large suitcase, and walked it over. The passenger of the rig took it, placed it on the ground and opened it. He then ran his hands over the large bills that were stacked in it, and then he looked back up at the driver and nodded.

All of a sudden, the head lamps of another car was spotted driving into the warehouse's compound. Nathaniel and his crew went into a defense mode, clutching their weapons. Then he shouted, "Who is that?"

"Calm down," the rig driver said, "That's our ride! You are going to need this rig to haul that shit, right? You do have somebody that knows how to drive this? Well, I hope so."

They all then stepped back and settled down.

"I guess my business is done here," Frank said as he turned and shook Nathaniel's hand.

"I guess it is, and I thank you."

They all then turned and walked to their vehicles.

Nathaniel walked up to two of his guys and said, "You two, take that to the vineyard." But little did Nathaniel know that the container had a tracker on it.

After driving away from the warehouse, Frank speed-dialed Andrew. "It's all yours!"

"Good job Frank! Oh, Frank, lock in on my phone's GPS, but keep your distance. You can come in when it's all wrapped up! I'll signal you."

After Frank hung up, he decided to pull over at a diner to set up the GPS. It was good timing for James too because he wanted set his phone's GPS for Christopher, so that he could get a heads up, and the lead on the story.

About fifty minutes later, the skies over Nathaniel's vineyard were filled with many helicopters, and on the ground, FBI units, along with SWAT teams, converged and circled Nathaniel and his crew of at least thirty men who were off-loading the containers.

Twenty minutes later, the FBI team was going through the process of arresting Nathaniel's White Supremacist crew. Suddenly, a metallic grey Acura sped up and came to a quick stop. As the dust settled around the vehicle, three doors opened and out stepped Christopher, his cameraman, and Steve, who was now employed with the news station, and was helping with the equipment.

Christopher was right on point with his coverage, as his cameraman caught great footage of Nathaniel and Richard being handcuffed, and pushed into the back of a panel van.

The following morning, Kenny Johnson, Andrew Anderson's partner, sat behind his computer checking emails, while simultaneously watching the breaking news. His computer screen abruptly glitched, and an email popped up that wasn't there before. It was one of the rerouted emails messages Brent Russell and Genevieve Martin had disseminated. He recognized the sender, but upon opening it, he realized it wasn't for him. What are the odds one would ask? His cousin, Mark Green, had sent an email to a militia group, warning them that the FBI was investigating them. Kenny slowly rubbed his chin, and then quickly hit print.

So what was it, a coincidence or divine intervention?

The snowball effect had begun throughout the populated continents of the world, North America, South America, Europe, Asia, Africa and Australia. Similar disseminated messages were rerouted via email and all of the other social media outposts, and sent to unsuspected people throughout the world. This created an uproar among all law abiding citizens of all nations globally. Nothing was held back! The authorities received tips at an alarming rate on suspected individuals who were involved in those groups that were behind the messages that were designed to desensitize the world, including families, friends, and neighbors. There was a clear difference between teaching and inciting. The 1/3 was starting to turn on its face.

In northern Europe, somewhere in an unknown city, six of the top ranking, fallen dark Angels Generals sat at a conference table on the top floor of an office building. They were all wearing designer suits, and yes, it was a group of splendor. The room was dimly lit, and in the dark far corner sat their leader—yes, Lucifer himself. Now that he could see his success in reigning supreme on the earth, he preferred them to call him Beelzebub. In a deep sounding voice, he asked, "Haven't you fools found the heaven stone yet?"

Leviathan, the general of the continent of Africa, raised his hand.

Beelzebub slowly beckoned to him to stand.

"Unfortunately, our message was broken before we could obtain the exact location. But we know this, it will be at a waterfall, one of the ten major waterfalls."

Verine, the general of Asia, chimed in by starting to call out all of the major significant waterfalls' names. "Niagara, Victoria....."

"Stop!" Beelzebub bellowed out. "Which one of the waterfalls is closest to the heavens?"

Berith, the general of South America, abruptly stood up and said, "Angel Falls is the highest."

"How fitting! We'll go there! Everyone gather all of our resources NOW!" Beelzebub bellowed out and then, he slowly faded away, disappearing from the dark corner where he had sat.

In the town of Canaima, Venezuela, the sounds of rolling thunder could be heard in the distance as the torrential rain came down. Dunstan, Angela, Julian and their tour guide, Luis, traveled up the Rio Carrao in a small boat (curiaras). Over three hours they endured the constant rain, for it was the rainy or off season for Angel Falls tours. Dunstan sat at the bow of the narrow boat, while Julian and Angela sat in the center, huddling under a canvas. The guide, who was used to the elements wore a rain coat. He sat at the rear, staring the outboard motor.

Twenty-five minutes later, Angela's head perked up alerted by the boat motor starting to decelerate. 'Oh, thank God at last,' she thought, 'finally they had arrived'. Dunstan felt terrible that he had to put them through this because of the extreme weather. Although Julian was a big guy, he was not really cut out for this. But then he lightened up on himself because it could have been a lot worse, especially since the dark side was hunting them too.

Surprisingly, the rain subsided as they were tying the boat up. Luis handed Julian and Dunstan the supplies. He was a twenty-nine-year-old Venezuelan native. He had been conducting these tours for ten years, so you can say that he knew his way around. During that time he had made it a point to study English, mainly because the majority of his clients spoke English. To him it seems as if the better English you spoke, the bigger tip you got. This tour topped them all because he still couldn't believe what Dunstan had given him so far.

"Luis, let's set up tent, and then I'll need you to take me to Lake Rabun," Dunstan said.

"No problem, it's not far," Luis responded. When their camp was set up, Dunstan walked over from it, and sat on a large rock. Then he opened up the little sack that held the heaven stone. He held it in the palm of his hand, and marveled at its mere sight. Suddenly, he jumped because he didn't see Angela approaching and hugging him from behind.

"What is that you have there, baby?"

"It's nothing," Dunstan said as he quickly folded his finger in an attempt to hide it.

"Ah, ha, bad Angel! I saw it! Come, let me see it!"

"Okay, don't you drop it? It's a heaven stone you know, and it's the reason we are here. It might help me to become a full-fledged Angel once again."

"But I love you the way you are. You promise you would stay with me."

Dunstan turned to Angela so that he could face her, and then he held her lightly by her chin and said, "Angela, as long as I can help it, I will never leave your side."

They both then reached out and hugged each other.

The forest had a peaceful feel to it, and although it was raining, it made everyone think about rolling over and going to sleep. The only sound that was heard was the chirping, crying and screaming of the many birds and animals of the wild life. Since the trip up the river began, Dunstan had heard and memorized all of the different sounds, taking note in his mind of all the names of the animals he had learnt throughout his lifetime.

It was 5:45 pm, and the sun would be setting at 6:07 pm, but they were forced to start the trip late because of the severity of the weather. Someone suggested to Dunstan that perhaps, he should postpone the trip until tomorrow. But he insisted on taking it today. He remembered Sam telling him, he should not waste any more time. He swiftly reached down to pick up his backpack along with a machete that he had brought to cut thick bushes and provide protection. He nodded to the others to do the same.

Luis turned to Dunstan and said, "Mr. Archer, wouldn't you much rather me show you the other beautiful lakes that are close by, since it will be dark in about twenty minutes. We can camp here tonight, and start fresh tomorrow with the entire day ahead of us."

Dunstan stood there to ponder the thought, and then decided to go alone. "You said it's not far, right? Point me in the right direction. I will go alone, but you can stay with them."

Angela immediately jumped in, "No, no, baby, wait until tomorrow! It will be okay."

"Tomorrow might be too late! In fact, ten minutes from now might be too late. It's not far. I will be a shouting distance away. Why don't you and Julian help Luis make a fire! I'll be back in time so that we can sit and get warm and cuddly under the moonlit night. Look, it's a full moon."

Angela immediately looked up, and yes, there it was, a full moon. Angela looked up at him and smiled, and then quickly pushed him off. "Okay, go quickly. Don't force me to wait up."

Dunstan started to make his way down the trail Luis had pointed out. Once again as he walked, he listened intensely to all of the different sounds of the animals. Suddenly, he stopped quickly because there was a sound that didn't fit. Dunstan stood silent for a minute, to listen for it again. When he didn't hear it anymore, he continued to walk.

Without warning a flapping sound like a wet raincoat descended on him. It was the unfeathered wings of a dark angel that was wrapped tightly around him. Dunstan's arms were pinned to his side. It was equivalent to the strength of duct tape bounding an average human being. Dunstan ran himself backwards into a tree, which he repeated over and over again, until the dark angel's grip released him. He powered himself from its grip and reached for his machete. He then flailed with relentless slashes until he dismembered every limb of the fallen angel. He quickly looked down on the steam from the failing breath of his attacker, and then looked up and swiftly climbed the trees that were extremely high. He leapt and swung from tree to tree, determined to reach Lake Rabun.

Angela quickly stood up, and held her head in fright because of the unusual noises and screams of the wildlife. She began breathing erratically as she reached for Julian, and then she screamed, "Dunstan, Dunstan! They've got him, let's go!" They both started to run down the path with Julian in tow, slipping as they ran on the muddy ground.

There were multiple dark angels descending on and around the trees. One flew at Dunstan, causing him to lose his grip. He slipped and fell twenty feet, only to regain himself on a branch of another tree. He stood there, gazed around, and noticed there were dark angels all through the trees, even on the ground. Beginning to despair, he peered through the trees, and saw Lake Rabun ahead.

The dark angels that were around him started to converge for an assault. Dunstan paused briefly, as he looked at his machete. Then he looked up and around and saw their numbers were increasing. Dunstan quickly took on an angelic warrior's stance. He mustered up from the bottom of his stomach, then through his lungs, a warrior's holler as loud as he could, and then took on an offensive run. He took out one, and slashed the second, but suddenly, they all crowded him. Just as he thought he was done, there was a glow of light, then there were two, and the fight quickly subsided. All of the dark angels turned to look, and there stood Raphael and Gabriel as the ground shook. The angels quickly descended to take on the fight, but it took a long time before the rest crawled out of sight.

Dunstan immediately started shedding tears as he said, "My brothers, my brothers, you saved me."

Both Gabriel and Raphael just smiled on him.

"Dunstan! Dunstan!" Angela shouted from below.

Dunstan looked down and shouted back, "I'm here my dear! I'm okay."

Without warning, there was a whirlwind and a roar, and like an eagle on its prey, Lucifer swept down and picked up Dunstan and flew him far up and away. Lucifer stopped to hover hundreds of feet in the air. He shouted down at Gabriel and Raphael, "Do you really care about this man? I will prove to you that he is just a wicked human," and then he dropped him from the air.

Angela's screams could be heard far, far away.

Gabriel and Raphael had taken on another assault as they hopelessly watched in dismay. A deafening silence followed after they defeated their attackers.

Down below, Angela was crying relentlessly as Julian tried to console her. She quickly tore away from him. Screaming, she ran towards Lake Rabun, where Dunstan had fallen.

As Julian quickly ran behind her to hold her back, he said, "I'm sorry, you can't, you can't! It's too dangerous."

3,200 ft. high above, on the precipice of Angel Falls, Lucifer stood jubilantly looking down on the chaos he had created. Suddenly, he heard a voice behind him.

"It's time!"

Lucifer spun around, and there stood before him, Michael, the Archangel.

"My, my, you've waited quite some time haven't you?"

"You are so ungrateful Lucifer, you had it all. Now look at you, the narcissistic behavior you engross yourself with up there, you put that plague on a 1/3 of your followers down here. You are an imbecile! You are shallow like your numbers," Michael responded.

Without waiting for a response, Michael came upon him like a ball of white heat, held him by the neck and let loose a series of blows to his face.

"Wait, wait! Look, look," Lucifer stammered as he nodded his head for Michael to look around.

The sound of a lion's groan came from deep within Michael as he panned his head around. Then he saw 350 or more dark angels standing on the cliffs, hills and mountain tops. Michael quickly spun Lucifer around, held him from behind and drew his sword. Even when Lucifer was in heaven, Michael's strength was much more brutal in comparison to Lucifer's.

Abruptly, Michael pushed Lucifer away, held his sword high, and then came a series of lightning strikes that lit up the skies. They were followed by a thunderous BOOM! A gigantic opening appeared in space, and a Milky Way looking cascade of angels rained down on the earth's surface. Tens of thousands of angels filled the mountains and hilltops, but the dark angels scattered and ran because they knew that there was no way they could stop them.

The glory of heaven lit up the dark night as Michael shouted throughout the land, "We will win this fight!"

Lucifer was bewildered as Michael slowly approached him and pointing down on Lake Rabun, and said, "Come, come, and look, look upon this splendor. Lake Rabun took on a magnificent array of colors. That was the manifestation of Angel Andrealphus. All the Angels held their hands high as Andrealphus surfaced the waters, and with the colorful wings of a peacock, he flew away up high.

Angela held Julian as she looked on amazed at her husband became an angel, who had risen up to fly away.

Lake Rabun's waters suddenly started to swirl into a black hole, and like a magnet it sucked all of the dark angels down into their dark world.

Michael turned to Lucifer and said, "That is all!" Then he threw him off the top and shouted, "Angel fall!"

༄

Three years later, on September 25th 2019, on a Psychic Ward in Virginia, a nurse explained to another, who was just recently employed, what to expect with certain patient behaviors. The new nurse quickly pointed to a faraway window in the corner of the room, at a man who was sitting there looking out of the window.

"Who is he?" she asked.

"Oh, him, he is no problem at all. Every day that's where he sits, but doesn't even talk much. Two and half years ago, a nice couple brought him in here. They explained that they found him on a tour while in Venezuela, the Angel Falls tour. He has a lot of money! They gave us his bank card and we are still running it."

"What is his name?" she asked.

"Dunstan Archer!" she replied.

༄

Faraway in heaven above, Andrealphus sat on a large rock by a running stream with his head in his hands. Some distance away, the noise of playing children could be heard, but he wasn't paying any attention to them.

Suddenly, a shadow came over him. Andrealphus looked up. It was Gabriel. Gabriel reached out his hand and said, "Come, Michael wants to see you."

Andrealphus slowly rose to his feet. Low on energy, he began to walk with Gabriel. Not far away on a hillside slope, Michael was sitting, waiting for them. He quickly stood up when he saw them approaching him. He reached out for Andrealphus and pulled him close. Then he whispered in his ear, "You can go!"

༄

Early one morning in Cleburne, Alabama, Angela sat on a park bench watching her three-year-old little boy, who was feeding the pigeons with the breadcrumbs she had given him. He was also running and laughing as he ran through the pigeons to make them fly.

Concerned for his safety, Angela kept repeating to him, "Be careful!" She turned to her right because her peripheral vision picked up someone approaching her. She couldn't quite see who it was because the sun was in her eyes. She only recognized who it was when she heard the voice say, "He likes birds!"

Immediately, Angela shot off the bench and ran towards the image that was approaching because she recognized his voice. Dunstan opened his arms to embrace her, and then spun her around as they started shedding tears. Finally, they settled down and Dunstan looked down at the little boy who was laughing at them both. He then asked him, "And what is your name?"

The little boy shouted out, "Aphus!"

Dunstan looked down and said, "That sounds as if it can be the short version of my middle name."

"Oh, what is your middle name because I never knew it?" Angela asked as she looked up at him.

Dunstan looked down, kissed her, and then said, "Andrealphus."

AMEN